新制多益
閱讀考題完全戰略

BASIC

Perfect Learning for the TOEIC Reading Comprehension!

作者：Ki Taek Lee
譯者：彭尊聖／陳依辰
審訂：Richard Luhrs

在英語評鑑考試中，多益是最有效、也是最值得信賴的考試。特別是從2018 年 3 月開始，增加了「整合型試題」，這類題型光靠背誦和解題技巧，是無法完全攻破的。在聽力的「整合型試題」中，例如「詢問對話者意圖」，考生一定要理解前後對話才能選出正確答案。另外在閱讀部分，以往應試舊制多益，只要看文章的一部分就能解題，新多益則融合了各式型態的文章來出題，也增加了許多「整合型試題」，例如「理解文章大意」題型，考生要看過全篇文章、知道文章的脈絡後才能答題，還有在正確位置放入句子的「文意填空」。另外，閱讀的文章類型也出現變化，還包括詢問即時通訊軟體的訊息、網路聊天室、三篇閱讀等。

本系列套書對新多益類型做了深層的分析，為了讓應試者能一眼看懂新多益試題，各單元（Part）也收錄了各類試題的詳細解說以及解題戰略。

聽力部分，Part 1 和 Part 2 的試題比重，較舊制降低許多，但選項句子的長度稍微增加了，句子的難度也有變難的傾向。Part 3 的簡短對話，大致會出對話者的意圖、三人對話，還有各式圖表資料同時出現的「整合型試題」。另外，Part 4 的簡短獨白在主題上沒有很大的變動，但是題型相當活用且具挑戰性，例如會問談話中的某特定句子，在整個對話中意涵為何，也會出附帶各式圖表資料的整合型試題。

閱讀部分改變也很多，因為會出現各式各樣的文章與試題，所以對考生來說，這是準備考試時感到最困難的部分。以 Part 7 單篇閱讀而言，共 10 篇 29題；雙篇閱讀共兩篇 10 題；多（三）篇閱讀共三篇 15 題，雙篇閱讀與多篇閱讀共 25 題。本書擺脫了舊制多益題型及文章類型，將閱讀分成單篇閱讀、雙篇文章、多篇閱讀，在呈現文章模式的同時，還有系統地說明了文章特徵、試題類型及戰略，讓應試者一眼就能看懂文章的特徵和試題類型，並收錄了幫助考生容易解題的詳盡分析。

《新制多益閱讀考題完全戰略 Basic》一書的架構與內容，期望讓應試者能在最短的時間，獲得最大的成果。為了幫助應試者熟悉新多益，本書大量收錄了新多益的試題。

期望各位考生，能獲得最大的學習效果，贏戰新制多益。

作者　Ki Taek Lee 李基宅

Contents
目錄

Part 7　閱讀理解

1. 因為缺乏理解英文含意的能力，初次接觸新多益閱讀測驗的讀者會覺得測驗困難。

2. 本書的單元安排將新多益閱讀測驗中，Part 5、6、7 常出的試題按題目類型分門別類。

3. 透過系統性訓練，培養能確實讀懂句子含意的閱讀能力。

▶ 綜上所述，各個單元最先出現的是題型綜覽和學習戰略區，使讀者一目了然測驗重點。

Parts Overview
題型綜覽

幫助多益考生剛開始研習該單元時，先透過例題，掌握一定要熟知的事項。因為是綜覽整個單元，所以請先試著無負擔地掃視，一面掌握多益試題的出題類型。該單元的類型全都學完後，再從頭瀏覽一遍，就能更信心十足地面對多益考試了。

學習戰略及試題類型
揭示各單元的學習方向

因為考生對多益完全陌生，所以開始學習前，本書整理試題的型式與學習重點，幫助考生理解吸收，並集合能得高分的常見句型，以及常考的試題模式，方便讀者集中練習。考生若剛開始因不熟而擔心害怕的話，可以學習了解該單元後，再熟讀常見句型與試題模式，作個完美的結束。

▶ 每 part 皆含「解題重點」、「題型暖身」和「命題分析」，透過階段式的訓練，不僅能充分理解，還能徹底提升考生的實力。

基礎文法和題型暖身
培養閱讀的基本實力

在多益應試者對試題不甚了解的情況下，一味地反覆解題，沒辦法培養英語實力。必須從文法到類型說明，仔細詳實地理解題目，自然而然培養出信心，累積多益英語的基本實力。

命題分析
仔細看清試題

為了讓考生在作答各類型試題的過程中,更容易掌握答題重點,本書用方框標示可能出現的考點,並作了條理清晰的說明。

實戰應用
解模擬試題

為了能確認學習成果,請考生透過「實戰應用」和 Mini Test 等,試著作答不同程度的模擬試題。

Actual Test
結束

讓考生作答真正符合多益試題水準的模擬試題,掌握自己的強項和弱點,不足處再學習補強。

這樣追上多益

多益是什麼？

多益（TOEIC, Test of English for International Communication）是美國教育測驗服務社（ETS: Educational Testing Service），為測定非英語母語人士，在商業上及國際上使用英語的流暢程度，而開發出的考試。重點放在會話溝通能力上，評斷在日常生活中，尤其是和商業相關的狀況下，實際使用英語的能力。

多益的結構

從 2018 年 3 月開始，多益考試有了下列的改變。

結構	Part	舊制多益		2018 新制多益		限制時間	分數
		各 Part 內容	題數	各 Part 內容	題數		
聽力測驗	1	照片描述	10	照片描述	6	45 分	495 分
	2	應答問題	30	應答問題	25		
	3	簡短對話	30 3 題 ×10 組	簡短對話	39 3 題 ×13 組		
	4	簡短獨白	30 3 題 ×10 組	簡短獨白	30 3 題 ×10 組		
閱讀測驗	5	單句填空 （文法／字彙）	40	單句填空 （文法／字彙）	30	75 分	495 分
	6	段落填空	12 4 題 ×3 篇	段落填空	16 4 題 ×4 篇		
	7	單篇閱讀 （9 篇）	28	單篇閱讀 （10 篇）	29		
		雙篇閱讀 （4 篇）	20	雙篇閱讀 （2 篇） 三篇閱讀 （3 篇）	25		
Total		7 Parts	200	7 Parts	200	120 分	990 分

這樣追上多益聽力測驗

從 2018 年 3 月開始改制的多益測驗,閱讀測驗的題數仍然是 100 題,不過各單元的題數不同了,且 Part 6 和 Part 7 追加了新類型的試題。

PART 5

- 測驗中的每一個句子皆缺少一個單字或詞組,從四個選項中選出最恰當的答案,以完成不完整的句子。
- 題型不變,題數縮減為 30 題。

PART 6

- 測驗中的文章可能是書信、電子郵件、公告、廣告、報導等各式各樣的商業文書,文章中的某些句子缺少單字、片語或句子,從四個選項中選出一個最適合放進空格的答案,以完成文章。每一篇文章出四道試題。
- 追加了新的試題類型,題數增加為 16 題。

新類型

將比較長的**片語**或**子句**,甚至是**一整個句子**填入空格中。不僅要費時解題,還必須掌握整篇文章的來龍去脈才能找出最合適的答案。

PART 7

- 測驗中的文章可能是書信、電子郵件、公告、廣告、報導、發票、訂購單、簡訊等各式各樣的商業文書,閱讀單篇文章,或是兩到三篇相關的文章,確實理解並回答問題。每篇或每組文章後會出現數個題目,從四個選項中選出最合適的答案。
- 追加了新的試題類型,題數增加為 54 題。

新類型

❶ 追加了**文字訊息**、**多人互動**的線上聊天等新穎、有關工作溝通的內容。

❷ 追加了將完整句子插入文章的試題。

❸ 追加了要閱讀三篇文章的**三篇閱讀文章**試題。

★ 請參考多益台灣區官方網站(http://www.toeic.com.tw),詳細閱讀注意事項,並看一下試題內容。

PART

5

單句填空

與舊制多益相比，新多益 Part 5 的試題從 40 題縮減為 30 題，類型和難度維持不變。多益測驗是全球最通行、也最具權威性的商業英語能力測驗，測驗內容側重於職場情境，從出勤狀況到下班之後的社交活動皆有可能作為出題重點，題材不僅多元，囊括的範圍也非常廣。

需要注意的是，多益測驗並不涉及過於專業的知識，而是測驗日常生活中英語使用的熟練程度，是以**字彙**、**文法**與**句型結構**在 Part 5 尤其重要，考生務必多背單字並熟悉英語語法；即便是基本文法都會有陷阱，甚至連母語人士都有可能會粗心大意，因此考生更應謹慎以對。

Example 1

When filling out the order form, please
------- your address clearly to prevent
delays.

(A) fix

(B) write

(C) send

(D) direct

Example 2

Ms. Morgan recruited the individuals
that the company ------- for the next
three months.

(A) will employ

(B) to employ

(C) has been employed

(D) employ

試題類型

1. B   2. A

試題大致可分為句型、字彙、文法以及慣用語四種試題。考生單看選項,就
要掌握試題屬於何種類型。倘若無法完整理解句子,則以句子結構和空格前
後來辨別。藉此判斷該題的類型,並以各種適用的解題戰略加以攻破。

1 基礎文法

- 名詞大致分為兩種：**可數名詞**（普通名詞、集合名詞）和**不可數名詞**（物質名詞、抽象名詞、專有名詞）。可數名詞前要加冠詞，沒有冠詞則要用複數形。
- 名詞是句子裡必備的成分，主要可當作**主詞**、**受詞**和**補語**使用。

1 名詞在句子裡的功能

① 主詞

- The sales department must attend the weekly staff meeting.
  銷售部門務必出席每週員工會議。

② 及物動詞的受詞

- Our charity will happily accept donations of used clothes or household items.
  本慈善機構將樂意接受二手衣物或家用品的捐贈。

③ 介系詞的受詞

- Franklin & Sons moved to a new location closer to the city.
  富蘭克林公司搬到離市區較近的新地點。

④ 補語

- A proper work-life balance for all employees is an advantage of working for our firm.
  在本公司上班的優點，是員工能取得工作和生活間的適當平衡。

2 可數名詞／不可數名詞

① 可數名詞需有不定冠詞，否則要用複數形。不可數名詞前不能有不定冠詞 a (an)；也不能使用複數形。

- I need desk with at least four draws.
  我需要至少有四個抽屜的書桌。
  → 因為 desk 是可數名詞，不能在沒有冠詞也不是複數形的情況下使用。要改成 a desk 或 desks。

- Prince & Company need a furniture / furnitures for their new offices downtown.
  普林斯公司需要為（其）市區的新辦公室準備家具。
  → furniture 是不可數名詞，所以前面不能有不定冠詞，也不能是複數形。

- 有些名詞的單複數同形，遇到這些名詞時，要特別注意動詞型態要用對。
  deer → deer 鹿   series → series 系列
  sheep → sheep 羊   salmon → salmon 鮭魚
  swine → swine 豬   trout → trout 鱒魚

② 可數名詞／不可數名詞的區分

可數名詞	
→ 指人／事物的普通名詞	manager, typist, ticket, letter . . .
→ 指集合名詞	family, majority, police, team, committee . . .

不可數名詞	
→ 特定人／事物的名字	Taipei, Hong Kong, Tom, Christmas . . .
→ 表概念／狀態／動作等	history, information, news, equipment . . .
→ 指天然資源、食物與化學元素等物質	paper, water, copper, glass, oil . . .

- 看起來像不可數名詞，實際上是可數名詞（有些常用複數形）：
a discount 折扣	a price 價格	a purpose 目的
a refund 退款	a relation 親戚	an approach 手段
a statement 敘述	a workplace 工作場所	a source 來源
a result 結果	belongings 財物	measures 措施
savings 存款	standards 道德準則	funds 資金

- 看起來像可數名詞，實際上是不可數名詞：
access 使用（或接近）的權利		advice 建議
baggage 行李	equipment 設備	information 資訊
luggage 行李	machinery 機械	news 新聞
stationery 文具用品	weaponry 武器	

- 不可數名詞可透過加上固定與其搭配的單位名詞，變成可數名詞：
  a sheet of paper 一疊紙
  a bottle of milk 一瓶牛奶
  a piece of information 一則消息
  I ate a slice of bread with cheese for lunch.
  我午餐吃了一片麵包搭配起司。

③ 不可數名詞變成可數名詞的情況

不可數名詞作為其他意思使用時，也可以變成可數名詞。當成可數名詞使用，就要加冠詞或變成複數形。

- I'll have a cup of coffee. 我要來一杯咖啡。
  ➡ coffee 在此為不可數名詞，必須與 a cup of 搭配使用。
- I'll have a glass of juice, please. 請給我一杯果汁。
- Two coffees, please. 請給我兩杯咖啡。
  ➡ coffee 作「一杯咖啡」使用時是可數名詞，所以本句 coffee 使用複數形。
- I'll have two juices, please. 請給我兩杯果汁。

④ 可數名詞和不可數名詞前表數量的量詞

> 表「很多、很少」的量詞，有些只能放在可數名詞前，有些則只能放在不可數名詞前。

● 無論是可數還是不可數名詞，量詞都必須放在它們前面。

many (of) 許多	a few (of) 一些	few (of) 極少數
fewer 較少	another 另一個	several (of) 好幾個
each (of) 每個	every 所有	plenty of 很多
a lot of/lots of 很多	most (of) 大多	some (of) 有些
any (of) 任何	all (of) 全部	no 無；沒有
other 其他	half (of) 半數	hundreds of 上百個
a/an, one, two 一個；兩個		

3 複合名詞

兩個或兩個以上的名詞組成一個詞，稱作複合名詞。一般來說，複合名詞的複數形，由後面的名詞來表現。

① 複合名詞是「名詞＋名詞」，前面名詞的位置，不能放形容詞、分詞或動詞。

account number 帳號	application form 申請表
arrival date 抵達日期	assembly line 生產線
attendance record 出席紀錄	communication skills 溝通技巧
conference room 會議室	confidentiality policy 保密政策
confirmation number 確認號碼	construction delay 施工延宕
convenience store 便利商店	currency market 貨幣市場
delivery company 快遞公司	enrollment form 登記表
exercise equipment 運動器材	expansion project 擴張計畫
expiration date 到期日	feasibility study 可行性研究
growth potential 成長潛力	identification card 身分證

installment payment 分期付款	interest rate 利率
investment advice 投資建議	marriage status 婚姻狀態
occupancy rate 住房率	performance appraisals/ evaluations 績效評估
product information 產品資訊	production schedule 生產時程表
reception desk 接待櫃檯	reference letter 推薦信
registration form 登記表	repair facility 維修廠
research program 研究計畫	retirement luncheon 退休午餐餐敘
return policy 退貨政策	safety inspection 安全檢查
security card 安全卡	service desk 服務台

② 複合名詞的複數形，是在後面的名詞後加 -(e)s。

- research program → research programs

TIP 複合名詞（名詞＋名詞）中，前面的名詞不能加 -(e)s，不過也有例外。

customs office 海關辦公室
public relations department 公關部門
electronics company 電子公司
earnings growth 盈餘成長
savings account/bank 儲蓄帳戶／銀行
sales division/promotion 銷售部門／促銷
human resources department 人力資源部

TIP	外來語的複數
on → a	phenomenon （現象）→ phenomena criterion （標準）→ criteria
um → a	datum （資料）→ data agendum （議程）→ agenda
is → es	basis （基礎）→ bases crisis （危機）→ crises
a → ae	alumna （女校友）→ alumnae larva （幼蟲）→ larvae

③ 在「數字＋單位名詞＋名詞」這型式中，單位名詞不能加複數 -(e)s。

- a five-**years**-old boy (x) → a five-**year**-old boy (o) 一名五歲男孩
- three **thousands** tickets (x) → three **thousand** tickets (o) 三千張票
- a three-**years**-old girl (x) → a three-**year**-old girl (o) 一名三歲女孩

常考的相似名詞

01
access 图 使用;接近
accessibility 图 無障礙;可理解
accession 图 登機;就職;加入
accessory 图 配件;附屬

02
advertisement 图 廣告;啟事
advertiser 图 廣告商
advertising 图 廣告業;廣告活動

03
advice 图 忠告;意見
advisor/adviser 图 顧問;指導者

04
agency 图 代理;仲介
agent 图 代理人;媒介

05
analysis 图 分析
analyst 图 分析師

06
appliance 图 器具;裝置
applicant 图 申請人;求職者
application 图 申請;應用
applicator 图 (藥物或化妝品等的)塗抹器

07
arbitration 图 仲裁;裁決
arbitrator 图 仲裁者

08
assembler 图 裝配工;裝配器
assembly 图 大會;集合;組裝

09
assistance 图 幫助;援助
assistant 图 助手;助理

10
attendance 图 出席;參加
attendant 图 陪伴者;侍者
attendee 图 出席者;在場者

11
author 图 作者
authority 图 權力;權威;權限
authorization 图 授權;委託

12
beneficiary 图 受益人
benefit 图 益處;補助費

13
certificate 图 證明;證書
certification 图 證明;審查

14
chemical 图 化學物質
chemist 图 化學家
chemistry 图 化學;化學現象

15
clearance 图 出清;淨空
clearing 图 清除;(林中)空地

16
close 图 結局;結束(口語用法)
closeness 图 接近;親密

17
collection 图 收集;聚集
collector 图 收藏者;收取(錢或票券)者

18
commitment 图 承諾;委託
committee 图 委員會

19
competence 图 能力;勝任
competition 图 比賽;競爭
competitor 图 競爭對手

20
complex 图 集合體;情節
complexity 图 複雜性

21
consultancy 图 顧問工作;顧問職位
consultant 图 顧問
consultation 图 諮商;會議

22
consumer 图 消費者
consumption 图 消費

23
continuation 图 繼續;續前
continuity 图 連續性;連貫性

24	contribution 图 貢獻；捐助 contributor 图 捐款人；貢獻者； 撰稿者
25	correspondence 图 符合；一致；通信連絡 correspondent 图 記者；通信者
26	developer 图 開發人員 development 图 開發
27	direction 图 方向 director 图 組長；導演
28	distribution 图 分送；分配物 distributor 图 發送者；銷售者
29	durability 图 耐用 duration 图 持續期間；持續
30	economics 图 經濟學；經濟情況 economist 图 經濟學家 economy 图 經濟；節約
31	effect 图 結果；作用；效果 effectiveness 图 效果
32	employer 图 雇主 employee 图 雇員 employment 图 僱用；就業
33	engineer 图 工程師 engineering 图 工程學；工程
34	entrance 图 進入；入口；登場 entry 图 入場；條目；參賽者（或 作品）
35	escalation 图 逐步上升 escalator 图 電扶梯
36	facilitation 图 簡便化；促進 facilitator 图 促進者 facility 图 設施；技能；簡易

37	incidence 图 發生 incident 图 事件；事情
38	inhalation 图 吸入空氣 inhaler 图 吸入器；人工呼吸器
39	interpretation 图 詮釋；口譯 interpreter 图 口譯員
40	management 图 管理 manager 图 經理
41	manufacturer 图 製造商；廠商 manufacturing 图 製造業；生產
42	observance 图 遵守（法律、風俗 等）；儀式 observation 图 觀察；察覺 observatory 图 天文台；瞭望台
43	opening 图 開口；開始 openness 图 坦承；誠實
44	producer 图 製作人；生產者 product 图 產品；產物 production 图 生產；產量 productivity 图 生產力
45	receipt 图 收到；收據 receptacle 图 容器；貯藏所 reception 图 接待；招待會；接納 receptionist 图 接待人員 recipient 图 接受者；收受者
46	servant 图 僕人 server 图 餐廳招待；伺服器 service 图 服務 serving 图 （食物或飲料的）一份
47	transport 图 運送；運輸；搬運 transportation 图 運送；運輸； 交通 transporter 图 運輸者；輸送機

Chapter 01

1. Montreal Steel impressed its
------- with perfect scores
for safety and environmental
standards.
   (A) inspection
   (B) inspecting
   (C) inspect
   (D) inspectors

2. The journal article outlines the
strategies and ------- the animal
uses to make the most of its
modern habitat.
   (A) adapted
   (B) adapter
   (C) adaptations
   (D) adapting

3. A number of wealthy individuals
funded a project dedicated to
the ------- of the historic Gola
Cathedral.
   (A) persuasion
   (B) expectation
   (C) preservation
   (D) dismissal

4. The catalog shows that
Hometime's lace curtains come
in a ------- of colors.
   (A) variety
   (B) priority
   (C) dimension
   (D) summary

5. In ------- to questions
about the drug's safety, the
pharmaceutical company held
an urgent press conference.
   (A) departure
   (B) exception
   (C) response
   (D) conclusion

基礎文法

已經出現過的名詞，不會重複使用，而是會用**代名詞**來代稱。

◆ 已經出現過的名詞稱為先行詞，代名詞用以代替先行詞。代名詞與名詞一樣有性別、人稱、數量之別，使用代名詞時務必切記，代名詞需與先行詞的性別與數量一致。代名詞依在句中的功能，分作主格、受格和所有格三種。

- I shut my dog in the closet, and my dog scratched the door.
  → I shut my dog in the closet, and it scratched the door.

  我把我的狗關進櫃子裡，於是牠用爪子刮門。

  → it 是為了避免前面出現過的名詞（my dog）重複出現，而用來代稱它的代名詞，並在子句裡當作主詞使用。
- The company employed more staff, and the staff were very efficient workers.
  → The company employed more staff, and they were very efficient workers.

  這家公司僱用了更多員工，他們都是有效率的工作者。

◆ 代名詞依性質分作人稱代名詞、反身代名詞、指示代名詞、不定代名詞等。

① 人稱代名詞（**I**、**you**、**she**、**he**、**they** 等）用來代稱人或事物。

- Anne quit her job because she didn't get along with her colleagues.

  安妮因為跟同事處不來，所以辭了工作。
- Henry just started his new job, but he does not get along with his new boss.

  亨利開始了新工作，但他跟新老闆處得不好。

② 反身代名詞（himself、herself、themselves 等）在人稱代名詞後
加 -self(-selves)，有「……自己」的意思，表人稱代名詞他自己。

單數	myself, yourself, himself, herself, itself
複數	ourselves, yourselves, themselves

- Jake talks to himself when he's thinking about something.
  傑克想事情的時候會自言自語。
- Norman devoted himself to the new project.
  諾曼投入這個新計畫。

③ 指示代名詞（this/these、that/those 等）是「這個（這些）」、「那
個（那些）」的意思，用來指特定的人或事物。這些代名詞也可以像指
示形容詞一樣，放在名詞之前修飾名詞。

- I have seen scenery like this. 我見過像這樣的景致。
- Those are my boys. 他們是我兒子。
- I haven't seen a film like this before. 我沒看過像這樣的電影。
- This winter will be very cold. 今年冬天會很冷。

④ 不定代名詞（some、any 等）表數量不明確的人或事物。它可以像不定
形容詞一樣，放在名詞前之前修飾名詞，當作「任何」、「某個」使用。

- Some of the students are married. 這些學生當中，有些已婚。
  Some students are married. 有些學生已經結婚了。
- Some of the employees are working overtime.
  這些員工當中，有些在加班。
  Some employees are working overtime. 有些員工正加班中。

上句中的 some，像不定代名詞一樣，指某些人中的「一些人」。而下句中的
some，則像不定形容詞一樣，當作「某些」使用。

1 人稱代名詞

① 人稱代名詞的種類

人稱	數／性		主格	所有格 形容詞	受格	所有格 代名詞
第一 人稱	單數		I	my	me	mine
	複數		we	our	us	ours
第二 人稱	單／複數		you	your	you	yours
第三 人稱	單數	男性	he	his	him	his
		女性	she	her	her	hers
		事物／動物	it	its	it	its
	複數		they	their	them	theirs

② 作為主格使用

- **They** were given complimentary tickets to the show.
  有人送他們表演的免費門票。
- **He** will go to the park with you as long as you take your bikes.
  只要你們騎自己的腳踏車,他就會跟你們去公園。

- 代名詞 it 本身沒有任何意義,可以當作表時間、距離、日子、天氣、頭銜等的「非人稱主詞」或「虛主詞」來使用。
  It may rain this evening. 今天晚上可能會下雨。
  It is about 30 minute's ride from here.
  從這裡過去大概 30 分鐘車程。
  It may be more expensive than we thought.
  它可能比我們想得貴。
  It is about 20 minutes away from the start of the show.
  從表演開始到現在大概過了 20 分鐘。

③ 所有格可以放在名詞前以修飾名詞,翻譯成「……的」

- Some people make decisions based on **their** own faulty judgement. 有些人根據他們錯誤的判斷做決定。
- Some of **my** coworkers had poorer sales performances than last year. 我的同事中,有些人的銷售表現比去年差。

④ 作為受格使用

- The advisor helped **them** to understand the legal situation.
  顧問協助他們弄懂法律形勢。
- The solicitor helped **them** to plan their course of legal action.
  律師協助他們規畫法律訴訟的程序。
- Mr. Williams works with **me**. 威廉斯先生和我一起工作。
- Greenwood Legal usually works with **us** because we have a long history together.
  青林法律事務所通常跟我們合作，因為我們有長期合作的經驗。

- 注意不要一看到介系詞，就選了人稱代名詞的受格。
  I am satisfied with me(→ **my**) job. 我滿意我的工作。
  ➡ 因為後面有名詞 job，所以要用所有格形容詞。
  I am very happy with me new(→ **my new**) position.
  我對於我新的職位感到開心。
  ➡ 因為後面有名詞 position，所以要用所有格形容詞。

⑤ 所有格代名詞代替「所有格＋名詞」，翻譯成「……的（東西）」

- My book is about plants generally, but **hers** specializes in herbs.
  我的書是關於一般植物，而她的（書）則專攻香草。
- My work is in the field of science, but **his** involves stock trading.
  我的工作是在科學領域，而他的（工作）則跟股票交易有關。

- 所有格形容詞後一定要接名詞，但所有格代名詞後一定不能有名詞。
  Many people make decisions based on theirs(→ **their**) emotions. 很多人依自己的情緒做決定。
  Many companies make decisions based on theirs(→ **their**) financial advisors' advice. 很多公司根據財務顧問的建議做決定。
  My report is about accounts, but her(→ **hers**) is about marketing. 我的報告是關於客戶的，而她的（報告）跟行銷有關。
  My job is in human resources, but her(→ **hers**) is in the accounting department.
  我的工作是在人力資源部門，而她的（工作）在會計部門。

2 反身代名詞

① 受詞指稱的人／事物，和主詞所指的人／事物相同時，受詞的位置就要放反身代名詞。這時反身代名詞不能省略。

- Sometimes I cook for **myself**. 有時候我會為自己下廚。
- I decided to go into business for **myself**.
  我決定為了自己走入商業這個領域。

② 為了強調主詞或受詞，可在強調的字詞後面，或句子的最後方，加上反身代名詞。這時反身代名詞可以省略。

- The manager **(herself)** guided the group to the laboratory.
  經理本人帶領了團體參觀實驗室。
- The tour guide **(himself)** guided the group to the cave.
  導遊親自帶著旅行團進入洞穴。
- She liked the house **(itself)**, but not the location or accessibility.
  她喜歡房子本身，但不喜歡地點，且去那裡的交通不方便。
- The only thing we have to fear is fear **(itself)**.
  我們唯一需要恐懼的是恐懼本身。

- 因為命令句的主詞 you 被省略了，所以即使主詞沒有出現，反身代名詞也要用 yourself。
  Don't try to do any repairs **yourself**. 勿嘗試自行修理。
  Do not operate the machinery by **yourself**. 勿自行操作機械。

TIP 和反身代名詞相關的慣用語

by oneself (= alone = on one's own) 獨自；單獨地
for oneself 為了自己　　　of itself 自動地　　　in itself 本質上

- She prefers to travel **by herself**. 她比較喜歡獨自旅行。
- You should judge **for yourself**. 你應該為自己做出判斷。

overeat oneself 暴飲暴食	avail oneself of 利用
absent oneself from 缺席	pride oneself on 引以為榮
apply oneself to 塗；敷	kill oneself 自殺
help oneself to 自便；自救	accustom oneself to 習慣
support oneself 支援	cry oneself to sleep 哭到睡著

3 指示代名詞

① 指示代名詞 that/those，用來代替出現過的先行詞

- Mr. Crane's performance is far superior to that [of his associates].
  克瑞先生的表現遠優於他同事（的表現）。
- Mr. Rigby's ability was far greater than that [of his teammates].
  瑞比先生的能力遠比隊友（的能力）好。
- I think the restaurants of Charleston are better than those [of Columbia]. 我認為查爾斯頓的餐廳比哥倫比亞的（餐廳）好。
- I think the company's products are better than those [of its competitors]. 我覺得這家公司的產品比對手的（產品）好。

② those 也可當作「那些做……的人」使用

- Those [who are responsible for this problem] will be submitted to disciplinary measures. 要為這個問題負責的人將被提送懲戒處分。
- Those [who are interested in joining the discussion] need to register. 有興趣加入討論者必須要登記。
- Those [who are interested in joining the weekend seminar] must fill out the online form.
  有興趣加入週末研討會者，必須填寫這線上表格。
  ➡ 這時，those 不是代替前面出現過的名詞，而是當作非限定用法的「某些做……的人」使用。those 後一定要接修飾語（關係子句、分詞、介系詞片語等）。

③ this/that 和 these/those，放在名詞前當作指示形容詞使用，表「這個／那個」、「這些／那些」

- This meeting will be tough. 這個會議將是一場硬仗。
- This financial year will be competitive. 今年的財政年度會競爭激烈。
- Those buildings were built 13 years ago.
  這些建築物興建於 13 年前。
- Those apartments are very high-priced. 這些公寓的價位很高。

- 指示形容詞 those，也可以當作 the 來使用。

  Those trainers (= The trainers) who wish to attend the meeting should register this month.
  想參加會議的訓練人員應該在本月登記。

  Those workers (= The workers) who wish to attend the company picnic must register this week.
  想參加公司野餐的員工必須在這星期登記。

④ 指示形容詞 this 也可以放在星期、季節、早上／下午／晚上、日／月／年前，表「今天、這次、本」。

- I saw James **this** evening. 我今天晚上看到詹姆士。
- I am going to have a meeting with Robin **this** afternoon.
  我今天下午會跟羅賓開會。

4 不定代名詞

① one / other / another

(1) one 代稱不確定的單數可數名詞。

- I lost my old bike and bought a new **one**.
  我弄丟了舊腳踏車，買了一台新的（腳踏車）。
- My old laptop broke so I bought a new **one**.
  我的舊筆電壞了，所以我買了一部新的（筆電）。
  ➡ one 前面一定要有 one 所代稱的先行詞。
- -
- one 的複數形是 ones，代稱不確定的複數可數名詞。

  I sold my old books and bought new **ones**.
  我賣了舊書，買了些新的（書）。

  I donated my old clothes and bought new **ones**.
  我捐了舊衣服，買了新的（衣服）。

(2) another 當作「除了已經提到的那個之外的另一個」使用。

- One of the students is from New Zealand. **Another** student is from Korea. (**Another** is from Korea.)
  這些學生中，有一位來自紐西蘭。另一位（學生）來自韓國。
- One of the new engineers is from America. **Another** is from Australia. (**Another one** is from Australia.)
  這些新工程師中，有一位來自美國。另一位（工程師）來自澳洲。
  ➡ another 當作形容詞使用時，後面接單數可數名詞。此外，another 前不能有 the。

(3) other/others 當作「除了已經提到的那個之外的其中幾個」使用。

- One of the students is from Mexico. Other students are from Ghana. (Others are from Ghana.)
  這些學生當中，有一位來自墨西哥。其他（學生）來自迦納。
- One of the technicians is from England. Others are from China. 這些技師中，有一位來自英格蘭。其他（技師）來自中國。
  ➡ other 只能當作形容詞使用，後接複數可數名詞。others 只能當作代名詞使用。

(4) the other(s) 當作「固定的東西中剩下的那些」使用。

- I have three books. Two are mine. The other book is yours. (The other is yours.) 我有三本書。兩本是我的，剩下那一本是你的。
- I bought four notepads. Three are mine. The other is yours.
  我買了四本筆記本。三本是我的，剩下那一本是你的。
- I have three books. One is mine. The other books are yours. (The others are yours.) 我有三本書。一本是我的，剩下的書都是你的。
- I have five apples. Three are mine. The others are yours.
  我有五顆蘋果。三顆是我的，剩下的都是你的。
  ➡ 剩下的只有一個的時候，用「the other ＋單數」來表示。剩下的有兩個以上時，則用「the other ＋複數」，或「the others」來表示。

② some/any, no/none, most/almost

(1) some 可當作代名詞或形容詞使用，表「一些、某些」，用在肯定句中。any 可當作代名詞或形容詞使用，表「一些、某些」，用在否定句、疑問句和條件句中。

- Some of the members didn't show up. 有些成員沒有出現。
  Some of the employees didn't come to work on time.
  有些員工沒有準時來上班。
- I'm going to buy some books. 我要去買幾本書。
  I'm going to purchase some new office furniture.
  我要去添購一些新的辦公室家具。
- There's some ice in the freezer. 冷凍庫有一些冰塊。
  There's some juice in the fridge. 冰箱有一些果汁。

- -

- We don't have any of the musical instruments.
  我們完全沒有這些樂器。
  We don't have any paper left for printing.
  我們已經沒有紙可以列印。

- Have you got **any** luggage? 你有沒有帶任何行李？
Have you got **any** of the new software yet?
你有買什麼新軟體嗎？
- If there are **any** letters for me, can you send them to this address? 如果有我的信，能幫我寄到這個地址嗎？
If there are **any** emails I should know about, please forward them to me. 如果有我應該知道的電子郵件，請轉寄給我。

(2) no 是形容詞，後面一定要接名詞。
none 是代名詞，單獨地放在名詞的位置。

- We had to walk home because there were **no** buses or taxis.
我們必須走路回家，因為沒有公車或計程車了。
We had to work from home because there was **no** Internet in the office. 我們必須在家工作，因為辦公室沒有網路。
- All the tickets have been sold. There are **none** left.
所有票券已售罄，一張不剩。
All of the products have been sold. There are **none** left.
所有商品皆已售罄，一無所剩。
- **None** of the shops was open. 沒有一家商店有營業。
None of the restaurants were open. 沒有一家餐廳有開。

(3) most 可當作代名詞或形容詞使用，表「大部分（的）」。
almost 當 作副詞使用，表「幾乎全部」。

- **Most** of the people enjoyed the party.
這些人大多喜歡這個派對。
Most of the staff came to the Christmas party.
大多數的員工都有來耶誕派對。
- **Most** people enjoyed the party. 大部分人都喜歡這派對。
Most team members worked well on the project.
團隊成員大多在這個專案上表現良好。
- **Almost** all the people enjoyed the party.
幾乎所有人都喜歡派對。
Almost all of the projects had been completed on schedule.
幾乎所有的專案都如期完成。

Chapter 02

1. After years of saving, Ms. Riley was finally able to purchase ------- home in a popular suburb.
   (A) her own
   (B) she
   (C) herself
   (D) hers

2. A customer service agent called Ms. Fox regarding the charge ------- had disputed on the bill.
   (A) her
   (B) herself
   (C) she
   (D) hers

3. The staff bought a card for Ms. Graham to cheer ------- up after her surgery.
   (A) hers
   (B) she
   (C) her
   (D) herself

4. All employees are required to arrive 10 minutes before ------- shift begins to make sure they are wearing the correct uniforms.
   (A) themselves
   (B) their
   (C) them
   (D) they

5. After more than a decade, Gregory Scott's manager finally promoted ------- to the head of the human resources department.
   (A) he
   (B) him
   (C) himself
   (D) his

Chapter 03 動詞

基礎文法

- **動詞**是句子裡最重要的敘述字。動詞的種類依後接句子的成分而定。
- 大致上,動詞可**依有無受詞**,而分作及物動詞和不及物動詞。
  依有無補語,而分作完全及物動詞、不完全及物動詞,以及完全不及物動詞、不完全不及物動詞。
- 上述在解答句子成分(主詞、受詞、補語)試題和句子結構試題,具有關鍵性的功能。

1 不及物動詞

① 主詞+不及物動詞:不及物動詞後面不接受詞。

appear 出現	die 死亡	exist 存在	thrive 成功;興旺
stand 站	be 是	dwell 居住	go 去
rise 升起;增加	stay 留下	come 來	emerge 浮現;出現
lie 欺騙	sit 坐	prevail 勝過;盛行;普遍	

- John's cat died the mouse. (×)
  ➡ 動詞 die 除少數特例情況外,是不及物動詞,後不可接受詞。
- John's cat can jump very high. 約翰的貓可以跳很高。
  ➡ 不及物動詞後面可接副詞或介系詞片語。

有些不及物動詞須和特定介系詞搭配成為動詞片語。

apply to . . . 申請	differ from / vary from . . . 與……不同
listen to . . . 傾聽	react to . . . 對……反應
respond to . . . 回應	specialize in . . . 擅長
consist of . . . 由……組成	differ in . . . 在……有所差異
originate from . . . 起源於	refer to . . . 提到
result in . . . 導致	result from . . . 起因於
serve as . . . 當作……使用	smile at . . . 對……微笑

② 主詞＋不及物動詞＋補語：不及物動詞不需要受詞，但要接補語才能完整表達意思。這樣的不及物動詞叫作不完全不及物動詞。

不完全不及物動詞（連綴動詞）	
● 基本動詞 be	am, are, is, was, were . . .
● become 動詞類（狀態的變化）	get, go, grow, turn, become . . .
● remain 動詞類（狀態的持續）	stay, keep, stand, remain . . .
● feel 感官動詞類（感覺）	smell, taste, sound, hear, feel . . .
● seem 動詞類（可能性）	look, appear, seem . . .

2　及物動詞

① 主詞＋及物動詞＋受詞：及物動詞一定要後接受詞。

answer 回答	discuss 討論	form 形成	lay 放下
raise 舉起；提高	enter 進入	hear 聽到	mention 提及
reach 到達；觸及	regret 後悔；遺憾	appreciate 欣賞；感謝	

- I regretted my decision. 我後悔做這個決定。
  　及物動詞　　　受詞

- John raised. (x) 約翰舉高。
  The company raised the prices of the products. (o)
  這家公司提高了產品售價。
  ➡ 及物動詞不能沒有受詞只有動詞。

表達感情時，受詞處放人稱代名詞的受格，這時及物動詞表「使（受詞）感覺……」。

amaze/surprise 使感到訝異、驚奇	bore 使感到無聊
disappoint 使感到失望	move 使感動
amuse 使開心	delight 使愉快
embarrass 使尷尬；使難為情	interest 使產生興趣

- The company was delighted with the catering service.
  公司很開心有外燴服務。
- The manager was embarrassed by his sales figures.
  經理為他的銷售數字感到很尷尬。
- The man was interested in the accountant's position.
  這名男子對會計師的職位很感興趣。

TIP 很容易誤認為是及物動詞的不及物動詞
→〈不及物動詞＋介系詞＝及物動詞〉

arrive in (at) = get to = reach 到達   add to = increase 增加

apologize to 對……道歉   complain of 抱怨

get into = enter 進入   object to 反對

reply to = answer 回覆；回答   wait for = await 等待

start from = depart from = leave from 從……離開

例：

- She **apologized** to the customer.
  她向顧客道歉。

- He **replied** to her email immediately.
  他馬上回覆她的電子郵件。

② 主詞＋及物動詞＋間接受詞＋直接受詞：此種動詞通常表「給某人某物」，所以也被稱為「授與動詞」。

give 給予   tell 告訴   buy 購買
send 寄送   bring 帶來；拿來   cost 花費
lend 借出   teach 教   show 顯示；露出

- Harry **sent** her some flowers.
  哈利送她一些花。

- Julia **lent** me her laptop computer.
  茉莉亞借我她的筆電。

- Robert **showed** me his cell phone.
  羅伯特給我看他的手機。

- Sam **taught** me to draw.
  山姆教我畫畫。

③ 主詞＋及物動詞＋受詞＋受詞補語：有受詞和受詞補語才能完整表達意思的動詞。

這時受詞和受詞補語之間，含有「主詞 — 述詞」的關係。

consider 視……為	find 認為……為
call 稱為	elect 推選……為

- They considered Jonathan a hard worker.
  他們認為強納森是認真的員工。
- He found the book interesting. 他認為這本書很有趣。
- The Board elected John Norman (as) the new Director.
  董事會選約翰·諾曼為新任董事。
- He considered her (to be) the best candidate for the job.
  他認為她是這個工作的最佳人選。

也有在受詞補語前加 as 的及物動詞。

define as 將……定義為……	identify as 認出；識別
describe as 將……描述成……	regard as 視……為……

- The worker described his manager as being very fair.
  這名員工形容他的經理為人公平。
- The CEO regarded the vice president as his close friend.
  執行長將副總裁視為好友。
- The reporter described the scene as wonderful and amazing.
  播報員形容這個場面美好而精彩。

3 容易混淆的不及物動詞和及物動詞

① 和介系詞搭配的不及物動詞

account for 是……的原因；對……有責任	complain about/of 抱怨
graduate from 從……畢業	reply to 回覆
wait for 等待	arrive in/at 到達；抵達
consent to 同意	interfere with 干涉
think of 思考；想到	

- She **accounted for** the mistake by saying she'd misplaced some documents. 她利用加班彌補錯放文件的失誤。
- He **graduated from** university with honors.
  他以優秀成績從大學畢業。

② 容易被誤認為是不及物動詞的及物動詞

answer 回答	attend 參加；出席
discuss 討論	explain 說明
describe 描述	enter 進入
mention 提及	resemble 像；類似

- They **discussed** the loan details with the bank.
  他們和銀行討論貸款細節。
- He **explained** the new project to his boss.
  他對老闆說明新計畫。

③ 有時是及物動詞，有時是不及物動詞

• 不及物動詞 grow	He **grew** weak from hunger. 他因為飢餓而逐漸虛弱。 He **grew** angry at his team members. 他對團隊成員動怒。
• 及物動詞 grow	Lucy **grows** vegetables in her garden. 露西在她的花園裡種菜。 Rowan **grows** all of the vegetables that he eats. 羅文種所有自己吃的蔬菜。
• 不及物動詞 pay	Hard work **pays**. 努力工作是值得的。 The manager always **pays** for dinner. 經理都會埋晚餐的單。
• 及物動詞 pay	He **paid** 100 dollars for the traffic fine. 他繳了 100 元交通違規罰單。 She **paid** 200 dollars for the parking ticket. 她繳了 200 元違規停車罰單。

- 不及物動詞
  develop

  Her business developed into a multinational corporation.
  她的生意茁壯成跨國公司。

  The company developed into a global leader in the market.
  這家公司成為市場上的全球龍頭。

- 及物動詞
  develop

  Exercise develops strength and endurance.
  運動鍛鍊強度和耐力。

  Healthy eating develops one's immune system.
  健康飲食會練就強壯的免疫系統。

Chapter 03

1. The members of the committee must ------- the quarterly budget by March 15.
   - (A) finalized
   - (B) to finalize
   - (C) be finalized
   - (D) finalize

2. The recall issued by Brant Manufacturing applies to dishwashers ------- between January and August of this year.
   - (A) bargained
   - (B) conducted
   - (C) purchased
   - (D) acknowledged

3. Workshop participants were divided into small groups and assigned a topic to ------- discussion.
   - (A) describe
   - (B) stimulate
   - (C) deny
   - (D) calculate

4. At the end of the tour, one of our artisans will ------- how the glass is shaped into beads, containers, and sculptures.
   - (A) allow
   - (B) speak
   - (C) provide
   - (D) show

5. The marketing director tried to ------- the board members to provide funding for a website upgrade.
   - (A) conclude
   - (B) persuade
   - (C) await
   - (D) endorse

時態

基礎文法

動詞的時態有**簡單式**，表事實、慣例或習慣等；有**完成式**，表已經完成的動作或狀態；有**進行式**，表動作正在進行。

◆ 動詞的時態包括時間與狀態，依此將動詞作各種不同的變化，稱作動詞變化。

- They **work** for the company. 他們為這家公司工作。
- John **works** on the paper a little bit every day.
  約翰每天都會寫一點報告。
- John **worked** on the paper last week. 約翰上週在寫報告。
- John **will work** on a paper tomorrow. 約翰明天會做報告。

如同上述例子，表動作的 work 有 works、worked、will work 等型態變化。
利用這些變化，表發生動作的時間與進行的狀態。

◆ 動詞的時態可依動作進行的狀態分為簡單式、完成式、進行式。

簡單式	表特定時間的動作或狀態，分別以「動詞 (s)」、「動詞＋ed」、「will ＋動詞」來表現。
● 現在	The company baseball team **meets** every Tuesday at 6 p.m. 這家公司的棒球隊每週二下午六點都會碰面。
● 過去	The staff members **met** to discuss the latest company changes. 職員碰面討論公司最新的變化。
● 未來	All employees **will attend** the meeting after work. 所有員工會在下班後出席會議。

完成式	以特定的某個時間為基準時間點，表在它之前發生的事或動作或狀態，一直持續到該基準時間點，用「have/has ＋ p.p.」來表現。
● 現在完成	Tim **has gone** home for the day. 提姆今天已經回家了。

● 過去完成	The plane **had** already **departed** when he arrived at the airport. 當他到機場時，飛機已經離開了。
● 未來完成	The new office **will have been** completed by next June. 到了明年六月，新辦公室就已經完工了。

進行式	表某一時間點動作持續進行，用「be + V-ing」來表現。
● 現在進行	Naomi **is talking** with her boss on the phone. 娜歐蜜正在跟老闆講電話。
● 過去進行	Krystal **was walking** with her dog when she met her friend. 克利斯朵遇到朋友時，她正帶著愛犬散步。
● 未來進行	Rob **will be taking** the subway to work because of highway construction. 因為高速公路施工，羅伯將會搭地鐵去上班。

1 簡單式

① 現在簡單式

現在簡單式表習慣的、規律反覆的事，或不變的真理。

- I **visit** my grandfather every week because he gets lonely.
  因為爺爺寂寞，所以我每週都會去探望他。
- She **plays** badminton with her best friend every weekend.
  她每個週末都會和最好的朋友打羽球。
- I **listen** to music on my way to work.
  我上班的路上都會聽音樂。
  ➜ 因為是每天習慣發生的事，所以用現在式。

② 過去簡單式

過去簡單式表過去發生的事，用動詞的過去式來表現。

- I **traveled** to my hometown several weeks ago.
  我幾個星期前去我的故鄉旅行。
- We **played** soccer last weekend at the local park.
  我們上週末在當地的公園踢足球。

③ 未來簡單式

未來簡單式表對未來狀況的推測，或表意志。

> - She **will go** to the movies with her friends tomorrow.
>   她明天會跟朋友去看電影。
>   ➡ 因為要表現明天會去看電影的意志，所以用未來式（will go）。

2 完成式

① 現在完成式

現在完成式表「過去發生且持續到現在的事」，或「已經完成的事」，如過去的經驗，或現在仍受過去發生的事影響。

> - She **has worked** for Hartman Accountants as a secretary for the last 12 years. 過去 12 年，她都在哈特曼會計師事務所擔任秘書。
>   ➡ 因為是過去 12 年前開始，一直持續到現在，所以要用現在完成式。（has worked）。
> - I **have** already **completed** most of the project.
>   我已經完成了大部分的專案。
>   ➡ 因為過去開始的專案現在完成了，要用現在完成式（have completed）。

② 過去完成式

過去完成式表「更早的過去」，或「過去的過去」，即過去某特定時間點之前已經完成的動作。

> - By the time the project finished, we **had** already **started** working on something new. 專案結束時，我們早就開始著手新工作了。
>   ➡ 表在過去特定時間點（專案結束時）之前，已經開始著手新的工作，所以要用過去完成式。

③ 未來完成式

未來完成式表「開始於過去」的動作，現在雖還沒完成，但「在未來某特
定時間點會完成」。

- I **will have worked** for this company for 10 years next
  January. 到明年一月，我就在這家公司工作 10 年了。
  ➡ 要表現從以前開始工作，到未來的時間點（next January）就工作 10 年
  了，所以要用未來完成式。

3　進行式

① 現在進行式

(1) 現在進行式表現在這個時間點正在進行的動作。

- He **is living** in France at the moment and working as a
  translator. 他目前住在法國，並擔任翻譯一職。
  ➡ 表現現在這個時間點（at the moment）正住在法國，所以要用現在進行
  式。

---

(2) 表反覆發生的動作，不能用現在進行式，要用現在式。

- Mr. Thornton is ~~usually giving~~(→ **usually gives**) a special
  weekend seminar each month.
  索頓先生通常每個月會辦特別週末研討會。
  ➡ 因為要表現反覆開研討會這個行動，所以不能用現在進行式（is usually
  giving），要用現在式（usually gives）。

---

(3) 表正在發生的動作，不能用現在式，要用現在進行式。

- The man ~~yells~~(→ **is yelling**) at the dog.
  這名男子正在對著狗吼叫。
  ➡ 因為是現在正在發生的行動，所以不能現在式（yells），要用現在進行
  式（is yelling）。

---

② 過去進行式

過去進行式表過去某個特定的時間點正在進行的事。

> ● They **were playing** basketball at the park yesterday afternoon.
> 昨天下午，他們正在公園打籃球。
> ➡ 表過去某個特定的時間點（yesterday afternoon）正在打籃球，所以要用過去進行式。

③ 未來進行式

未來進行式表未來某個特定的時間點正在進行的事。

> ● At this time tomorrow, we **will be traveling** to New York on a business trip. 明天的這個時候，我們會出差到紐約。
> ➡ 表未來某個時間點（At this time tomorrow）正在紐約旅行，所以要用未來進行式。

4 沒有進行式的字彙

> ● 情感動詞
>
> | surprise 使……驚喜 | shock 使……吃驚；使……震撼 |
> |---|---|
> | hate 厭惡 | prefer 偏好 |
> | want 想要 | believe 相信 |
>
> ● 狀態動詞
>
> | include 包括 | need 需要 | |
> |---|---|---|
> | be 是（表示狀態） | know 知道 | exist 存在 |

● I am preferring(→ **prefer**) the sound of the sea.
我偏好海洋的聲音。
➡ 因為情感動詞沒有進行式（am preferring），所以要用現在簡單式（prefer）來表現。

● The president is being(→ **is**) out of the office.
總裁現在不在辦公室。
➡ 因為狀態動詞沒有進行式（is being），所以要用現在簡單式（is）來表現。

Chapter 04

1. Last month, Fred Garland ------- to the city council to replace a member who had stepped down.
   (A) is electing
   (B) was elected
   (C) elects
   (D) elected

2. If you cannot attend the board meeting yourself, please ------- someone to represent you.
   (A) to appoint
   (B) appoint
   (C) appointed
   (D) appoints

3. The photo used on the front of the package will ------- to a wide range of customers.
   (A) appealing
   (B) appealed
   (C) appeals
   (D) appeal

4. Those applying for the accountant's position must prove that they ------- the professional exam.
   (A) passing
   (B) have passed
   (C) to pass
   (D) passes

5. The policy that requires businesses to provide medical insurance applies only to those ------- more than 25 people.
   (A) employs
   (B) employ
   (C) employed
   (D) employing

① 不定詞

基礎文法

1　不定詞的型態和特性

- 不定詞，正如它的名字，指的就是**沒有特定功能的詞**。它在句中可以扮演名詞、形容詞或副詞的角色，因此不定詞可以拿來當主詞、受詞或補語。

- 不定詞是動狀詞，由動詞演變而來，在句中雖具動詞特性，卻擔任其他詞類的角色，不能放在主詞之後當作句子的動詞來使用。

① 不定詞最基本的形式是 to ＋原形動詞

- To work early in the morning is difficult for me.
  早上工作對我來說很困難。

- I need a bigger house to live in with my parents.
  我需要一間大房子才能與父母同住。

- I work hard to have a better life. 我努力工作，才能過更好的生活。

② 不定詞雖然不能當作句子的動詞來使用，但是因為具有動詞的性質，所以後面可以接受詞或補語，也可以被副詞修飾。

- I want to learn how to play the violin. 我想學拉小提琴。

- I want to be a company director within 10 years.
  我希望在十年內成為公司總監。

- I need to wake up early in the morning to get ready for work.
  我早上得早起，為上班做準備。

2 不定詞的功能

不定詞具有**名詞**、**形容詞**、**副詞**的功能。

① 當名詞使用時，放在主詞、受詞、補語的位置。

● 主詞	To exercise regularly is one way of keeping in shape. 定期運動是維持身材的一種方式。
● 受詞	You need to read the newspaper to stay up to date on current affairs. 你要看報紙才能掌握最新時事。
● 主詞補語	This company's mission is to become one of the top five firms in the country. 這家公司的使命是成為國內前五大公司。
● 受詞補語	James helped Jessica to write a letter of application for the position she wanted. 詹姆士幫忙潔西卡為她想要的職位寫求職信。

② 當形容詞使用時，放在名詞後修飾它。

- She has a project to complete. 她有個案子要完成。
- I have some friend to help me. 我有些朋友可以幫我。
- He has a secretary to assist him with his work. 他有一個秘書可以協助他工作。

③ 當副詞使用，修飾動詞以表目的，或修飾形容詞。

● 修飾動詞，表目的	I am calling to inquire about your new insurance policies. 我打電話來是想詢問新的保單。 The accounting team worked very hard to discover a more efficient way to file taxes. 會計團隊研發出新軟體，以找出更有效率的報稅方法。
● 修飾形容詞	The company is pleased to grant Mr. Price the position of senior vice president. 這家公司很高興能給予普萊斯先生資深副總裁的新職位。

3 for ＋名詞＋不定詞

不定詞的邏輯主詞與句子的主詞不相同時，可以用**介系詞 for** 引導出不定詞主詞。

- It is almost impossible for John to finish the work by tomorrow.
  約翰幾乎不可能明天前完成工作。
- The company's goal was for its new software to become one of the biggest products on the market.
  公司的目標是讓他們的新軟體成為市場上最大的產品之一。

4 與不定詞搭配使用的動詞、名詞和形容詞

① 與不定詞搭配使用的動詞

allow 允許	consider 考慮	encourage 鼓勵	invite 邀請
permit 許可	require 要求	want 希望	ask 請求
convince 說服	expect 期待	need 需要	persuade 勸告
tell 告訴	warn 警告	cause 致使	enable 使能夠
force 強迫	order 命令	remind 提醒	urge 敦促

- He allowed the staff to leave work early. 他允許員工提前下班。
- He encouraged his team to work harder. 他鼓勵團隊加倍努力。
- They required their employees to wear formal attire.
  他們要求員工穿著正式服裝。
- She convinced her colleagues to change the design.
  她說服同事變更設計。

② 與不定詞搭配使用的名詞

ability to 有能力做		authority to 有權限做
capacity to 有能耐（能力）做		chance to 有機會做
claim to 主張	decision to 決定	effort to 努力做
need to 需要做	opportunity to 有機會做	plan to 計畫做
readiness to 準備好	right to 有權利做	time to 是時候做
way to 做……的方式	wish to 希望	

- He has the **ability to** fix computers. 他有修電腦的能力。
- He has the **authority to** access the supply room.
  他有進入材料室的權限。
- She had the **capacity to** work very hard. 她有賣力工作的能耐。

③ 與不定詞搭配使用的形容詞

be able to 有能力	be ready to 準備好做
be willing to 樂意做	be likely to 可能做

TIP　It is＋（表人的性質或特徵的形容詞）＋ of ＋受詞＋不定詞

➡ S（人）＋ be ＋（表評論意味的形容詞）＋不定詞

> 表評論意味的形容詞：
> good, fine, bad, kind, unkind, cruel, wise, clever, stupid, rude, foolish, silly, generous, polite, thoughtful, considerate, careful

- It is very kind of you to say so. 你這麼說，你人真好。
  - ➡ You are very kind to say so. 你這麼說，你人真好。
  - ➡ How kind (it is) of you to say so! 你這麼說，真是大好人呢！
- It is very rude of you to arrive late. 你遲到實在是很失禮。
- It is thoughtful of you to think of me. 你能想到我真是貼心。
- It is very generous of you to ask me to lunch.
  你邀我吃午餐真是非常大方。
- It is very clever of you to make friends with the boss.
  你去跟老闆交朋友是很聰明的。

④ 和不定詞片語有關的用語

> 序數、最高級、最後（last）、唯一（only）＋（名詞）＋不定詞片語：
> 第幾次去做……的、最……的去做……的、最後一個去做……的、
> 唯一一個去做……的

- It was **the first** air conditioner **to be sold** at the convention.
  這是大會賣出去的第一部冷氣機。
- He was **the youngest** employee of the company ever **to be promoted** to department manager.
  他是公司內有史以來最年輕就被升為經理的員工。

> 疑問詞（how、what、whom、when、where）＋不定詞片語：
> 要去做……的方法、要去做……、誰要去做……、什麼時候要去做……、
> 要去哪裡做……

- I've decided **what to wear** to my interview at the law firm on Friday. 我已經想好週五要穿什麼去律師事務所面試。

> 形容詞／副詞＋ enough ＋不定詞片語
> enough ＋名詞＋不定詞片語：足夠……而可以……

- Bruce is **old enough to start** working as a mechanic at his factory. 布魯斯的年紀已經大到可以在工廠機械部門裡工作。

5 不帶 to 的不定詞

① 使役動詞（**make**、**let**、**have**）＋受詞＋不帶 to 的不定詞（即原形動詞）

- Mr. Grinley **let** us **take** the rest of the afternoon off because we had worked hard to complete an important project.
  努力完成重要專案後，葛林利先生讓我們下午的時間都休息。

② 準使役動詞 **help**（＋受詞）＋不帶 to 的不定詞／帶 to 不定詞

- Jonathan **helped** Julie **(to) understand** the new accounting software. 強納森幫助茱莉學習新的會計軟體。
  ➡ 不帶 to 的不定詞和帶 to 的不定詞，都可以當作準使役動詞 help 的受詞補語。

③ 感官動詞（**hear**、**see**、**watch**、**notice**）＋受詞＋不帶 to 的不定詞／現在分詞

- I **saw** her **walk** across the bridge. 我看到她走路過橋。
- I **saw** her **walking** across the bridge. 我看到她正走過那座橋。
  ➡ 不帶 to 的不定詞和現在分詞，都可以當作感官動詞 saw 的受詞補語。用現在分詞則更強調動作的進行。

6 獨立不定詞

- **To tell the truth**, I think we need to update our safety policy.
  說實話，我認為我們必須升級安全政策。
- **To make a long story short**, I was finally offered the job.
  長話短說，我終於拿到那個工作了。
- **To be frank (with you)**, the manager is not satisfied with our
  work. 不瞞你說，經理對我們的工作不滿意。

② 動名詞

基礎文法

1 動名詞的型態和特性

動名詞同時具有動詞和名詞的性質，所以也兼具動詞和名詞的含意。簡言之，它是一個「**將動詞名詞化的詞**」。

- 動名詞（V-ing）在句子裡不當作動詞使用，而是要當作名詞使用。

  - **Designing** buildings is a difficult job. 設計建築物是一椿困難的差事。
  - I like **sewing** dresses. 我喜歡縫製洋裝。

- 動名詞仍然具有動詞的性質，所以可以像動詞一樣，後接受詞或補語，也可以接受副詞的修飾。

  - I like **using** computer software. 我喜歡使用電腦軟體。
  - **Becoming** a doctor takes many years of study and practice.
    要成為醫師得花上好幾年的學習和練習。
  - **Working** quickly can lead to careless errors.
    倉促工作可能會導致粗心之過。

① 動名詞的功能、型態和意義上的主詞

(1) 動名詞具有**名詞**的功能，可放在主詞、受詞、補語的位置。

- 主詞位置
  Providing your online password will allow us to access your account details much faster.
  請提供線上密碼，讓我們快速取得您的帳號資料。

- 動詞受詞的位置
  Steven enjoys playing badminton with some of his coworkers on weekends. 史蒂芬喜歡在週末和幾位同事打羽球。

- 介系詞受詞的位置
  The new company director is good at eliminating unnecessary expenses. 公司的新主管善於縮減不必要開支。

- 補語位置
  John's main role in the company is making promotional materials using computer software.
  約翰在公司的主要角色，是利用電腦軟體製作促銷內容。

(2) 被動用法： be ＋ being ＋ p.p.

- The company is being merged with a larger corporation.
  這家公司正與一個大型企業合併。

② 與動名詞搭配使用的動詞

(1) 只能用動名詞作受詞的動詞。

enjoy V-ing 喜愛；享受	recommend V-ing 建議
consider V-ing 考慮	finish V-ing 完成
quit V-ing 放棄；戒除	discontinue V-ing 停止；不再繼續
postpone V-ing 延遲	dislike V-ing 不喜歡
deny V-ing 否定；否認	mind V-ing 介意
avoid V-ing 避免	

- I **enjoy riding** a bicycle by the river. 我喜歡在河邊騎腳踏車。
- I **considered buying** a new computer. 我考慮買一部新電腦。
- I **finished marking** the assignments. 我改完作業了。
- I **discontinued ordering** from that supplier.
  我不再跟這個供應商訂貨了。
- I **postponed delivering** the package until Friday.
  我把遞送包裹延到週五。
- I **avoided driving** to work because of the traffic.
  因交通之故，我避免開車上班。

(2) 與動名詞和不定詞搭配使用，意義均相同的動詞。

begin 開始	start 開始	continue 繼續	plan 計畫
attempt 嘗試	cease 中止	like 喜歡	love 熱愛
neglect 忽視	prefer 偏好	intent 想要	
(can't) bear 無法承受			

- I can't **bear to see** her cry.
  I can't **bear seeing** her cry. 我不忍看到她哭。
- He couldn't **bear to see** his product fail in the market.
- He couldn't **bear seeing** his product fail in the market.
  他無法忍受看到自己的產品在市場上失敗。
- They couldn't **begin building** the house until the plans
  were completed.
  They couldn't **begin to build** the house until the plans
  were completed. 他們要等平面圖完成後才能開始蓋房子。

(3) 動詞＋受詞＋介系詞＋動名詞片語

accuse . . . of 指控……罪	congratulate . . . on 恭喜……事
forgive . . . for 原諒……事	prohibit . . . from 禁止……做
stop . . . from 阻止……做	thank . . . for 感謝……因為
blame . . . for 指責……事	discourage . . . from 勸阻……事
ban/prevent/keep . . . from . . . 禁止……事	suspect . . . of 懷疑……事
punish . . . for 處罰……事	
warn . . . against 警告……不要	

- Jeff accused me of lying. 傑夫指控我說謊。
- The company prohibited employees from leaving work before 4 p.m. 這家公司禁止員工在四點前下班。
- He thanked her for helping him finish his work on time. 他感謝她協助他準時完成工作。
- He was warned against arriving late for work. 他被警告上班不可以遲到。
- They blamed him for making that terrible mistake. 他們責怪他犯下致命錯誤。
- The car accident prevented him from walking for more than six months. 最近這場車禍使他六個多月不良於行。

(4) 很容易被誤以為要與不定詞搭被使用，其實後面要接**動名詞**的動詞：

be accustomed to 習慣於	be opposed to 反對
look forward to 期待	be dedicated to 為……而設；奉獻
be related to 跟……有關	contribute to 對……有貢獻
object to 反對	be devoted to 奉獻
be used to 習慣	lead to 導致
resort to 訴諸	

- He was accustomed to working on a team. 他習慣在團隊裡工作。
- She was opposed to merging with the other company. 她反對跟另一家公司合併。
- He was looking forward to working with the new manager. 他期待和新經理共事。
- The case study is related to waiving the charge, as they are our valued customers. 這則案例是關於免除他們的費用，因為他們是我們尊貴的顧客。
- Because I used to work as a truck driver, I am used to driving at night. 我做過卡車司機，所以習慣在夜間開車。
- Because he found it unfair, Tim objected to changing the rule regarding staff vacation time. 提姆反對改變員工假期時間的規定，因為他覺得不公平。

2 動名詞的慣用句型

① 和動名詞片語有關的句型

- **have ＋ trouble / difficulty / a hard/difficult time ＋ in ＋動名詞片語**

  Due to her inexperience with the software, Julie had trouble (in) solving the problem.

  茱莉對軟體不熟，所以無法解決問題。

  When she arrived at the airport her cell phone didn't work, so I had a hard time (in) finding her.

  她到機場的時候，手機無法使用，所以我找不到她。

- **go ＋動名詞片語**

  Because we have to work on Sundays, we usually go dancing on Friday nights.

  因為我們週日必須上班，所以常會在週五晚上去跳舞。

② 用動名詞當受詞，和用不定詞當受詞，意思上有不同的時候。

- I remembered ordering the goods. 我記得我有訂貨。
- I remembered to order the goods. 我記得要去訂貨。

③ 分詞和分詞片語

分詞具有**動詞**的性質，卻不當成動詞使用，而是在句子中擔任**形容詞**的角色。分詞分成兩種，一種是具有主動和進行中含意的**現在分詞**，另一種是具有被動和完成含意的**過去分詞**。分詞和不定詞、動名詞一樣，不能成為句子的動詞，而是**動狀詞**。

◆ **分詞**（現在分詞、過去分詞）雖然從動詞衍生而來，但在句子中卻不是扮演動詞，而是扮演形容詞的角色。

◆ 分詞仍然帶有**動詞**的性質，所以可以像動詞一樣後接受詞和補語，且接受副詞的修飾。

- There were many people **enjoying** the concert.
  很多人喜歡這個演唱會。
- The computer which was **fixed** yesterday is working well.
  昨天修好的電腦現在正常運作了。

1 分詞的型態和特性

① 分詞具有形容詞的功能。

② 像形容詞一樣，放在名詞前或後來修飾名詞。

- Because of the **increasing** price of materials, we have to reduce production. 因為原物料漲價，所以必須減產。
- He left the computer **running**. 他讓電腦繼續運作。

2 分詞的種類

① 修飾名詞時，分詞和被修飾名詞之間的關係是主動的話，用現在分詞；是被動關係的話就用過去分詞。

- We have seen a notice **recommending** that we read the new tax laws.
  我們看過一個公告，建議我們要讀新稅法。
  ➡ 因為接受修飾的名詞（a notice）和分詞的關係，是主動的「公告推薦」，所以要用現在分詞（recommending）。

- The special offer is only valid for products **purchased** in our stores. 特別優惠只適用於在店內購買的商品。
  ➡ 因為接受修飾的名詞（products）和分詞的關係，是被動的「被購買的商品」，所以要用過去分詞（purchased）。

② 分詞作主詞補語或受詞補語使用時，和主詞或受詞的關係是主動的話，用現在分詞，是被動的話就用過去分詞。

- The movie became **interesting**. 電影變得有趣了。
  ➡ 因為主詞（The movie）和補語的關係是主動的「電影給出趣味」，所以要用現在分詞（interesting）。

③ 分詞作為分詞片語使用時，和主要子句主詞的關係是主動的話，用現在分詞，是被動的話就用過去分詞。

- You must read the terms of the contract carefully before **signing** it.
  在簽約前，你務必要詳讀合約條款。
  ➡ 因為主要子句的主詞（You），和分詞片語的關係是主動的「你簽名」，所以要用現在分詞（signing）。

- **Located** on the first floor of the building, the café is frequented by employees.
  咖啡店就在建築物一樓，所以常受到員工的光顧。
  ➡ 因為主要子句的主詞（the café），和分詞片語的關係是被動的「咖啡店位在」，所以要用過去分詞（located）。

描述某人的感覺是什麼，用過去分詞；要描述引起這種感覺的人、事物、情形、事件，就用現在分詞。

- **The excited audience** all sang together.
  興致高昂的觀眾一起唱了起來。
- There are lots of **interesting exhibitions**. 有很多有趣的展覽。

3　分詞片語

分詞片語的功能和特徵

(1) 作副詞用的分詞片語，具有表**時間**、**原因**、**條件**、**連續動作**等的功能。

- **Having failed the screening process**, I returned to training camp. 因為我沒有通過篩選流程，所以又回到訓練營。
- **Feeling confident**, Sam delivered his speech well.
  = Because Sam felt confident, he delivered his speech well.
  山姆因為有自信，因此他的演講很成功。
- **Marketed properly**, our new summer range will sell well.
  = If it is marketed properly, our new summer range will sell well. 好好行銷的話，我們新的夏季系列會熱銷。
- The pet store added a new exotic pet section, **featuring animals from Asia and Australia**.
  = The pet store added a new exotic pet section, and it featured animals from Asia and Australia.
  寵物店多了異國寵物區，特色是有來自亞洲和澳洲的動物。

(2) 作形容詞用的分詞片語，置於被修飾的名詞後面。表發生的狀況時，要用「with ＋受詞＋分詞片語」這型式。

- Mrs. Grey walked by **with papers falling** out of her briefcase.
  葛雷太太走經過的時候，紙從公事包掉了出來。

Chapter 05

1. The warehouse workers were asked ------- the manager when new shipments arrive.
   (A) to notify
   (B) notified
   (C) notification
   (D) notifying

2. Foreman Jake Haines was praised for ------- several shipping processes to improve efficiency.
   (A) consolidation
   (B) consolidated
   (C) consolidating
   (D) consolidate

3. Author Gloria Haggins is praised for ------- the unique characters in the genre.
   (A) creative
   (B) creation
   (C) created
   (D) creating

4. The relaxation therapy greatly reduced Ms. Trevor's anxiety, but it did not eliminate the problem -------.
   (A) outside
   (B) unlike
   (C) altogether
   (D) entire

5. To have her belongings professionally moved, Ms. Kerr paid $949, ------- applicable taxes.
   (A) inclusion
   (B) include
   (C) including
   (D) inclusive

06 介系詞

基礎文法

◆ 介系詞放在名詞或代名詞前，表場所、時間、原因等。

- We had dinner **at** a Thai restaurant.
  我們在一家泰國餐廳享用晚餐。
- The city hosts a drama festival **in** the summer.
  該城市在夏天舉辦了戲劇節。
- It is usually colder **on** the beach because of the breeze.
  海灘上因為有微風，所以通常比較冷。

◆ 介系詞片語在句子中扮演修飾名詞的形容詞角色，或修飾動詞的副詞角色。

- The box **on** the table is empty. 桌上的盒子是空的。
- I exercise **in** the evening. 我晚上會運動。

1 介系詞的用法

① 時間和場所

(1) 表時間的介系詞 in/at/on

介系詞	用法	舉例
in	月、年度 季節、世紀 在 …… 時間後、早上／下午／晚上	• in October 在十月 • in 2018 在 2018 年 • in the 21st century 在 21 世紀 • in two days 在兩天內 • in the morning/afternoon/evening 　在早上／下午／晚上
at	（具體的）時刻、時間點	• at nine o'clock 九點時 • at noon/night/midnight 　在中午／晚上／午夜 • at the beginning/end of the month 　在月初／月底

| on | 日期、星期、特別的日子 | ● on August 15th 在 8 月 15 日
● on Friday 在週五
● on Christmas Day 在耶誕節 |

(2) 表場所的介系詞 in/at/on

介系詞	用法	舉例
in	大空間內的場所	● in the world/country 　在世界上／在國內 ● in the city/room/town 　在城市中／房間內／鎮上
at	地點、地址	● at the intersection 在十字路口 ● at the bus stop 在公車站
on	平面的上面、 一直線上的地點	● on the table 在桌上 ● on the Donau River 在多瑙河上 ● on the 1st floor/level 在一樓

② 各種交通方法

　　by ＋交通工具／通信手段（無冠詞名詞）

> She came here │ by train. 她搭火車來。
> 　　　　　　　　│ on a train
> 　　　　　　　　│ by a train (x)
> He came here on foot. 他走路來。
> He came here on horseback. 他騎馬來。

| by | air 空運
plane = on a plane 搭飛機
steamer 搭汽船
train = on a train 搭火車
bicycle = on a bicycle 騎單車
bus = in a bus 搭公車
car = in a car 搭車；開車
express 快遞
sea 海運
coach 搭遊覽車 | by | taxi = in a taxi 搭計程車
ship = in a ship 搭船
land 陸運
mail 郵寄
word of mouth 藉口耳相傳
telegram 用電報
letter 以信件
cable 以海外電報
telephone 透過電話
wireless 透過無線通信 |

③ 表「移動」的介系詞

- She slowly walked **into** the office. 她慢慢走進辦公室。
- The company could not take any funds **out of** its accounts.
  公司無法從他們的帳戶取出資金。

-----

across 穿越；各處　　along 沿著

- He walked **across** the bridge on his way to work.
  他在上班途中越過這座橋。

④ 表「位置」的介系詞

above 在……上面　　over 在……之上　　at 在……地點
under 在……之下　　below 在……下面　　on 在……上
beneath 在……之下　　up 在……上　　down 在……下
in 在……內

- The files were **below** the books. 檔案在書本下方。
- Alice just lives one floor **down** from me. 艾莉絲就住在我家樓下。
- The files were **in** the man's desk. 檔案在這位男士的書桌裡。

⑤ in/at/on 慣用語

in	
in time 及時	in between 在期間
in the coming year 來年	in place 到位；就位
in the sales department/division 在銷售部門	in the foreseeable future 在可預見的未來
in a campaign 在活動中	in any case 無論如何
in consideration of ... 考慮到	in lieu (of) 替代
in addition to 除了……外	in all probability 在所有的可能性中

- The team had to work overtime to complete the project **in time**.
  團隊必須加班才能及時完成專案。
- The company participated **in a charity event** for the community.
  公司為了社區而參與了慈善活動。

- We expect sales of our new products to be high **in the coming year**. 我們預期來年新產品的銷售量會飆高。

- Because of low profits, a new marketing strategy was put **in place**. 因為低利的緣故，採用了新的行銷策略。

- The company has three new employees **in the sales division**. 公司銷售部門有三名新進員工。

- The manager expected higher sales **in the coming financial year**. 經理預期明年會計年的營收將攀升。

- Thornley & Sons hired a new marketing team **in a campaign** to increase sales. 索恩利公司為提高銷量的活動，僱用了新的行銷團隊。

- **In consideration of** market changes, Swinley Industrial was forced to reduce its staff. 顧及市場的改變，斯溫利工業被迫裁員。

- **In lieu of** a birthday party, Sandra had an expensive dinner with her parents. 珊卓沒有舉辦生日派對，而是和父母吃了一頓昂貴的晚餐。

- **In addition to** footwear, the shop sells various accessories. 該店除了販賣鞋襪外，也販售不同的飾品。

- **In all probability** we will finish early. 我們很可能提前完成。

at	
at once 立刻；馬上	at a good pace 快速地
at the rate of ... 以……的速度	at times 有時；不時
at (a) high speed 高速	at the age of ... 在……歲時
at least 至少	at a low price 以低價
at a price/cost of ... 以……為代價	at the latest 最晚
at 60 miles an hour 以時速 60 英哩	at your leisure 當你有空時
at one's expense ... 以……為代價；在犧牲……的狀況下	at regular intervals 每隔（一定時間或距離）
at your earliest convenience 盡早	at a loss 虧本的；困擾的
at any rate 不管怎樣	at a premium 以高價；以溢價
at any cost 不惜代價	at best 充其量
at most 最多	at hand 在手邊；即將到來
at every turn 處處；隨時	at liberty 自由的

- The team worked **at a good pace**. 這個團隊快速運作。
- **At times** we must clean the equipment. 我們不時都要清潔設備。
- He became manager **at the age of** 25. 他在 25 歲時當上經理。
- Jim was driving **at 60 miles an hour**. 車子以每小時60英哩的速度前進。
- Next week you can arrive at work **at your leisure**. 下週你有空就可以來工作。
- Employees must take breaks **at regular intervals**. 員工每隔一段時間就必須休息。
- The business was running **at a loss**. 公司的經營面臨虧損。
- The company's products sold **at a premium**. 公司的產品以高價售出。
- The accounting team expected a 10 percent sales increase **at best**. 會計團隊預期營收成長率最多只有 10%。
- We can offer a 10 percent discount **at most**. 我們最多只能打九折。
- The project encountered problems **at every turn**. 這個專案到處都遇到問題。
- The man was not **at liberty** to tell the truth. 這位男士沒有說出實話的自由。

on	
on time 準時	on the waiting list 在候補名單上
on a regular basis 定期	on the recommendation of ... 依……的推薦
on approval 不滿意可以退的	on call 隨時待命
on board 在飛機上；在船上	on duty 值勤

- The restaurant was busy, so customers were put **on the waiting list**. 餐廳很忙，所以顧客被放在等候名單上。
- We must update our software **on a regular basis**. 我們必須定期更新軟體。
- He was hired **on the recommendation** of his former employer. 他受到前任雇主的推薦而被僱用。
- The company bought the new furniture **on approval**. 公司買了不滿意可退貨的新傢俱。
- Staff must be **on call** until midnight this week. 這個星期，員工到午夜前都必須隨傳隨到。
- There weren't many passengers **on board** the plane. 登上這個班機的乘客並不多。
- The security guard was **on duty** for 12 hours. 保全人員值班 12 小時。

2 介系詞的選擇

時間點和期間

表時間點的介系詞	
since 自從	from 從
until/by 直到／不晚於；早於	before/prior to... 在……之前

- I have worked here **since** I was 18 years old.
  我從 18 歲就開始在這裡工作了。

- We are open **from** 9 a.m. to 5 p.m.
  我們從早上九點開到下午五點。

- Today we have to work **until** 10 p.m.
  我們今天必須工作到晚上十點。

- We must finish this project **by** next week.
  我們必須在下週前完成專案。

- Please check your uniform **before** coming to work.
  上班前請檢查制服。

- Please check all your documents **prior to** sending in the application. 在申請這個職位前，請檢查你所有的文件。

表期間的介系詞	
for 達；計	over/through(out)... 整個；從頭到尾
within... 在……之內	during... 在……期間

- The manager has been working there **for** seven years.
  經理在這裡工作已經七年了。

- The accounting department was busy **during** the tax period.
  會計部門在報稅期間很忙碌。

- Staff had to work **over** the weekend to finish the project.
  員工整個週末都必須工作以完成專案。

- The marketing team worked **through** the night to complete the project. 行銷團隊通宵工作以完成專案。

- The construction company had to complete the building **within** six months. 建設公司必須在六個月內蓋好這棟建築。

(1) **for** 是表「已經持續多久」，**during** 是表「在這段時間內」。

> - The CEO had been running the company **for** over 20 years.
>   執行長已經營這家公司超過 20 個年頭。
> - The staff members were required to work overtime **during** the Christmas holiday. 員工被要求在耶誕節期間加班。

(2) in 也可以接「一段時間」，表「在……期間」。

> - Your package will arrive **in** seven business days.
>   您的包裹將在七個工作天內送達。

(3) **by**, **until**

> - by 在……之前   by six o'clock 在六點之前
> - until 直到   until two hours later 直到兩小時後
>
> -
>
> - We should receive the funds **by** five o'clock this afternoon.
>   我們應該在今天下午五點前就收到款項。
> - This credit card is valid **until** July 2020.
>   這張信用卡有效期限到 2020 年 7 月。
>   ➜ by 是不要晚於下午五點／在下午五點前的意思。第二句，因為信用卡到 2020 年 7 月仍有效，所以用 until。

(4) **for**, **during**, **since**

> - for ＋期間   for three months 三個月內
> - durning ＋期間   during the Christmas holidays 聖誕假期期間
> - since ＋時間點   since 2000 從 2000 年起
>
> -
>
> - Construction will continue **during** the winter / **for** 12 months.
>   施工會持續整個冬天／施工會持續 12 個月。
> - The factory workers had to work **for** six more hours to meet the deadline. 這些工廠工人必須加班六個小時以趕上期限。
> - Shintech Technologies has been operating **since** 2005.
>   新科科技公司從 2005 年開始營運。
>   ➜ for 後接期間，since 後接特定的時間點。

3 位置

表位置的介系詞	
above/over 在……上面	below/under 在……下面
beside / next to 在……旁邊	between 在（兩者）之間
near 靠近	among 在（三者或以上）之間
around 環繞；在……四處	within 在……裡面

- He lifted his hands above/over his head. 他將雙手高舉過頭。
- He held the ball above his head. 他將球高舉過頭。
- He threw the ball over his head. 他將球高丟過頭。
- Look in the cupboard below/under the sink. 看一下水槽下的櫥櫃。
- Look in the cabinet below the desk. 看一下書桌下的櫃子。
- The file is under those books. 檔案在那些書本下方。
- I sat down beside / next to my wife. 我在我太太旁邊坐下來。
- Please sit beside your manager. 請坐在你的經理旁邊。
- He sat next to his coworker. 他坐在同事的旁邊。
- There's a table between the two chairs. 兩張椅子中間有一張桌子。
- There's a bathroom between the two offices.
  兩間辦公室之間有一間廁所。
- The midday meal was served between two and four o'clock.
  兩點到四點間會供應午餐。
- The workers had their lunch break between one and two o'clock.
  工人在一點到兩點間會有中餐休息時間。
- They walked among the crowd. 他們在人群中走著。
- He was the best candidate among all the interviewees.
  他是所有面試者中最棒的人選。
- I'd like to sit near a window. 我想坐在靠窗的位置。
- His office desk was near a large window. 他的辦公桌靠近大窗戶。
- All staff should be aware of activities within the company.
  所有員工都應該要知道公司內部的動靜。
- There are over 60 bus lines operating within the city.
  市區內有超過 60 條公車路線行駛。
- Some of the travelers wanted to walk around the night market.
  這些遊客中，有些人想逛一逛夜市。
- The new workers were shown around the factory.
  新員工被帶四處參觀工廠。

① between 是「在兩個東西之間」，也可以用來表「在兩個位置之間」或「在兩個時間之間」。among 是「在三個以上的事物／人之間」。

② above/over 和 below/under 也有「……以上」和「……以下」的意思。

- You have to be over 19 to see this film.
  你必須年過 19 才能看這部電影。
- You can't see this film if you're under 19.
  如果你未滿 19 歲，就不能看這部電影。

---

over	
have the edge over 有優勢	over the hump 渡過最困難的階段
over the counter 不需處方箋	over someone's head 難以理解

- Because of his training he had an/the edge over the competition. 他因為受過訓練，在這場競賽中佔有優勢。
- The medicine was available over the counter.
  這款藥不需處方箋就能購買。
- The joke went over his head. 這笑話超過他所能理解。

under	
under new management 在新的管理下	under investigation 接受調查
under close supervision 在嚴密監控下	under review 接受審查
under one's current contract 依目前的合約	under consideration 被考慮
under control 受到控制	under discussion 在討論中
under development 發展中	under pressure 在壓力下

- The company resumed operations under new management.
  公司在新經營團隊帶領下恢復運作。
- Due to its tax problems, the company was under investigation.
  這家公司因為稅務問題正在接受調查。
- New staff members must be kept under close supervision.
  新進員工必須受到嚴密監督。
- All employees will be under review this month.
  所有員工本月將會被考核。

- **Under your current contract** you are entitled to health insurance. 根據現在的合約，你享有健康保險。
- The building manager had the project **under control**. 這個建案在工程經理的掌握之中。
- The new manager was **under pressure** from the board of directors. 新任經理處於董事會的壓力之下。
- A new marketing strategy is currently **under development**. 新的行銷策略目前還在發展階段。

between

a difference/gap between A and B 在 A 與 B 之間有差距／落差

- There was a big **difference between** the two suppliers' prices. 這兩個供應商的價格有大差距。

within

within a radius of	within the organization
在⋯⋯半徑範圍內	在組織內

- All testing must be done **within a radius of** 10 kilometers. 所有測試必須在半徑十公里內進行。
- **Within the organization** there were 100 employees. 組織中有 100 名員工。

around

around the world	around the corner
全世界；世界各地	在轉角；在附近；即將發生

- After 10 years, the company had expanded **around the world**. 十年後，這家公司已擴張到全世界。
- There was a bank **around the corner**. 以前轉角有一家銀行。

4 方向

表方向的介系詞	
from 從	to 到
across 穿越	through 穿過；在各處
along 沿著	for 往（表目的）
toward(s) 往……方向	into 到……裡面
out of 在……外；離開	

- The necessary documents are available **from** the front counter.
  必要文件可在前台取得。
- The package will be sent directly **to** the head office.
  包裹將直接送到總公司。
- The popularity of the new product spread **across** the world.
  新產品受歡迎的程度傳遍全球。
- I walked **through** the woods. 我步行穿越林地。
- All staff members must enter **through** the security gate.
  所有員工必須從安全門進入。
- Newman walked **along** the street.
  紐曼沿著街道行走。
- They walked **along** the boulevard on their way to work.
  他們沿著大街走路去上班。
- I'm leaving **for** Taichung. 我將前往臺中。
- The marketing team aimed **for** a successful campaign.
  行銷團隊的目標是成功辦好活動。
- She walked **toward** me. 她朝我走過來。
- The manager was working **toward** a promotion.
  經理為了升遷而努力。
- We moved all the luggage **into** the room.
  我們把所有行李搬進房內。
- The company put all of its money **into** developing new product.
  這家公司傾注所有資金到研發新產品上。
- I took the key **out of** my pocket. 我從口袋中拿出鑰匙。
- He took the money **out of** his account.
  他從他的戶頭中領出這筆錢。

from

| from one's point of view
從……的觀點 | from the cradle to (the) grave
從生到死；一輩子 |

- **From the manager's point of view**, the new advertisement was successful. 從經理的角度來看，新廣告很成功。
- He lived in the small town **from the cradle to the grave**. 他這輩子都住在那個小鎮上。

to

to the relief of 使……鬆了一口氣；使……放心	to a great extent 到很大的程度
to my knowledge 就我所知	to be sure 確保
to one's satisfaction 讓……滿意	

- The project was finally completed, **to the relief of** all the staff members. 專案最後終於完成，所有員工鬆了一口氣。
- The new staff members' performance had improved **to a great extent**. 新進職員的表現大有進步。
- **To my knowledge**, there have been no changes in the company policy. 就我所知，公司政策並沒有改變。
- Please double-check all your work **to be sure** it is free of errors. 請再檢查一次你的工作，確保沒有錯誤。
- All work must be completed **to the CEO's satisfaction**. 所有工作必須完成，讓執行長滿意。

along/across

| along the shore 沿著岸邊 | across the street 越過街道 |
| across from the post office 在郵局對面 | |

- The man took a long walk **along the shore** in the morning. 男子早上沿著岸邊走了一大段路。
- The new head office was **across the street** from the old one. 新的總部辦公室在舊的辦公室對街。
- The bank is directly **across from the post office**. 銀行在郵局的正對面。

● out of	
out of date 過時	out of reach 手搆不著；無法達成的
out of order 故障	out of room 沒有空間了
out of print 絕版	out of stock 沒有存貨了
out of season 非當季的；過季的	out of control 失控
out of town 出城了	out of paper 沒有紙了

- Many of the items delivered were **out of date**.
  寄送的東西有許多已經過時。
- Most of the printers were **out of order**.
  這些印表機多半都故障了。
- The new range was so popular it was **out of stock** in 24 hours.
  新系列大受歡迎，24 小時內就銷售一空。
- The vegetables were quite expensive because they were **out of season**. 因為不是當季的蔬菜，所以價格相當昂貴。
- The manager was **out of town** on a business trip.
  經理因公出城去了。
- The printer had run **out of paper**. 印表機的紙已經用完了。

5 原因、讓步、目的、除外、附加

表原因、讓步、目的的介系詞
because of / due to / owing to /on account of 因為；由於
despite / in spite of / regardless of 儘管；雖然；不管
for 為了

- We were late **because of** the rain.
  因為下雨，我們遲到了。
- The company reduced its staff **because of** budget cuts.
  公司因為預算縮減而裁員。
- The company has a lot of money **owing to** its recent success.
  因為最近的成功，這家公司有很多錢。
- The employees continued working hard **regardless of** their results.
  不論成果如何，員工依然繼續勤奮工作。
- **Despite** a poor economy, the shop has been doing well.
  儘管經濟不好，這家店依舊做得有聲有色。

- **Despite** recent changes in the market, the company has continued to do well.
  儘管最近市場出現變化，這家公司依舊表現良好。
- **In spite of** the bad weather, the farmer continued to work.
  雖然天候不佳，農人還是繼續工作。
- The club is hosting a party **for** all its members.
  俱樂部正在為所有成員舉辦一個派對。
- This weekend the company will hold a retirement party **for** its CEO. 這個週末，公司將會為執行長舉辦退休派對。

含有介系詞 for 表某目的的片語

for your convenience 為了你方便	for future uses 供未來使用
for future reference 作為日後參考	for safety reasons 基於安全因素
articles for sale 待售物件	

- **For your convenience**, the café opens at 7 a.m.
  為了你方便，咖啡廳上午七點開門。
- I filed the documents away **for future uses**.
  我把文件歸檔，以備未來之用。
- **For safety reasons**, please fasten your seat belts during the flight.
  基於安全考量，請在飛行期間繫緊安全帶。

表除外、附加的介系詞

except (for) / excepting / aside from / apart from 除……之外
instead of 代替；而不是
in addition to / besides 除……之外

- I cleaned all the rooms **except (for)** the bathroom.
  除了浴室沒掃之外，我打掃了其他所有房間。
- All staff can leave early today **except for** the accounting department. 除了會計部門之外，所有員工今天都可以提早下班。
- The new employees were all doing well, **aside from** one.
  除了一位之外，所有新進員工都表現良好。
- The employees all received bonuses, **apart from** several of the new interns. 除了幾位實習新人外，所有員工都收到紅利。
- We used graphics **instead of** words. 我們使用圖像而不是文字。
- We will be using a new software program **instead of** our current one. 我們會用新的軟體程式，取代目前用的這個。

- **In addition to** the new offices, the building has a coffee shop on the first floor. 除了新辦公室外，這棟建築物的一樓有個咖啡廳。
- We stock several other brands **in addition to** our own. 除了我們自己的商品外，我們也庫存了幾個他牌商品。
- **Apart from** writing novels, he also worked in an office. 除了寫小說之外，他也有正職。
- **Besides** writing summaries, she proofreads all of the professor's work. 除了撰寫摘要外，她校對教授的所有作品。

- I don't know anything about wine, except for that(→ **except that**) I like it. 除了說我喜歡紅酒外，我對紅酒一無所知。
➡ except 用在後接「連接詞＋子句（主詞＋動詞）」的情況，不能和 for 搭配使用。

---

6 關於

表「關於」的介系詞		
about 關於	on 關於	over 與……有關
as to 關於；至於	as for 關於；至於	
concerning 就……而言	regarding 關於；至於	
with/in regard to 關於；至於	with respect to 就……而言	
with/in reference to 論及	when it comes to 談到……時	
as far as sb./sth. is concerned 在……看來		

- She speculated **about/on** my motives. 她推測我的動機。
- There is no point in arguing **over** this. 爭論這個沒有意義。
- **As to** when is the deadline, we'll talk about that later. 至於期限是什麼時候，我們之後再說吧。
- The employee was asked to meet with management **concerning** his performance review. 這名男子因績效考核之故，被要求和管理階層見面。
- **With regard to** health and safety, all factory workers are required to conform to company regulations at all times. 基於健康與安全考量，所有工廠工人在任何時候都必須遵守公司規定。
- **As far as** I concerned, what the manager said doesn't make any sense. 在我來看，經理說的話毫無道理。

7 和動詞、名詞、形容詞搭配使用的介系詞片語

和動詞搭配使用的介系詞片語

account for 解釋；成為……的原因	depend on (= rely on = count on) 依賴；取決於
associate A with B 將 A 和 B 聯想在一起	add to 加到
sympathize with 同情；諒解	congratulate A on B 因 B 恭喜 A
comply with 遵守	wait for 等待
direct A to B 指示 A 到 B	consist of 由……組成
keep track of 掌握……的發展	return A to B 將 A 歸還給 B
contribute to 對……有貢獻	employ A as B 僱用 A 擔任 B（職位）
transfer A to B 將 A 調動到 B	

- The manager was asked to **account for** the lack of sales in his department. 經理必須為自己部門的銷售不佳負責。
- The manager knew he could **depend on** his team to work hard.
  經理知道他可以信賴他的團隊努力工作。
- A new range of menswear was released to **add to** the winter collection. 男性服飾新系列已上市，加入冬季精選。
- Due to his own experience, the manager had to **sympathize with** his staff.
  基於個人經驗，經理必須同情他的員工。
- The CEO called the marketing team to his office to **congratulate** them **on** their achievement.
  執行長把行銷團隊叫進辦公室，恭喜他們的成就。
- All staff members are required to **comply with** the new health and safety policy.
  所有員工必須遵守新的衛生安全政策。
- The man had to **wait for** seven days to find out if he had gotten the job.
  這名男子必須等七天才會知道他是否得到這份工作。
- Most of the new staff members' work will **consist of** record-keeping. 多數新進員工的工作包含記帳。
- The new policy states that employees must **keep track of** all travel expenses.
  新政策要求員工記錄所有旅費。

- Because of a problem with the product, the man returned it to the store.
  因為產品有問題，男子把它退回店裡。
- All staff members are expected to contribute to the charity event this weekend.
  這個週末，所有員工都要為慈善活動貢獻己力。
- The manager decided to employ her as his new assistant.
  經理決定僱用這名女性當他的助理。
- Because of Gail's performance, the manager decided to transfer her to the head office.
  有鑑於蓋兒的表現，經理決定將她調到總公司。

動詞＋介系詞

apologize for 為……道歉	consist of 由……組成
benefit from 因……受惠	depend on / rely on / count on 仰賴
listen to 聆聽	result in 導致
suffer from 受苦；患病	believe in 相信
belong to 屬於	contribute to 對……有貢獻
interfere with 干涉；妨礙	pay for 支付
succeed in 成功	think of 思考；想到
apply A to B 將 A 應用於 B	compare A with B 將 A 與 B 相比
lead A to B 帶領 A 到 B	provide B with A 提供 A 給 B
remind A of B 提醒 A 有 B	substitute B for A 以 A 取代 B
compare A to B 將 A 比做 B	define A as B 將 A 定義為 B
pay A for B 為了 B 支付 A	prevent/keep A from B 防止 A 做 B；使 A 遠離 B
regard A as B / consider A B 視 A 為 B	

和形容詞搭配使用的介系詞片語

absent from 缺席	equivalent to 等同於
identical to 與……相同	consistent with 與……一致
responsible for 對……負責	comparable to 比得上
similar to 與……類似	

- He was **absent from** work because of personal issues.
  他因個人因素而沒有去上班。

- The quality of the new product was **equivalent to** that of the competitior's.
  新產品的品質等同於競爭對手的。

- The new cell phone was almost **identical to** the older version.
  新手機幾乎和舊版一模一樣。

- All staff members must ensure that their work is **consistent with** company requirements.
  所有員工必須要確保他們的工作成果符合公司要求。

- All employees are **responsible for** recording their travel expenses.
  所有員工有責任記錄他們的差旅費。

- The company offered him a new contract that was **comparable to** his old one.
  這家公司提供這位男子能跟他舊合約相提並論的新合約。

- The company's new tablet computers are quite **similar to** its competitor's models.
  這兩家公司的平板電腦彼此雷同。

形容詞／過去分詞＋介系詞

accustomed/used to 習慣於	anxious about/for 對……感到焦慮、掛念
capable of 有能力	famous for 因……出名
interested in 對……有興趣	pleased with 對……感到滿意、開心
responsible for 對……負責	tired of 對……感到厭煩
afraid of 害怕	wrong with 出問題
disappointed with 對……失望	free from 免於
necessary for 對……是有必要的	related to 跟……有關
satisfied with 對……滿意	

access to 使用	exposure to 接觸
advocate for/of ……的提倡者或支持者	cause/reason for ……的原因
concern over 對……感到憂心	lack of 缺乏
permission from 從……取得許可	problem with 有……的問題
dispute over 爭論	respect for 尊敬
effect/impact/influence on 對……有影響	
question about/concerning/regarding 對……有疑慮	
decrease/increase/rise/drop in ……的減少／增加／提升／下降	

- The new key cards will give staff **access to** the parking lot.
  新的門禁卡讓員工可以使用地下停車場。

- The charity's ad campaign raised **exposure to** their work overseas.
  這個慈善機構的廣告增加了他們海外工作的曝光度。

- The charity worked hard **for a good cause**.
  這個慈善機構為了良善的目標而奮鬥。

- There is growing **concern over** recent stock market trends.
  近期股市的變化受到愈來愈多關注。

- Factory workers who need to use the toilet must ask for **permission from** the floor manager.
  想要上廁所的工廠工人必須得到經理的同意。

- Many of the staff were having **problems with** the new software.
  許多員工搞不定新軟體。

名詞＋介系詞

advance in ……的進步	capability of ……的能力
decrease in ……的減少	example of ……的例子
influence on ……的影響	possibility of ……的可能性
approval of ……的許可	contribution to 對……的貢獻
demand for 對於……的需求	increase in ……的增加
interest in 對……的興趣	use of ……的使用

Chapter 06

1. VIP guests were invited to sit ------- the front row during the lecture.
   (A) in
   (B) down
   (C) without
   (D) of

2. ------- some confusion regarding her reservation when she checked in, the CEO's stay at Harrison Hotel was pleasant.
   (A) As for
   (B) On the contrary
   (C) In addition to
   (D) Notwithstanding

3. Passengers are not allowed to board the aircraft ------- a boarding pass from the airline.
   (A) against
   (B) owing to
   (C) without
   (D) about

4. Water from a broken pipe spilled ------- the floor and caused minor damage.
   (A) onto
   (B) at
   (C) until
   (D) aside

5. The check-in desk provides name tags ------- participants in the technology conference.
   (A) in
   (B) of
   (C) by
   (D) for

形容詞

基礎文法

形容詞是表現數量、性質、模樣、大小、顏色等的字，放在名詞前用來**修飾名詞**，或當作**補語**用來補充說明主詞或受詞。

◆ 形容詞用來限定或說明名詞的性質或狀態。

- I see a cute baby. 我看到一個可愛的嬰兒。
- The baby is cute. 這個嬰兒很可愛。
  ➡ 形容詞可置於名詞之前，作修飾名詞之用；也可置於連綴動詞之後，當補語以補充名詞之涵義，使句意完整。

◆ 形容詞大致都是以 -able、-al、-ible、-ic、-tive、-ous、-ful、-y 等為字尾。

advisable 明智的；適當的	formal 正式的	responsible 負責任的
specific 指定的；特定的	scientific 科學的	previous 先前的
doctrinal 教義的；學說的	effective 有效的	heavy 重的；沉重的
unbelievable 難以置信的	talkative 健談的	envious 嫉妒的
predictable 可預測的	beautiful 美麗的	pretty 漂亮的
successful 成功的		

也有以 **-ly** 結尾的形容詞，這些字要特別注意不要誤以為是副詞了。

likely 有可能的	lively 精力充沛的	costly 昂貴的	deadly 致命的
friendly 友善的	lovely 可愛的	lonely 寂寞的	silly 愚蠢的
ugly 醜陋的	timely 及時的	oily 油膩的	holy 神聖的

複數普通名詞

the rich = rich people 有錢人	the poor = poor people 窮人
the dead = dead people 死人	the wounded = wounded people 傷患
the new = new things 新事物	the wise = wise people 聰明人

the young = young people 年輕人

the old = old people 老人家

the learned = learned people 學識淵博的人

the dying = dying people 將死之人

the known = things that are known 已知的事物

the unknown = things that are not known 未知的事物

the suffering = people or things that suffer 受苦的人或物

the horror = something that is horrible 可怕的事物

the miserable = people or things that are miserable 悲慘的人或物

the redhead, blonde, or brunette = a person with that hair color
紅髮、金髮、深色頭髮的人

單數普通名詞

the deceased 最近去世的人	the accused 被告
the pursued 偵探	the condemned 死刑犯

單數抽象名詞

the true = truth 真相	the good = goodness 善
the beautiful = beauty 美麗	

1 形容詞的功能

① 形容詞作修飾名詞的位置

（冠詞）＋（副詞）＋形容詞＋名詞

- I will send you that **particular** email soon.
  我很快就會寄給你那封電子郵件。
- The **truly happy** person is successful at work and at home.
  真正快樂的人，家庭事業皆有成。

形容詞＋複合名詞（名詞＋名詞）

- The player scored with a **powerful** slam dunk.
  球員靠強而有力的灌籃得分。

名詞＋形容詞

- Our copier makes **perfect** copies. 我們的影印機每次列印都完美。

(1) 只能修飾名詞的形容詞：live、little、mere、total、golden、main

- He was a **mere** boy of 16 when he graduated from university. (o)
  The boy was a **mere** 16 (years old) when he graduated from university. (x)
  他大學畢業時不過是個年僅 16 歲的男孩。
- The acting troupe has an **alive** performance every night. (x)
  The acting troupe has a **live** performance every night. (o)
  劇團每天晚上都有現場演出。

(2) 只能當作補語的形容詞：alive、alike、afraid、asleep、awake、aware、sorry、sure、well

- When the ambulance arrived, the woman who had been in the car accident was still **live**. (x)
  When the ambulance arrived the woman who had been in the car accident was still **alive**. (o)
  救護車抵達時，這位出車禍的婦女還活著。
- The doctor kept the patient **live**. (x)
  The doctor kept the patient **alive**. (o)
  醫師維持著這位病患的生命。

(3) **頻率／程度副詞**：放在一般動詞前，或放在助動詞或 be 動詞後。

頻率副詞＋一般動詞

- He **often** studies till late at night.
  他常常讀書讀到很晚。

助動詞＋頻率副詞＋一般動詞

- He **rarely ever goes** to class on time.
  他幾乎不曾準時去上課。

---

be 動詞＋頻率副詞

- He **is almost** always working hard.
  他幾乎總是非常努力。

- He **is sometimes** nervous when he speaks a foreign
  language. 當他說外語的時候，有時會緊張。

② 形容詞放在補語的位置

形容詞放在主詞補語的位置

- There is more to being **successful** than just being **rich**.
  成功不只是變富有而已。

- Roy often remains **quiet** when having a meeting.
  羅伊開會時通常很安靜。

形容詞放在受詞補語的位置

- Working out really makes me **hungry**.
  運動真的會讓我飢腸轆轆。

- Even the thought of bungee jumping makes me **anxious**.
  光想到高空彈跳就讓我焦慮。

③ 形容詞的位置不能放副詞或名詞

- The manager was a very practically(→ pratical) practical.
  經理是個非常務實的人。
- It was a high-power(→ powered) engine. 這是強力的引擎。

2 數量用語

① 放在可數名詞、不可數名詞前的數量用語

可數名詞前			不可數名詞前	可數名詞、不可數名詞前	
單數名詞	複數名詞				
a/an 一個	one of 其中一個	each of 當中每個都	little 少到幾乎沒有	no 沒有	all 全部
each 每個	few 少到幾乎沒有	fewer 較少的	a little 一些	more 更多	most 大多
one 一個	a few 一些	many 許多	less 較少的	some 一些	any 任何
every 每個	both 兩者都	numerous 眾多的	much 許多	lots of 許多	a lot of 許多
another 另一個	several 數個	a variety of 各式各樣的	a great deal of 大量的	plenty of 許多	other 其他
a single 單一個	various 各種的	a number of 一些	a large amount of 大量的		
	a couple of 一些				

- Much(→ Many) customers benefited from the service.
  許多顧客都受惠於這項服務。
  ➡ 因為 customers 是可數名詞，所以它前面不能放修飾不可數名詞的數量用語（much），要放修飾可數名詞的數量用語（many）。

② **all**、**more**、**lots of**、**plenty of**、**other** 和可數名詞搭配使用時，要放在複數名詞前。

> ● These days more student(→ students) study in the library than at home. 最近，到圖書館自習的學生比待在家裡的多。

③ 數量用語和名詞之間加入 **of the**，表限定名詞的一部分或全部時，不能省略 **of** 或 **the**。

> one/two　each　all　both　none
> many/much/most/several　　　　} ＋ of the ＋名詞
> some　any　(a) few　(a) little
>
> ● **Several of** the workmen arrived late at the construction site this morning. 今天早上好幾個工人晚到工地。
> ➡ 數量用語（several）和名詞（workmen）之間，of 和 the 不能只出現一個，兩個都要有才行。

3　主要的形容詞型態

① 容易混淆的形容詞

(1) 拼法相似但意義不同

appreciable 可估計的；可察覺的	appreciative 有欣賞力的
argumentative 爭辯的；爭論激烈的	arguable 可辯論的；可論證的
beneficial 有助益的	beneficent 慈善的
careful 小心的	caring 有愛心的
considerable 相當多的	considerate 體貼的；考慮周到的
comparable 可比較的	comparative 用比較方法的；相對的
comprehensible 可理解的	comprehensive 廣泛的
economic 經濟學上的；經濟上的	economical 節省的

exciting 令人興奮的	excitable 容易激動的
impressive 給人好印象的	impressionable 易受影響的
informational 含有資訊的	informative 教育性的；提供資訊的
persuasive 有說服力的	persuasible 可說服的
probable 可能成真的；可能發生的	probabilistic 可能性的
profitable 有利的；營利的	proficient 精熟的
prospective 預期的；未來的	prosperous 繁榮的；富足的
reliable 可靠的	reliant 依賴的
respectable 可敬的；可觀的	respectful 恭敬的；尊重人的
responsible 有責任的	responsive 有反應的
satisfactory 尚可的；算滿意的	satisfying 讓人心滿意足的
seasonal 季節的；季節性的	seasoned 經驗豐富的；有調味的
successful 成功的	successive 連續的
understanding 善解人意的；通情達理的	understandable 容易理解的

(2) 拼法或用法相似

advice

advisable 形 適當的；明智的	advisory 形 顧問的；勸告的

conclusion

concluding 形 結束的；結局的	conclusive 形 決定性的

confirmation

confirmatory 形 確定的；證實的	confirmed 形 成習慣的；被證實的

evidence

evident 形 明顯的　　　　　　evidential 形 作為證據的

expectation

expecting 形 懷孕的　　　　　expectant 形 期待的；懷孕的

health

healthy 形 健康的；有益健康的　healthful 形 有益健康的

identification

identifiable 形 可識別的　　　identical 形 完全相同的

inflation

inflatable 形 可充氣的　　　　inflationary 形 通貨膨脹的

interest

interesting 形 讓人有興趣的　　interested 形 感到有趣的

prevention

preventable 形 可預防的　　　preventive 形 預防的

protection

protective 形 保護的　　　　　protecting 形 受（法律）保護的

satisfaction

satisfactory 形 尚可的；算滿意的　satisfying 形 讓人心滿意足的
satisfied 形 感到滿意的

service

serviceable 形 堪用的；耐用的　serving 形 現任的

strategy

strategical 形 戰略上的　　　strategic 形 戰略上的

comparison

comparable
形 可比較的；比得上的　　　comparative 形 比較的；對比的

prosperity

prosperous 形 繁榮的；富足的　　　prospering 形 繁盛的

consciousness

conscious 形 有意識的；有知覺的　　　conscientious 形 認真的；憑良心的

difference

different 形 不同的　　　differential 形 有所區別的

continuity

continual 形 不間斷的　　　continuous 形 連續的

confidentiality

confidential 形 機密的　　　confident 形 有信心的

access

accessible
形 可接近的；可使用的　　　accessional 形 附加的

close

close 形 親近的　　　closed 形 關閉的

competition

competitive 形 競爭的　　　competent 形 有能力的；能幹的

complication

complicated 形 複雜的   complicating 形 複雜的

confidence

confident 形 有信心的   confided 形 幽禁的

disappointment

disappointed 形 失望的   disappointing 形 令人失望的

economy

economical 形 符合經濟效益的   economic 形 經濟的

excitement

exciting 形 令人興奮的   excited 形 興奮的

foresee

foreseeable 形 可預見的   foreceeing 形 預見的

involve

involved 形 複雜的   involving 形 涉及的

live

live 形 活的；現場的
alive 形 活的   living 形 在世的；現存的
lively 形 熱烈的；生動的

local

local 形 當地的；區域的   localized 形 本地化的

numeral

numerous 形 許多的   numerical 形 數字上的

persuade

persuasive 形 有說服力的　　persuadable 形 可說服的

reliability

reliable 形 可信賴的　　reliant 形 依賴的

understand

understandable 形 容易理解的　　understanding 形 善解人意的

revise

revised 形 修訂過的　　revisable 形 可修改的

distribute

distributed 形 分散的　　distributive 形（數學）分配（律）的

subject

subject 形 易受……的；受限的　　subjective 形 主觀的

clear

clear 形 清澈的；清楚的　　cleared 形 清除的；清空的

less

less 形 較少的
least 形 最小的；最小的
（little 最高級）

lesser 形 次要的

operation

operational 形 操作上的　　operative 形 使用中的；有效的

90

transfer

transferable 形 可轉移的 | transferred 形 轉換的

industry

industrial 形 工業的；產業的 | industrious 形 勤奮的

addition

additional 形 額外的；多的 | added 形 附加的

approximation

approximate 形 近似的；大概的 | approximative 形 近似的

concurrence

concurrent 形 同時發生的；一致的 | concurring 形 意見相同的

exact

exact 形 精確的；嚴格的 | exacting 形 需付出極大努力的

favorite

favorite 形 最喜歡的 | favorable 形 有利的；適合的

hesitate

hesitant 形 遲疑的 | hesitating 形 遲疑的

presume

presumptive 形 可推定的 | presumptuous 形 放肆的；冒昧的

regret

regrettable 形 令人遺憾的；不幸的 | regretful 形 懊悔的；遺憾的；惋惜的

security

securable 形 可獲得的；安全的　　　secure 形 安全的

temporary

temporary 形 暫時的；臨時的　　　temporal 形 世間的；世俗的；現世的

volunteer

voluntary 形 志願的　　　volunteer 形 志願的

custom

customary 形 習慣上的　　　customable 形 可徵關稅的

compliance

compliant 形 順從的　　　complying 形 順從的

reflect

reflective 形 反射的；沉思的　　　reflexive 形 反射的；本能的

include

including 形 包括的
inclusive 形 包括一切的　　　included 形 包括在內的

lower

lowering 形 （天空）烏雲密佈的
lowly 形 低等的；卑微的　　　low 形 低的；少的

renew

renewable 形 可再生的　　　renewed 形 更新的

- Background music has an appreciative(→ appreciable) effect on employee productivity. 背景對員工的生產力有相當的影響。

- The outside consultant suggested that management needs to be more responsible(→ responsive) to rank-and-file employees.
  外部顧問建議管理階層對基層員工要更加關照。

- My manager said my presentation was very impress(→ impressive).
  我的主管說我的簡報讓人印象深刻。

② 「be ＋形容詞」慣用語

形容詞放在 **be** 動詞後，可以組成如下這樣的慣用語。

be apt to do = be likely to do = be liable to do 易於做……的；常做……的	be aware of = be conscious of = be cognizant of = be careful of 小心；留意
be available to do 有空	be available for 可取得的
be capable of V-ing 有能力做	be comparable to 比得上
be consistent with 與……一致；符合	be eligible for/to do 適合；有資格
be subject to 易受……的；受限於	be subjective to 對……很重要
be responsible for/to 對……負責	be skilled in/at 擅長於
be willing to do 樂意去做	be expected to do 被期望去做

- Sales **are likely to** increase this season due to high consumer confidence.
  因為消費者信心高，這一季的營收可能會上升。

- Everyone should **be aware of** the dangers of secondhand smoke.
  人人都該了解二手菸的危害。

- Everyone should **be aware of** the new rules by now.
  到現在大家都應該要知道新規定。

- John said he would **be available to** work overtime this weekend if it were necessary.
  約翰說，必要的話他這個週末可以加班。

- Patricia Wells **is** usually **available for** private consultation on weekends only.
  派翠西亞·威爾斯通常只有週末可以提供私人顧問的服務。

- This conference room **is available for** meetings anytime after next week.
  下週之後，會議室隨時可以用來開會。

- You should **be careful of** Dan; he is in a bad mood.
  你要小心丹，他心情不好。

- The department **is capable of** providing specialized rescue service.
  這個部門可以提供特殊救援服務。

- This airplane **is capable of** flying at the speed of sound.
  這部飛機能以音速飛行。

- Export figures from this year **are comparable to** those from the past two years.
  今年開始的外銷數字可以和過去兩年的統計數字相比。

- Sales figures this month **are comparable to** those from this time last year.
  本月銷售數字可以跟去年同期的銷售數字相比。

- Product quality and design must **be consistent with** what customers demand.
  產品品質和設計必須符合顧客的要求。

- Company rules must **be consistent with** all state and federal laws.
  公司內規必須要符合所有州和聯邦法規。

- Freelance workers **are** not **eligible for** the company pension plan.
  自由工作者不適用公司的年金計畫。

- Only employees with 20 or more years of service **are eligible for** the company pension plan.
  只有服務 20 年以上的員工適用公司年金計畫。

- I heard that Tom **was eligible to** apply for a Fulbright grant.
  我聽說湯姆有資格申請傅爾布萊特獎助金。

- Part of this presentation may be subject to revision.
  簡報的部分內容可能會調整。

- These rules are subject to change at any time without notice.
  這些規定隨時會變更，不另行通知。

- The city police were responsible for the accident.
  市區警察對這起意外有責任。

- Who is responsible for this mess? 這麼亂是誰弄的？

- The chairman of the board said he was only responsible to the shareholders.
  董事會主席說他只對股東負責。

- People who are skilled in website design are in high demand these days.
  擅長網路設計的人最近很搶手。

- People who are highly skilled in foreign languages find it easy to get jobs.
  有外語能力強的人容易找到工作。

- Dick is highly skilled at computer programming, but he does not have the people skills to be a manager.
  迪克擅長編寫電腦程式，但他不具作為經理要有的人際能力。

- He is willing to do whatever it takes to succeed.
  為了成功，他什麼都願意做。

- She said she was willing to do what was necessary to finish the project on time.
  她說，她願意做一切必要努力，準時完成專案。

1. Laguna National Park's
------- campsites make it a
popular destination among
outdoor enthusiasts.
   (A) many
   (B) every
   (C) each
   (D) much

2. For the duration of the
construction, the west entrance
will be -------, so customers are
asked to use the main doors.
   (A) irresponsible
   (B) illogical
   (C) unexpected
   (D) inaccessible

3. The solar power plant will
provide clean, ------- energy
to thousands of homes in the
surrounding area.
   (A) renews
   (B) renewable
   (C) renewals
   (D) renew

4. The selection of merchandise at
Tyler department stores is
------- depending on the
branch.
   (A) entire
   (B) occasional
   (C) successive
   (D) variable

5. The insurance company would
not insure any homes in this
area because they are very
------- to flood damage.
   (A) vulnerable
   (B) obtainable
   (C) structural
   (D) intensive

Chapter *08* 副詞

基礎文法

1 副詞的功能和種類

① 副詞具有修飾除名詞之外其他詞類的功能，除了可修飾形容詞、副詞、動詞之外，還可修飾片語、子句和整個句子。

修飾形容詞

- The cakes were **really** delicious. 這些蛋糕實在很美味。
- The flowers were **very** beautiful. 這些花朵非常美麗。

修飾其他副詞

- The dog can run **very** fast. 這隻狗可以跑很快。
- The cat can jump **very** high. 這隻貓可以跳很高。

修飾動詞

- He **carefully** opened the gift. 他小心翼翼地拆開禮物。
- He **slowly** closed the door. 他慢慢地關門。

修飾片語

- We finished the work **shortly** after 6 p.m.
  我們在下午六點後不久就完成了工作。
- The store will close **just** after 9 p.m. 商店過晚上九點就關門。

修飾子句

- She arrived **just** after the meeting began.
  她在會議開始後才出現。
- He arrived **long** after the beginning of his shift.
  他在他的班開始很久後才到。

- **Usually**, we are open seven days a week. 通常我們一週開七天。
- **Usually**, the manager works from Monday to Saturday.
  經理通常從週一工作到週六。

② 大部分的副詞從「形容詞 + **ly**」衍生而來。

(1) 就像 calmly、completely、entirely、temporarily 這些副詞，大致都是以 -ly 結尾。不過也有像 ahead、just、only、still、well 等不是以 -ly 結尾的副詞。

- He **calmly** told his manager that he was leaving the company.
  他冷靜地告訴經理他要離開這家公司了。

(2) 另外要注意像 costly、elderly、friendly、silly、ugly、worldly 這樣的以 -ly 結尾的形容詞，不要把它們誤認為是副詞了。

- The new machinery was very **costly**. 新的機械非常昂貴。

形容詞和副詞同形

- 形容詞 **early**：
  She was very upset after the **early** death of her dog.
  她遭逢愛犬早逝，非常悲傷。
- 副詞 **early**：
  Ban always gets up **early**. 班都起得很早。

	形容詞意義	副詞意義		形容詞意義	副詞意義
early	早的；提早的	早；初期	long	長的；長久的	長久地
fast	快速的	快速地；牢牢地	wide	寬的；寬的	完全；大大地
hard	堅固的；困難的	辛苦地；辛勤地	far	遙遠的	久遠地
high	高的	高處	right	右邊的；正確的	恰好；正確地
late	遲的；晚期的	遲地；晚地	just	正義的；恰當的	恰好；僅僅
wrong	錯誤的	錯誤地	close	接近的；密切的	接近；緊緊地
near	近的	不遠；接近	great	巨大的；偉大的	（表示強調）特別

2 副詞的功能和種類

① 修飾動詞以外的詞時，副詞要放在被修飾詞的前面。

> ● The speaker's words were particularly profound, and inspired the crowd.
> 講者的話非常有深度，激勵了群眾。

② 副詞的位置不能放形容詞。

> ● Expense accounts for traveling employees have been cut substantial(→ substantially). 員工差旅費用的帳戶已被大幅刪減。
> ➡ 要修飾動詞（have been cut），不能用形容詞（substantial），要用副詞（substantially）。
>
> ● The location that you choose to live in is entire(→ entirely) up to you. 決定要居住在哪裡完全操之在你。
> ➡ 要修飾片語（up to you），不能用形容詞（entire），要用副詞（entirely）。

3 副詞主要的型態

① 型態類似但意思不同的副詞

要注意不要搞混外型類似但意思完全不同的副詞。

hard 困難地	hardly 幾乎不
high 高地	highly 非常；很
great （表示強調）特別	greatly 非常
late 晚地；遲地	lately 最近
most 多數地	mostly 主要地；通常
near 接近	nearly 幾乎（= almost）

- Please ensure that you continue working **hard** on this project.
  請確保我們會持續在這個專案上努力。

- There was **hardly** enough time to complete their work.
  他們幾乎沒有足夠時間完成工作。

- You have to hit the ball as **high** as possible. 你必須把球打得愈高愈好。

- Admittedly, I think **highly** of our company's founder.
  坦白說，我非常尊敬本公司的創辦人。

- Due to weather conditions, there was a **great** large increase in the cost of produce. 因為天候狀況，農產品成本大大增加。

- In spite of a lack of practice, her writing has **greatly** improved.
  雖然缺乏練習，她的寫作還是大有進步。

- Many staff members arrived **late** for work because of bad traffic.
  許多員工因為交通狀況不佳而上班遲到。

- **Lately** there have been several changes in company policy.
  近來公司政策有許多變革。

- The new product is the **most** successful in our company's history.
  這個新產品是本公司史上最成功的作品。

- The business began to focus **mostly** on making computer software. 公司開始將大部分的重心放在製造電腦軟體。

- The new office is **near** the company headquarters.
  新辦公室在公司總部附近。

- We have **nearly** finished the project months ahead of our deadline.
  我們幾乎是比期限早好幾個月完成了專案。

② 時間副詞 already/still/yet、ever/ago/once

(1) already/still/yet

already 當作「已經」（肯定句）使用。

- He was **still** working on his presentation after 9 p.m.
  過了九點他還在準備簡報。

still 當作「仍然」（肯定句、否定句、疑問句）使用。

- The marketing team **still** has to design the new posters.
  行銷團隊仍然必須設計新海報。

yet 當作「尚未」（否定句）、「已經」（疑問句）使用，詢問一件猜測的事有沒有發生。

- Our new product line was released several weeks ago, but the company's stock price has not increased yet.
  新產品推出好幾週後，這家公司的股票還沒上漲。

have yet to ＋原形動詞：還沒有……

- She has yet to turn in her project.
  她還沒交出她的計畫。

finally（終於、最後），表等待已久的事終於發生。

- After months of waiting for approval, we can finally begin construction.
  等待許可好幾個月之後，我們終於可以開始施工。

soon（立刻），表預測不久之後將發生某事，或某事已經發生。

- The new office furniture should arrive soon.
  新的辦公家具應該很快就會到。

(2) ever/ago/once

ever 用在表不確定的過去的某個時間點，搭配否定句或疑問句使用。

- The new accounting department hardly ever makes errors in its records. 新的會計部門的紀錄幾乎沒出錯過。

ago 表時間剛過不久，以現在為基準不久前發生的事。

- The meeting began two hours ago.
  會議兩小時前就開始了。

once 用在表不確定的過去的某個時間點時，也可以用來修飾形容詞。

- Once-thriving fish markets stand deserted and in ruins.
  昔日熱鬧的魚市如今遭到廢棄，滿目瘡痍。

③ 頻率副詞

(1) 表頻率的副詞，用來表事情「多久、多常」發生，通常放在**一般動詞前**，或放在**助動詞**、**be 動詞之後**。

always 總是	almost 幾乎
often 常常	frequently 頻繁地
usually 通常地	sometimes 有時
hardly/rarely/seldom/scarcely/barely 幾乎不	never 從不

- The company **often** updates its products to remain competitive.
  這家公司常常會更新產品，以維持競爭力。
- Due to market changes, the company can **hardly** reach its sales targets. 因為市場變化，這家公司幾乎達不到銷售目標。

(2) **usually** 或 **often**，可以放在句子的**最前面**或**最後面**，但 always 則不行。

- Always(→ Usually), the pizza is delivered within 15 minutes of our order. 通常，披薩會在接到訂單後 15 分鐘內送達。
- All orders always(→ usually) arrive within seven business days.
  所有訂貨通常都會在七個工作天到貨。
- I go there always(→ often). 我常去那邊。

(3) 因為 hardly、rarely、seldom、scarcely、barely 含有**否定的含意**（表幾乎沒有），所以**不能**再跟 not 或其他否定字一起搭配使用。

- She had hardly never(→ ever) eaten lunch outside of the office.
  她幾乎不曾在辦公室外吃午餐。
  ➡ 因為 hardly 已經有否定含意，所以不能再跟 never 搭配使用，故要將 never 刪除或改成 ever。

(4) 為了強調這樣的否定副詞，而將它們放到句首的話，「**主詞—動詞**」就要**倒置**。

- Never have we had a harder worker than our newest employee.
  從來沒有比這個新員工更認真的人了。

④ 連接副詞

(1) 連接副詞是**連接前後子句**的副詞。

besides 此外	moreover 此外；並且
furthermore 此外；再者	therefore 因此；於是
hence 因此	consequently 因此；結果
however 然而；可是	nevertheless 然而；不過
nonetheless 但是；仍然	otherwise 否則；不然
then 那麼	meantime/meanwhile 同時

- All departments besides the sales team must attend the seminar this weekend.
  除了業務團隊之外的所有部門，都必須出席週末的研討會。

- The company faced a low-profit year; therefore budget cuts had to be made.
  這家公司面臨低利潤的一年，因此預算刪減勢在必行。

- The new product was priced fairly; however, the sales were lower than expected.
  新產品訂價合理，但銷售量還是低於預期。

(2) 連接副詞不能和**副詞子句連接詞**重複使用。

- Even though the employees were tired, ~~nevertheless~~ they continued to work.
  員工儘管很疲勞，還是繼續工作。
  ➡ 因為連接副詞 (nevertheless) 不能和副詞子句連接詞 (even though) 重複使用，所以要刪除 nevertheless。

(3) **then** 是例外，即便放在在 if 子句之後，它也能出現。

- If you complete the design today, then we can begin planning construction.
  如果你今天以前可以完成設計，那我們就可以開始規畫施工。

⑤ 強調副詞

(1) **just**、**right**（正、就）要放在 **before** 或 **after** 之前強調。

- All factory workers must ensure they are wearing the appropriate safety wear just before beginning work.
  工廠工人在開始工作之前，都必須確認已穿上適當的安全服裝。

(2) **only**、**just**（只）強調**介系詞片語**或**名詞片語**。

- The company hires new staff only at the beginning of the year. 這家公司只會在年初僱用新員工。

(3) **well**（好得多）強調**介系詞片語**。

- Jack's new salary was well over what he had expected.
  傑克的新待遇遠比他預期的高。

(4) **quite**（相當地）放在「**a/an ＋名詞**」前強調。

- The new archiving system is quite a success.
  新的檔案管理系統相當成功。
- Our new range of winter clothing has been quite a success among adults.
  新的冬衣系列在成人顧客中相當成功。

(5) nearly（幾乎）、almost（幾乎）、just（正、就）強調原級，much、even、still、far、a lot、by far（得多）強調**比較級**，by far、quite（顯然、遠超過）強調**最高級**。

- He's just as good at playing basketball as his two older brothers. 他跟他兩個哥哥一樣很會打籃球。
- There is a much quicker way to the office than this.
  有更快可以到辦公室的方法。

⑥ 程度副詞

(1) so 和 such 兩個都是「非常」，不過 so 是**副詞**，修飾**形容詞**和**副詞**；such 則是**形容詞**，修飾**名詞**。

> ● The office was ~~such~~(→ so) full that it had to be moved to a larger building.
> 辦公室非常擁擠，以至於他們必須要搬到更大的大樓。

(2) very（非常）意思和 so 一樣，但和 so 不同的是，它後面**不能接 that 子句**。

> ● The explanation in the book is very clear.
> 這本書中的解釋非常清楚。
>
> ● The new employee was ~~very~~(→ so) good at programming **that** he was given a promotion.
> 新員工非常擅長程式設計，因而獲得升遷。

(3) too（太）和 so/such/very 不同，**too . . . to . . .** 含有「太……而不能……」這**否定**的含意。

> ● John's report was too long to read all at once.
> 約翰的報告太長了，一次看不完。
> ➡ 具有「報告太長，沒辦法一下子全部讀完」這否定的含意。

1. The packaging for the protein shake was ------- designed in order to appeal to young adults.

   (A) boldest
   (B) bold
   (C) boldly
   (D) bolder

2. Due to its lightweight design, the Greco 360 vacuum cleaner glides ------- across any surface.

   (A) potentially
   (B) effortlessly
   (C) attentively
   (D) generously

3. These dishes are made ------- from locally grown organic ingredients, and do not contain any processed food.

   (A) reluctantly
   (B) exclusively
   (C) negatively
   (D) alternatively

4. Mr. Menard ------- sent thank-you cards to the volunteers who worked on the project.

   (A) thought
   (B) thoughts
   (C) thoughtfully
   (D) thoughtful

5. The technician advised against relying ------- on basic anti-virus software to protect our computer network.

   (A) harshly
   (B) solely
   (C) genetically
   (D) besides

Chapter

09 比較級與最高級

基礎文法

用形容詞或副詞的比較級／最高級,來表現「比……;更……」或「最……」。
比較對象是**兩個**時,用**比較級**來表現;比較對象是**三個以上**,則可以用**最高級**
來表現。

◆ **比較句**,是比較兩個以上東西的數量或性質的句子,依據比較對象的數量和
比較方法,可分成**三種句型**。

- **兩個對象是同等的比較句,用「原級」句型。**
  Peter is **as** old **as** John. 彼得跟約翰年紀一樣大。

- **兩個對象中有一個比較優越,用「比較級」句型。**
  Peter is older **than** John. 彼得比約翰年長。

- **三個以上的對象中,有一個最優越,用「最高級」句型。**
  Peter is **the** oldest man in the band. 彼得是樂團中年紀最長的。

◆ 在原級、比較級、最高級中,形容詞和副詞分別有不同的型態。
  形容詞或副詞是**單個音節**的單字,或字尾是 **-el**、**-ow**、**-some** 的兩個音節的
  單字時,則參考下表的型態,即原級、比較級和最高級的基本型態。

原級 （形容詞或副詞的 一般型態）	比較級 （原級＋ er）	最高級 （原級＋ est）
old	older	the oldest
clever	cleverer	the cleverest
slow	slower	the slowest

-y 結尾的單音節形容詞則**去 y** 加 **ier** 或 **iest**。

形容詞或副詞字尾是 **-able**、**-ful**、**-ous**、**-ive** 的**兩個音節**或**三個以上音節**的單字時，則參考下表的型態。

原級 （形容詞或副詞的 一般型態）	比較級 （more ＋原級）	最高級 （the most ＋原級）
useful	more useful	the most useful
important	more important	the most important

某些形容詞和副詞，不用 -er/-est，而是有它**固定的比較級／最高級**型態。

原級	比較級	最高級
good/well	better	best
bad/badly	worse	worst
many/much	more	most
little	less	least
slow	slower	slowest

1 原級

原級以「as ＋形容詞／副詞＋ as」，來表示兩個對象是同等的。

- The order was shipped to the customer as quickly as possible.
  訂貨會盡快出貨給顧客。

2 比較級

① 比較級以「形容詞／副詞的比較級＋ than」，來表示兩個對象中有一個比較突出。

- This year's sales were bigger than last year's.
  今年銷量比去年多。
- The manager behaved more cleverly than usual.
  經理的行為舉止比平常精明。

② 比較級以「more/fewer/less ＋名詞＋ than」，來表示「比……更多的名詞／更少的」。

- More candidates are applying to our company this year than applied last year. 來我們公司求職的人比去年多。

③ 雖然比較級中不用 the，但如下這個例外的比較級句型，就一定要加 the。

- the 比較級，the 比較級（愈……就愈……）
  The more you exercise, the healthier you will become.
  多運動，就會越健康。

④ 強調形容詞／副詞的比較級用語，有 much、even、still、far、a lot、by far 等，表「得多」。

- The effort you make to achieve your dream is much more valuable than the dream itself.
  為追求夢想付出的努力比夢想本身珍貴許多。
  ➜ 出現比較級的話後面一定要有 than，出現 than 的話前面一定要有比較級。

3 最高級

① 最高級以「最高級＋ of / in / that 子句」，來表示在三個以上的對象中，有一個最突出。

- Robert is the funniest (one) of all the employees.
  羅伯特是全員工中最有趣的人。
- This is the thickest book in the world.
  這本書是全世界最厚的。
- It is the most exciting movies (that) I've ever seen.
  這是我看過最刺激的電影。

② 強調形容詞／副詞的最高級的用語，有 by far、quite 等。

- John was by far my best coworker. 約翰是最好的同事。

- 有 of、in、that 子句，這些表「在……中」的片語時，就要用最高級。
  Matthew is the fastest of all the workers.
  馬修是所有員工中最快的。
  This building is the tallest (that) I have ever seen.
  這棟建築是我見過最高的。

4 副詞的最高級前不能加 the。

- This train goes the fastest in the world. (x)
- This train goes fastest in the world. (o)
  這是全世界跑最快的火車。

5 不規則變化型態

部分單字，不遵照既定的規則，有它固定的比較級和最高級型態。

原級	比較級	最高級
good/well	better	best
bad/badly	worse	worst
many/much	more	most
little	less	least
far	father	farthest
far	further	furthest
old	older	oldest
old	elder	eldest
late	later	latest
late	latter	last

6 慣用語

比較級用語

more than 比……更多	less than 比……更少
no later than 在……之前	no longer 不再
no sooner . . . than 一……就……	other than 不同於；除了
rather than 與……相比	would rather . . . than 寧願

- There are **more than** 100,000 books in the library.
  圖書館有十萬冊以上的藏書。

- **Less than** 30 percent of our subscribers chose not to renew.
  不到三成的訂戶決定不再續訂。

- The supervisor expects us to come to work **no later than** nine o'clock. 主管希望我們不要超過九點進來上班。

- Bill **no longer** uses makeup. 比爾不再使用化妝品了。

- **No sooner** had Alice put the phone down **than** it rang again.
  艾莉絲才放下電話，電話又再響起。

- **Other than** yogurt, milk and eggs are the only breakfast foods he eats. 除了優格，奶類和蛋是他最愛的早餐食物。

- The workers want to continue to work **rather than** quit.
  員工想繼續工作，不是想離職。

- I **would rather** work at home **than** drink beer with my friends.
  我寧願在家工作而不是跟朋友喝啤酒。

Part 5

Chapter 09

1. These cables are made from the ------- materials in the world.
   (A) stronger
   (B) strongest
   (C) strong
   (D) strongly

2. WebTime provides the ------ designs for online businesses and other sites.
   (A) most innovative
   (B) innovation
   (C) innovate
   (D) innovatively

3. The study's shocking findings suggest that shaking hands could be as ------- as smoking due to the potential spread of germs.
   (A) dangers
   (B) dangerous
   (C) dangerously
   (D) danger

4. The safety problem with its latest cell phone battery is the ------- issue the company has ever faced.
   (A) seriousness
   (B) most serious
   (C) more serious
   (D) serious

5. Cell Net's new range of smartphones has been very successful, as they are even ------- than those of the company's competitors.
   (A) slim
   (B) slimmer
   (C) slimming
   (D) slims

假設語氣與被動語態

1 假設和條件

① 條件子句

條件子句是用來表達事件發生的條件或環境，通常由表條件的從屬連接詞 if 引導。當條件子句指的是可能的未來事件，用現在簡單式表未來的含義。然而，當條件子句表達的並非事實，而是與事實相反的想像，則用過去簡單式或過去完成式表示 (即條件不存在)。

- **If we hear anything from the company, we'll contact you.**
  如果我們有公司的消息，就會跟你聯絡。
  ⇨ 現在簡單式的條件子句，表可能的未來

- **If the worker made a mistake, I could fire him.**
  如果員工犯了錯，我會開除他。
  ⇨ 過去簡單式的條件子句，表與事實相反

② 與現在或未來事實相反的假設

用 if 表示與現在或未來事實相反，且不真實或不可能發生的事情時，if 子句用動詞過去式。這裡的過去式並不指過去時間，而是意味著不真實的、不可能的假設語氣。這時否定的內容可以用肯定來表現，讓對方感覺更善意一點，意思是「如果……的話，就會……」。

- **條件子句**：if ＋主詞＋動詞的過去式（if 子句裡的 be 動詞不分人稱和單複數，一律用 were。）
- **主要子句**：主詞＋ would/should/could/might ＋原形動詞
  If you knew how much I lost, you wouldn't ask me to help you.
  如果你知道我失去了多少，就不會找我幫忙。

③ 與過去事實相反的假設

用 if 表達非真實的過去事件（過去沒有發生的事情）時，if 子句要用過去完成式，意思是「如果做了……的話，就會……了」。

● **條件子句**：if ＋主詞＋ had ＋ p.p.

● **主要子句**：主詞＋ would/should/could/might ＋ have ＋ p.p.

If I hadn't been so tired, I could have worked on the project.
如果我沒這麼累，就可以做這個案子。

If John hadn't moved to the USA, he could have lived with me.
如果約翰沒搬去美國，就可能跟我住。

What would have happened to the company if it hadn't replaced its chairman?
那家公司如果沒撤換總裁，會變成怎樣？

---

④ 混合句型

當 if 子句和主句所涉及的時間不一樣時，那麼假設語氣就要使用混合句型，意思是「如果做了……的話，現在就會……」。

● **條件子句**：if ＋主詞＋ had ＋ p.p.

● **主要子句**：主詞＋ would/should/could/might ＋原形動詞

If we had had more money, we wouldn't live like this now.
如果我們當時比較有錢，現在就不會落到這步田地。

The company wouldn't be so prosperous now if it hadn't developed that software program.
如果公司當時沒有開發軟體程式，現在就不會這麼發達。

---

2 被動語態

① 主動語態和被動語態的比較

主詞是動詞的行為者時，叫作**主動語態**；主詞是動詞的承受者時，叫作**被動語態**。

> (1) Our company has given many benefits to us.
> 本公司提供我們很多福利。
>
> (2) Many benefits have been given to us by our company.
> 很多福利由公司提供給我們。

這兩個句子的意思一樣。不過，講話時關注的焦點不同。像 (1) 這樣，主詞是行為者時，叫作主動語態。像 (2) 這樣，主詞承受動詞的行為時，叫作被動語態。

② 句子型式

主動語態的構成是「主詞＋動詞＋受詞」，被動語態的構成是「**主詞＋be＋動詞的過去分詞（＋by 行為者）**」。標示行為者的介系詞，基本上會隨動詞而不同。

> * 主動語態：
>
> The H&D auto company makes more than 100,000 cars a year.
> H&D 汽車公司年產十萬輛以上的汽車。
>
> * 被動語態：
>
> More than 100,000 cars a year are made by the H&D auto company. 一年有十萬輛以上的汽車被 H&D 公司製造出來。

③ 使用被動語態的情況

> * 為了配合主題而使用。
>
> Thomas has run the shop for 18 years. It was built in 2000.
> 湯瑪斯經營這家店 18 年了。這家店成立於 2000 年。
>
> Vitamin C keeps people healthy. It is needed to fight illness.
> 維他命 C 讓人保持健康，為了打擊疾病這是必須的。

④ 現在簡單被動語態

> ● 型態：主詞＋ am/are/is ＋ p.p.
> More staff members are employed in the marketing
> department. 更多職員被僱用到行銷部。
> All workers are asked to participate in the seminar this
> weekend. 所有員工被要求參加週末的研討會。

⑤ 過去簡單被動語態

> ● 型態：主詞＋ was/were ＋ p.p.
> Many of these products were made by machines.
> 許多產品由機器製造。
> A lot of cars were exported to China last year.
> 去年有很多車外銷到中國。

⑥ 未來簡單被動語態

> ● 型態：主詞＋ will / be going to ＋ be ＋ p.p.
> More oil will be needed in the coming year.
> 明年對石油需求更大。
> The company's policies will be partially changed within the
> next month. 公司政策下個月會部分變更。

⑦ 情態動詞被動語態

> ● 型態：主詞＋ will/shall/can/may/would/should/could/might/must
> ＋ be ＋ p.p.
> The manager may be replaced this month.
> 經理可能會在這個月被撤換。
> All factory workers must be given safety gear.
> 工廠所有員工必須獲得安全配備。

⑧ 動名詞被動語態

> ● **型態**：主詞＋ am/is/are/was/were ＋ being ＋ p.p.
> The rights of the workers **are being neglected**.
> 員工權利正遭受忽略。
> When I arrived at the station, the train **was being loaded** with luggage. 當我到車站時，火車正載著許多行李。

⑨ 完成式被動語態

> ● **型態**：主詞＋ have/has/had ＋ been ＋ p.p.
> Many mistakes **have been found** in her reports.
> 她的報告被發現有很多錯誤。
> Some of the hotel's reservations **have been canceled**.
> 這家旅館有些預定已經取消了。
> A lot of improvements **have been made**.
> 已經有一堆新公司被設立了。

⑩ 使用 **by** 以外的介系詞

被動語態的句子，也會有在「be 動詞＋過去分詞」之後，使用 **by** 以外的介系詞的情形。

be based on 基於	be crowded with 擠滿……的
be interested in 對……感興趣	be known for 因……出名
be provided with 被提供	be surprised at 對……感到驚喜
be composed/comprised of 由……組成	be disappointed with 對……失望
be known as 因（某身分）而出名	be pleased with 對……感到欣慰、開心
be satisfied with 對……感到滿意	be used for 被用來
be amused at 被……逗樂了	be delighted with 對……感到高興
be gratified with 對感到高興	be disappointed at 對……失望
be astonished at 對……感到震驚	be frightened at 受……驚嚇

be shocked at 對……感到震驚	be worried about 憂心
be concerned about/with 擔心	be bored with 對……覺得無趣
be tired of 對……感到厭倦	be ashamed of 對……可恥
be convinced of 深信	be alarmed of 被……嚇一跳
be involved in 涉入；涉及	be engaged in 從事
be associated with 跟……聯繫在一起	be related to 跟……有關
be absorbed in 專注於	be exposed to 暴露於；接觸
be devoted to 致力於	be dedicated to 為……而設；奉獻於
be skilled in/at 對……熟練	be equipped with 有……配備
be covered with/in 被……覆蓋	

- Sara is interested in cooking.
  莎拉喜歡烹飪。

- Brenda has been satisfied with the results so far.
  布蘭達到目前為止對結果都很滿意。

- The company is equipped with computers and printers.
  公司備有電腦和印表機。

- The bankruptcy of the company is closely related to the corruptions of its owner.
  公司破產跟公司持有人的貪腐密切相關。

Part 5

Chapter 10

1. Should the car salesperson give ------, the buyer will feel more comfortable making the purchase.
   - (A) assures
   - (B) assurance
   - (C) assured
   - (D) assure

2. Harlington Construction is ------ for its ability to quickly provide fair estimates for a wide range of services.
   - (A) well know
   - (B) knowing
   - (C) well known
   - (D) to know

3. The results of the survey showed that customers were highly ------ with our new range of products.
   - (A) satisfied
   - (B) satisfy
   - (C) satisfying
   - (D) satisfaction

4. In order to avoid any damage to our manufacturing equipment, strict safety guidelines have been ------ in place.
   - (A) put
   - (B) putting
   - (C) to put
   - (D) puts

5. The online marketing team did an excellent job of exposing our products to consumers who ------ might not have heard about them.
   - (A) otherwise
   - (B) beforehand
   - (C) near
   - (D) seldom

Chapter
11 連接詞

基礎文法

1 連接詞

① 連接詞具有連接單字和單字、片語和片語、子句和子句的功能。

(1) **對等連接詞**：將單字和單字、片語和片語、子句和子句對等地連接起來。

(2) **從屬連接詞**：將主要子句和從屬子句連接起來。

② 連接詞的位置

從屬連接詞可以引導從屬子句放在主要子句的前面，也可以放在後面，放在主要子句前面時，要加逗點區隔連接。

> ● If you work hard, I will promote you.
> 如果你認真工作，我會讓你升遷。
>
> ● When you see Joe, please tell him to call me back.
> 如果你遇到喬，請他回我電話。

2 子句

子句由「**主詞＋動詞**」組成，並依在句中的功能，可分為名詞子句、形容詞子句和副詞子句。句子由一個子句構成的話，叫作**單句**；由對等連接詞連接兩個子句的話，叫作**合句**；用從屬連接詞連接兩個子句的話，叫作**複句**。

> ● **單句**：由一個**子句**構成的句子
> John put the bag on the table. 約翰把袋子放到桌上。

> ● **合句**：用**對等連接詞**連接的句子
> Peter had planned to take a trip to Japan, but it was canceled. 彼得計畫去日本旅行，但後來取消了。

- **複句**：用從屬連接詞連接的句子
  The L&T camp will help managers to be more decisive **when** dealing with employees.
  L&T 營隊將幫助經理在面對員工時能更果決。

3 對等連接詞

① **and**：對前面的句子，再追加訊息時使用。

- Alice plays the piano, **and** Sara the violin.
  愛麗絲彈鋼琴，莎拉拉小提琴。

② **but**：對前面的句子，提出相反的訊息時使用。

- John is tall, **but** Susan is short. 約翰個子高，而蘇珊矮小。

③ **or**：在前面的句子和後面的句子中，選擇一個時使用。

- Ernie can now choose to stay with the company, **or** he can retire early.
  爾尼可以選擇留在公司，或是提前退休。

④ **so**：對前面的句子，作出決定的時候使用。

- Jason already had a lot of experience, **so** I put him in charge of the whole marketing department.
  傑森已經有豐富的經驗，所以我讓他管理整個行銷部門。

⑤ **for**：對前面的句子，提出原因的時候使用。

- I need to save a lot of money, **for** I plan to study abroad.
  我需要存很多錢，因為我有出國讀書的計畫。

4 對等相關連接詞

both A and B A 和 B 兩者都	either A or B 不是 A，就是 B
neither A nor B 不是 A，也不是 B	not A, but B 不是 A，而是 B
not only A, but (also) B 不只 A，還有 B	

A as well as B A 和 B

- John has buildings in both New York and Paris.
  約翰在紐約和巴黎都有房子。

- Either you or I should go to the marketing seminar this Friday.
  你或我其中一人應該要參加週五的行銷研討會。

- Neither the company nor its employees wanted to continue the negotiations regarding working conditions.
  不管公司或員工都不想繼續協商工作條件。

- The accounting office is not on the first floor, but on the third floor.
  會計辦公室不在一樓，而是在三樓。

- The RG Bakery not only offered discounts, but also gave away small souvenirs.
  RG 烘培坊不只打折，還送小紀念品。

5 從屬連接詞

從屬連接詞可用以引導**名詞子句**或**副詞子句**。引導名詞子句的連接詞有：that、if、whether、疑問詞（who、how、when、where、what、why、which）等。

① that

從屬連接詞 that 只起連接作用，在受詞子句中不扮演主詞或受詞的角色，引導受詞子句時常可以省略。

- **That** Branda passed the exam is exciting.
  布蘭達考試通過了，這件事振奮人心。
- It is possible **that** the company will be successful.
  這家公司會成功是一件可能的事。
- The best thing about it is **that** she will be able to take her children with her. 最棒的是，她可以繼續帶著孩子。
- Sara keeps saying **that** she loves me very much.
  莎拉不停說著她深愛著我。

② whether、if

連接詞 whether/if 意味「**是否**」，用來連接**主句**和**受詞子句**，在子句中不扮演任何角色。兩者意思上雖然相近，但在用法上是有差異的，要特別注意。

- BB Bank is not sure **whether/if** it will reduce the number of its branches. BB 銀行不確定是否要縮減分行。
- Peter asked **whether/if** I could continue to work with him.
  彼得問我是否能繼續跟他共事。

③ whether 子句能縮減成 whether ＋不定詞，但是 if 子句不能縮減成 if ＋不定詞。

- We haven't decided yet whether to host an incentive travel in Hawaii or Guam. (o)
- We haven't decided yet if to host an incentive travel in Hawaii or Guam. (x)
  我們還沒決定獎勵旅遊要辦在夏威夷或是關島。

④ whether 子句能縮減成 whether or not，但是 if 子句不能縮減成 if or not。

- John told me to let him know whether or not I was prepared for the presentation. (o)
- John told me to let him know if or not I was prepared for the presentation. (x)
  約翰要我讓他知道我是否為簡報做了準備。

⑤ whether 子句能成為介系詞的受詞，但是 if 子句不能成為介系詞的受詞。

- There was disagreement among our company directors about whether we should merge with HB Bank. (o)
- There was disagreement among our company directors about if we should merge with HB Bank. (x)
  關於是否要與 HB 銀行合併，我們公司的董事間有歧見。

1. Mr. Wu has worked at several of our overseas branch offices, ------- Ms. Browning has been stationed exclusively at our headquarters.
   (A) even
   (B) regardless of
   (C) aside from
   (D) whereas

2. A courier from Vargas Shipping dropped off a package, ------- the receptionist signed for it.
   (A) and
   (B) else
   (C) whether
   (D) or

3. The merger will be considered complete ------- the documents have been signed by both parties.
   (A) which
   (B) during
   (C) that
   (D) when

4. All charges for customized must be paid in advance ------- the manager has approved a different payment plan.
   (A) throughout
   (B) rather
   (C) that
   (D) unless

5. Drivers are required to present a valid license ------- they rent a car.
   (A) over
   (B) when
   (C) toward
   (D) but

Chapter *12* 關係詞

基礎文法

關係詞分為關係代名詞、關係形容詞和關係副詞。關係詞若是引導一個從屬子句，並與句子裡的一個名詞或代名詞有關聯的代名詞，稱作**關係代名詞**，指代前面已經出現過的名詞（先行詞）。最具代表的關係詞，一般包括**關係代名詞** who、whose、whom、which、that、what 和**關係副詞** when、where、how、why。

1 關係代名詞 who

關係代名詞 **who**，用在先行詞是**人**的時候。

- Sara, who is one of my best friends, is good at writing stories.
  先行詞　　　　關係詞子句
  我的摯友莎拉善於寫故事。

2 關係代名詞 which 和 that

關係代名詞 **which** 或 **that**，用在先行詞是**事物**的時候。

- I bought some books. 我買了一些書。
- I would read them before going to bed. 我會在上床前看這些書。
  → I bought some books which I would read before going to bed.
  　　　　　先行詞　　　　　　　　　關係詞子句
  我買了一些上床前會看的書。

當事物先行詞有 the first、the last、the next、the only、every、any、no、all 這些限定字限定它時，關係代名詞就不能用 which，要用 **that**。

- Peter knew the first thing that he had to do.
  彼德知道他要做的第一件事。
- All that glitters is not gold. 閃閃發亮的並非都黃金。(虛有其表)

3 關係代名詞 what

關係代名詞 **what** 沒有特定的先行詞，它就是自己所要代替的名詞。

- I owe what I have to my wife. 我所擁有的一切都是因為我太太。
- What I want to do most is develop the best possible program.
  我最想做的是發展出最好的計畫。

4 關係代名詞 whose 和 whom

依先行詞後接句子是何種功能，來判斷要用關係代名詞所有格 whose 還是關係代名詞受格 whom，來代替該先行詞。

關係代名詞所有格 whose 後要接名詞。當先行詞是所有格時，就要用 whose。

- I hired a man. 我僱用了一個人。
- His mother is one of my mother's best friends.
  他媽媽是我媽媽的好友。
  ➡ I hired a man whose mother is one of my mother's best friends.
  我僱用的人，他媽媽是我媽媽的好友。

5 關係代名詞的用法

① 關係代名詞的格

先行詞	主格	受格	所有格
人	who	whom, who	whose
事物、動物	which	which	whose, of which
人、事物、動物	that	that	-

② 關係代名詞的省略

關係代名詞當作**受詞**使用時**可以省略**，但當**主詞**使用時則**不能省略**。關係代名詞也可當作介系詞的受詞使用，直接放在**介系詞後**時也**不能省略**。另外，關係代名詞 that 除了介系詞 **in** 之外，不能放在其他的介系詞後。

- The book (that/which) my daughter gave me is very exciting.
  我女兒給我的書很有趣。
- Do you know the woman (whom/who/that) John is hanging out **with**? 你認識跟約翰往來的那位女士嗎？
- Do you know the woman **with** (who/that) **whom** John is hanging out? 你認識跟約翰往來的那位女士嗎？
- Do you know the woman with John is hanging out? (x)
  你認識跟約翰往來的那位女士嗎？

③ 「關係代名詞＋ be 動詞」的省略

- The building (which was) chosen for our new offices is very beautiful. 選來做我們新辦公室的大樓非常漂亮。
- I want to hire people (who are) responsible for these positions. 我想任用會對自己工作負責的人。
  ➡ 「主格關係代名詞＋be動詞」(which was / who is / which is)可以省略，只留下後面的分詞 (chosen) 或形容詞 (responsible)。

6 關係副詞

依先行詞的種類，來使用不同的關係副詞。

先行詞	關係副詞
時間	when
原因	why
場所	where
方法	how（the way 不能和 how 一起使用。兩個中只有使用一個。）

- Monday is the day **when** the new employees meet.
  週一是新雇員碰面的第一天。
- The place **where** I had dinner with my girlfriend has a great salad bar. 我跟女友去吃晚飯的地方有很棒的沙拉吧。
- The report explained the reason **why** the accidents had happened.
  報告說明了意外發生的原因。
- I tried to learn **the way/how** the machine works.
  我試著學習機器運作的原理。

Chapter 12

1. Please call our hotline for more information about ------- new businesses should do before registering with the tax department.
   (A) which
   (B) how
   (C) where
   (D) what

2. The staff at Aruga Airlines will do ------- we can to ensure that you have a safe and relaxing flight.
   (A) each
   (B) every
   (C) above
   (D) whatever

3. Ms. Chun left me a voice mail saying that she had taken one of the company cars, but she didn't mention ------- one it was.
   (A) whoever
   (B) which
   (C) either
   (D) every

4. ------- what time of the day or night it is, the security staff monitoring your CCTV will quickly respond to any suspicious activity.
   (A) Even so
   (B) As though
   (C) As if
   (D) No matter

5. ------- is interested in joining the company softball team, please send Julian an email before Friday.
   (A) One
   (B) Whoever
   (C) Anyone
   (D) Someone

Actual Test   PART 5

閱讀試題，選出最適合填入空格中的選項。

1. The head security officer at the international airport used his ------- to deny a suspicious passenger the right to board.
   (A) authority
   (B) authorized
   (C) authoritative
   (D) authorizes

2. The hiring manager is looking for an experienced business developer who will take the ------- in finding new clients.
   (A) supplement
   (B) initiative
   (C) circumstance
   (D) advice

3. Aside from reducing household odors, the cleanser has many other practical -------.
   (A) use
   (B) useful
   (C) usefully
   (D) uses

4. Bailey's Grill provides diners with a ------- of steak, seafood, and pasta dishes.
   (A) beneficiary
   (B) preference
   (C) maintenance
   (D) selection

5. Axyl Communications will form a partnership with a Mumbai-based telephone company to solidify its ------- in India.
   (A) presence
   (B) repetition
   (C) courtesy
   (D) description

6. The number of full-time staff at Khan Beverages recently ------- with the opening of a new plant.
   (A) convened
   (B) doubled
   (C) charged
   (D) released

7. The employees at Niko Games always ------- to create unique and entertaining software that will appeal to the public.
   (A) designate
   (B) strive
   (C) hesitate
   (D) assume

8. A consumer survey was carried out to ------- young adults' interest in online education.
   (A) persuade
   (B) gauge
   (C) combine
   (D) administer

9. Some employees of Jenson Consulting ------- within a few miles of the office.
   (A) live
   (B) take
   (C) use
   (D) have

10. The newspaper article confirms that the allegations ------- by the appointed committee next week.
    (A) investigating
    (B) have been investigating
    (C) investigated
    (D) will be investigated

11. Andrew Gray is an ------- composer who has written a number of award-winning musicals.
    (A) admires
    (B) admire
    (C) admired
    (D) admiringly

12. Candidates must clearly explain their strengths and weaknesses when ------- interviews.
    (A) are attending
    (B) attend
    (C) to attend
    (D) attending

13. There are two new employees that need to go through ------- before they can begin working.

    (A) orienting
    (B) oriented
    (C) orientation
    (D) to orient

14. One of the biggest ------- of automobiles in the country has just announced that it will be expanding into Asia.

    (A) distributing
    (B) distributors
    (C) distribute
    (D) distribution

15. If our company is ------- to go on a leadership retreat this summer, we should all agree on the location.

    (A) to go
    (B) going
    (C) of going
    (D) to going

16. Every strategy that we have employed so far has ------- to our benefit.

    (A) working
    (B) worked
    (C) to working
    (D) work

17. Do you have any suggestions for ------- our advertising?

    (A) improving
    (B) to improve
    (C) improve
    (D) improved

18. The company needs to make an aggressive move if it plans on ------- the necessary raw materials at a reasonable rate.

    (A) acquire
    (B) acquired
    (C) acquiring
    (D) acquires

19. Our first priority is to ------- the members of our community who need our help the most.

    (A) are serving
    (B) serve
    (C) served
    (D) serving

20. The purpose of the new fountain downtown is ------- people from out of town into our commercial center.

    (A) to attract
    (B) attracting
    (C) for attract
    (D) attract

21. When processing the claims of multiple companies, it is important to communicate fully with all parties -------.

    (A) are involved
    (B) involving
    (C) involvement
    (D) involved

22. ------- ratings have led us to conclude that our target audience is being reached.

    (A) To be increased
    (B) To increase
    (C) Increased
    (D) Increase

23. The upgraded network allow employees to edit and transfer documents more -------.

    (A) easy
    (B) easily
    (C) ease
    (D) easing

24. If the professor decides to conduct her research, she could wind up taking an ------- leave from the school.

    (A) extend
    (B) extends
    (C) extending
    (D) extended

25. When ------- sensitive information, you should use an encrypted server.
    (A) transmit
    (B) transmits
    (C) transmitted
    (D) transmitting

26. The director was quoted as saying that KG, Inc should not ------- with Hub Corp. Because of the difficulty of integrating such vastly different corporate cultures.
    (A) resign
    (B) merge
    (C) establish
    (D) extend

27. When you described the new sales plan, you really ------- me of its effectiveness.
    (A) convince
    (B) convincingly
    (C) convinced
    (D) convincing

28. The government is ------- a new campaign to increase tourism.
    (A) promoting
    (B) promoted
    (C) promote
    (D) to promoting

29. The percentage of our market share ------- increasing every year since we opened the branch downtown.
    (A) is
    (B) was
    (C) had
    (D) has been

30. Be sure to proofread your résumé carefully before ------- it to potential employers.
    (A) sent
    (B) send
    (C) sends
    (D) sending

PART

6

段落填空

一、試題要點

Part 6 是一篇文章，文章中的某些句子挖空單字或詞組。考生閱讀文章，從四個選項中選出最適合的答案來完成文章中的空格。

Part 6 和 Part 5 一樣，依據空格所在的**上下文文法**和**句意**，選出最合適的字彙、詞類、介系詞、連接詞等來完成文章。然而 Part 5 只要探究一個句子的結構，Part 6 要探究的是**句子和句子間的關係**。而新制多益更是出現了新的試題類型，考生須選出一個完整句子來填入空格。因此與舊制多益相比，更要知道整篇文章的來龍去脈才能解題。

Part 6 的文章會以商業書信或電子郵件、廣告、公告、報導及介紹等各式文章來出題。以**字彙選擇**的試題為最多，另外動詞時態、主被動語態、副詞與連接詞的使用也經常出現。填入完整句子的試題尤其講究邏輯，要透過連接子句和子句、句子和句子的連接詞連續關係才能解題。Part 6 一篇文章出四道試題，共有四篇文章 16 道試題。

① **符合句意的字彙試題**：掌握空格所在句子的句意，或前後文的文意。
② **完成句子的試題**：掌握空格前後的字彙，並留意代名詞所代替對象的性別和數量是否一致。
③ **動詞型態變化的試題**：同上也是詞類的問題，專門測驗動詞時態之掌握。必須完整理解句子和前後文的文意，與不定詞、現在和過去分詞等的動詞變化。
④ **選出一個句子以完成整篇文章的邏輯試題**：理解整篇文章的來龍去脈，掌握連接詞／副詞等，和選項句子與整篇文章的邏輯關係。

二、應試策略

Step1　掌握**文章的類型**，可能是商業書信、廣告、新聞報導等。

Step2　依選項掌握**試題的類型**。

Step3　掌握句子「**主詞＋動詞＋（受詞）**」的結構，以便確知空格要放入哪種詞類。除了有空格的句子外，也要掌握**上下文的邏輯關係**。

Step4　填入句子的試題，可以透過連接句子與句子的**連接詞**，或是段落與段落的**轉承詞**（如 for example、furthermore、in addition、as a result、by the way、however 等）來掌握選項和文章的邏輯關係。

Example

Questions 1-4 refer to the following announcement.

Thank you for shopping at Larson's China. Our products are known for their modern and unique patterns and color combinations, as well as ------- **1.** and strength. ------- **2.** Please note however, that repeated drops and rough handling will ------- **3.** eventual breakage. We suggest you store them carefully and that you don't use harsh chemicals, steel sponges, or ------- **4.** scrubbing when cleaning them. Please visit our website at www.larsonchina.com for information about handling and care, or call us at 555-1234 if you have any questions or concerns.

1. (A) durable
   (B) durability
   (C) durableness
   (D) durable

2. (A) Larson's utensils and silverware go great with our dinnerware.
   (B) Our most popular line, the spring flower china, is sold out at most locations.
   (C) Visit our store to check out our other beautiful products.
   (D) They are dishwasher- and microwave-safe, and we're confident that you'll be using them for years to come.

3. (A) result in
   (B) occur to
   (C) ending at
   (D) stop with

4. (A) ambitious
   (B) combative
   (C) aggressive
   (D) complacent

1. B 2. D 3. A 4. C

試題類型

在新制多益中，Part 6 的試題有了很大的改變，即增加了需要填入完整句子的題型，考生必須要理解整篇文章的來龍去脈，才能加以解題。試題數也從每篇文章三道題增加為四道；且文章數也從三篇文章增至四篇。

除此之外，Part 6 也增加了一些以前舊制多益沒有的題目類型。尤其是邏輯試題，正確答案不能只在空格所在的那句找，更要看前後文；甚至只看前後句仍不夠，還要確實讀懂整篇文章才能解題。選項不只是片語而更有完整句子，因此題目的變化更多了，而句子的位置，可能會在文章的開頭、中間或是結尾，相當多樣。

電子郵件

1 題型暖身

STEP 1 試題 1—2 與下列電子郵件有關。

To: Craig Pittman <craigpittman@lovemail.com>
From: Tina Michaels <tm2304@ttmail.com>
Date: October 21
Subject: Re: Looking for a Job?

Dear Mr. Pittman,

Yes, what you have heard is correct. I left my position at One Way Consulting back in September. Since I was tired of working in Manhattan, I decided to search for a job ------- **1.** . I recently ------- **2.** my application to a promising start-up in Albany that is looking for a PR representative. The company seems like a perfect fit for me. I will be having an interview with them next Monday. Although it is not easy to be between jobs, I find this opportunity very appealing. Thanks again for your support. I'll let you know when I have more news. Wish me luck!

Tina Michaels

---

1. (A) elsewhere
    (B) instead
    (C) later
    (D) further

2. (A) corrected
    (B) accepted
    (C) resigned
    (D) submitted

STEP 2 確認正確答案及翻譯和解說。

收件人：克雷格‧皮特曼 <craigpittman@lovemail.com>

寄件人：蒂娜‧麥可斯 <tm2307@ttmail.com>

日期：10 月 21 日

主旨：Re：正在找工作嗎？

皮特曼先生您好：

是的，誠如您所聽到的消息，我在九月時已從單行顧問離職。由於我不想在曼哈頓工作，打算到他處另謀發展。最近我寄了求職信到奧爾巴尼一家前景看好的新創公司，他們在徵一位公關代表。那家公司看起來很適合我，我下週一會去面試。儘管待業的這段期間心情並不好過，我還是對這次機會充滿期待。再次謝謝您的支持，有什麼消息都會跟您說。祝我好運吧！

蒂娜‧麥可斯

字彙

promising 可為的；有前途的　　representative 代表　　opportunity 機會

正確答案

1. (A) elsewhere

2. (D) submitted

解說

1. 空格前面提到蒂娜對於在曼哈頓工作感到疲累，所以從上下文意，應選到其他地方找工作（elsewhere），正確答案為 (A)。

從句意上來看，不是要找其他工作來代替（instead），所以不能選 (B)。選項 (C) 則和後文的文意不合，也不能選。用更進一步（further）則和前句意思相反，所以 (D) 也是錯誤答案。

2. 句意是向公司提出履歷，這時空格只能放 (D)，表「提出、提交」。其他的選項意思分別為 (A) 更正 (B) 接受 (C) 辭職。

To: Emily Childes <e_childes@chemiohi.com>
From: Curtis Stephenson <c_stephenson@chemiohi.com>
Date: October 2
Subject: Employment Delay

Dear Ms. Childes,

I want to fill you in on what is happening with our company's new Indonesian engineer, Mr. Ade Hatta. Currently, his paperwork is being processed by the immigration office. Our plan was for him to begin working here at the beginning of October. However, it appears that there is some ------- on the part of the
3.
immigration officials to grant his visa. They think that the V8 visa we applied for may not be the correct type for his line of work. Therefore, we might have to apply for another visa. ------- When they reply to us, I will contact you
4.
immediately.

Sincerely,

Curtis Stephenson
Human Resources
Chemio Heavy Industries

3. (A) agreement
    (B) consideration
    (C) attitude
    (D) reluctance

4. (A) Thank you for using our services; we hope to hear from you again.
    (B) We have contacted the immigration office to inquire about other types of visas.
    (C) The employment period is contracted to finish in March.
    (D) All applications should be processed as soon as possible.

STEP 2 確認正確答案及翻譯和解說。

收件人：艾蜜莉・柴爾德斯 <e_childes@chemiohi.com>
寄件人：柯蒂斯・史蒂芬森 <c_stepheson@chemiohi.com>
日期：10 月 2 日
主旨：延遲僱用

柴爾德斯女士您好：

我想跟您更新一下本公司印尼籍新進工程師阿蒂・哈達先生的近況，移民署正在跑他的書面流程。我們本來計畫讓他十月開始上班，但看起來移民署還不會發給他簽證。他們認為我們申請的 V8 簽證不適用他的行業，必須再申請另一種。我們已向移民署詢問其他簽證種類。如果他們有回覆，我會立刻與您聯絡。

柯蒂斯・史蒂芬森 敬上
人力資源部門
卡蜜歐重工業公司

字彙

immigration 移民；移居　　grant 給予；同意

正確答案

3. (D) reluctance

4. (B) We have contacted the immigration office to inquire about other types of visas.

解說

3. 空格所在的本句以 however 開頭，所以可以知道接下來的內容會和前面所述相反，即簽證的過程並不順利。(A) 表「同意」，與文意相反，(C) 表「態度」，和上下文完全無關，所以它們都可以刪除。

　　(B) 是「考慮」，乍看之下好像可以，不過從上下文來看，在出現了問題的狀況下，移民署有些「不願意」的意思更順，所以 (D) 是正確答案。

4. 從空格的前後句中找答案。後句提到了代名詞 they，由此可知空格內所填的句子必須有可以讓 they 代稱的先行詞。選項中，只有 (B) 提到了相當於 they 的團體，那就是移民署，所以正確答案是 (B)。

電子郵件（email）

多益測驗中的電子郵件一般都是公司和消費者間，或公司和公司間往返的信件。此類試題通常會考**寄件人**、**收件人**以及**寄件主旨**等。尤其是和寄件人或收件人有關的代名詞、和職位有關的內容等等，一定要看清楚。

STEP 1　試題 1—4 與下列電子郵件有關。

To: Sarah Grissom
From: Laura Nicholson
Date: May 6
Subject: Museum Request

Dear Ms. Grissom,

I am Laura Nicholson, the director of exhibits here at the National Museum. I understand that you keep a collection of your famous grandmother's clothes ----1.---- your residence. We are interested in exhibiting some of the most famous dresses made by the late designer Victor Valentine. ----2.---- We are especially interested in the dress she wore to the Academy Awards in 1963 and the lovely wedding dress she wore in 1966. Is it possible to set up an appointment so that I can personally visit you and view some potential pieces for the exhibit? We can discuss compensation and other details at our meeting if you choose to ----3.---- us the dresses. I hope you will consider our request. I look forward to ----4.---- from you.

Sincerely,

Laura Nicholson
Director of Exhibits
National Museum

1. (A) to
    (B) for
    (C) at
    (D) with

2. (A) If you are interested in purchasing some of his dresses, please contact me.
    (B) Your grandmother wore quite a few of his pieces.
    (C) His designs are timeless and classic today.
    (D) We need to find some of his vintage dresses that were worn by famous actresses in the past.

3. (A) credit
    (B) allowance
    (C) loan
    (D) borrow

4. (A) heard
    (B) hearing
    (C) has heard
    (D) hear

STEP 2 確認正確答案及翻譯和解說。

收件人：莎拉・葛里森
寄件人：蘿拉・尼克爾森
日期：5 月 6 日
主旨：博物館的請求

葛里森女士您好：

我是國家博物館展覽主任蘿拉・尼克爾森。我知道您在住處珍藏了您名人祖母的衣物。我們計畫展出已故設計師維克多・華倫泰最著名的禮服。您祖母穿過不少他的作品。我們對她在 1963 年出席奧斯卡頒獎典禮的那件禮服，和 1966 年婚禮穿的禮服特別感興趣。不知道有沒有機會跟您碰面，我想親自拜訪並看一下想要邀展的禮服。如果您願意出借，我們可以在碰面時討論報酬和其他細節。希望您能考慮我們的請求，並期盼您的回覆。

蘿拉・尼克爾森 敬上
展覽主任
國家博物館

字彙

exhibit 展覽　　residence 住所；宅邸　　late 已故的　　potential 潛在的
compensation 報酬；賠償　　consider 考慮　　piece 作品　　vintage 復古的
allowance 補貼；零用錢　　borrow 借入　　loan 借出

1. (C) at

2. (B) Your grandmother wore quite a few of his pieces.

3. (C) loan

4. (B) hearing

1. residence 是住宅、宅邸,所以用表「在……地點」的介系詞 at 是最合適的,正確答案是 (C)。

2. 維克多·華倫泰不是收信人的祖母,而是知名的服裝設計師。這位設計師和收信人祖母間的關係,應該就是空格的內容。選項中唯一提到兩者間的關係的,就只有 (B) 了,祖母穿過許多他設計的服裝。

3. loan 和 borrow 之間的差別要弄清楚,borrow 是「借入」,loan 是「借出」。空格的主詞是 you,是寄件人,也就是要借出衣服給博物館展覽的人,所以要用借出 loan,正確答案是 (C)。

4. 這裡的 hear 不是直接「聽到對方聲音」,而是表示「收到對方的回音、聯繫」,整句是「期望收到您的回音」。look forward to 這個片語後要接動名詞,最好背下來。正確答案是 (B)。

Chapter 02 公告與通知

1 題型暖身

STEP 1 試題 1—2 與下列公告有關。

To: Residents of Pine Knoll Apartment Building No. 3
From: SOE Gas Company
Date: September 15
Subject: Gas Line Work

Please note that SOE Gas Company will be shutting off your gas on September 23 from 10 a.m. to 1 p.m. in order to repair and replace old gas lines. While SOE Gas Company is working on the gas lines, residents of Pine Knoll Apartment Building No. 3 are ------- to vacate the property for health
1.
and safety reasons. We apologize for any inconvenience this might cause you, and we thank you in advance for your -------.
2.

1. (A) requiring
   (B) requires
   (C) required
   (D) require

2. (A) negotiation
   (B) cooperation
   (C) publication
   (D) investigation

收件人：松丘公寓大廈第三棟所有住戶

寄件人：SOE 瓦斯公司

日期：9 月 15 日

主旨：瓦斯管線工程

請留意，SOE 瓦斯公司將於 9 月 23 日上午 10 點到下午 1 點間暫停供應瓦斯，以維修和替換老舊瓦斯管線。基於健康安全理由，在 SOE 瓦斯公司施工期間，請松丘公寓大廈第三棟所有住戶暫時離開住處。如有造成任何不便，敬請見諒。感謝您的配合。

字彙

replace 更換；取代　　residents 居民　　vacate 空出；騰出

正確答案

1. (C) required

2. (B) cooperation

解說

1. 本句是「要求住戶離開住處」的意思，因為主詞是住戶，所以空格應該放「被要求」，選項中的被動語態是正確答案。

2. 這句是「如有造成任何不便，敬請見諒。感謝您的配合。」空格放 (B)「合作」最合適。因為沒提到住戶獲得補償，所以 (A) 的「協商」不能選。而 (C) 的「發表」和 (D) 的「調查」，和句子的內容完全無關，所以也都刪除。

L.A. Top Planning, which promotes tourist attractions in Los Angeles, is looking to hire the best and brightest people we can find. To be a part of our team, you have to have a master's degree or higher in business management with a GPA over 3.5. For more information, including a full list of the ------- you need to
3.
satisfy and the duties you will be performing. Please visit our website at www. latopplanning.com. ------- Any application received after this date will not be
4.
considered. Applicants will hear back from us by February 15.

3. (A) claims
   (B) supplies
   (C) engagements
   (D) requirements

4. (A) Thank you for taking the time to complete the survey.
   (B) We accept applications from students with GPAs below 3.5.
   (C) The website will be completed by the first of January.
   (D) Applicants must submit all of the necessary documents before the end of December.

推廣洛杉磯觀光景點的 L.A. 頂尖規畫公司正在招募一流的優秀人才。想加入團隊者，至少要有商業管理碩士學位，在校平均成績必須高於 3.5。詳情（包括各項必要條件和工作內容）請參閱本公司網站 www.latopplanning.com。應徵者必須在 12 月底前提交所有必要文件。逾時的應徵將不受理。我們會在 2 月 15 日前與應徵者聯絡。

字彙

tourist attraction 觀光景點　　duty 責任；義務　　application 申請

正確答案

3. (D) requirements

4. (D) Applicants must submit all of the necessary documents before the end of December.

解說

3. 能夠和表「滿足；符合」的 satisfy 搭配使用的單字，選項中只有 requirements（條件）了。所以 (D) 是正確答案。其他選項都不是能「滿足或符合」的名詞，選項意思分別為 (A) 聲明 (B) 供給 (C) 訂婚。

4. 空格後的句子，是「逾時的應徵將不受理。」所以要放進空格裡的這句話，裡面一定要提到特定的時間，因此只剩 (C) 和 (D) 可以考慮。(C) 的文意不對所以不能選。(D) 則提到了提交文件的特定時間，故為正確答案。

2 命題分析

公告與通知（announcement/notice）

● 公告與通知是對在特定時間點和場所中的人，介紹或說明事項的文章。一篇文章出四道試題。試題類型分別為：**文法試題**（一至二題）、**字彙試題**（一至二題）、**慣用語試題**（至多一題），還有新類型「**文意選填**」的類型。

● 解題策略如下：

➡ 文法試題，可以在空格所在句的前後句中，找到正確答案線索。

➡ 字彙與慣用語試題，要勤背常考的字彙片語。

➡ 文意選填試題，要分析談話的主旨、前後文的關係，以及因果關係，還要知道整篇文章的來龍去脈。當你選定一句話後，也需分析整篇文章通順與否。

STEP 1　試題 1—4 與下列通知有關。

Attention all Home Depot staff. There are some changes ------- made to the
　　　　　　　　　　　　　　　　　　　　　　　　　　　　　　1.
company's retirement packages. This notice will likely not affect many of

you because you will move on to other jobs. For those of you ------- make a
　　　　　　　　　　　　　　　　　　　　　　　　　　　　2.
career with us here at Home Depot, however, we ask you to please take part

in the question and answer seminar we have set up for this coming Saturday.

3.
Please note that this announcement only ------- to employees who were hired
　　　　　　　　　　　　　　　　　　4.
after January 2nd of this year.

1. (A) be
   (B) being
   (C) was
   (D) to being

2. (A) wish to
   (B) wished to
   (C) wishing
   (D) wishing to

3. (A) We understand this is a
       weekday, but it is important.
   (B) We know this will cut into your
       weekend, but it is important.
   (C) You don't have to make any
       decisions about the schedule.
   (D) The management will be taking
       meal requests for next week's
       lunches.

4. (A) impacts
   (B) associates
   (C) applies
   (D) reminds

家得寶員工請注意。退休方案會有些變更。而這項公告可能不會影響太多人，因為你們會繼續從事其他工作。如果你有意願要留在家得寶繼續奮鬥，請出席本週六舉辦的問答座談。我們知道這樣會犧牲週末假期，但這件事情很重要。

請注意，本公告僅適用於今年 1 月 2 日後受僱的員工。

字彙

package 方案；包裹　　affect 影響
make a career with 與……合作　　take part in 參與

正確答案

1. (B) being
2. (D) wishing to
3. (B) We know this will cut into your weekend, but it is important.
4. (C) applies

解說

1. 因為空格位在退休方案變更的動詞的位置，而且可以知道，做出變更（change）的動詞 make，要改成被動語態。另外，又因為變更事項現在正在實施或在不久的將來即將實施，所以時態要用現在進行式（being made）或未來式（to be made）。注意到要用被動語態，並仔細觀察句子的結構，就能立刻解題了。正確答案是 (B)。

2. make a career with 是「與……合作」的意思。把想留下來繼續工作的人（you）當作主詞，「想要去……」是 wish to，由於省略關係代名詞 who，wish to 要改成現在分詞 wishing to，正確答案是 (D)。

3. 選項中的 this 或 it，都是指星期六要舉辦的問答座談，而根據前後文，是要求員工前來參加該座談會。開會的時間是星期六，不是週間（weekday），所以 (A) 錯了。(D) 和文章完全無關。(C) 的時間表（schedule）沒有在文章中出現，所以也不對。正確答案是 (B)。

4. 本句沒有動詞，是以可以判斷空格處放的應是動詞，與 to 搭配使用。選項 (A) 的 impact 是給予衝擊，通常與介系詞 on 搭配使用，所以不能選。表關聯的 (B) associates 的介系詞是 with；表提醒的 (D) reminds 則常和介系詞 of 連用，兩者都不能選。

正確答案是與 to 形成 apply to，表「適用於」的 (C)，以告知公告的「適用範圍」。

Chapter 03 廣告

1 題型暖身

STEP 1 試題 1—2 與下列邀請函有關。

October 1

David Cooper
64 Stonewall Road
Vancouver V2H 1M4

Dear Mr. Cooper,

Stargazer Coffee would like to invite you to our first anniversary celebration as a thank-you for the business you have done with us. Last October 15th we -------- our business, and exactly one year later on the same date we will
1.
celebrate this special day with a fun party. It will start at 7 p.m. and end at 10 p.m. We would really appreciate it if you would join us. We are looking forward to -------- you soon.
2.

Sincerely,

Amy Heller, Store Manager
Stargazer Coffee

---

1. (A) are opening
    (B) would open
    (C) opened
    (D) should have opened

2. (A) meet
    (B) met
    (C) meets
    (D) meeting

10 月 1 日
大衛 · 庫柏
石牆路 64 號
溫哥華 V2H 1M4

庫柏先生您好：

觀星咖啡敬邀您參加我們一週年感恩活動，謝謝您對我們的支持。我們從去年 10 月 15 日開始營運，一年後的同一天，我們將舉辦一個好玩的派對，以慶祝這特別的一日。派對將從晚上七點開始，到十點結束。我們會非常感謝您的參與，期待與您見面。

艾咪 · 海勒 敬上
觀星咖啡店經理

字彙

anniversary 週年；週年紀念日　　celebrate 慶祝　　appreciate 感謝；欣賞

正確答案

1. (C) opened
2. (D) meeting

解說

1. 句意是「去年 10 月 15 日咖啡店開幕」，動詞的時間點是過去。
正確答案是過去式的 (C)。
2. 表期待的動詞片語 look forward to 後面要接動名詞，正確答案是 (D)。

We at the Diamond Theater are proud to announce our 27th Annual Spring Performance, featuring special guest Antonio Vietto. Mr. Vietto is a -------
3.
operatic tenor who has sung in many opera houses all around the world, including La Scala in Milan and the Sydney Opera House. He is especially well known for his performance as the opening singer at the last Olympic Games, where he sang the official Olympic theme song. The Diamond Theater will offer a special discount for this event to all season ticket holders. This once-in-a-lifetime event will take place on April 15 at 8 p.m. Tickets start from $250, and the event will be followed by a black tie cocktail party at the theater.

4.

3. (A) temporary
   (B) tedious
   (C) renowned
   (D) predictable

4. (A) The theater will open at 6:30 p.m., after the show.
   (B) To book tickets, please visit our website at www.diamondtheater.com.
   (C) Please ensure that all the necessary documents are attached.
   (D) A memo will be sent to all performers regarding the Olympic opening ceremony.

鑽石劇院很榮幸宣布我們第 27 屆的年度春季表演，特別來賓是安東尼歐·維埃托。他是知名歌劇男高音，曾在全球許多著名歌劇院演唱，包括米蘭的斯卡拉大劇院及雪梨歌劇院。他最著名的演出是在上屆奧運擔任開場歌手，演唱奧運主題曲。持有季票的觀眾可享有這場演出門票的特別折扣。這場千載難逢的難得演出，將於 4 月 15 日晚上八點開演。一般票券售價從 250 元起，演出結束後，劇院內會有正式晚宴。購票請洽我們的網站：www.diamondtheater.com。

字彙

once-in-a-lifetime 一生一次的　　book 預約

正確答案

3. (C) renowned

4. (B) To book tickets, please visit our website at www.diamondtheater.com.

解說

3. 從特別來賓安東尼歐·維埃托在世界許多歌劇院演出過這點可以知道，他相當有名，所以空格應該放具有類似含意的單字。選項意思分別為 (A) 暫時的 (B) 沉悶的 (D) 可預測的，這些單字都和句意不符，所以正確答案是表「知名的」的 (C)。

4. 空格的前面告知了日期和票價，要放進空格內的句子，除了說明訂票事項的 (B) 之外，其他選項都和訂票無關。(A) 提到表演後劇場開門的時間，(C) 提到文章中沒有提到的必備文件，(D) 提到和文章主題完全無關的奧林匹克，所以上述都是錯的。

2 命題分析

廣告（advertisement）

產品或服務所做的廣告文章也會拿來出題。廣告的內容通常會提到，產品或服務的特徵、價格、折扣、折扣期間、日期、場所、優惠細節等。一篇文章出四道試題。試題類型分別為：**文法試題**（一至二題）、**字彙試題**（一至二題）、**慣用語試題**（至多一題），還有新類型「**文意選填**」的類型。試題類型雖然和 Part 5 類似，但要理解整篇文章才能找出正確答案。解題時尤其要注意文章內的**轉承詞**、**主旨**、**前後文關係**和**因果關係**。

STEP 1 試題 1—4 與下列廣告有關。

Do you like chocolate? Of course you do! ---‑---.
1.

This Saturday, be sure to come on down to the grand opening of Mitch

Wilson's Chocolatiers!

Mitch Wilson ---‑--- handcrafted chocolates for over 30 years. Originally
2.

trained in Belgium, Mitch recently decided to bring his skills and experience

back to his hometown of Maplewood.

Mitch Wilson's Chocolatiers ---‑--- handing out information on the sourcing
3.

of our ingredients, as well as giving away ---‑--- of free samples. Be sure to
4.

mark it on your calendar and come on down!

1. (A) Well, vanilla is delicious too!
    (B) How about Belgian Chocolate?
    (C) Dutch chocolate is our specialty!
    (D) Chocolate is on every plate in Spain!

2. (A) has been creating
    (B) has created
    (C) has creating
    (D) was created

3. (A) was
    (B) will
    (C) will be
    (D) will being

4. (A) tons
    (B) some
    (C) many
    (D) a few

你喜歡巧克力嗎？肯定是喜歡的！那你喜歡比利時巧克力嗎？

本週六，請一定要來米奇・威爾森巧克力店的盛大開幕！

米奇・威爾森先生手工製作巧克力已有 30 年以上的經驗。他最早在比利時學藝，最近決定帶著技藝和經驗回到故鄉楓木鎮。

米奇・威爾森巧克力店將會提供原料來源的相關資訊，也會發送大量免費試吃品。

一定要在日曆上記下這一天，來參加吧！

字彙

chocolatier 巧克力店　　hand out 發出　　sourcing 來源；來源
ingredient 成分　　specialty 特製品；專長

正確答案

1. (B) How about Belgian Chocolate?

2. (A) has been creating

3. (C) will be

4. (A) tons

解說

1. 廣告的第一句話和最後一句話，通常是宣傳標語出現的地方，本題就是要考第一句該放入什麼樣的句子。第二句話在宣傳說巧克力店的開幕，所以 (A) 不會是正確答案。內容中沒有出現荷蘭巧克力（Dutch Chocolate）和西班牙巧克力（Spanish Chocolate），故 (C) 和 (D) 也都可以刪除。

　　而根據文章，提到米奇・威爾森在比利時受訓後回故鄉開店，所以提到比利時巧克力很合理，正確答案是 (B)。

2. 本句中有表特定期間的介系詞 for，米奇・威爾森製作手工巧克力到現在已經超過 30 年，要用現在完成式。又因為製作巧克力的行為沒有停止，故須使用現在完成進行式，正確答案是 (A)。

3. 空格後的動詞是現在分詞，所以 (B) 和 (D) 可以不用考慮。另外因為活動是在這星期六，還沒發生，故過去式的 (A) 也可以刪除，正確答案是 (C)。

4. 文章的內容是廣告，本題要找出最適合的分送免費樣品（free samples）的數量，知道這個立刻就能解題了。作為吸引人的誘因，廣告商免費分送的樣品數量是不會少的，所以 (D) 不用考慮。

　　另外，如果 (B)、(C)、(D) 是正確答案的話，那 free samples 前就要加定冠詞。正確答案是用誇張法來表示樣品數量的 (A)。

Chapter 04 書信

1 題型暖身

STEP 1 試題 1—2 與下列信件有關。

September 2

Emma Blair
Hartman Design Co.
1200 31st Street
Santa Monica, CA 90405-3012

Dear Ms. Blair,

This is Francis Hardy from Glorious Fashions. I am sending you some samples of the new shoe line High Steps, which we have produced in ------- **1.** with designer Sarah Adams. We are hoping to ------- **2.** our new products this winter in various fashion magazines. We trust that your company can create some eye-catching ads for us. Our goal is to present a deluxe and elegant image for this line. However, since the shoes are mainly marketed toward a younger urban demographic, the ads should not be too formal. Please see the enclosed guidelines for more information. If you have any questions, just let me know.

Sincerely,

Francis Hardy
Glorious Fashions

1. (A) cooperation
   (B) cooperatively
   (C) cooperate
   (D) cooperative

2. (A) import
   (B) promote
   (C) postpone
   (D) vote

9月2日
艾瑪·布萊爾
哈特曼設計公司
31 街 1200 號
聖塔莫尼卡，加州 90405-3012

布萊爾女士您好：

我是榮耀時裝的法蘭西斯·哈蒂，這次寄給您本公司新的鞋子產品線「高步」的一些樣本，這系列是我們和設計師莎拉·亞當斯合作的成果。我們希望今年冬季能在各時尚雜誌中推廣我們的新商品。我們相信貴公司能為我們設計出吸睛的廣告。我們的目標在於呈現品牌奢華高雅的形象。但是，由於這些鞋款主打年輕的都會族群，廣告不能太正式。請參閱附件中的詳細說明。有任何問題，也請您告知。

法蘭西斯·哈蒂 敬上
榮耀時裝

字彙

sample 樣品　　eye-catching 吸引目光的；吸睛的　　deluxe 高級的；豪華的
urban 城市的　　demographic 特定族群（常指消費族群）

正確答案

1. (A) cooperation
2. (B) promote

解說

1. 片語 in cooperation with 是「和⋯⋯合作」的意思。因為空格剛好就是這個片語，所以空格要放名詞型的 cooperation，正確答案是 (A)。

2. 因為不會自己進口自己的產品，所以 (A) 不考慮。也沒有延後的理由，(C) 也不能選。(D) 的 vote 則和產品完全無關，很明顯是錯誤答案。文章是想要促銷自己的產品，所以 (B) 的 promote 最合適。

We have recently reviewed your account and noticed that you are eligible to increase your credit limit by 50 percent. If you would like to do so, we would be pleased to extend your credit limit. This would be an excellent way to prepare for your future. We are now also looking at the best loan options with regard to purchasing your new home.

To take advantage of this --------, please visit our local branch or call us at
3.
1-800-555-0698. --------.
4.

Sincerely,

Erik Stapleton
Credit Card Representative
Everton Bank

3. (A) discount
    (B) offer
    (C) investment
    (D) mortgage

4. (A) We appreciate your feedback
        regarding our products.
    (B) We are not able to increase
        your credit limit at this time.
    (C) Alternatively, you can contact
        me directly at 555-6262.
    (D) The new loan has a 10-percent
        interest rate.

我們最近檢視了您的帳戶，發現您符合提高 50% 信用額度的資產。如果您有此意願，我們將樂意為您提高信用額度。這是為未來做好準備的好方法。我們也正在研究對您購置新屋最有利的貸款方案。想要把握好康，請親洽分行或撥打電話 1-800-555-0698。也可以直接與我聯絡，來電請撥 555-6262。

艾瑞克 · 斯特普爾頓 敬上
信用卡專員
艾佛頓銀行

字彙

account 帳戶　　eligible 有資格的；合適的　　credit 信用　　branch 分店

正確答案

3. (B) offer

4. (C) Alternatively, you can contact me directly at 555-6262.

解說

3 信件的主旨在於通知收信人，可以提高信用額度，並非打折，所以 (A) 不會是正確答案。也沒提到「投資」和「貸款」的優惠，所以 (C) 和 (D) 也不對。

　　(B) 表提案、建議，就是指前面提到的事項（提高信用額度），所以是正確答案。

4. 建議收信人接受「信用額度提高」這個提案，是本文的目的。告知相關訊息後，最後一定是揭示聯絡方法，所以跟聯絡方法無關的選項 (A) 和 (D) 不用考慮。和文章內容無關的選項 (B) 也是錯誤答案。正確答案是 (C)。

2 命題分析

書信（mail）

書信類試題和電子郵件基本上很類似，內容可能涉及公司和公司之間，或公司和客戶之間。信件的**主題**以及**寄件人和收件人兩者間的關係**要特別注意。文法類試題和時態類試題、關係詞和連結詞的試題也常出。除了確實讀懂整篇文章的來龍去脈外，也要細心地分析全文。

Council Member Mark Zing

2874 Hill Street
Lexington, IN 93872

Dear Council Member Zing,

I am writing on behalf of the community of Lexington. As more people
------- not to drive, we are seeing an increase in the number of cyclists
     1.
around our community. ------- I am requesting the development of more
                       2.
bike lanes around our small community, since over half the population either
walks or bikes to work. -------, there has been an increase in the number of
                        3.
bicycle shops around here as both tourists and locals rent or buy bicycles to
get around town. I believe creating more bike lanes will help our community
become more environmentally conscious, help people ride safely to and from
their destinations, and increase tourism in our area. Please consider this
request. The community of Lexington can only ------- from such a project.
                                              4.
Thank you in advance for your help.

Sincerely,

Ron Henderson

1. (A) choose
   (B) chose
   (C) have chose
   (D) are chosen

2. (A) But the roads are often too
       filled with rush-hour traffic.
   (B) In fact, everyone I know is
       starting to bike to work.
   (C) However, we don't have
       enough bike lanes.
   (D) The cyclists need a safe
       place to ride around.

3. (A) As a result
   (B) Furthermore
   (C) Therefore
   (D) In contrast

4. (A) profit
   (B) assistance
   (C) interest
   (D) benefit

市議員馬克‧辛

希爾街 2874 號

列克星頓，印地安納州 93872

馬克‧辛議員您好：

我謹代表列克星頓社區寫信給您。愈來愈多人選擇不開車，我們看到社區裡騎單車的人變多了，但我們缺乏足夠的腳踏車道。畢竟有超過半數的人不是走路去上班就是騎單車，因此我來信請求在這個小社區內鋪設更多腳踏車道。此外，隨著觀光客和本地人開始或租或買單車四處晃晃，這一帶單車店也變多了。我相信鋪設更多單車道將有助於提升社區的環保意識，讓人們能更安全地騎行通勤，並促進社區內的觀光活動。請考慮我的請求，這對列克星頓社區只有好處。先謝謝您的幫助。

朗‧韓德森 敬上

字彙

community 社區　　cyclist 單車騎士　　lane 車道；通道　　rent 租用；借入
environmentally conscious 有環保意識的；保護環境的　　destination 目的地
in advance 事前；預先

正確答案

1. (A) choose

2. (C) However, we don't have enough bike lanes.

3. (B) Furthermore

4. (D) benefit

解説

1. 仔細觀察空格所在句的句意，再看到空格後面提到「騎自行車人數增加」，be 動詞是現在進行式。「騎自行車人數增加」是結果，所以以 as 引導的原因，也要用現在式。正確答案是 (A)。

2. 空格之後的句子，句意是希望增加「更多的」自行車道（more bike lane），不是希望「有」自行車道或是「缺乏」自行車道。所以空格放進表自行車道不夠的 (C) 意思最順。

3. 空格前的句子提到乘坐自行車的人數增加，空格後的句子則提到自行車店增加，所以空格要選一個能將兩句作最好連接的連接詞。(C) 表「結果」，很容易誤認為是正確答案，然而空格前後的兩個句子不是因果關係，而是並列、累增的關係，所以表「更進一步」的 (B) 最合適。

4. 只要正確掌握動詞的含意就可以解題。(A) 的 profit 是「得到利潤、利息」，即儲蓄或投資獲得利金的意思，所以不對。正確答案是「得到益處」的 (D)。

1 題型暖身

STEP 1 試題 1—2 與下列報導有關。

November 2—Shelby Moore says that starting early next year her store, Books and Moore, will begin constructing an expansion on its east side in order to increase the capacity of the main building in Lyndonville. In addition, Books and Moore, one of the most popular bookstores in the area due to its massive collection of books and locally brewed coffee, is currently developing ideas to ------- its locations to other cities. Given the possibility of creating new jobs in
   1.
construction, Ms. Moore believes this project can help boost the economies of surrounding areas. "The most ------- thing for any economy is jobs," she says,
                        2.
"and we would like very much to create some."

1.   (A) broadened
    (B) broadens
    (C) broaden
    (D) broadening

2.   (A) improper
    (B) confidential
    (C) mutual
    (D) beneficial

STEP 2 確認正確答案及翻譯和解說。

11 月 2 日

雪比 · 摩爾說，摩爾書屋明年初將在其建築物東側展開擴建，以擴張林頓維爾這棟主要建築物的容納量。此外，摩爾書屋因豐富藏書和在地烹煮的咖啡而大受歡迎，也計畫到其他城市擴點。此項工程會創造新的工作機會，摩爾女士相信這項開發案有助於帶動周邊區域的經濟。「對任何經濟體最有利的是工作，而我們很樂意創造工作機會。」

字彙

expansion 擴展；擴張　　construction 建造；建設　　capacity 容量；能量

正確答案

1. (C) broaden

2. (D) beneficial

解說

1. 因為空格前有 to，所以可以知道這是不定詞，to 後面要接原形動詞，正確答案是 (C)。

2. 空格之後的內容是，對經濟會有幫助並創造工作機會。由此可以推知，空格應該要放具有肯定且重要含意的字彙。選項中最合適的字是 beneficial（有益的），所以正確答案是 (D)。選項其他意思為 (A) 不合適的 (B) 機密的 (C) 互相的，都和句意不符。

March 24—Sunnyville police reports can now be viewed on any electronic

------- . Officer Eric Jackson of the public relations department says this new
3.

technology is going to help police officers as well as civilians.

------- Officer Jackson says, "With this new technology, our officers will now be
4.

able to focus on serving our community rather than sitting behind a desk."

3. (A) device
    (B) publishing
    (C) purse
    (D) signature

4. (A) The department stated that officers and the community should have access to the same information.
    (B) The devices can be charged using a mobile phone.
    (C) Officers will now have less information than citizens.
    (D) More time will now be spent on desk work.

STEP 2 確認正確答案及翻譯和解說。

3月24日

現在可以在任何電子設備上看桑尼維爾的警政報告了。公關部門的艾瑞克·傑克森警官說，這項新科技對警員和市民都有益處。

該部門表示，警員和社區應該要有管道接觸到一樣的資訊。傑克森警官說，「有了這個新科技，員警更能好好服務社區，而不是單純坐在辦公桌前。」

字彙

technology 科技

正確答案

3. (A) device

4. (A) The department stated that officers and the community should have access to the same information.

解說

3. 選項中最有可能瀏覽報告的東西，除了 (A) 的設備（device）外，沒有更合適的了。其他選項意思為 (B) 處罰的 (C) 錢包 (D) 簽名，和報告毫無關係，所以都不能選。

4. 因為空格前一句的內容是，市民和警察全都可以瀏覽報告，故空格可能會是此描述的附加說明。另外因為空格後的內容是，傑克森警官說警察能更專注在服務上，所以放進空格的句子，應該會同時提到市民或警察。故正確答案是 (A)。

選項 (B) 提到可以透過手機充電，還有和本文意思完全相反的 (C) 和 (D)，都是錯誤答案。

報導（article）

報導類試題會從報紙或雜誌上，選出有關社會、政治、教育、健康、環境等各式各樣**時事文章**來出題。也會出文法、字彙以及片語、時態等等的試題。由於報導內容種類繁多，字彙會比較難，所以平時要多看英文文章並背好字彙，做好充分的準備。

STEP 1 試題 1—4 與下列報導有關。

SEATTLE (April 9)—The Keenan Group ------- today that Alan Jordan will
1.
become the vice president of international trade and marketing for the third-
largest food company in America. Many ------- labels such as Pradles Chips,
2.
Cobbler Cookies, and Jammin Soda are connected to the Keenan Group.
Mr. Jordan will oversee international marketing strategies in Europe and Asia
and work to expand into markets in South America and the Middle East.
Mr. Jordan was ------- the company's regional director of operations in Asia
3.
and successfully launched several of Keenan's most popular snacks in China,
Japan, and South Korea. Mr. Jordan has stated that his 30 years of experience
in the company, and his hands-on approach to the work involved, have helped
make many of his ideas come to life and brought success to the Keenan Group.
------- .
4.

1. (A) will announcing
   (B) announces
   (C) are announcing
   (D) has announced

2. (A) usual
   (B) customary
   (C) familiar
   (D) frequent

3. (A) previously
   (B) prematurely
   (C) currently
   (D) earlier

4. (A) He has stated that he looks forward to creating more beloved snacks.
   (B) He hopes his tenure as vice president of international trade and marketing will further the company's goals.
   (C) He has stated that the company will merge with its biggest rival under his leadership.
   (D) He hopes that his innovations, along with advances in technology, will benefit the company.

西雅圖（4月9日）——其南集團宣布艾倫・喬丹將會成為這家全美第三大食品公司的國際貿易行銷副總經理。許多耳熟能詳的品牌，如普拉多洋芋片、科博餅乾和詹米汽水，都與其南集團有關。喬丹先生將掌理歐亞地區的國際行銷策略，並盡力擴張市場到南美國家和中東地區。喬丹先生之前任職公司區域主管，負責亞洲營運，曾在中日韓三國推出許多公司最受歡迎的零食。喬丹先生表示，他在公司 30 年的經驗及親力親為的工作態度，幫助他實現了許多理念，並為公司帶來成功。他期待作為國際貿易行銷的副總經理，能幫助其南集團達到更多目標。

字彙

vice president 副總裁、副總統　　international trade and marketing 國際貿易行銷
label 標籤　　oversee 監督；管理；俯視　　Middle East 中東　　regional 區域的
hands-on approach 親力親為的態度　　customary 習慣上的
premature 過早的；不成熟的；早產的　　tenure 任期　　merge 合併

正確答案

1. (D) has announced

2. (C) familiar

3. (A) previously

4. (B) He hopes his tenure as vice president of international trade and marketing will further the company's goals.

解說

1. 主詞是單數專有名詞其南集團，所以複數的 (C) 可以立刻刪除。(A) 缺少 be 動詞，因此也不對。由於報導撰寫的時間是已經公告完了的狀況，所以表現在的 (B) 也不對。正確答案是 (D)。

2. 空格前一句告知其南集團是第三大的食品公司，它旗下的眾多產品會給人什麼感覺，就是解題的關鍵。表「熟悉的」的 (C) 是最合適的。其他選項的意思為 (A) 尋常的 (B) 傳統的 (D) 經常的。

3. 掌握了描述艾倫・喬丹的動詞就能立刻解題。如今喬丹即將擔任的職位是副總經理（vice president），所以擔任什麼特定工作，或在什麼地區工作，這些都是在講他以前的事蹟，尤其空格所在的句子說他在亞洲的成功。由此可知，正確答案是 (A) previously（以前）。其他選項意思為 (B) 過早地 (C) 目前 (D) 早一點。

4. 文章中沒有提到企業合併，所以 (C) 可以立刻刪除。也沒提到艾倫・喬丹有所創造或是未來科技的內容，因此 (D) 也可以刪除。因為喬丹之前的工作不是產品開發，而是專注在特定國家的市場擴張上，所以 (A) 也不對。正確答案是提到他未來的職位和工作的 (B)。

Questions 1-4 refer to the following email.

To:	Bob Johnson <bjohnson@happy.net>
From:	Kaspar Rekstad <tkr@human source.net>
Date:	November 29
Subject:	Refund?

Dear Mr. Johnson,

I purchased several pairs of pants from the Happy Emporium downtown on Clairmont Avenue last week. They ------- all labeled as having a 38-inch waist and a 32-inch inseam. However, when my brother tried them on, they were ------- the wrong size. I still have the receipt, so can I bring them back for an exchange or refund? ------- Please write me back and let me know. I don't live in Wallingford, so ------- would have to make a special trip and don't want to waste my time.

All the best,
Kaspar Rekstad

1. (A) is
   (B) was
   (C) were
   (D) weren't

2. (A) obvious
   (B) clearly
   (C) clarifying
   (D) clear

3. (A) I can return the pants to your store if you're willing to send me replacements that are the right size.
   (B) I hate to drive, but I'm willing to go back to your store if necessary.
   (C) My brother doesn't need the pants anymore.
   (D) I think my brother must have gained a lot of weight.

4. (A) she
   (B) you
   (C) I
   (D) he

Questions 5-8 refer to the following notice.

Lakewood Community Center

Lakewood Community Center is conducting a survey to determine what improvements need ---5.--- made to the facilities and services that are provided to Lakewood residents. The community center is planning a full-scale restructuring program ---6.--- will take about two years. The information gathered from survey responses will help with this restructuring.

The survey can be accessed in ---7.--- at the information desk in the main lobby or online at www.lakewoodcommunity.com/survey. Residents are encouraged to participate in the survey. ---8.--- Lakewood Community Center is open every day from 9 a.m. to 7 p.m. For more information, please visit our website or call us at 555-1234.

---

5. (A) be
   (B) to be
   (C) being
   (D) were

6. (A) when
   (B) what
   (C) which
   (D) who

7. (A) directly
   (B) person
   (C) face
   (D) office

8. (A) Your participation may have a direct impact on the types of changes that are made.
   (B) Without your support the center would not exist.
   (C) We need more volunteers.
   (D) The changes will be announced once the plans have been finalized.

Questions 9-12 refer to the following article.

(Hargrove City, Oct. 23) Labor Force has just announced an expansion of its delivery operations into neighboring Newton beginning next month. ----9.---- The new move comes just a month after Labor Force opened a state-of-the-art factory right here in Hargrove City.

Labor Force has been ----10.---- employer in Hargrove City for over 25 years. At this time last year there was fear that it would have to ----11.----. Fortunately, the city passed a bill to grant funding to Labor force and allow it to upgrade all of its facilities. Thanks to this intervention by the city council, Labor Force was able to update its permits and ----12.----.

9. (A) This is another sign of a major turnaround for Labor Force.
   (B) Newton is in competition with Hargrove City.
   (C) This can't be good news for competitors.
   (D) This will cause deliveries to take longer.

10. (A) the leader
    (B) a leading
    (C) a leader
    (D) leading

11. (A) close
    (B) expand
    (C) remodel
    (D) divest

12. (A) carried on
    (B) carry on
    (C) care on
    (D) cared on

Questions 13-16 refer to the following notice.

We ------- for amateur athletes from all over the country to sign up for
13.
a friendly tournament at Grand Stadium in New York. We welcome
baseball players of all ages to join us and represent your hometowns.
This event is being sponsored by Adimas and Cougar Gear. ------- You
14.
will also have a chance to meet professional baseball stars who will be
in attendance, and teams will have the chance to win ------- awards and
15.
prizes.

Please visit our website at www.gstournament.com/baseball for full
details. Teams must sign up before the deadline in order to qualify, and
professional athletes are not ------- for the competition. The meet-up at
16.
Grand Stadium will be on April 20th. We hope you will sign up and join
us for this exciting event!

13. (A) look
    (B) have looked
    (C) are looking
    (D) had to look

14. (A) Please consider buying their
        products.
    (B) They have graciously agreed to
        support our event.
    (C) Both companies are famous for
        their baseball gear and athletic
        wear.
    (D) Participants will get free hats
        and jackets from our proud
        sponsors.

15. (A) various
    (B) distinct
    (C) separate
    (D) diversified

16. (A) acceptable
    (B) suitable
    (C) eligible
    (D) preferable

PART 7

閱讀理解

一、試題要點

Part 7 閱讀文章並解題。文章類型涵蓋公告、通知、廣告、報導、書信,或新題型的簡訊(text message)、線上聊天或討論等。出題類型有三:

1. 單篇文章共 10 篇,總計 29 道試題。
2. 兩篇文章共 2 組,總計 10 道試題。
3. 三篇文章共 3 組,總計 15 道試題。

可能是網頁文章—電子郵件—公告、電子郵件—書信—行程表、公告—電子郵件—其他各種形式文章等。新制多益中,測定綜合思考能力的複合式文章題目大幅增加,務必注意文章之間的共通點。

① 從文章前出現的**題目介紹**,來掌握文章類型。

② 問題中可能會出現**詢問文章訊息**的類型,因此字彙能力在 Part 7 尤其重要。確實讀懂文章、掌握單字含意還不夠,選項中不一定會出現一模一樣的字,因此也必須熟記**相似(同義)字**,才能快速並正確的作答。

③ 文章中若出現**表格**,如行程表、日程表、菜單、報價單等等,便很有可能會出與**數字**相關的試題,因此必須特別留意。

④ 若是新聞報導,可以透過**報導標題**,掌握其扼要內容,並找出文章主旨。

⑤ 有時答案並不一定逐字逐句出現在文章裡,要注意字裡行間的線索,邏輯推演,一步一步導出確知的結論。

⑥ 除了新制多益新增的三篇文章外,考題也新增了插入整個句子的「**文意選填**」,和詢問**撰文者意圖**的試題。這種題目需要理解並統合整篇文章意義才能解題。因此一面閱讀、一面分析文章、理解它的來龍去脈,培養專注力與耐心,才是奪得高分的必要條件。

二、解題策略

STEP 1 一般來說,出題順序會依循文章內容,所以讀文章前先**掃視試題**,以便知道要掌握哪些內容。

STEP 2 如果文章有標題,要**先讀標題**,以便掌握文章主題或內容。

STEP 3 集中注意在**試題**和**與試題有關的內容**,遇到生字也不要驚慌遲疑,繼續一面讀一面從上下文中找出正確答案。

STEP 4 兩篇文章和三篇文章的複合式文章類型,特別講究**多篇文章內容的關聯性**,因此要整合理解文章和文章、或文章和各式圖表資料之間的關係,找出相關或相同之處。

Example

Questions 1-2 refer to the following text message chain.

Judy Lynch   **10:12**
Will we be able to charge this dinner gathering to the company credit card?

Nathan Lee   **10:13**
Unfortunately, no. The company policy changed just last month. Only meetings conducted with clients during lunch or dinner can be covered as company expenses.

Judy Lynch   **10:14**
That's too bad. I guess we'll just have to split the bill this time.

Nathan Lee   **10:14**
Yes, but at least we can go to any restaurant we want.

1. Why does Judy contact Nathan?
   (A) To get him to pay for dinner
   (B) To get information about company expenses
   (C) To ask if he wants to join her for dinner
   (D) To get recommendations for a good restaurant

2. At 10:14, what does Judy mean when she writes "we'll just have to split the bill"?
   (A) They will charge the company.
   (B) They will ask the accounting department.
   (C) They will have to decide who will pay.
   (D) They will each have to pay a portion of the cost.

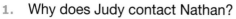

1. B   2. D

試題類型

新制多益中，Part 7 變化幅度尤其大。增加了簡訊、線上聊天或線上討論等文章。試題方面，增加了需要插入一整句以完成文章的「文意選填」，以測驗考生是否充分理解整篇文章的來龍去脈。除了舊有的兩篇文章，還增加了三篇文章之考題，共 15 道試題。不僅要理解整篇文章的主旨，還須具備將各式各樣文章互相理解融會貫通的能力。

單篇閱讀

① 表格、圖表、折價券

- 具體訊息類型：**數字**在表格類文章尤其重要，考題可能會出詢問特定訊息對應的具體數字，或是單純詢問文章的一些訊息。
- 邏輯推演類型：經由**文章細節**推知正確答案的試題。

1 命題分析

STEP 1 試題 1—2 與下列兌換券有關。

---

❶ This Voucher Is Good for One Free Cleaning!

❷ In celebration of our first year serving the Brighton area, All-Bright Dentistry is offering all new patients a free checkup and cleaning from January 1st to February 14th.

❸ This offer is only valid for new patients and cannot be used for any services other than cleaning. The checkup includes X-rays and fluoride treatment.

---

① 揭示對象和主題
文章的對象和主題，會在標題揭示出來。

② 傳達具體訊息
關於對象和主旨的細節，通常會在文章的首句或第一段揭示。具體訊息往往是考題的出題來源，要特別注意日期和數字等等。

③ 傳達追加訊息
雖然不是文章主旨，但是同樣重要，通常提供與主旨相關的備註，也是出題的可能來源。

1. What is suggested about All-Bright Dentistry?
   (A) It has been in business for many years.
   (B) It has just opened.
   (C) It is celebrating its anniversary.
   (D) It is trying to collect coupons.

2. What is true about the coupon?
   (A) It expires at the end of January.
   (B) It can be used for X-rays only.
   (C) It can be used for X-rays, fluoride treatment, and a cleaning.
   (D) It can be used for procedures of similar cost to a cleaning.

STEP 2 確認正確答案及翻譯和解說。

憑兌換券可享一次免費洗牙！

為了慶祝我們在布萊頓區服務滿一年，從 1 月 1 日起至 2 月 14 日止，潔白齒科提供所有新病患一次免費檢查和洗牙。

兌換券僅供新病患使用，除洗牙外不得用於其他服務。檢查包括 X 光和塗氟處理。

1. 從本文可得知潔白齒科什麼事？
(A) 他們已經營業好幾年了。
(B) 他們才剛開始營業。
(C) 他們正在慶祝週年。
(D) 他們正在收集兌換券。

2. 關於兌換券，以下敘述何者正確？
(A) 兌換券一月底到期。
(B) 只能兌換 X 光檢查。
(C) 兌換券包括了 X 光檢查、塗氟、洗牙服務。
(D) 只能用於等價的療程。

字彙

voucher 禮券；兌換券　　checkup 檢查
valid for . . . 對……有效的　　fluoride 氟化物

正確答案

1. (C) It is celebrating its anniversary.
2. (C) It can be used for X-rays, fluoride treatment, and a cleaning.

解說

1. 從本文第一句中可推知紀念時間是一週年，所以 (A) 是錯的。(B) 在本文中沒有提到，(D) 則和分送兌換券的本文完全相反，所以也不能選。正確答案是 (C)。

2. 從本文第一段可知兌換券的使用日期是一月到二月，所以 (A) 是錯的。在本文的最後一段提到服務除了照 X 光外，還有塗氟處理，所以 (B) 也錯了。文章有說使用兌換券能提供新病患一次免費檢查和洗牙；第二段提到檢查包括 X 光和塗氟處理，所以包含照 X 光、塗氟處理、清潔牙齒，全都說明得很清楚的 (C) 是正確答案。

Questions 1-4 refer to the following form.

DOVER QUALITY

Dover Quality congratulates you on your new purchase. We are a time-honored company that has been operated by the Green family for three generations. We would appreciate it if you, our valued customer, would fill out the following survey. Results from the survey will help us improve our services and our customers' experience. After we receive your completed form, you will receive a small thank-you gift in return. Thank you so much for your time.

Name: Jamie Bridges

Email: jbridges@frescosh.com

Address: 98 Eagle Heights Dr., Dover, MN 55929

Product ID Number: F4556Y56

Product Description: Front-Loading Washing Machine

How did you find out about our store?
One of my coworkers recommended it.

How did you find our customer service?
The customer service agent was very kind.

What recommendations can you make for our company?
An easy-to-use online forum for asking questions would be helpful.

---

1. What can Mr. Bridges receive by completing the survey?
   (A) A free giveaway
   (B) Some store credit
   (C) A discount coupon
   (D) A lifetime membership

2. What did Mr. Bridges buy?
   (A) A piece of recreational equipment
   (B) A home appliance
   (C) A fashion accessory
   (D) A replacement part

3. How did Mr. Bridges find out about the store?
   (A) He saw an advertisement on TV.
   (B) He works at a nearby store.
   (C) A coworker mentioned it to him.
   (D) He visited a website.

4. In Mr. Bridges' opinion, how could Dover Quality improve?
   (A) By keeping the store more orderly
   (B) By hiring more in-store staff members
   (C) By offering an additional customer service option
   (D) By extending its warranty period

② 簡訊

- 簡訊固定會出**一題**。
- 內容通常是職場同事為了**處理業務**而彼此交換訊息或傳達意見。
- 會出現**省略主詞**的口語體句子，務必特別留意。

1 命題分析

STEP 1 試題 1—2 與下列文字訊息有關。

❶ 10:35 a.m.   **Jennifer Cosmo**
Hey Brian, why are you quitting the company?

10:45 a.m.   **Brian Cee**
Uhhhhh, sorry, Jennifer. I should have told you that I was leaving. My coworkers are driving me nuts!

❷ 10:47 a.m.   **Jennifer Cosmo**
Yeah, I was worried that would happen. Your office is full of weird people.

11:00 a.m.   **Brian Cee**
It's not just them; the staff in room 311 are so pretentious. I just had to find a more relaxed atmosphere.

❸ 11:05 a.m.   **Jennifer Cosmo**
I understand; I get that from 311, too. Well, please stay in touch!

11:06 a.m.   **Brain Cee**
Will do!

(1) 人物關係及對話主題
透過對話最前面的部分，可以知道參加討論者之間的關係。

(2) 傳達具體訊息
揭示對話主題和相關的細節。內容主要是相互交換的訊息。

(3) 傳達追加訊息
在最後會揭示之後要採取的行動、要做的事，或請求事項等。

1. What does Brian Cee indicate he will do?
   (A) Start a new job
   (B) Meet with HR and discuss his issues
   (C) Look for work in a more competitive environment
   (D) Continue to be friends with Jennifer Cosmo

2. At 10:45 a.m., what does Brian Cee most likely mean when he says, "My coworkers are driving me nuts!"?
   (A) His clients are diligent.
   (B) His colleagues make him very upset.
   (C) His supervisor is a difficult person.
   (D) The competition is too much for him.

STEP 2 確認正確答案及翻譯和解說。

珍妮佛・卡司莫（上午 10:35）
嗨！布萊恩，你為什麼要離職呢？

布萊恩・席（上午 10:45）
唉呀，對不起，珍妮佛，我應該有跟你提過我要離職。同事快把我逼瘋了。

珍妮佛・卡司莫（上午 10:47）
喔，我擔心過會那樣。你辦公室有一堆怪人。

布萊恩・席（上午 11:00）
不只我辦公室那些人，在 311 室的人太假了。我真的需要輕鬆一點的氣氛。

珍妮佛・卡司莫（上午 11:05）
我知道，我對 311 室也有同樣感覺。好吧，保持聯絡吧。

布萊恩・席（上午 11:06）
會的！

1. 布萊恩・席說他會做什麼？
   (A) 開始新工作
   (B) 跟人力資源部討論他的問題
   (C) 找個有競爭環境的工作
   (D) 會繼續跟珍妮佛・卡司莫維持朋友關係

2. 上午 10 點 45 分，布萊恩・席說「my coworkers are driving me nuts（我同事把我逼瘋了）」最可能是什麼意思？
   (A) 他的客戶很勤奮。
   (B) 他的同事讓他不悅。
   (C) 他的主管是個難相處的人。
   (D) 對他來說競爭太激烈了。

字彙

drive someone nuts 把……逼瘋　　pretentious 矯飾的
atmosphere 氣氛；大氣　　HR (human resources) 人力資源
competitive 競爭的

正確答案

1. (D) Continue to be friends with Jennifer Cosmo
2. (B) His colleagues make him very upset.

解說

1. 由於布萊恩只提到他要離職，並沒有説會尋找新工作，所以 (A) 和 (C) 不能選。而完全沒有提到的 (B) 也不對。布萊恩在訊息中的最後一句話是會的（Will do!），本句省略主詞 I（我），表對於珍妮佛要求保持聯絡（stay in touch）的肯定答覆。由此可知 (D) 是正確答案。

2. upset 除了生氣之外，還可以表示沮喪、心情不好等的負面情緒。用它來替代「把我弄瘋了（drive me nuts）」也可以，所以正確答案是 (B)。

Questions 1-2 refer to the following text message chain.

Chan Whatley (1:23 p.m.)
Hey Gail, I need you to come in to work early tomorrow, OK?

Gail Sayers (1:34 p.m.)
How early is early? I already get there at 6 a.m., and most of the customers don't come in for their morning coffee until at least seven.

Chan Whatley (1:45 p.m.)
Yeah, I know, but we have to do a total inventory and I want to be sure we are all cleaned up and ready to open when we are done.

Gail Sayers (2:00 p.m.)
Gotcha. Soooo . . . what time, then?

Chan Whatley (2:10 p.m.)
Let's make it five?

Gail Sayers (2:15 p.m.)
Done. See you there, but you owe me!

1. For what type of business does Chan Whatley most likely work?
    (A) An auto shop
    (B) A café
    (C) A lunch restaurant
    (D) An art gallery

2. At 2:10 p.m., what does Chan Whatley mean when he writes "Let's make it five?"
    (A) Five people should be there.
    (B) They should take five minutes to think.
    (C) They should meet at five in the morning.
    (D) He thinks Gail needs five cups of coffee.

③ 公告與通知

- **公告**可能是公家機關、旅行社、商店等，揭示設施及服務的使用說明、缺失更正、行程的說明及變更等的文章。
- 公告的**具體訊息**和**主旨**一定會列入考題。
- 一定要掌握**數字**部分的細節，特別是變更處、公告日期、生效日期等。

1 命題分析。

STEP 1 試題 1—2 與下列公告有關。

❶ **Dear Covington Garden Visitors,**

Due to the increasing amount of garbage that our staff has been finding on the grounds over the past month, we will be instituting a new monitoring system.

❷ Beginning on the 1st of June, we will be checking identification at the park entrance, and operating a system of surveillance cameras throughout the park. People who are recorded leaving their trash in the park will be issued a fine according to the local ordinances of Covington. Please enjoy the park responsibly.

The Management

(1) 目的：通常在標題中揭示

公告和通知的對象還有目的，通常會在標題中揭示出來。透過這些可以掌握整篇文章的主題。

(2) 傳達具體訊息

具體訊息包括變更的狀況以及生效的日期。

1. Where would the notice most likely appear?
   (A) In the restrooms
   (B) In the newspapers
   (C) At the entrance to a garden
   (D) In the local ordinances

2. Why will the park begin checking identification?
   (A) The security cameras are new.
   (B) There are too many visitors.
   (C) There is a problem with littering.
   (D) There is a problem with garbage cans.

STEP 2 確認正確答案及翻譯和解說。

親愛的科文頓花園訪客，您好

過去一個月，我們的同仁發現地上有愈來愈多垃圾，因此決定啟用新的監視系統。

從 6 月 1 日起，我們會開始在公園入口檢查身分，並在公園全區啟動監視攝影機系統。被拍到在園區丟垃圾者，會依科文頓地區的規定開罰。請帶著責任心遊賞本園。

公園管理組

- -

1. 這則公告最可能出現在哪裡？
   (A) 廁所
   (B) 報紙
   (C) 花園入口
   (D) 當地規定

2. 為什麼公園要開始檢查身分？
   (A) 因為監視攝影機是新的。
   (B) 因為有許多遊客。
   (C) 因為有亂丟垃圾的問題。
   (D) 因為垃圾桶有問題。

字彙

institute 制定；開始　　identification 身分
surveillance camera 監視器；監視攝影機　　issue 核發
ordinance 條例　　litter 亂丟垃圾

正確答案

1. (C) At the entrance to a garden

2. (C) There is a problem with littering.

解說

1. 掌握公告的對象以及發出公告的人是誰，就很容易解題了。這是公園管理組向所有遊客發出的公告，所以張貼公告的地方應該是所有遊客可以看到的地方，因此 (C) 是正確答案。條例、規定（ordinance）不適合用來表示地點，故 (D) 是錯的。

2. 檢查身分證是新的管理辦法，掌握為什麼要有新的管理辦法，就能解題了。本文第一句即提到因為「愈來愈多的垃圾」，才導引出了新的規定。動詞 litter 是「亂丟垃圾」，所以 (C) 是正確答案。

2 實戰應用

Questions 1-4 refer to the following flyer.

Aspen Credit Union

55 Carlton Street
Aspen, Colorado 25234
www.aspencreditunion.com

We thank you for being a loyal customer of Aspen Credit Union since we were established a decade ago. We would like to inform you that Aspen Credit Union will be introducing a selection of new banking services in the new year.

You can look forward to the following:
- You can check your balances, transfer money, and pay bills more conveniently by using our new mobile banking apps.
- We will now be open on Saturdays in order to better serve our customers.
- We will be providing additional loan options and guidance for those in need of personal loans as well as financing options for small businesses.

Aspen Credit Union is currently running a promotional event available to elderly clients who open a new senior citizen's savings account with us in the month of January. They will receive a $100 deposit upon registration!

There is more information about our new banking services on the back of this flyer.

1. What is indicated about Aspen Credit Union?
   (A) It has recently relocated.
   (B) It is hiring new employees.
   (C) It has been in operation for 10 years.
   (D) It will open a new branch in January.

2. What is NOT a service that Aspen Credit Union will offer next year?
   (A) Lower interest rates
   (B) More types of loans
   (C) Expanded business hours
   (D) More convenient mobile services

3. The word "running" in paragraph three, line one, is closest in meaning to
   (A) withdrawing
   (B) rotating
   (C) moving
   (D) operating

4. According to the flyer, how can elderly clients receive a $100 deposit?
   (A) By applying for a credit card
   (B) By filling out a survey
   (C) By downloading a mobile app
   (D) By opening a special account in January

④ 電子郵件

- 電子郵件通常與工作等**商務情境**有關。
- 一般來說，開頭會揭示**主旨**或**目的**，並以**請求**或**建議**等內容收尾。
- 電子郵件的主旨通常是廣告、祝賀、感謝、道歉、建議、訊息提供、請求等。

1 命題分析

STEP 1 試題 1—2 與下列電子郵件有關。

❶ **To:** Bob Pendergrass <bp@gmc.net>
From: Mishli Koomarakam
　　　　<mkoomarakam@zip.com>
Date: Oct. 30
Subject: Zippers

❷ Dear Mr. Pendergrass,

My name is Mishli Koomarakam, and I represent the offices of Zip Co., the leading supplier of industrial-strength zippers in lower Bridgeport. The reason I am contacting you today is that I saw an article that you had written in the *Business Journal* on October 28th. In the article you seemed to imply that the model of zipper that is being produced by our competitor, Ace Zippers, is a superior product to all comparably priced zippers. Although you are certainly entitled to your opinion, I would like the opportunity to change your mind.
❸ Zip Co. would like to send you a selection of our zipper lines for you to test against the performance of Ace Zipper's lines. Should our zippers impress you, all we request is that you make mention of this zipper challenge in a future article for *Business Journal.*

All the best,

Mishli Koomarakam
Sales and Marketing Director, Zip Co.

(1) 收件人（To）和寄件人（From）
文章的文頭首先列出收件人和寄件人。確認他們的名字，再來掌握他們的關係，試題問的對象是收／寄件人還是第三者也要注意。另外，透過主旨（Subject）可以推知整篇文章大概的內容。

(2) 目的：一般揭示在信件的前半部
有時電子郵件的主旨寫得過於籠統，便需要看過整篇文章才確知主題。此時可以先看其他試題，最後再回來主題試題，節省時間。

(3) 請求事項及追加事項
電子郵件的結尾處通常會有請求事項或追加事項，需要特別留意。最後署名的地方，會揭示寄件人的職位及所屬單位。

1. What is suggested about Bob Pendergrass?
   (A) He is a celebrity.
   (B) He is a business journalist.
   (C) He is a mechanical engineering journalist.
   (D) He is a sports journalist.

2. Why does Mishli Koomarakam write to Bob Pendergrass?
   (A) He wants him to retract his support of Ace Zippers.
   (B) He wants him to join Zip Co.
   (C) He wants him to try Zip Co.'s products.
   (D) He wants to pay him to write an article about Zip Co.

STEP 2 確認正確答案及翻譯和解說。

收件人：鮑勃‧潘達葛拉斯 <bp@gmc.net>

寄件人：密絮里‧庫瑪拉坎 <mkoomarakam@zip.com>

日期：10 月 30 日

主旨：拉鍊

潘達葛拉斯先生您好：

我是密絮里‧庫瑪拉坎，謹代表拉拉鍊公司跟您聯繫。本公司是位於下橋港的工業用強力拉鏈大廠。

今天之所以跟您聯絡，是因為我在 10 月 28 日的《商業雜誌》看到您寫的一篇文章。您在文中似乎暗示，我們對手艾斯拉鍊公司製造的拉鍊優於所有同價位的拉鍊。您當然有權有您自己的見解，但我還是想藉此機會讓您改觀。

拉拉鍊公司想讓您試用一些拉鍊產品，並與艾斯拉鍊的產品評比。如果我們的產品讓您驚豔，希望您在《商業雜誌》未來的文章能提及這次的拉鍊試用評比。

祝您萬事如意

密絮里‧庫瑪拉坎

拉拉鍊公司銷售與行銷主任

1. 從本文可得知鮑勃‧潘達葛拉斯什麼事？
   (A) 他是位名人。
   (B) 他是商業記者。
   (C) 他是機械工程記者。
   (D) 他是體育記者。

2. 密絮里‧庫瑪拉坎為什麼要寫信給鮑勃‧潘達葛拉斯？
   (A) 他希望鮑勃‧潘達葛拉斯退回艾斯公司的拉鍊。
   (B) 他希望鮑勃‧潘達葛拉斯能加入拉拉鍊公司。
   (C) 他希望鮑勃‧潘達葛拉斯能試用拉拉鍊公司的產品。
   (D) 他想付費請鮑勃‧潘達葛拉斯寫一篇拉拉鍊公司的文章。

正確答案

1. (B) He is a business journalist.

2. (C) He wants him to try Zip Co.'s products.

解說

1. 掌握電子郵件的寄信原因就能立刻解題了。郵件的第二段提到，看到寄件人看到潘達葛拉斯在《商業雜誌》寫的報導（article）後，決定要跟他聯絡。由此可知，潘達葛拉斯是在《商業雜誌》的財經記者。正確答案是 (B)。

2. 選項 (A) 說將報導撤回（retract），這是陷阱選項。retract 是將發出去的東西再收回的意思，但文章明確提到寫這封電子郵件的目的，是希望潘達葛拉斯試用拉拉鍊公司的產品，以後再寫相關報導時，能提到他們產品的正面評價，所以 (A) 是錯的。正確答案是 (C)。

2 實戰應用

Questions 1-4 refer to the following email.

From: John Steele <jsteele@starburst.com>

To: Mary Hampton <mhampton@starburst.com>

Date: September 22

Subject: Media Relations Manager Position

Dear Ms. Hampton,

Hello, this is John Steele in the marketing department. I am emailing you about the current job opening for a media relations manager in your department. I would like to suggest Jessica Hardy for the position. I think she is highly suitable for the role. As head of the marketing department, I have overseen her work for the past three years, and she has been an exceptional team member. In our marketing department, she has led a variety of marketing campaigns that have increased the profitability of our products.

I think Ms. Hardy would also be successful in your media relations department. Through her work as an experienced marketing specialist, she has been regularly communicating with many journalists and broadcasters in the field. She has superb communication skills and would therefore do an excellent job in a managerial position in media relations.

As our company continues to grow in size, I think it is important that we promote our long-term employees to higher positions. If you would like to know more about Ms. Hardy, please don't hesitate to contact me. My extension number is 2315. I am usually in the office except on Monday and Wednesday mornings.

I look forward to hearing from you soon.

John Steele, Director

Marketing Department

Starburst Incorporated

1. What is the purpose of the email?
   (A) To recommend an employee for a job
   (B) To advise a client about a purchase
   (C) To propose a meeting agenda
   (D) To promote an investment opportunity

2. What does the letter indicate about Ms. Hardy?
   (A) She is in the same department as Ms. Hampton.
   (B) She currently works in the marketing department.
   (C) She used to be a journalist for a newspaper.
   (D) She is not available on Monday mornings.

3. According to the email, what is necessary to work as a media relations manager?
   (A) Innovative marketing strategies
   (B) Long-term planning
   (C) Strong interpersonal skills
   (D) Computer programming proficiency

4. What is suggested about Starburst Incorporated?
   (A) It is considering downsizing its workforce.
   (B) It recently won a new contract.
   (C) Its operations are expanding.
   (D) It was founded three years ago.

⑤ 廣告

- 分為**商品廣告**（產品、服務、不動產、活動等）和**求才廣告**。
- **商品廣告**，在揭示產品名稱、產品特徵及優點後，會以購買方法及聯絡方式收尾。
- **求才廣告**，在揭示職位和負責的工作後，會以揭示應徵方法及聯絡方式收尾。

1 命題分析

STEP 1 試題 1—2 與下列廣告有關。

---

❶ Rellington Square Condos

Wonderful listing available for those in the market for a state-of-the-art condominium. Rellington Square is the premier development in the greater Hillside area, and these properties don't stay on the market for long at only 145 grand!

(1) 宣傳商品的廣告
文章標題和廣告開頭，會開宗明義說明所宣傳的商品、業者，還有服務的種類。

❷ Amenities include:
- Hardwood floors
- 10-foot ceilings
- All modern kitchen appliances including refrigerator, dishwasher, range, and convection oven
- Washer and dryer
- Security
- Parking garage
- Full gym with an indoor lap pool

(2) 商品的優點及特徵
中段會揭示商品及服務的優點和特徵。這部分會出具體資訊的試題。

❸ An open house is scheduled for 2 p.m. on Friday the 23rd of June, or you may book a private showing by contacting us at appointments@rellingtonsquarereality.com.
We look forward to meeting with you.

(3) 購買方法與聯絡方式
廣告的最後通常會以購買方法與聯絡方式收尾，務必多加留意，另外優惠日期和期限也要注意。

---

1. What is indicated about Rellington Square?
   (A) It is not popular.
   (B) It is desirable.
   (C) There are many vacancies.
   (D) People have to pay to see it.

2. How much is the asking price?
   (A) $145
   (B) $1,450
   (C) $14,500
   (D) $145,000

3. According to the advertisement, what should interested buyers do?
   (A) Call Rellington Square for an appointment
   (B) Email Rellington Square to reserve a spot on Friday the 23rd
   (C) Show up at the condo at 2 p.m. on the 23rd
   (D) Come to the headquarters of Rellington Square

STEP 2 認正確答案及翻譯和解說。

芮林敦廣場公寓大樓

市場上想找高級現代公寓大樓的人有福了。芮林敦廣場是大山邊區重要的開發案，這些房地產不會在市場上閒置太久，只要 14 萬 5 千美元就能入手！

設施包括：

- 硬木地板
- 10 英呎高天花板
- 先進的廚房電器，如冰箱、洗碗機、爐連烤和旋風烤箱
- 洗衣機和乾衣機
- 保全
- 車庫
- 完善健身房和室內小型泳池

開啟參觀日訂於 6 月 23 日週五下午兩點，您也可以寄電子郵件到 appointments@rellingtonsquarereality.com 跟我們預約個人看屋。

期待與您見面。

1. 從本文可得知芮林敦廣場什麼事？
   (A) 芮林敦廣場不受歡迎。
   (B) 芮林敦廣場很搶手。
   (C) 還有許多空戶。
   (D) 需要付款才能看屋。

2. 賣方報價是多少？
   (A) 145 美元
   (B) 1,450 美元
   (C) 14,500 美元
   (D) 145,000 美元

3. 根據這則廣告，有興趣的買家應該怎麼做？
   (A) 打給芮林敦廣場約時間看屋
   (B) 在 6 月 23 日週五當天寄電子郵件給芮林敦廣場預訂一戶
   (C) 在 6 月 23 日下午兩點出現在這棟公寓大樓
   (D) 到芮林敦廣場總部

字彙

premier 首要的；最先的　　grand 一千美元　　amenity 便利設施
convection oven 旋風烤箱　　lap pool 小型泳池　　reserve 保留；預定

正確答案

1. (B) It is desirable.

2. (D) 145,000

3. (C) Show up at the condo at 2 p.m. on the 23rd

解說

1. 找到修飾芮林敦廣場公寓的形容詞立刻就能解題了。本文第一段提到它最先進的公寓大樓，也是該地區重要的開發案，又說在市場上不會閒置太久，意思就是立刻就會被賣掉。(A) 和內容完全相反，不能選。文章中並沒有提到公寓的數量或空房有多少，所以 (C) 無法確認。正確答案是透過表肯定的形容詞來描述它的 (B)。

2. grand 是一千元的意思，所以正確答案是 (D)。

3. 根據本文的最後，有興趣的購買者，可能會參加 6 月 23 日的開放參觀日，也可能透過電子郵件預約看屋，所以兩者之一就是正確答案。(C) 是第一種方法，所以是正確答案。(B) 乍看之下是第二種方式，但它的日期卻是開放日的時間，所以不對。本文中出現的聯絡方法是發電子郵件，不是打電話，所以 (A) 也不對。至於 (D) 則無法從本文中確認。

Questions 1-2 refer to the following advertisement.

Apply for Membership in the Bexton Entrepreneurs' Organization

Join now the most influential community of business leaders and entrepreneurs in the area.

To apply, you must be a business owner. Your business must earn at least one million dollars per year. Additionally, you must have five employees or more.

Joining our community will help you to grow your business and become more competitive. As you know, interaction with other business leaders is one of the most important factors in the business world. Our database connects you with various business owners who are excited to share their experience and knowledge. Never underestimate the insight and expertise of your fellow businesspeople. We are interested in your success.

Apply in September and we will waive your first monthly membership fee. For detailed information, please visit our website, www.bextoneo.com, or call us at 555-8974.

PART
7

Chapter
01

單篇閱讀

1. What is NOT mentioned as a requirement for application?
   (A) Ownership of a business
   (B) An academic degree
   (C) A certain number of workers
   (D) Minimum annual earnings

2. According to the article, what does the Bexton Entrepreneurs' Organization offer?
   (A) A monthly newsletter
   (B) Conveniently located office spaces
   (C) Networking opportunities
   (D) A reduced annual rent

⑥ 新聞報導與社論

- 文章主題包羅萬象，揭示各式各樣的事實及意見。
- 具體的**統計資料**或**日期時間**時常會是出題重點，要特別注意；還有報導的主體是人、公司企業或活動，也要確實掌握。
- 主題通常會在文章**最初**或**最後**的地方揭露。

1 命題分析

STEP 1 試題 1—2 與下列新聞報導有關。

❶ (October 4) A new business park has been approved for the waterfront area in downtown Bristol. —[1]— The park will be developed by the HN Winchester Group. The HN Winchester group was responsible for the successful development last June of a similar park in Renton that holds 40 businesses. —[2]—

❷ Once the park is complete, HN Winchester will auction off the parcels during an open bidding session. —[3]— This session will be announced by the city planning department and all qualified bidders will be welcome.

❸ According to Frank Harris, the CEO of HN Winchester, the park in Bristol will be able to support twice as many businesses as the Renton Park. —[4]— The resulting revenue will have a tremendous impact on the tax base of Bristol.

(1) 報導目的及主題
報導和社論的主題通常會在文章開頭處揭示，但也會出現要看過整篇文章才知道主題的情形。此時應該繼續往下，了解具體訊息再來解主題試題。

(2) 揭示具體訊息
此處通常會有具體的時間及統計資料，很多都和正確答案密切相關，可能出的問題除了循席類試題，也可能出邏輯推演試題。

(3) 附加說明
此處可能會提到關於報導主題或對象的附加說明，此類額外資訊也可能成為考題。

1. In which of the positions marked [1], [2], [3], and [4] does the following sentence belong?

   "The park will also be able to support 150 single-dwelling apartments and 50 multi-occupant apartments."

   (A) [1]　　　　(B) [2]
   (C) [3]　　　　(D) [4]

2. What is the article about?

   (A) A new ferry terminal that is being built
   (B) A change in the administration of HN Winchester
   (C) The business competition between Bristol and Renton
   (D) A new construction project

3. According to the information in the article, what is most likely true?

   (A) Frank Harris will become the CEO of HN Winchester.
   (B) The Bristol project will feature 80 businesses.
   (C) The Bristol project will feature 150 businesses.
   (D) The Bristol project will feature fewer businesses than the Renton Park.

STEP 2　確認正確答案及翻譯和解說。

（10 月 4 日）布里斯托市中心水岸區的新商業園區已被核准。—[1]— 園區將由 HN 溫徹斯特集團負責開發。六月時 HN 溫徹斯特集團也成功在倫敦，開發了一個可容納 40 個企業的類似園區。—[2]—

一旦園區完工，HN 溫徹斯特集團將會公開招標。—[3]— 競標由市府規畫處公布，屆時歡迎所有符合資格的標商參與。

據 HN 溫徹斯特集團執行長——法蘭克・哈瑞斯——指出，布里斯托的園區可容納比倫頓園區多兩倍的公司行號。—[4]— 園區所創造的收入將對布里斯托的稅基帶來重大影響。

----

1. 文中的 [1]、[2]、[3]、[4] 四個位置中，何者最適合插入這句「The park will also be able to support 150 single dwelling apartments and 50 multi-occupant apartments.（園區將可容納 150 個獨立公寓和 50 棟多住戶公寓）」？

   (A) [1]　　　　(B) [2]　　　　(C) [3]　　　　(D) [4]

2. 本報導的主題是什麼？
(A) 新的渡輪終點站正在施工
(B) HN 溫徹斯特集團的管理將有所變革
(C) 布里斯托和倫頓在商業上彼此競爭
(D) 一個新的營建開發案

3. 根據文中資訊，以下何者最可能是正確的？
(A) 法蘭克‧哈瑞斯將成為 HN 溫徹斯特集團執行長。
(B) 布里斯托園區可容納 80 個公司行號。
(C) 布里斯托園區可容納 150 個公司行號。
(D) 布里斯托園區容納的公司數比倫頓少。

字彙

approve 核准　　waterfront 濱水區　　auction off 拍賣出去
parcel（土地）一塊　　qualified 符合資格的　　revenue 收益；歲入
dwell 居住　　occupant 居住者　　competition 競爭

正確答案

1. (D) [4]
2. (D) A new construction project
3. (B) The Bristol project will feature 80 businesses.

解說

1. 該句出現了副詞「也」（also），所以可以知道本句的主詞（園區）不是第一次出現。只要掌握住這點，立刻就能解題了。

本句用未來式來描述園區，可以知道此園區是指未來要在布里斯托建立的商業區域，而非已經建好的倫頓園區。〔4〕之前的句子也在詳細說明該商業園區，所以本句放在〔4〕是最恰當的。

2. 這是一篇關於布里斯托新商業園區的報導，報導詳細描述了該園區的細節，以及它所產生的影響。所以將這說成是「一個新的營建開發案」的 (D) 是正確答案。(B) 和 (C) 皆無法在本文中確認，而 (A) 也是在本文中沒有出現的內容。

3. twice as many A as B 片語是「A 是 B 的兩倍」的意思。文中提到，比起六月開發的倫頓商業園區（可容納 40 個企業），布里斯托商業園區是它的兩倍，所以 (B) 是正確答案。因為法蘭克‧哈里斯現在已經是 HN 溫徹斯特的執行長了，不能用未來式來敘述，所以 (A) 是錯的。

2 實戰應用

Questions 1-4 refer to the following article.

Solving the Housing Shortage

MAYTON, June 23—The city of Mayton is currently holding city council meetings to propose solutions to the problem of the growing number of citizens who cannot find housing that fits within their budget. According to city officials, measures need to be taken to increase the housing supply in the short term through immediate policy initiatives and reform plans.

In order to make housing prices more reasonable for residents, city officials recommended carrying out a comprehensive survey of current housing needs. The city government then plans to offer low-income citizens subsidized housing paid for through tax revenues. Additionally, it is said that the city government is considering approving a law requiring developers to include inexpensive units for low-income citizens in any new apartment development.

City officials and local residents hope that these measures will help alleviate the housing crunch that has been affecting Mayton residents. The housing problem will be a very important issue in the upcoming elections, when a new mayor, city councilors, and school board members will be elected.

1. What problem is Mayton experiencing?
   (A) A shortage of labor
   (B) An influx of refugees
   (C) A lack of affordable housing
   (D) A population decrease

2. What is NOT listed among the recommendations?
   (A) Subsidizing housing costs
   (B) Passing new legislation
   (C) Building new schools
   (D) Conducting a survey

3. The word "alleviate" in paragraph three, line one, is closest in meaning to
   (A) solicit
   (B) attest
   (C) facilitate
   (D) relieve

4. What is indicated about Mayton?
   (A) It will hold municipal elections soon.
   (B) It has an irresponsible city government.
   (C) It is trying to attract more tourists.
   (D) It has postponed a construction project.

⑦ 線上聊天與討論區

- 線上聊天與討論區每次都會出現**一篇**。
- 通常是關於職場同事之間**閒暇時聊天**的內容。
- 線上聊天的特性與簡訊一樣，時常會出現省略主詞的**口語英語**。

1 命題分析

STEP 1 試題 1—4 與下列線上聊天有關。

❶ Jason Chan: [10:24 a.m.]
Hey guys, has anyone had any experience with Hope Realty? I need to find a new apartment and their advertisement sure seemed to imply they were the experts.

❷ Mario Lopez: [11:02 a.m.]
Yeah, I've seen the commercials that have been running lately, but I'm not too sure you can trust them. You know what they say: if it seems too good to be true, it probably is.

Jane Johnson: [11:31 a.m.]
No way! Hope Realty is the best. The same owner has been running the business for the last 15 years. They helped me find an apartment when I moved into town, and another when I had to relocate for my job. Trust them!

Marie Lo: [11:40 a.m.]
I'm with Jane Johnson on this one. They are for real. They are totally trustworthy. When my landlord tried to evict me they even recommended a good lawyer.

Mario Lopez: [12.23 p.m.]
Really? They do that? Well, if that is the case then I will definitely use them in the future. I might have to find a bigger place when my wife gives birth, and that might mean breaking my lease.

❸ Marie Lo: [1:00 p.m.]
Mario, Jason, ask for Sean; he is the one who helped me! They can suggest an attorney too if you need one!

Jason Chan: [1:03 p.m.]
Thanks! Will do!

(1) 人物的關係及對話主題
對話的主題經常在第一段對話中揭露。

(2) 具體討論內容
從後續的討論中可以看出，對話參與者對該主題的意見與反應。

(3) 請求及建議
在後半部，以說話者之後的行動、該做的工作、請求事項等結論作結尾。

1. At 11:40 a.m., what does Marie Lo mean when she says, "They are for real"?
   (A) She is going to get an apartment with Jane.
   (B) She thinks that Hope Realty is an actual company.
   (C) She believes that they are a good company.
   (D) She thinks that the ad is too good to be true.

2. According to the discussion, what service does Hope Realty provide?
   (A) Moving services
   (B) Transportation
   (C) Legal representation
   (D) Help with finding a place to live

3. What will Jason Chan most likely do?
   (A) Use Hope Realty
   (B) Stay where he lives
   (C) Ask for legal help
   (D) Use another realtor

4. Why does Mario Lopez think he might need to use Hope Realty?
   (A) He wants to find a better apartment.
   (B) His family will get larger.
   (C) He thinks he will get evicted.
   (D) He might need help moving.

STEP 2 確認正確答案及翻譯和解說。

杰森・詹（上午 10:24）

嗨，各位，有沒有人找過希望房屋？我要找房子，他們的廣告看起來好像很專業。

馬利歐・羅佩茲（上午 11:02）

對，我有看到他們最近一直在播的廣告，但我不確定你可以信任他們。你知道人們怎麼說的：如果好到不像真的，那就大概不是真的。

珍・強森（上午 11:31）

不可能！希望房屋是最棒的。他們已經營業 15 年了，沒有換過老闆。我剛來這裡的時候，就是靠他們幫我找到房子，後來換工作要搬家也是找他們。相信他們！

瑪莉・羅（上午 11:40）

我跟珍・強森看法一樣。他們認真做事，很值得信任。我房東要趕我出來的時候，他們還推薦我一個好律師。

馬利歐・羅佩茲（下午 12:23）

真的嗎？他們會這樣？如果是真的，我以後一定會找他們。我太太生完孩子後，我可能就要找大一點的房子，也就是說，我可能要提前解約。

瑪莉・羅（下午 1:00）

馬利歐、杰森，你們可以找尚恩。他就是當時幫我的人！如果有需要，他們也可以推薦律師喔！

杰森・詹（下午 1:03）

謝謝。我會的。

1. 上午 11: 40 時，瑪莉‧羅說「They are for real.（他們認真做事）」是什麼意思？
(A) 她將會跟珍找一個房子。
(B) 她認為希望房屋是一家真實的公司。
(C) 她認為希望房屋是好公司。
(D) 她認為廣告好到不真實。

2. 根據這段討論，希望房屋提供什麼服務？
(A) 搬家服務　　(B) 貨運
(C) 法定代理　　(D) 找房子

3. 杰森‧詹最可能會採取什麼行動？
(A) 請希望房屋協助
(B) 繼續住在原來的地方
(C) 尋求法律協助
(D) 找另一家房地產仲介

4. 馬利歐‧羅佩茲為什麼認為他有機會找希望房屋來幫忙？
(A) 他想找比較好的公寓。
(B) 他的家庭有新成員。
(C) 他認為他會被房東趕出來。
(D) 他可能需要有人幫忙搬家。

字彙

expert 專家　　relocate 轉換地點；重新安置　　trustworthy 值得信任的
landlord 房東　　evict 逐出　　give birth 生產　　break a lease 提前解約

正確答案

1. (C) She believes that they are a good company.
2. (D) Help with finding a place to live
3. (A) Use Hope Realty
4. (B) His family will get larger.

解說

1. They are for real.（他們認真做事），表對特定公司的服務肯定和支持。所以只要在選項中找出對該公司給予正面評價的句子，立刻就能解題了。選項 (B) 是直接從字面上來解釋公司存不存在，不是本文討論的內容，因此不能選。正確答案是 (C)。

2. 這是很容易讓人選錯的試題，所以要仔細閱讀本文才能找出正確答案。選項 (C) 用法律代表來稱呼律師，也就是文中提到的 lawyer 和 attorney，文中提到希望房屋會推薦好的律師，但這不是他們主要需求的服務，所以不能選。

本文提到該公司辦理不動產業務是值得信賴的（trustworthy），而這才是希望房屋的主要事業，(D) 是正確答案。

3. 杰森‧詹最後一句話說「我會的」（will do），意思就是他會去找尚恩，也就是會與希望房屋聯絡，所以正確答案是 (A)。

4. 因為馬利歐‧羅佩茲直接提到，太太生產後將會去找更大的房子，將會解除租屋合約（breaking my lease），所以會找希望房屋幫忙的原因，是因為家庭規模將變大，正確答案是 (B)。

2 實戰應用

Questions 1-4 refer to the following online chat discussion.

Pepe Juarez [10:12 a.m.] Hey, when is the staff meeting today? I have a dentist's appointment at 1 p.m.

Colin Coward [11:00 a.m.] Pepe, where are you? The meeting is starting in 30 minutes. Be here.

Pepe Juarez [11:01 a.m.] I messaged everyone earlier but got no response. How long will it last?

Joachim Fitzgerald [11:02 a.m.] It will last as long as it takes to get all of the protocols written up for the convention.

Colin Coward [11:04 a.m.] Pepe, you have an important job organizing security for this event. Don't blow it.

Richard Burton [11:06 a.m.] Everyone is planning on being here at 11:30, right? If we start on time we should finish before one. I'll be taking roll.

Colin Coward [11:08 a.m.] Yes, sir. I'm already here setting up the conference room. Joachim, make sure you bring the projector.

Pepe Juarez [11:12 a.m.] Ok, I'll cancel my appointment. You can count on my being there. Just chill.

Joachim Fitzgerald [11:15 a.m.] The projector is already there but it's hidden. I didn't want anybody taking it. I'll grab it before we start. See you all in a bit.

1. What will be the subject of the meeting?
   (A) Investment banking
   (B) Security screening
   (C) Sports and recreation planning
   (D) Organizing for an event

2. At 11:12 a.m., what does Pepe Juarez mean when he writes "Just chill"?
   (A) He wants a cool drink.
   (B) He wants people to stop worrying.
   (C) He wants to go to his appointment.
   (D) He wants people to wait for him.

3. What job does Richard Burton most likely have?
   (A) Head coordinator
   (B) Caterer
   (C) Decorations manager
   (D) Secretary

4. What will Joachim Fitzgerald most likely do next?
   (A) Go to lunch
   (B) Call Pepe for an update
   (C) Retrieve the projector
   (D) Contact Richard Burton

⑧ 網頁

- 內容可能與**公司**、**企業**、**活動**等有關。
- 會針對公司介紹、產品說明、後記、FAQ（常被詢問的問題）等來出題。
- 和網頁內容有關的訂購、預約、申請等的各式表格，也常會拿來出題。

1 命題分析

STEP 1 試題 1—3 與下列網頁有關。

---

❶ AAA Movers—We Ship for YOU!

Thank you for choosing AAA Movers. We are always trying to improve our business, and a big part of that quest for perfection involves listening to our customers. Please take the time to fill out the following questionnaire as honestly as possible. Don't worry; you won't hurt our feelings!

❷ Customer Name: <u>Eric Holder</u>

Date of Move: <u>September 23</u>

Lead Mover's <u>Name: Harrison</u>

From Address: <u>231 Axle Road</u>

To Address: <u>87 Park Drive</u>

On a scale of 1 to 10, with 1 being poor and 10 being perfect, how would you rate the following aspects of our service?

Professionalism of staff: <u>3</u>

Cost of the move: <u>8</u>

Efficiency of the move: <u>8</u>

Care taken with your possessions: <u>8</u>

Safety of our team: <u>7</u>

---

(1) 網站及形式介紹
文章一開始會介紹網站的內容以及網站的形式。

(2) 網站的細節資訊
關於網站所提供的服務、說明等等，此處會有更詳細的解釋，要和試題對照，仔細地閱讀。

Would you be likely to use our service again? <u>No</u>.

Would you recommend our service to a friend or family member? <u>No</u>.

Comments: <u>To begin with, I was really shocked by the appearance of the staff. All of the movers were wearing street clothes, not uniforms. They all had visible tattoos and some even had facial piercings. I was quite frightened of them. All of my things were moved successfully, but it just seemed like you had hired some thugs off the street. Please at least require your staff to wear uniforms.</u>

1. How will AAA Movers most likely use the information that they collect from the form?
   (A) To better map their moving routes
   (B) To train their drivers
   (C) To improve their customer relations
   (D) To become a safer company

2. What does Eric Holder indicate about the condition of his belongings?
   (A) He felt they didn't belong.
   (B) They were all successfully moved.
   (C) Objects were broken.
   (D) He felt his stuff was unsafe.

3. What does Eric Holder indicate about the service he received?
   (A) He thought the movers performed well.
   (B) He didn't like the movers' informal style.
   (C) He wanted more movers.
   (D) He thought it was an unsafe way to move people's things.

STEP 2 確認正確答案及翻譯和解說。

AAA 搬家公司「我們為您搬運！」

謝謝您選擇 AAA 搬家公司。我們一直盡力改善我們的營運，而追求完美的過程包括了傾聽客戶意見。請您撥冗填寫以下問卷，請盡量如實以告，別擔心，您不會傷害我們的感情。

顧客姓名：<u>艾瑞克・厚德爾</u>

搬家日期：<u>9 月 23 日</u>

搬運工頭：<u>哈瑞森</u>

起點：<u>艾克索路 231 號</u>

終點：<u>帕克大道 87 號</u>

以 10 分量表，1 分表示很差，10 分表示完美，請您評分以下服務內容：

人員專業程度：3

搬運費用：8

搬運效率：8

搬運過程中對您財物的細心程度：8

本公司團隊的安全：7

您是否會再選擇本公司的服務？否。

您是否會向親友推薦本公司的服務？否。

其他意見：首先，你們人員的外表真的嚇到我了。所有搬運人員各穿各的，不是穿制服。看得到大家有刺青，有些人甚至臉上有穿洞。我真的有點怕他們。我所有的東西都搬好了，只是你們好像聘用了街上的混混。請至少要讓求員工穿著制服。

---

1. AAA 搬運公司最可能如何運用意見表蒐集來的資訊？
(A) 改善運送路線的地圖
(B) 訓練司機
(C) 改善顧客關係
(D) 成為更安全的公司

2. 艾瑞克·厚德爾說他的物品狀態如何？
(A) 他覺得東西沒有搬到對的地方。
(B) 物品安然搬好。
(C) 物品有破損。
(D) 他覺得他的東西不安全。

3. 艾瑞克·厚德爾提到他得到的服務是如何？
(A) 他認為服務很好。
(B) 他不喜歡人員不正式的風格。
(C) 他希望來更多的幫手。
(D) 他認為這樣搬運物品不安全。

正確答案

1. (C) To improve their customer relations
2. (B) They were all successfully moved.
3. (B) He didn't like the movers' informal style.

解說

1. 文章開頭便開宗明義指出，該公司為了提供顧客更好的服務，會充分利用這份問卷，所以正確答案是 (C)。

2. 艾瑞克·厚德爾在「搬運過程中對您財物的細心程度」這一項，給了很高的分數（8 分），在其他意見也提到所有的東西都搬好了，由此可知正確答案是 (B)。

3. 艾瑞克·厚德爾在其他意見中指出，搬運人員沒有穿制服，且身上有刺青和穿洞，讓他感到害怕。所以正確答案是 (B)。

Questions 1-3 refer to the following web page.

Welcome to Amazing Animals, the ONLY website that creates custom-made stuffed animals based upon your own pet!

We offer service to all types of pet owners. Cats and dogs are of course the most popular, but we have done fish, lizards, snakes, and even pigs!

All you have to do is fill out our order form with payment and delivery instructions, then upload three to five jpegs of your pet. Within 24 hours we will send you a digital image and a quote. If you want us to proceed, we will process your payment and get started.

Amazing Animals make great gifts, and can really help people who have recently lost a beloved pet.

Refer to our handy price guide below to get an estimate on your Amazing Animal!

- Small pets (up to three kg in weight and less than one cubic meter) $24.95
- Medium pets (up to 10 kg in weight and less than two cubic meters) $59.95
- Large pets (over 10 kg and greater than two cubic meters) $89.95*

*Amazing Animals cannot create products larger than four cubic meters.

Place your order today!

1. What type of animal could Amazing Animals NOT create for its customers?
   (A) A snake
   (B) An elephant
   (C) A bird
   (D) A cat

2. What is suggested by the web page?
   (A) This product is for children.
   (B) This product is good for people whose pets have passed away.
   (C) This product must be supervised.
   (D) This is a complicated process.

3. What is stated about Amazing Animals?
   (A) They are the sole providers of custom-made stuffed animals online.
   (B) They guarantee satisfaction.
   (C) They use state-of-the-art equipment.
   (D) They are expanding into exotic pets.

⑨ 書信

- 書信是出題頻率非常高的文章類型。
- 特別會出掌握**寄信人**和**收信人關係**的試題，以及從傳達的內容中推知事實的邏輯型試題。
- 信件的**意圖**和**目的**也時常會考，所以閱讀時要特別注意。

1 命題分析

STEP 1 試題 1—4 與下列書信有關。

❶ April 3
Myra Lewis
Hollaway Properties
101 Eastlake Plaza
Wyclef, NV

Dear Ms. Lewis,

❷ The Wyclef Planning Commission has received Hollaway Properties' application for a variance of a zoning variance in the Upland Park area to construct the "Newtown Condominiums." The application is to allow a residential development in an area zoned as commercial. The application as written has been rejected. This letter details the changes that Hollaway Properties will have to make in your application should you want it to succeed.

❸ To begin with, the proposed location of the condominiums will interfere with traffic going to the Upland Park shopping center. In order for this problem to be solved, Hollaway Properties will have to pay for the installation and construction of a controlled intersection at Grove Street and Pine Avenue.

Another major obstacle to the granting of the variance is the burden it will place on the water system in the area. The sewers and water mains were not built to handle the

(1) 收信人資訊
書信的信頭會揭示收信人的資訊。確認收信人的姓名，掌握試題問的對象是信件的當事人還是第三者。

(2) 信件目的
通常會出現在文章的首段，不過有時也可能必須閱讀完整篇文章後才知道，這時要先解其他試題，之後再解主題試題，這樣才能節省時間。

(3) 揭示具體訊息
和主題有關的細節也是考題重點。

volume of a residential apartment complex. In order to remedy this, Hollaway Properties will have to upgrade the existing infrastructure in the Upland Park area.

④ If Hollaway Properties is willing to follow the recommendations contained in the letter, then the Wyclef Planning Commission is confident the variance can be allowed. Please submit a revised proposal including plans to address the issues mentioned above by the 30th of this month if you would like to proceed.

Dennis Hopper
Wyclef Planning Commission

(4) 請求事項及追加事項
信末通常會提到請求事項或附加訊息，最後署名的地方會點出寄信人的職位和所屬單位。

1. Why does Dennis Hopper write to Myra Lewis?
   (A) To help her succeed with an application
   (B) To discourage her from moving forward with a development
   (C) To tell her why Hollaway Properties have succeeded with their application
   (D) To tell her Upland Park does not want Hollaway Properties to build there

2. What is suggested about Upland Park?
   (A) It is a busy urban area.
   (B) It is an area without a lot of infrastructure.
   (C) It is an area with plenty of residential housing.
   (D) It is an area that needs more businesses.

3. What is indicated about the proposed Newtown Condominiums?
   (A) They will be an easy project to complete.
   (B) Hollaway Properties will have to make a lot of improvements around Upland Park in order to build them.
   (C) The Wyclef Planning Commission does not want the project to proceed.
   (D) Hollaway Properties will abandon the project.

4. What does Dennis Hopper ask Myra Lewis to do if Hollaway Properties wants to proceed with the Newtown Condominiums?
   (A) Revise the plans completely
   (B) Send a new proposal by May 30th
   (C) Figure out a way to solve the problems mentioned in the letter
   (D) Write a letter explaining how the project would benefit Wyclef

4 月 3 日

米拉‧露易絲

荷拉偉地產公司

東湖廣場 101 號

懷克里夫，內華達州

露易絲女士您好：

懷克里夫規畫委員會已收到荷拉偉地產公司申請，變更鄂普蘭園地的土地用途，以興建「新城公寓大樓」一案。此申請是為了核准在商業區開發住宅的建案。如書面文件所示，申請已駁回。本公文將詳細說明荷拉偉地產公司必須做哪些變更，才能通過申請。

首先，地產公司提出的新城公寓大樓預定地，將會干擾鄂普蘭園購物中心的交通。為了解決此問題，荷拉偉地產公司必須支付在葛羅夫街和松林大道交叉口建置交通控管的費用。

另一個攸關允許變更的障礙是，本建案會造成該區供水系統的負擔。原先的下水道和自來水總管無法負荷住宅公寓的用量。為了解決這個問題，荷拉偉地產公司必須升級鄂普蘭園現有的基礎建設。

如果荷拉偉地產公司願意採取文中建議，懷克里夫規畫委員會有信心此變更申請將可獲准。如果您希望本案繼續進行，請在本月 30 日前，重新提交更新版本，並提出上述問題的解決方案。

丹尼斯‧哈波

懷克里夫規畫委員會

---

1. 丹尼斯‧哈波致信給米拉‧露易絲的目的是什麼？
(A) 協助她申請成功
(B) 阻止她繼續進行這個開發案
(C) 通知荷拉偉地產公司申請成功
(D) 通知她鄂普蘭園不希望地產公司在那邊蓋房子

2. 從本文可得知鄂普蘭園什麼事？
(A) 鄂普蘭園是繁忙的都會區。
(B) 本區並沒有太多基礎設施。
(C) 這一帶有許多住宅。
(D) 這一帶需要更多商家。

3. 本文提到「新城公寓大樓」提案的什麼事？
(A) 這是個能順利完成的案子。
(B) 荷拉偉地產公司必須負責改善鄂普蘭園許多設施。
(C) 懷克里夫規畫委員會並不希望本案持續進行。
(D) 荷拉偉地產公司會放棄這個案子。

4. 如果荷拉偉地產公司希望持續進行「新城公寓大樓」建案，丹尼斯‧哈波要求米拉‧露易絲做什麼事情？
(A) 全面重寫計畫
(B) 在 5 月 30 日前提交新計畫
(C) 想辦法解決公文中提出的問題
(D) 寫一封信說明此案為何有利於懷克里夫

字彙

planning commission 規畫委員會　　variance 變化；變動
zoning 都市區域劃分　　residential 住宅的　　commercial 商業的
succeed 成功　　intersection 十字路口　　sewer 下水道
water main 自來水總管　　infrastructure 基礎建設　　urban 都市的
abandon 拋棄；丟棄

正確答案

1. (A) To help her succeed with an application

2. (B) It is an area without a lot of infrastructure.

3. (B) Hollaway Properties will have to make a lot of improvements around Upland Park in order to build them.

4. (C) Figure out a way to solve the problems mentioned in the letter

解説

1. 寫這封信的原因可以在以 this letter（本信）為主詞的句子裡找到，也就是第一段的第四行，detail 當動詞使用時是「陳述細部事項」。

　　這句話提到，這封信將陳述要變更的事項，暗示將這幾項令人擔心的地方變更的話，申請就會核准通過了。所以正確答案是 (A)，幫忙收信人通過申請。

2. 一一檢視各選項正確與否。選項 (A) 無法從本文中確認。選項 (C) 的顎普蘭園是購物中心，目前並有住宅，所以也是錯的。選項 (D) 也是本文沒有提到的內容。要讓公寓大樓的建案通過，需要建設交叉路口的交通設施和水管設施，由此可以間接知道，基礎建設嚴重不足，所以正確答案是 (B)。

3. 懷克里夫規畫委員會拒絕申請的原因，是因為有兩個設施方面的問題點，若將這點予以改進，就能通過申請。將這意思換一種説法，説成是「荷拉偉地產公司必須負責改善鄂普蘭園許多設施。」意思是一樣的，所以 (B) 是正確答案。

4. 選項 (A) 的動詞 revise 是更改的意思，很容易讓人誤選，以為這是正確答案。不過 revise completely 是將申請計畫全面重寫，提出一份新的申請，不適合用來説明只要改進兩個問題點就可以了的狀況。所以説「想辦法解決公文中提出的問題」的選項 (C) 是正確答案。

Questions 1-4 refer to the following letter.

Winsor Outdoor Apparel

September 27

Jeannie Tyler
12 Fowler Street
Crosby, MI 49618

Dear Ms. Tyler,

To celebrate the start of the fall season, Winsor Outdoor Apparel is offering discounted prices on all of our fall fashions! We hope to see you at our store soon when you take advantage of this great opportunity!

This event will begin at our Lansing location on Monday, October 1. At our Detroit location, these special offers will be available starting October 2. The event will run at both stores for about a week, finishing on the same day, October 7.

We will be selling a wide variety of fall apparel ranging from jackets and skirts to hats and scarves. We will also be selling specialized outdoor apparel for camping, biking, and running. Many of these items are brand-new and are expected to sell out quickly. Additionally, we will have extra employees on hand at each store to accommodate the increased number of customers.

Our Lansing location is at 45 Willow Street, just past the Fulton department store, and our Detroit location is at 137 Pine Street, between the Maxwell Theater and Hoshi, a Japanese restaurant.

You can get more information on this special event by reading the enclosed detailed brochure. Please don't hesitate to stop by next week!

Sincerely,

John Waters
Marketing Manager
Winsor Outdoor Apparel

1. Why was the letter written?
   (A) To promote a new online store
   (B) To advertise a seasonal sale
   (C) To introduce new employees
   (D) To solicit customer feedback

2. When will the event hosted by Winsor Outdoor Apparel end?
   (A) On September 27th
   (B) On October 1st
   (C) On October 2nd
   (D) On October 7th

3. What is NOT mentioned about the event?
   (A) Its dates
   (B) Its locations
   (C) Its prices
   (D) Its items

4. What will Ms. Tyler most likely do for more information?
   (A) Contact Mr. Waters
   (B) Visit the Winsor Outdoor Apparel website
   (C) Read the document inside the envelope
   (D) Stop by a store

雙篇閱讀

信件為主的兩篇文章

第一篇文章是電子郵件或信件，第二篇文章可能是另一篇電子郵件或信件，或廣告、表格等。

廣告為主的兩篇文章

第一篇文章是商品廣告或求才廣告，第二篇文章可能是另一篇廣告，或電子郵件、信件回覆等。

公告為主的兩篇文章

第一篇文章是公務公告或消息通知，第二篇文章可能是電子郵件或信件，或表格、報導等。

表格為主的兩篇文章

第一篇文章是合約或表格，第二篇文章可能是另一份表格，或電子郵件、信件、報導等。

① 信件為主的兩篇文章

命題分析

STEP 1 試題 1—5 與下列電子郵件和信件有關。

To: Natalie Park <npark@acemail.com>
From: Marcus Beauchamp <beauchamp@theaternet.net>
Date: March 22
Subject: Scheduling

Hello Natalie,

I'm glad to hear that more people have chosen to join our membership programs. This probably means that our advertising is paying off. Thank you for the good news. We'll keep promoting our programs on our website and around the theater. Hopefully news will also spread by word of mouth from our members.

As for your question about Angela Bower's performance, we're still in contact with her managers and working out a contract that will please both sides. I'm hopeful that she will perform in the summer as planned, but she has been asked to make a brief appearance in a movie that will film during the same period since another actress may drop out due to scheduling conflicts. Until that is all resolved, we won't know for certain whether she will be able to perform at our theater. I'll let you know as soon as everything has been arranged.

Cheers,

Marcus

Vancity Theater, March 25
Mr. Jake Monogram
224 Thorton Street
Washington, DC 93847

Dear Mr. Monogram,

Thank you for joining our membership program for the spring and summer season. On behalf of the Vancity Theater, I'd like to welcome you. Your benefits as a member include two seats at three of our plays in July and August. Members also receive email alerts on upcoming plays and performances before tickets are sold to the general public. I have enclosed your tickets to the three plays. Information about the plays, biographies of the performers, and other information is available on our website at www.vancitytheater.com. If you have further questions, you can also call the theater at 555-1234.

I hope you will enjoy the benefits of your membership. Feel free to contact us at any time. Please also note that performance dates and times are subject to change.

Sincerely,

Natalie Park

Managing Director of Theater Patrons
Vancity Theater

1. What is Mr. Beauchamp pleased about?
   (A) The number of theater members is increasing.
   (B) A famous actress has signed to perform at the theater.
   (C) More plays and performances are planned for this season.
   (D) The theater has received positive reviews from critics.

2. Why is Mr. Beauchamp concerned?
   (A) Dress rehearsals are behind schedule.
   (B) The costs for some of the plays are over budget.
   (C) An appearance by a famous performer has not yet been confirmed.
   (D) Some members have not received their schedules.

3. In paragraph one, line two of the email, the expression "paying off" is closest in meaning to
   (A) bills will be paid
   (B) successful
   (C) a profit has been made
   (D) meaningful

4. Why did Ms. Park send the letter to Jake Monogram?
   (A) To give details of upcoming performances
   (B) To thank him for his contributions to the theater
   (C) To remind him to renew his membership
   (D) To provide information about his membership

5. According to the letter, what can members do on the theater's website?
   (A) Buy tickets
   (B) Find information about plays
   (C) Ask questions
   (D) Contact performers

收件人：娜塔莉‧帕克

寄件人：馬可斯‧波強

日期：3 月 22 日

主旨：檔期

娜塔莉你好：

很開心得知愈來愈多人加入我們的會員，這大概表示我們的廣告奏效。謝謝你捎來的好消息。我們會持續在網站上和戲院推廣我們的方案。也希望這個消息透過會員的口耳相傳而散布出去。

至於你詢問的安琪拉‧鮑爾的演出，我們仍在聯絡她的經理人，並盡力達成讓雙方都滿意的合約。我樂觀地認為她會如期在夏天演出。但是，她受邀參與一部電影的串場演出，這部電影必須在夏天同時開拍，否則同劇另一位女演員會因撞期而退出。在這件事情解決之前，我們無法確定她是否會在我們戲院登臺。一切安排妥當後，我會馬上通知你。

謝謝你，

馬可斯

梵希堤劇院，3 月 25 日

傑克‧莫諾格蘭

索頓街 224 號

華盛頓特區，93847

莫諾格蘭先生您好：

謝謝您加入我們的春夏兩季會員方案。謹代表梵希堤劇院歡迎您的加入。會員福利包括七八月分三場演出門票各兩張。同時，我們也會在票券向大眾開賣之前，寄發電子信件告知會員近期登場的戲劇和表演。在此附上三場演出門票。關於劇目、表演者簡介及其他資訊，請上網站 www.vancity.com。如果您有其他問題，請撥打劇院電話 555-1234。

希望您喜歡我們提供的會員福利。歡迎隨時與我們聯繫。也請您留意，表演日期和時間可能會有改變。

娜塔莉‧帕克 敬上

劇院贊助管理經理

梵希堤劇院

1. 波強先生對於什麼感到欣慰？
   (A) 劇院會員人數正在增加。
   (B) 一位知名女演員已簽約登臺。
   (C) 這一季規畫了更多戲劇和表演。
   (D) 劇院得到劇評正面的評價。

2. 波強先生為什麼覺得擔心？
   (A) 著裝彩排進度落後。
   (B) 有些表演超過預算。
   (C) 一場知名演員的演出尚未定案。
   (D) 有些會員還沒收到演出時間表。

3. 本封信第一段第二行的
   「is paying off（成功；有效）」
   意思最接近下列何者？
   (A) 帳單會有人付錢的
   (B) 成功的
   (C) 有利可圖的
   (D) 有意義的

4. 帕克女士為何要致信杰克・莫諾格蘭？
   (A) 提供近期演出的細節
   (B) 謝謝他對劇院的貢獻
   (C) 提醒他續會
   (D) 提供會員相關資訊

5. 根據這封信，會員可以上劇院網站做什麼？
   (A) 購買票券
   (B) 查詢演出相關訊息
   (C) 詢問問題
   (D) 聯絡表演者

字彙

advertising 廣告　　pay off 帶來好結果；成功　　promote 推廣；促進
be in contact with ... 與……有聯絡　　contract 合約
brief 簡短的；短暫的　　appearance 出現　　drop out 脫離
resolve 解決；決心　　on behalf of 代表　　alert 提醒
upcoming 即將來臨的　　enclose 附上　　biography 傳記
patron 贊助者；常客

正確答案

1. (A) The number of theater members is increasing.

2. (C) An appearance by a famous performer has not yet been confirmed.

3. (B) successful

4. (D) To provide information about this membership

5. (B) Find information about plays

1. 在馬克斯 • 波強寫的電子郵件第一句便提到，他很高興劇場的會員數增加了，所以 (A) 是正確答案。

2. 在電子郵件的第二段提到了劇院目前的問題，也就是知名女演員安琪拉 • 鮑爾因為檔期的關係，可能不能來參加演出，所以 (C) 是正確答案。

3. is paying off 的前一句是說，很高興劇院的會員增加了，所以可以推知這是因為廣告很成功的緣故。因此 is paying off 應該是成功的意思，(B) 是正確答案。

4. 必須確實讀懂整篇文章，才能理解帕克女士寫信的用意。整個第二篇文章都是帕克女士在向新加入的會員傑克 • 莫諾葛蘭，提供會員的相關訊息，所以正確答案是 (D)。

5. 第二篇文章揭示了預知更多關於表演劇目和表演者簡介等資訊，請洽劇院網站，所以正確答案是 (B)。

② 表格為主的兩篇文章

命題分析

STEP 1 試題 1—5 與下列表格、電子郵件有關。

Omega Supplies

Client name:　　R & R
Client address: 405 Devon Street, New York, NY 18827
Date:　　　　　April 7

Item Number	Description	Quantity	Unit Price	Total
C88391	large paper cups with lids, red	3,000	$0.50	$1,500
C43771	small napkins, red and blue trim	5,000	$0.10	$500
C83872	small paper cups with lids, red	3,000	$0.30	$900
C28763	paper carriers for two cups, red	1,000	$0.25	$250

If you have any questions, please contact your sales representative Jason Chow at jasonchow@omegasupplies.com.

To: Jason Chow <jasonchow@omegasupplies.com>
From: Ron Ronson <ronron@randr.com>
Date: April 11
Subject: Invoice

Hello Jason,

I have received the invoice that you sent, as well as all the supplies I ordered for my business. However, I do have a slight concern about the napkins that I ordered. The red and blue trim is usually very crisp and separated, but the batch that I've just received has the red and blue bleeding into each other. It's not that big a deal, but it's a bit unsightly for my taste. I would like to return them for a new batch with clean lines. Furthermore, I notice that the paper carriers for the cups are now $0.25 a unit. I know that some of your items have increased in price, but I thought that they were still $0.15 a unit. Can you please confirm the unit price for me? Other than that, I'm happy with the supplies and hope to continue doing business with you.

I'll return the napkins by post this afternoon, but I need the replacement as soon as possible. I'm worried, which we may not have enough, especially during the weekend which gets busy for us here at the café.

Thank you,

Ron Ronson
Owner of R & R

1. What, most likely, is R & R?
   (A) A coffee shop
   (B) A supply store
   (C) A hotel
   (D) A clothing company

2. What do all of the products ordered have in common?
   (A) Their cost
   (B) Their unit price
   (C) Their color
   (D) Their amount

3. What product did Mr. Ronson think cost less than he was charged?
   (A) The large paper cups with lids
   (B) The small napkins
   (C) The small paper cups with lids
   (D) The paper carriers for two cups

4. What is suggested about R & R in the email?
   (A) It is a small business.
   (B) It gets busy on weekends.
   (C) It is closed on Sundays.
   (D) It is a new customer of Omega Supplies.

5. What is NOT suggested in the email?
   (A) Mr. Ronson has ordered from Omega Supplies before.
   (B) Some of the supplies have increased in price.
   (C) Some of the items will be returned.
   (D) Mr. Ronson forgot to place an order for medium-sized cups.

PART

7

Chapter

02

雙篇閱讀

歐米嘉耗材公司

客戶名稱：R & R

客戶地址：德文街 405 號，紐約市，紐約州 18827

日期：4 月 7 日

貨號	商品內容	數量	單價	總價
C88391	附蓋大紙杯，紅色	3,000	$0.50	$1,500
C43771	小餐巾紙，紅藍色邊飾	5,000	$0.10	$500
C83872	附蓋小紙杯，紅色	3,000	$0.30	$900
C28763	紙製兩杯架，紅色	1,000	$0.25	$250

有任何問題，請與業務杰森・周聯絡，來信請寄 jasonchow@omegasupplies.com。

收件人：杰森・周 <jasonchow@omegasupplies.com>

寄件人：朗・朗森 <ronron@randr.com>

日期：4 月 11 日

主旨：發票

杰森您好：

我收到您寄來的發票和之前我訂購的所有貨品，但我對我訂的餐巾紙有個小疑慮。紅色和藍色的邊飾線條通常乾淨分明，但我收到的這批貨，紅色和藍色油墨互相暈染，這雖然不是什麼大不了的問題，但對我來說是有點不賞心悅目。我希望可以退貨，換一批勾線分明的。此外，我發現杯架的單價現在是 0.25 元，我知道你們公司有些品項價格調漲，但這些東西應該還是一個 0.15 元。能否請您幫我確認一下單價呢？除此之外，我很滿意這些商品，也希望未來能繼續跟你交易。

我今天下午會寄還這些紙巾，但我希望能盡快收到新的。我擔心我這邊庫存不足，尤其我們咖啡店週末會特別忙碌。

謝謝你，

朗・朗森

R & R 負責人

----

1. R & R 最有可能是什麼？

   (A) 咖啡店   (B) 備品公司

   (C) 旅館   (D) 服裝公司

2. 朗・朗森訂購的貨品有什麼共通性？

   (A) 價格一樣   (B) 單價一樣

   (C) 顏色相同   (D) 數量一樣

3. 朗森先生認為哪個商品的價格應低於他實際支付的金額？

   (A) 附蓋大紙杯

   (B) 小餐巾紙

   (C) 附蓋小紙杯

   (D) 紙製兩杯架

4. 由本文可得知 R & R 什麼事？
　　(A) 是一家小店。
　　(B) 週末會很忙。
　　(C) 週日公休。
　　(D) 是歐米嘉耗材公司的新客戶。

5. 這封電子郵件沒有提到以下何者？
　　(A) 朗森先生跟歐米嘉耗材公司訂過貨。
　　(B) 有些商品已經漲價。
　　(C) 有些品項會退回。
　　(D) 朗森先生忘記訂中型紙杯。

字彙

supply 供給；供應　　unit price 單價　　trim 裝飾
sales representative 業務專員　　invoice 發票；收據　　slight 輕微的
crisp 酥脆的；乾淨俐落的　　batch 批　　bleed （印刷）出血；超出邊界
unsightly 不好看的

正確答案

1. (A) A coffee shop

2. (C) Their color

3. (D) The paper carriers for two cups

4. (B) It gets busy on weekends.

5. (D) Mr. Ronson forgot to place an order for medium-sized cups.

解說

1. 在第二篇的電子郵件中，最後一句朗森先生擔心存貨不足，因為咖啡店在週末會特別忙碌，由此可知 R & R 應該是咖啡店，所以 (A) 是正確答案。

2. 從第一篇的表格中，其中說明處（Description）記載的事項，可以知道全部產品都是紅色的，所以 (C) 是正確答案。

3. 在第二篇的電子郵件中，朗森先生提到紙製兩杯架的單價似乎有所變動，他認為實際價格應該比帳單上的價格更低，所以 (D) 是正確答案。

4. 在第二篇的電子郵件中，最後一句朗森先生擔心存貨不足，因為咖啡店在週末會特別忙碌，由此可知 R & R 週末會很忙，所以 (B) 是正確答案。

　　由於朗森先生說他知道有些品項價格有調漲，故可知他不是歐米嘉耗材公司的新客戶，因此 (D) 不能選。

5. 第一篇文章是歐米嘉耗材公司給朗森先生的發票，第二篇文章是收到這張發票後，朗森先生回覆的電子郵件，由此可知朗森先生有跟歐米嘉耗材公司下過訂單，選項 (A) 是正確的。

　　另外第二篇文章中朗森先生提到，他知道有些商品的價格上漲了，所以 (B) 也是正確的。在第二篇文章的最後提到，朗森先生會在今天下午退回紙巾，因此 (C) 也是正確的。唯一沒有提及的內容是 (D)，故 (D) 是正確答案。

三篇閱讀

網頁—電子郵件—公告

第一篇文章是網頁,第二篇文章是電子郵件,第三篇文章是公告。

電子郵件—信件—行程表

第一篇文章是電子郵件,第二篇文章是信件,第三篇文章是各式各樣行程表。

公告—電子郵件—表格

第一篇文章是公告,第二篇文章是電子郵件,第三篇文章是各式各樣表單或行程表。

報導—評論—信件

第一篇文章是報導,第二篇文章是有關該篇報導的評論,第三篇文章是信件。

介紹—線上評論—電子郵件

第一篇文章是介紹,第二篇文章是線上評論,第三篇文章是電子郵件。

STEP 1 試題 1—5 與下列兩封電子郵件和表單有關。

To: Customer Service <cservice@starinteriors.com>
From: John Brown <jbrown@zipnet.com>
Date: October 16
Subject: Wallpaper Exchange

Dear Customer Service,

I recently purchased five rolls of Spring Rain wallpaper from you online. The wallpaper does not match the pictures on the Internet. I would like to exchange Spring Rain for Summer Season if I could. I have never bought anything from your company before, so I am not sure what to do about a return.

Sincerely,

John Brown

To: John Brown <jbrown@zipnet.com>
From: Rachel Jenkins <cservice@starinteriors.com>
Date: October 16
Subject: Exchange

Dear Mr. Brown,

We would be happy to exchange your wallpaper. Just send us back your shipment of Spring Rain and we will send Summer Season to you. Would you like us to send you a sample of the Summer Season wallpaper to make sure it is all right? Although we are happy to make the exchange, you will have to pay for the return shipping. Please fill out the enclosed return form and write us back to let us know if you would like a sample first.

Thank you,

Rachel Jenkins
Star Interiors Customer Care

Star Interiors Return Order Form

Product Name	Amount	Length required	Price per yard	Reason for exchange
Spring Rain	5 boxes	100 yards	$3.00	Didn't match the photo online

1. Why did John Brown write to Star Interiors?
   - (A) To get a refund
   - (B) To order new wallpaper
   - (C) To report the nondelivery of his wallpaper
   - (D) To exchange wallpaper designs

2. What is indicated about Spring Rain wallpaper?
   - (A) It doesn't fit John Brown's color scheme.
   - (B) It is defective.
   - (C) It doesn't match the photo shown online.
   - (D) It was delivered to the wrong address.

3. What does Rachel Jenkins tell John Brown about the return?
   - (A) He must pay for the shipping of Spring Rain.
   - (B) He must pay for the shipping of Summer Season.
   - (C) He must order a sample.
   - (D) The order cannot be returned.

4. What does Rachel Jenkins offer to do for John Brown?
   - (A) Pay for his shipping
   - (B) Send him a sample of Summer Season
   - (C) Send him a different roll of Spring Rain
   - (D) Explain the new designs for the upcoming season

5. What job does Rachel Jenkins most likely have?
   - (A) CEO
   - (B) CFO
   - (C) Customer service representative
   - (D) Sales representative

STEP 2 確認正確答案及翻譯和解說。

收件人：客服 <cservice@starinteriors.com>

寄件人：約翰・布朗 <jbrown@zipnet.com>

日期：10 月 16 日

主旨：壁紙換貨

客服部門你好：

我最近在你們的網站上購買了五捲「春雨」壁紙。實品跟網路圖片不同。可以的話，我想把「春雨」換成「夏季」。我以前沒有跟你們買過東西，所以不知道如何處理退換。

約翰・布朗 敬上

收件人：約翰・布朗 <jbrown@zipnet.com>

寄件人：瑞秋・詹金斯 <cservice@starinteriors.com>

日期：10 月 16 日

主旨：換貨

布朗先生您好：

我們很樂意幫您換貨。只要您將「春雨」寄還給我們，我們就會寄出「夏季」壁紙。您是否想要我們寄「夏季」壁紙樣品給您，以確認這是您要的東西呢？雖然我們很樂意為您換貨，您還是要自付退貨運費。請填寫附件表格，並回覆我們您是否需要樣品。

謝謝您，

瑞秋・詹金斯

繁星傢飾客服部

繁星傢飾退貨單

品名	數量	需求數量	每碼單價	換貨原因
春雨	5 捲	100 碼	3 元	實品與網路上照片不符

1. 約翰・布朗為何要寫信給繁星傢飾？
(A) 要求退款
(B) 訂購新壁紙
(C) 回報壁紙有瑕疵
(D) 更換不同設計的壁紙

2. 本文可得知「春雨」壁紙什麼事？
(A) 與約翰・布朗的色彩配置不搭。
(B) 有瑕疵。
(C) 跟網路上的照片不符。
(D) 寄到錯誤的地址。

3. 瑞秋・詹金斯告知約翰・布朗關於退貨的什麼事項？
(A) 約翰・布朗必須付「春雨」壁紙的運費。
(B) 約翰・布朗必須付「夏季」壁紙的運費。
(C) 約翰・布朗必須購買樣品。
(D) 無法退貨。

4. 瑞秋・詹金斯要幫約翰・布朗做什麼？
(A) 幫他付運費
(B) 寄給他「夏季」壁紙樣品
(C) 再寄給他一捲「春雨」壁紙
(D) 說明新一季的設計

5. 瑞秋・詹金斯可能做什麼工作？
(A) 執行長
(B) 財務長
(C) 客服人員
(D) 銷售人員

字彙

shipment 運送；運送的東西　　return 退貨　　enclosed 附上的
refund 退款　　defective 有瑕疵的　　CFO (= chief financial officer) 財務長

正確答案

1. (D) To exchange wallpaper designs
2. (C) It doesn't match the photo shown online.
3. (A) He must pay for the shipping of Spring Rain.
4. (B) Send him a sample of Summer Season
5. (C) Customer service representative

1. 從約翰‧布朗寫給繁星傢飾的第一封電子郵件中可以找出答案。出問題的是已經配送到府的壁紙，電子郵件的第二句提到與實務與網路照片不符，接著第三句話直接闡明了想要換貨（exchange）的意願，所以正確答案不是退錢，也不是回報壁紙的瑕疵，而是要換壁紙，因此 (D) 是正確答案。

2. 掌握了「春雨」壁紙的具體細節就能解題了。因為並沒有提到顏色的問題，所以 (A) 不對。且訂購的壁紙已經收到了，所以不是地址的問題，(D) 也不能選。由於並未揭示春雨壁紙有什麼缺陷，因此 (B) 不能選。只有選項 (C) 清楚說明了電子郵件中提到的問題，也就是實體和網路照片不符，故 (C) 是正確答案。

3. 在第二封電子郵件中，客服部門的瑞秋直接詢問要不要先寄樣品，所以 (C) 不對。瑞秋告訴布朗先生，他必須要支付退貨的運費（you will have to pay for the return shipping），意即「春雨」的退貨（return）費用必須由布朗先生支付。所以正確答案是 (A)。

4. 在第二封電子郵件中，客服部門的瑞秋直接詢問要不要先寄樣品，要注意的是這題並沒有在問瑞秋願不願意提供換貨，而是瑞秋的提議，也就是寄送樣品，所以 (B) 是正確答案。

5. 在第二封電子郵件的最後署名的地方，提到瑞秋任職於客服部，所以 (C) 是正確答案。

To: Aaron Damon <adamon@acemail.com>
From: James Host <holtrain@zipnet.net>
Date: Jan. 12
Subject: Earnings Report

Dear Aaron,

Could you please resubmit your earnings report in the proper format? If you recall, we had a meeting at the end of the last quarter where everyone agreed to standardize our reports. Please see the example attached to this email.

Kind regards,

James

Earnings Report Form

Name : James Host	Division	Account Balance	% Change from Last Quarter
Acct. 32	Tech	$35,356	+1.2%
Acct. 37	Logistics	$10,032	+1.6%
Acct. 40	Servicing	$16,078	+1.1%

To: James Host <holtrain@zipnet.net>
From: Aaron Damon <adamon@acemail.com>
Date: Jan. 12
Subject: Earnings Report

James,

Sorry I didn't send the report in the correct format. It will not happen again.
I am trying to fill this new form out properly, but one of my accounts is
new this quarter. I don't know what I should do with the field asking for the
percentage change from last quarter. Any advice?

All the best,

Aaron

6. What is most likely true about James and Aaron?
   (A) They are competitors.
   (B) James is Aaron's supervisor.
   (C) Aaron is James's supervisor.
   (D) They are business owners.

7. What is indicated about Aaron's report?
   (A) He did not send it in the proper format.
   (B) The fields are not filled in correctly.
   (C) There are problems with his budget.
   (D) He will have to use it for a presentation.

8. According to the information provided, what is true about Aaron?
   (A) He has a lot of experience with the company.
   (B) He needs more sales.
   (C) He has a new client this quarter.
   (D) He will have to work harder for better results.

9. According to the report, what is true about James Host?
   (A) He is struggling with sales.
   (B) He has the best accounts.
   (C) His sales have increased since the last quarter.
   (D) He needs to help Aaron with his report.

10. According to the information, what is Aaron struggling with?
    (A) His sales figures
    (B) His morale
    (C) His secretary
    (D) The new form

確認正確答案及翻譯和解說。

收件人：亞倫‧戴蒙 <adamon@acemail.com>

寄件人：詹姆士‧侯司特 <holtrain@zipnet.net>

日期：1 月 12 日

主旨：營收報告

亞倫你好：

麻煩你用正確格式重傳營收報告。如果你記得的話，我們在上一季末開過會，當時大家都同意要統一報告格式。請見附件的範本。

祝福你，

詹姆士

營收報告表

名字： 詹姆士‧侯司特	部門	餘額	相較上一季的變化
帳戶 32	技術	$35,356	+1.2%
帳戶 37	物流	$10,032	+1.6%
帳戶 40	服務	$16,078	+1.1%

收件人：詹姆士‧侯司特 <holtrain@zipnet.net>

寄件人：亞倫‧戴蒙 <adamon@acemail.com>

日期：1 月 12 日

主旨：營收報告

詹姆士：

抱歉，我沒有依正確格式寄出報告。我不會再犯一樣的錯了。我還在想辦法將表格填妥，但我這一季有個新客戶，不知道這樣要如何填寫相較上一季的百分比變動。你有建議嗎？

祝好，

亞倫

6. 關於詹姆士和亞倫的敘述，以下何者最可能正確？
(A) 他們是競爭關係。
(B) 詹姆士是亞倫的主管。
(C) 亞倫是詹姆士的主管。
(D) 他們都是老闆。

7. 從電子郵件中可得知亞倫的報告有什麼狀況？
(A) 他沒有用正確格式寄出報告。
(B) 表格填寫錯誤。
(C) 他的預算有些問題。
(D) 他必須使用報告去做簡報。

8. 根據文中提到的資訊，關於亞倫的描述以下何者正確？
(A) 他在這家公司有豐富經驗。
(B) 他需要更多銷售量。
(C) 他今年有新的客戶。
(D) 他需要加倍努力才有更好的成效。

9. 根據這個報告，關於詹姆士‧候斯特何者正確？
(A) 他正在努力改善銷售量。
(B) 他有最好的客戶。
(C) 他的銷售量比上一季多。
(D) 他必須幫亞倫處理報告。

10. 根據資訊，詹姆士正在為什麼而努力？
(A) 銷售數字
(B) 他自己的士氣
(C) 跟秘書處不好
(D) 填寫新的表格

字彙

earning 營收　　proper 適當的　　format 格式　　recall 記得
quarter 季；四分之一　　standardize 標準化　　correct 正確的
form 表格　　account 客戶　　supervisor 主管　　budget 預算
struggle with . . . 努力；奮鬥

正確答案

6. (B) James is Aaron's supervisor.

7. (A) He did not send it in the proper format.

8. (C) He has a new client this quarter.

9. (C) His sales have increased since the last quarter.

10. (D) The new form

6. 透過詹姆士寫給亞倫的電子郵件，他們曾經一起開過會，所以可以知道兩人是同一家公司的員工。再從這裡推測兩人的關係，並找到正確答案。詹姆士要求亞倫重填報告表格，而亞倫又詢問詹姆士關於報告書的細節與建議，由此可知詹姆士的職位較亞倫的高，所以正確答案是 (B)。

7. 從第一封電子郵件，詹姆士要亞倫根據所附的表格再重寫報告，便可以知道亞倫原先寄的資料表格有問題，所以正確答案是 (A)。

8. 選項 (A) 和 (D) 的內容並沒有出現在本文中。亞倫寄給詹姆士的電子郵件中有提到，由於在這一季有新的客戶，不知道該如何填寫上一季百分比變化的表格，因而詢問詹姆士的意見。所以正確答案是 (C)。

9. 從表格中可以看出，詹姆士的所有收益都較上一季增加了，所以 (A) 是錯的，而正確答案是 (C)。

至於其他選項，因為沒有提供其他人的收益報告書，所以無從比較，因此 (B) 不對。選項 (D) 的助動詞 needs 表示必須幫忙亞倫，但是亞倫並沒有要求幫忙，只是詢問詹姆士「有沒有什麼建議」，所以不能選，這點要注意。

10. 看到亞倫的電子郵件中提到不知道（don't know）的地方，立刻就能解題了。亞倫不知道再有新客戶的這一季，應該如何正確填寫表格，所以正確答案是 (D)。選項 (A)、(B) 和 (C) 都無法從本文中確認。

PART

7

Chapter

03

三篇閱讀

To: Evelyn Chase <echase@bizcorp.com>
From: Helen Thomas <helenthomas@yjconsulting.net>
Date: June 5
Subject: Scheduling

Dear Ms. Chase,

I have been looking over my schedule for the coming week and I see that I have you booked to come into our office for a consultation this Thursday at 1:30 p.m. Will that work for you? I could always fit you in on Friday morning if that would be more convenient. Let me know.

Helen Thomas
Senior Consultant, YJ Consulting

To: Helen Thomas <helenthomas@yjconsulting.net>
From: Evelyn Chase <echase@bizcorp.com>
Date: June 6
Subject: Rescheduling

Dear Ms. Thomas,

I think that I am going to be too busy on Thursday to make it over to your office after all. I will take you up on the offer to switch to Friday morning. Ten-thirty works for me, if it's good for you. I hope that you will have my portfolio ready. I need those photos to be perfect for my gallery opening. Have a great day!

Take care,

Evelyn Chase

Helen Thomas Weekly Planner

	Mon.	Tue.	Wed.	Thu.	Fri.
9:00	Planning	Molly	Jack	Paul	Dennis
10:30	Jenny	Mindy	James	Peter	Evelyn
Lunch	*	*	*	*	*
1:30	Gym	Planning	Carter	Sally	James

11. When was Evelyn Chase's original appointment?
    (A) Friday morning
    (B) Thursday morning
    (C) Thursday afternoon
    (D) Thursday evening

12. What is indicated by the first email?
    (A) Helen Thomas is not good at her job.
    (B) Helen Thomas is flexible with her scheduling.
    (C) Helen Thomas needs Evelyn Chase to change her scheduled appointment.
    (D) Helen Thomas is not interested in working with Evelyn Chase.

13. According to Helen Thomas's schedule, what is true?
    (A) Evelyn Chase kept her original appointment.
    (B) Evelyn Chase canceled her appointment completely.
    (C) Evelyn Chase changed her appointment to Friday morning.
    (D) Evelyn Chase will have lunch with Helen Thomas.

14. Based upon the weekly schedule, what can be inferred?
    (A) Helen Thomas needs clients.
    (B) Helen Thomas exercises daily.
    (C) Helen Thomas starts work at 9 a.m.
    (D) Helen Thomas enjoys eating large lunches.

15. Based upon the second email, what can be inferred about Evelyn Chase?
    (A) She is an architect.
    (B) She opens galleries.
    (C) She is a photographer.
    (D) She is friends with Helen Thomas.

收件人：艾芙琳‧吉斯
　　　　<echase@bizcorp.com>
寄件人：海倫‧湯瑪斯
　　　　<helenthomas@jyconsulting.net>
日期：6 月 5 日
主旨：預約

吉斯女士您好：

我在看我接下一週的行程表，發現我跟您約好這週四下午一點半來我辦公室諮詢。您還是方便這個時間來嗎？如果週五上午比較方便的話，我有空檔可以保留給您。請您再跟我確認。

海倫‧湯瑪斯
YJ 顧問公司資深顧問

收件人：海倫‧湯瑪斯
　　　　<helenthomas@jyconsulting.net>
寄件人：艾芙琳‧吉斯
　　　　<echase@bizcorp.com>
日期：6 月 6 日
主旨：重新約時間

湯瑪斯女士您好：

我想我週四可能會忙到無法到您辦公室碰面。那我就改到週五上午。如果你也有空，我十點半可以到。我希望您已看過我的作品集。我需要這些照片很完美，作為藝廊開幕時用。祝您今天順利！

保重，
艾芙琳‧吉斯

海倫‧湯瑪斯週計畫表

	週一	週二	週三	週四	週五
9：00	計畫中	茉莉	傑克	保羅	丹尼斯
10：30	珍妮	明蒂	詹姆士	彼得	艾芙琳
午餐					
1：30	健身房	計畫中	卡特	莎莉	詹姆士

11. 艾芙琳‧吉斯女士原先約定的時間是何時？
(A) 週五上午　　　　(B) 週四早上
(C) 週四下午　　　　(D) 週四晚上

12. 從第一封電子郵件可以得知什麼事？
(A) 海倫‧湯瑪斯不擅長她的工作。
(B) 海倫‧湯瑪斯時間安排是彈性的。
(C) 海倫‧湯瑪斯要請艾芙琳‧吉斯改時間。
(D) 海倫‧湯瑪斯不想跟艾芙琳‧吉斯合作。

13. 根據海倫‧湯瑪斯的時程表，以下何者敘述正確？
(A) 艾芙琳‧吉斯維持原來的時間。
(B) 艾芙琳‧吉斯完全取消會議。
(C) 艾芙琳‧吉斯把會議改到週五上午。
(D) 艾芙琳‧吉斯會跟海倫‧湯瑪斯吃午餐。

14. 根據這個週計畫表，可以得到以下何種
推論？
(A) 海倫·湯瑪斯需要新客戶。
(B) 海倫·湯瑪斯每天運動。
(C) 海倫·湯瑪斯早上九點開始工作。
(D) 海倫·湯瑪斯喜歡中午吃得很豐盛。

15. 從第二封電子郵件，可得知艾芙
琳·吉斯女士什麼事？
(A) 她是建築師。
(B) 她開設多間藝廊。
(C) 她是攝影師。
(D) 她跟海倫·湯瑪斯是朋友。

字彙

book 預約　　consultation 諮詢　　fit someone in on . . . 把……放到（某日）
after all 畢竟　　original 原本的；最初的

正確答案

11. (C) Thursday afternoon
12. (B) Helen Thomas is flexible with her scheduling.
13. (C) Evelyn Chase changed her appointment to Friday morning.
14. (C) Helen Thomas starts work at 9 a.m.
15. (C) She is a photographer.

解說

11. 從兩封電子郵件中找出相關事項就能解題。試題問的是原來（original）約定
的時間，而第一封郵件提到原本約定的時間是星期四下午一點半，之後又說，
如果方便的話換成星期五也可以，並詢問要不要改期，就是第一封電子郵件的
主要目的。原定時間是星期四下午一點半，所以正確答案是 (C)。選項 (D) 的
evening 通常是指傍晚七點左右的時間，這點要注意。

12. 海倫·湯瑪斯並未提到改期的原因，只說她什麼時間都可以配合，如果艾芙
琳·吉斯方便改成星期五也可以，所以 (B) 是正確答案。更改時間不一定代表
工作有了問題，因此 (A) 是錯的。

13. 將表格和電子郵件仔細對照，立刻就能解題了。第一封電子郵件提到，如果
艾芙琳·吉斯方便，也可以將原來約定的時間改成星期五上午；再看到海倫·
湯瑪斯的圖表，星期五十點半的空格裡人名是艾芙琳，可見這是收到艾芙琳同
意更改時間的郵件後，做過修正的時間表，所以正確答案是 (C)。

14. 海倫·湯瑪斯運動的時間只有星期一，所以 (B) 是錯的。除了午餐時間之外，
幾乎所有時間都有預約，可見沒有客戶不足的問題，選項 (A) 也可以刪除。選
項 (D) 則未在本文出現，所以正確答案是 (C)，每天開始工作的時間是上午九
點。

15. 有關艾芙琳工作的訊息，是在第二封電子郵件最後，艾芙琳希望海倫能看一下
她作品集的照片，以作為藝廊開幕之用。從此可知艾芙琳是攝影師，正確答案
是 (C)。選項 (B) 的藝廊是複數，動詞是原形動詞，表習慣或常做的事，所以
整句話的意思是她開很多家藝廊，因此 (B) 不能選。

Questions 1-2 refer to the following notice.

Keller Community Center Welcomes Dona Pitts

We are excited to announce that Dona Pitts will be running a dog-training workshop at the Keller Community Center on the weekend of July 22nd to July 23rd. Ms. Pitts is a popular animal trainer who has recently made appearances on various TV talk shows such as *Your Sunny Morning* and *Nightly Report.* Those who plan to attend are asked to bring a dog leash and keep their dogs restrained at all times.

During her long career as a professional trainer, Ms. Pitts has worked with many celebrities such as singer Gina Winston and actor Jason Quinn to teach them about animal behavior and obedience training. You can view instructional videos and read more about Ms. Pitts' training methods by visiting her website, www.donapitts.com.

Available spots are expected to fill up fast, so interested individuals should call the community center early to register their dogs for this great opportunity.

1. What type of event is being advertised?
   (A) A dog show awards ceremony
   (B) A pet shop opening
   (C) A television show premiere
   (D) An animal-training class

2. What are attendees asked to do?
   (A) Arrive before the official start time
   (B) Provide personal information
   (C) Control their pets
   (D) Contact the community center

Questions 3-4 refer to the following message chain.

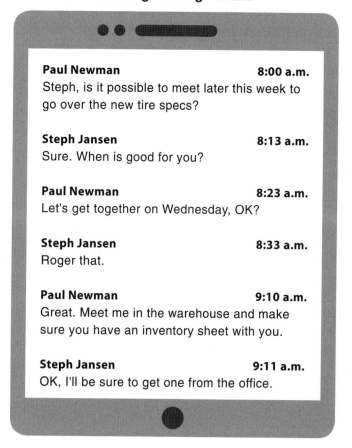

Paul Newman   8:00 a.m.
Steph, is it possible to meet later this week to go over the new tire specs?

Steph Jansen   8:13 a.m.
Sure. When is good for you?

Paul Newman   8:23 a.m.
Let's get together on Wednesday, OK?

Steph Jansen   8:33 a.m.
Roger that.

Paul Newman   9:10 a.m.
Great. Meet me in the warehouse and make sure you have an inventory sheet with you.

Steph Jansen   9:11 a.m.
OK, I'll be sure to get one from the office.

3. For what type of company does Steph Jansen most likely work?
   (A) Financial
   (B) Construction
   (C) Automotive
   (D) Programming

4. At 8:33 a.m., what does Steph Jansen mean when she writes "Roger that"?
   (A) She thinks Roger should do it.
   (B) She understood Paul's message.
   (C) She will be there on Wednesday.
   (D) Roger already did it.

Questions 5-7 refer to the following email.

To: Product Development Staff
From: David Swanson
Date: August 28
Subject: Customer Feedback

As you may know, our newest toys were put to the test by JD Consulting Group. Vesta's popular toy models continue to sell steadily well, but we haven't experienced any increase in sales in over six years. All of our newest toys have launched to disappointing sales. In order to assess what it is that customers are looking for, we contacted JD Consulting Group to help us determine what types of toys consumers are gravitating towards and what they dislike about our new toys.

I'm happy to note that the newest prototypes for children five years old and under look to be promising. The multi-learning and educational-type toys seem to be popular with consumers, and if these trends continue I'd like to have the prototypes developed so that we can begin producing them and introduce them in time for the holiday toy rush. Hopefully, they will develop into the hottest must-haves for the holidays.

I appreciate your hard work and hope you will continue to bring innovative products to our lineup.

Sincerely,

David Swanson
Senior Director

5. What is the purpose of the email?
   (A) To ask for survey participants
   (B) To arrange a meeting
   (C) To provide information about a new development
   (D) To encourage employees to work harder

6. In line six of the second paragraph of the email, "must-haves" is closest in meaning to
   (A) Essential products
   (B) Trendsetters
   (C) Should buy
   (D) Creative

7. What is implied about Vesta Toys?
   (A) Its sales have been steadily increasing for the last few years.
   (B) Its sales have been steadily decreasing for the last few years.
   (C) A new toy it has in development looks promising.
   (D) It specializes in electronic toys.

Questions 8-11 refer to the following online chat.

Leslie Appleton   **8:09 p.m.**
OK, everybody, what are the terms of our deal?

Josie Kim   **8:17 p.m.**
The people from the wholesale company said we could have everything in the warehouse for 20 percent. That includes all of the golfing equipment.

Robert Jackson   **8:21 p.m.**
Twenty percent? That is a really strong offer. Can we handle all of that inventory?

Josie Kim   **8:22 p.m.**
Definitely. Our warehouse is not that big, but I believe that most of their stock can be sold during our Spring Fitness Blastoff on the 13th.

Robert Jackson   **8:25 p.m.**
Perfect. I'll contact the moving company and set up some trucks to meet us at their warehouse, then.

Josie Kim   **8:35 p.m.**
Awesome! I'll get started on adding their products to our sales advertisements.

Leslie Appleton   **8:45 p.m.**
This sounds amazing, you guys. I know it's only my first week at the helm, but everything is running like a dream.

8. Where do the people most likely work?
   (A) A bank
   (B) A video game company
   (C) A sporting goods company
   (D) A catering service

9. At 8:45 p.m., what does Leslie Appleton mean when she writes "everything is running like a dream"?
   (A) She thinks things are going well.
   (B) She doesn't believe this is real.
   (C) She wants things to run better.
   (D) She has a problem waking up.

10. What job does Leslie Appleton most likely have?
    (A) Shipping secretary
    (B) Manager
    (C) Warehouse staff
    (D) Truck driver

11. What will Robert Jackson most likely do next?
    (A) Arrange for a pickup
    (B) Go get coffee
    (C) Create promotional materials
    (D) Contact Leslie for directions

Questions 12-14 refer to the following article.

Lawson Coffee, a popular coffee shop that was founded in Denver seven years ago, is planning to open a new store in the neighboring town of Aurora next year. This was announced yesterday during the opening event of a new store in Lakewood. James Heller, marketing and public relations manager of Lawson Coffee, commented, "We're really excited to open new locations in the main cities of Colorado, and to make long-lasting connections with these communities."

Lawson Coffee was started by Linda Lawson, then a university student, with a specific mission: to provide excellent coffee at affordable prices in a cozy and relaxed atmosphere. Ms. Lawson's coffee shop gradually became known by word of mouth within the community, and it became a popular meeting place for groups of local residents and office workers. Last year it received the Best Coffee Shop Award from the National Coffee Board, and its popularity and reputation have been skyrocketing ever since.

Lawson Coffee is currently searching for a suitable location to open its new store in Aurora. Ms. Lawson emphasizes that the new location must have enough space for comfortable tables and chairs, and face south to let in bright sunlight. She also says there must be a spacious parking lot.

Those with serving or cooking experience are encouraged to apply for possible positions at the new location in Aurora. They can reach Eva Wright, customer service manager, directly at 720-555-2349. More information about Lawson Coffee can be found at www.lawsoncoffee.com.

12. What is the purpose of the article?
   (A) To announce the recipient of an award
   (B) To report on a business expansion
   (C) To advertise a new product
   (D) To explain a revised policy

13. What is NOT mentioned as a requirement for the Aurora location?
   (A) Sufficient room for seating
   (B) A heating and cooling system
   (C) A large parking space
   (D) Abundant natural lighting

14. According to the article, who is encouraged to contact Ms. Wright?
   (A) Restaurant equipment suppliers
   (B) Interested investors
   (C) Food journalists
   (D) Potential employees

Questions 15-17 refer to the following news item.

Prescott Daily News

(November 2) After seven months of construction, the Prescott Convention Center will open its doors to the public tomorrow. The convention center will provide services to the greater Prescott area, and in addition to offering state-of-the-art facilities, it will be able to host events for up to 10,000 people. —[1]—

The Maxin Corporation has spent north of 10 million dollars on the planning and development of the convention center. —[2]— Although this is a substantial amount of money, the city of Prescott had to match this amount in order to get the project completed. The Prescott Convention Center is hoping to recoup the cost of construction through a series of conferences already scheduled for the coming year. —[3]—

The opening ceremony will begin at noon and the mayor of Presoctt will be present for the ribbon-cutting. —[4]— All members of the community are welcome to attend; complimentary food will be provided by the permanent vendors who have rented space at the center.

15. What is the article about?
(A) A new construction project set to begin
(B) The opening of a new business facility
(C) The work being done in the Prescott area
(D) Maxin Corporation's investment

16. What will the mayor of Prescott do?
(A) Introduce Maxin Corporation's president
(B) Provide complimentary food
(C) Formally announce the convention center's opening
(D) Hold a conference

17. In which of the positions marked [1],[2],[3], and [4] does the following sentence belong?

This will mark the fourth time a new facility has been opened by her this year.
(A) [1]
(B) [2]
(C) [3]
(D) [4]

PART
7
Actual Test

Horton University

January 20

Linda Gott

2789 Roosevelt Road
Minneapolis, MN 52985

Dear Ms. Gott,

I am so glad you have agreed to be a speaker at this year's Kansas Business Conference in Wichita, Kansas. I think it will be a great opportunity to bring together investment bankers, tax analysts, financial auditors, and other specialists in one place to meet and learn from each other.

The conference begins on Monday, February 13th. Please arrive at the conference center no later than 10 a.m. and visit the conference information desk, where we will issue you a name tag, conference schedule, and your hotel key. Because you will be speaking on the first day of the conference, you might want to arrive a little early to prepare. Also, please keep in mind that all guests must check out before 3 p.m. on Friday, February 17th.

The Wichita Conference Center is just a 10-minute drive from the airport. If you take a taxi from the airport, you should not have any trouble getting here.

I enjoyed your speech at a recent conference in Colorado, and am really looking forward to hearing you speak again in Wichita. If you have some free time after your speech, we could meet for lunch and enjoy each other's company. Let me know your schedule.

Sincerely,

Michael Trenton

Chief Organizer, Kansas Business Conference

18. What is NOT mentioned in the letter?
    (A) The event location
    (B) Registration procedures
    (C) Travel costs
    (D) Networking opportunities

19. How does Mr. Trenton know Ms. Gott?
    (A) He was introduced through a mutual friend.
    (B) He saw her at a previous event.
    (C) He read her recent book.
    (D) He went to the same university as her.

Questions 20-22 refer to the following flyer.

International Student Orientation

Trenton University is pleased to welcome
new international students for the upcoming academic year.
Trenton University Student Union
September 3, 9:00 a.m.–1:00 p.m.

Orientation Schedule	
9:00 a.m.	Class Registration: How to decide what courses to take (Room 108)
10:00 a.m.	Academic Success: Tips for studying and receiving help on campus (Room 202)
11:00 a.m.	Immigration: Understanding visa rules (Room 114) / Life in the U.S.: How to adapt to a new culture (Room 111)
12:00 noon	Residence Hall Life: Regulations regarding residential life (Room 120)

Please note that all international students are required to attend the orientation. At the beginning of the first orientation session, student identification cards as well as course catalogs will be distributed. If you cannot attend, please contact Drew Nelson at 432-555-8924 in advance.

Do not hesitate to ask our staff questions at this time. This orientation is an opportunity for international students to feel more comfortable and welcome at our university.

Once the orientation is done, international students are encouraged to join our administrators for a free lunch at the cafeteria. Attendees will be given meal vouchers that can be redeemed at the cafeteria only on September 3rd.

Once again, we thank you for choosing Trenton University.

20. For whom is the flyer most likely intended?
    (A) Visiting professors
    (B) European immigrants
    (C) Students coming from abroad
    (D) The faculty of Trenton University

21. What is indicated about the event?
    (A) Attendance is mandatory.
    (B) Seating will be assigned.
    (C) Tickets should be purchased in advance.
    (D) Identification is necessary for entry.

22. According to the flyer, what can attendees do immediately after the event?
    (A) Register for classes
    (B) Ask the staff questions
    (C) Meet some professors
    (D) Have a complimentary meal

The Georgetown Museum Council is excited to announce that the groundbreaking ceremony for the city's new science museum will be held at 11 a.m. on Saturday, March 21st. The museum will be built on the west side of Georgetown, next to the George Young Memorial Park. It will be a total of five stories tall, making it the third-tallest building in Georgetown. Additionally, an entire floor of the museum will be used for educational purposes. The museum council wants to inspire children to develop an interest in science.

The Georgetown Science Museum is being built thanks to the support of many individual donors. In particular, the single largest donation of two million dollars comes from well-known local philanthropist Brandon Bolt. Mr. Bolt is a renowned scientist who taught genetics for over 20 years at Henson University and founded a multinational agricultural corporation, Bolt Food Company, Inc. "I always think about how I can help my hometown," he said in several interviews. In honor of his generous donation, the natural history section of the museum will be named the Brandon Bolt Natural History Exhibit Hall.

The groundbreaking ceremony will be open to the public. Georgetown mayor Greg Wright and 23 donors, including Mr. Bolt, will be in attendance at the event. More detailed information and images of the museum and the event will be released next Monday on the official website at www. georgetownsciencemuseum.org.

23. What is the article mainly about?
   (A) The results of scientific research
   (B) The opening of a new government office
   (C) The beginning of a construction project
   (D) The schedule of a science fair

24. What is implied about the Georgetown Science Museum?
   (A) It will be the tallest building in the area.
   (B) It will be completed next week.
   (C) It belongs to Brandon Bolt.
   (D) It was funded by private donations.

25. According to the article, how can people learn more about the science museum project?
   (A) By going to a construction site
   (B) By reading the local newspaper
   (C) By visiting a website
   (D) By contacting Mayor Wright

Questions 26-29 refer to the following email.

From: Debra Stills <dstills@comclast.com>
To: Henry Ward <hward@kansasbuilders.com>
Date: December 18
Subject: Satisfied
Attachment: kitchen.jpg

Dear Mr. Ward,

I'm Debra Stills, and I live in Hendersonville. I'm emailing to express my gratitude and satisfaction with the work your firm, Kansas Builders, has done at our home. We hired you to redesign and modernize our guest bathroom, and we couldn't be happier with the results. Not only did it turn out exactly the way my husband and I wanted, but we were also able to stay within our budget.

We have some relatives coming for the holidays, and they will be staying in the guest room. We are so grateful that you were able to finish the job before they arrived. I was thoroughly impressed by your team's professionalism.

As I told you before, the new house we just moved into still needs a lot of renovations. Because we are so satisfied with your work, we plan to ask for your help with future projects. First, please send me an estimate for renovating our kitchen. I have attached a picture of it for your reference.

Thanks again and happy holidays.

Sincerely,

Debra Stills

---

26. What is Kansas Builders?
    (A) An accounting firm
    (B) A remodeling company
    (C) A fitness club
    (D) A real estate agency

27. Why did Ms. Stills want the work done quickly?
    (A) She is moving out.
    (B) She is hosting a party.
    (C) She is renting out her guest room.
    (D) Her family is visiting.

28. The word "thoroughly" in paragraph two, line two, is closest in meaning to
    (A) Meticulously
    (B) Gradually
    (C) Generally
    (D) Completely

29. What does Ms. Stills imply in the email?
    (A) She will use Kansas Builders' services again.
    (B) She is in the process of finalizing a budget.
    (C) She hopes that Mr. Ward will visit during the holidays.
    (D) She will send her payment within the next few days.

The Shoe Closet

The Shoe Closet's annual clearance sale is on from February 6th–8th. Grab any of these items at 75 percent off the retail price before they sell out. Hurry while supplies last!

Women's Georgia Ankle Boots—Made from real leather. Available in smooth black leather, black suede, brown leather, grey leather, and red patent leather. Heel height is nine cm. Built for comfort and style, whether at the office or out on the town. Item Number: GB387. Price: $85.

Women's Kensington Knee-Length Boots—Available in smooth black leather, black suede, and navy blue suede. Side zipper detail with 10-cm heel height. These sleek boots are must-haves to complete an outfit with a bold statement. Item Number: KB472. Price: $129.

Men's Bedford Loafer—Available in black or brown leather. Lined with wool for warmth during the winter months. Dress up any casual outfit, whether at the office or out on the town. This classic style will become a staple of your wardrobe for years to come. Item Number: BL327. Price: $99.

Men's Bradley Work Boots—Made from durable cowhide. Only available in tan color. Features waterproof rubber soles and grooves that make them ideal boots for snowy and icy winter conditions. Lined with wool for warmth, this boots are perfect for winter. Item Number: WB382. Price: $125.

Prices do not include tax. Tax will be calculated at checkout.

Shipping Information: Items will have a flat shipping rate of $7 dollars for purchases up to $100. Items over $100 will be shipped for free. Domestic shipping only. Shipments will take three to five business days.

The Shoe Closet

Https://www.theshoecloset.com

Name: Jonathan Brown

Address: 3827 Orion Avenue

City: Seattle

State: Washington

Phone Number: 101-555-1234

Email: jbrown@email.com

Item Number: BL327   Size: 11

Color: Black   Quantity: 1

If you have finished entering items to purchase, please click "Submit" to calculate the total, including taxes and shipping costs.

30. What is indicated about the Shoe Closet?
   (A) Its products are geared towards office workers.
   (B) It has a clearance sale every year.
   (C) It sells only women's shoes.
   (D) It specializes in boots.

31. What information is NOT given in the advertisement?
   (A) The colors of the items
   (B) The materials the products are made of
   (C) The sizes the items come in
   (D) The names of the products

32. What types of items are mainly advertised for the clearance sale?
   (A) Winter footwear
   (B) Women's shoes
   (C) Men's shoes
   (D) Work shoes

33. What is Mr. Brown buying from The Shoe Closet?
   (A) Ankle boots
   (B) Knee-length boots
   (C) Loafers
   (D) Work boots

34. How much will Mr. Brown probably have to pay in shipping costs?
   (A) $0   (B)$7
   (C) $99   (D)$125

Welcome to the Newsline Weekly Magazine Website

The Newsline Weekly Magazine offers advertising for local businesses and pages dedicated to community announcements.

Our prices include one-week publications, one-month publications, and one-year publications for both our print and online magazines. Options also include full double layout ads, full-page ads, and small 50-word-limit ads. Check out the prices below.

Double layout: $600 for one-week publications, $650 for one-month publications, and $800 for one-year publications.

Full-page layout: $400 for one-week, $450 for one-month, and $600 for one-year.

Small layout: $100 for one week, $150 for one month, $300 for one year.

To send us your information, please complete the form below here and include any picture attachments.

Ordered by: | Dream Travel

Advertisement layout: | full-page layout, one-month

Date of submission: | July 1

Date of publication: | July 8

Text:

Full package deal to Hawaii for just $500. Price includes five days' and four nights' stay at a four-star hotel (complimentary breakfast included), round-trip flight with Bell Airlines, and tours to Waikiki Museum, scuba diving, cultural exhibitions, and magic show. This promotion is only for the month of August. Book your trip today!

Photo attachment: | Hawaiipic

Options: | Full-color picture

35. What is being advertised?
    (A) A free trip to Hawaii
    (B) Advertising pages
    (C) Email notifications
    (D) Subscriptions to a magazine

36. What is suggested about Newsline Weekly Magazine?
    (A) It is a local magazine.
    (B) It publishes every month.
    (C) New subscribers are given discounts.
    (D) It is a business magazine.

37. How much did Newsline Weekly Magazine probably charge Dream Travel?
    (A) $650
    (B) $400
    (C) $450
    (D) $150

38. What does Dream Travel want to advertise?
    (A) Cheap flights
    (B) Hotel promotions
    (C) Four-star restaurants
    (D) Travel packages

39. What is indicated in Dream Travel's advertisement?
    (A) Hawaii is a good place for honeymoons.
    (B) The promotion lasts for only one month.
    (C) The flights include business class seats.
    (D) All meals are included in the package.

Questions 40-44 refer to the following web page and form.

Mount Valley International Airport

The Mount Valley International Airport lost and found office is located on the second floor in Terminal A. An elevator next to the information desk in Terminal A will take you directly to the office. All unclaimed items found around the airport, waiting areas, parking lots, curbside areas, and any shops and restaurants inside the airport are stored at the office for 90 days. If an item remains unclaimed after this 90-day period, it will be put up for auction at the end of the year. Items found inside airplanes are kept by the respective airlines, so passengers are asked to contact the airlines directly.

To request help in locating a missing item, please click on the LOST & FOUND tab on this page. Fill out the application form in as much detail as possible. Be sure to include your contact information and a detailed description of the missing item. Once the item is located, a representative will contact you. Valuable items must be claimed in person, and a signature will be required for the release of the item. Other items can be shipped to your residence for a small shipping fee, but they must also be signed for.

Mount Valley International Airport
Lost Property Report

Today's date:	June 20
Date the item was lost:	June 19
Name:	Claudia Lee
Address:	482 Milton Street, Mount Valley, IL
Home phone:	101-555-2837
Work phone:	
Email:	lee837@email.com
Preferred method of contact:	home phone
Preferred time of contact:	anytime

Description of missing item and where it was left:

Duty-free shopping bag from Totorro Airport with a brand-new Puccia handbag inside it. The bag is black leather with gold details on it. It is a shoulder bag. I was waiting for my husband at gate 8D. I accidentally left it on one of the benches near gate 8D when I went to help my husband with his luggage and bags. It was a gift my husband had brought back for me from his business trip.

---

40. According to the web page, what is there a charge for?
(A) Calling an airline
(B) Requesting a lost item search
(C) Storage of a lost item
(D) Shipping a lost item

41. What is true about Claudia Lee?
(A) She came back from a business trip.
(B) She bought herself a handbag.
(C) She picked her husband up at the airport.
(D) She works at the airport.

42. What is indicated about the missing item?
(A) It was given as a gift.
(B) It is an old item.
(C) It is a piece of luggage.
(D) It was left on an airplane.

43. Based on the web page information, what is missing from Ms. Lee's form?
(A) An address
(B) A flight number
(C) A work phone number
(D) A date

44. Why will Ms. Lee have to provide a signature?
(A) To confirm that she has received the item
(B) To confirm that her identity is correct
(C) To confirm a flight
(D) For the airline's records

Young Artist Realizes Dream

A prodigy at the tender age of 18, Martin Sanders is already selling his paintings for $10,000 and more. Sanders has been featured in *Art Life* Magazine and even made an appearance on the Oprah Winters show.

His longtime art teacher Valentine Summers explains, "He has a very special talent that very few people are blessed with. From the age of 10 he was creating masterpieces. I'm very proud of him."

His parents knew that he had talent, but as Mr. Sanders says, "I never in a million years would have thought that Oprah, of all people, would pay for his paintings. We've even had CEOs calling about his paintings."

Martin Sanders' paintings are in such high demand now that he will only sell from his new workshop at the Galleria Plaza. His paintings are also a popular attraction at the Balmont Art Museum, where his pieces are on display for this month only. Visitors will have a chance to see the vibrant colors and dreamlike quality of his work. Those who wish to purchase a piece must contact Martin Sanders for a private viewing at his workshop. Only serious inquiries will be considered.

From:	Bill Grant
To:	Martin Sanders
Date:	September 3
Subject:	An Inquiry

Dear Mr. Sanders,

I am Bill Grant, the owner and general manager of the Stevenson Hotel in downtown Parkview. I am looking to purchase one of your pieces for my office at the hotel. I first saw a painting of yours on the wall of a colleague of mine and was instantly impressed. I also visited the Balmont Art Museum last week and was further impressed by your exhibit there. I especially enjoyed your landscapes. Is it possible for me to tour your workshop and select a painting that you have for sale? My work hours at the hotel are very flexible, unless I have a sudden meeting to attend, so I can meet you at your convenience. I hope that you will consider my request. I look forward to hearing back from you.

Sincerely,

Bill Grant

45. What is the article about?
   (A) An art museum
   (B) A young businessperson
   (C) A beautiful painting
   (D) An art teacher

46. In paragraph one, line three of the article, the phrase "made an appearance" is closest in meaning to
   (A) Selected   (B) Gained fame
   (C) Painted   (D) Showed up

47. According to the article, what is true about Galleria Plaza?
   (A) It is the location of Martin's workshop.
   (B) It has Martin's artwork on display this month.
   (C) It is a famous museum.
   (D) It is where Martin took painting lessons.

48. Why was the email sent?
   (A) To make a request
   (B) To give advice
   (C) To offer congratulations
   (D) To confirm a meeting

49. Where did Mr. Grant first see Martin's artwork?
   (A) At the museum
   (B) On the Oprah Winters show
   (C) At a colleague's place
   (D) In a magazine

Questions 50-54 refer to the following article, web page, and certificate.

October 8 – The Organofoods Supermarket Company has launched an online shop where consumers can purchase products from the comfort of their homes without having to go out into their neighborhoods to shop. Organofoods supermarkets are known for selling fair trade products, organic foods, vegan and vegetarian foods, and for donating two percent of their profits to charities. Because Organofoods is one of the few corporations that considers social responsibility a high priority, the company has been growing in popularity, especially among millennials and Gen-Xers.

The new online shop offers all kinds of products that can be found in Organofoods stores, but fresh produce, meats, and dairy products can only be delivered in areas where distribution centers are near by. The company wants to wait and see how the online market responds before expanding. So far the response has been positive and a larger consumer base continues to be exposed to Organofoods, which so far has only 128 stores around the country. For more information, visit the company's website at www.organofoods.com.

Organofoods Supermarket began as a small gathering of eight farmers who decided to start a farmers' market in the small town of Bingsley, Washington. Only local produce and handcrafted items and products were allowed. It soon grew into a successful year-round market. The farmers then decided to set up a cooperative (or co-op) where private farmers could sell their goods to a larger market, and the Organofoods Supermarket was born. To this day, original farmer's market at Bingsley continues to draw large crowds, and the farmers all agree that corporate interests and greed have no place in their co-op. Organofoods Supermarket prides itself on the fact that 100 percent of the products it sells are organic, environmentally safe, and fair.

The Organization for the Integrity of Corporations
Is pleased to present this certificate of recognition to
Organofoods Supermarket.

This award recognizes not only the wonderful achievements of Organofoods Supermarket, but also the integrity it continues to espouse in the corporate world. We are pleased to see that your company gives back to society and encourages the ethical treatment of workers and farmers. Most importantly, this award honors your work in spreading awareness of the importance of social responsibility.

Kevin Lamonte
President

50. What is indicated about Organofoods Supermarket?
    (A) It just opened a new franchise in another country.
    (B) It gives part of its earnings to charity.
    (C) It only sells vegan and vegetarian food.
    (D) It is a very old company.

51. What is NOT true about Organofoods Supermarket?
    (A) It is popular among younger adults.
    (B) It is a growing company.
    (C) Its products are very cheap.
    (D) It places importance on social responsibility.

52. On the webpage, the word "draw" is closest in meaning to
    (A) Attract
    (B) Paint
    (C) Imagine
    (D) Examine

53. What is true about the Bingsley farmers' market?
    (A) It no longer exists.
    (B) It sells a variety of imported products.
    (C) It only sells produce.
    (D) It became the Organofoods Supermarket.

54. Who is Kevin Lamonte?
    (A) The president of Organofoods Supermarket
    (B) President of the OIC
    (C) A member of the Farmers' Association
    (D) A customer

New York (February 9) – K-Beauty has swept the beauty industry in recent months, bringing with it a growing demand for South Korean beauty products here in the United States. This is why the leading South Korean makeup brand, Arumdaeun, has announced that it will open its first American store and supply center right here in New York City. A few Arumdaeun products are being sold at the makeup counters in some department stores here, but a full shop dedicated to the brand is set to open in the summer. Already, the products that are currently being sold are ranked among the top sellers at Norman Markus, Harrin's, and Sikes Avenue Department Stores. The general manager of Norman Markus says, "The demand for Korean makeup and skincare products is overwhelming our supply. We are happy to hear that Arumdaeun will open a center in New York. This will definitely make customers happy.

Positions Available at Arumdaeun's New York Branch

Over 100 positions are available immediately at Arumdaeun including warehouse jobs, administrative and management positions, customer service, sales, and beauty consulting. Experience is preferred but not necessary for all positions except management. Candidates for management positions should have at least two years' experience in a related field and two reference letters. For customer service jobs, fluency in English and an additional language—especially French, Spanish, Chinese or Korean—is desirable. Interested candidates should send their completed application forms and résumés to www.arumdaeunbeauty.com. Group interviews will take place at the Horton Hotel in conference rooms B and C on March 15th. Second interviews for selected applicants will take place at a later date.

From:	Judy Hamilton
To:	Linda Marks
Date:	April 3
Subject:	Special Thanks

Dear Linda,

I really appreciate the reference letter you gave me for my application to Arumdaeun. I am very happy to announce that I passed both interviews and have been accepted for the position I applied for. I certainly could not have done it without your help. I've learned so much working here at Esteemed Beauty. I can't believe that it's already been five years since I started working here. How time flies! Although I am excited to start a new chapter of my life, I will also greatly miss everyone here.

I begin work next week, which is sooner than I had anticipated. I know that my leave begins in two weeks. I'll try to continue working here until my official leave starts, but I am needed for the orientation next Monday. I've asked Samantha to cover my shift. I hope this is not a problem.

As always, thank you for your understanding.

Sincerely,

Judy

55. What does the article mention about Arumdaeun?
    (A) It is a New York company.
    (B) Some of its products are already available in the US.
    (C) It is South Korea's first beauty company.
    (D) It is the leading beauty company in America.

56. According to the article, what does Arumdaeun plan to do?
    (A) Open an official shop in New York
    (B) Manufacture its goods in America
    (C) Export more products from South Korea
    (D) Expand to other countries

57. Which of the following is NOT an entry-level position and requires previous experience?
    (A) Administrative
    (B) Customer service
    (C) Management
    (D) Beauty consulting

58. In paragraph one, line five of the email, "How time flies!" is closest in meaning to
    (A) A bird flew by.
    (B) The years passed by slowly.
    (C) Judy feels old.
    (D) Time passes very quickly.

59. For what job was Ms. Hamilton most likely hired?
    (A) Administrative
    (B) Customer service
    (C) Management
    (D) Sales

Brick House Restaurant

Enjoy any of the following lunch and dinner sets this week. Choose from the menu below and enjoy a variety of our house specials at a discounted price.

Set A Lunch	Enjoy a large tomato pasta, roast chicken, tossed garden salad, and vanilla ice cream. Price $12.99 per person.
Set B Lunch	Comes with our special cream of mushroom soup, grilled prawns, pasta salad, tossed salad, and fresh fruit tarte. Price $19.99 per person.
Set C Dinner	Starts with our popular clam chowder, garlic bread sticks, our special six-cheese lasagna, and tossed garden salad, and ends with our signature chocolate cake. Price $29.99 per person.
Set D Dinner	Enjoy our best-selling Caesar salad, homemade tomato soup, our special fire-grilled cheeseburgers with large potato wedges on the side, and some grilled vegetables, and end your dinner with our lemon tarte. Price $36.99 per person.

*Note that set menus are only available for groups of two or more people.

From:	Brick House Restaurant
To:	Rodney Smith
Date:	September 28
Subject:	Re: Business Dinner

Dear Mr. Smith,

Thank you for your inquiry. We do have private rooms for business meetings. They seat up to 12 people, which should be more than enough for your party of eight. We have set menus for larger groups, which can be more cost-effective than ordering dishes separately. You mentioned that you have seafood allergies. I hope that the second dinner set menu we have is to your liking, as it includes no seafood.

As for your other question, unfortunately we don't have set menus before lunch, but I have attached information on a number of our house specials and best-selling dishes along with their prices for your further reference and future business meetings here.

Thank you and we look forward to hearing from you again.

Sincerely,

Cindy Lowland

Here is a sneak peek at some of Brick House Restaurant's upcoming house specials and customer favorites.

Seasonal Classic: Grilled Lobster Omelette*	$29.99
Brick House Best-Selling Breakfast: Stacked Blueberry Pancakes with Bacon and Eggs	$27.99
Chef's Special: Bacon, Eggs, and French Toast	$19.99
A Customer Favorite: Waffles with Whipped Cream	$12.99

*The lobster omelette will be available starting in October.

60. Which set menu will Mr. Smith most likely choose for his meeting?
   (A) Set A Lunch
   (B) Set B Lunch
   (C) Set C Dinner
   (D) Set D Dinner

61. What is implied about Mr. Smith?
   (A) He has food allergies.
   (B) He is a strict vegetarian.
   (C) He is the CEO of his company.
   (D) He has been to Brick House Restaurant before.

62. How many people will be attending the meeting?
   (A) Two
   (B) Four
   (C) Eight
   (D) Twelve

63. What is most likely true about the meeting?
   (A) It will take place in the morning.
   (B) It will take place at noon.
   (C) It will take place in the evening.
   (D) It will get cancelled.

64. In the attached memo, the term "sneak peek" is closest in meaning to
   (A) Secret menu
   (B) A brief showing
   (C) A picture
   (D) A sample taste

PART

7

Actual Test

Chapter 01 p. 022

名詞

1. D 2. C 3. C 4. A 5. C

1.

翻譯 蒙特婁鋼鐵公司在安全和環境標準上得到完美分數，讓檢查員印象深刻。

解說 空格位在所有格人稱代名詞 its 之後，可以知道空格應填寫接受 its 修飾的名詞。在名詞 inspection（檢查、檢核）和 inspectors（檢察員、監督官）中，表現出對蒙特婁鋼鐵公司印象深刻的是 inspectors，故正確答案是 (D)。

字彙 impress 使印象深刻；感動
safety 安全
environmental standard 環境標準
inspector 檢查員

2.

翻譯 這篇期刊文章描述了該動物採取了何種策略和適應方法，來充分運用現在的棲地。

解說 空格前是 and，可以知道空格和 and 前的 strategies 是並列的關係。空格後的句子結構是「主詞（the animal）＋動詞（uses）＋（受詞）＋不定詞（to make）」，該子句沒有受詞，由此可知該句是省略了受格關係代名詞的子句。故空格是關係代名詞的先行詞，與 strategies 並列，因此名詞的 (C) 是正確答案。

字彙 journal 期刊 article 文章
outline 概述 strategy 策略
modern 現代的 habitat 棲息地
adaptation 適應

3.

翻譯 一些有錢人資助了維護有歷史意義的哥拉教堂的計畫。

解說 persuasion 是「說服」，expectation 是「期待」，preservation 是「保存、維持」，dismissal 則是「解僱、解散、免除」。根據句意，(C) 是最合適的答案。

字彙 a number of 若干；一些
wealthy 富有的 individual 個人
fund 資助；贊助 dedicated to 奉獻
historic 歷史的 persuasion 說服
expectation 期待 preservation 保存
dismissal 解散；解雇

4.

翻譯 這本目錄顯示居家時光的蕾絲窗簾有各種顏色。

解說 空格位在不定冠詞 a 之後，由此可知空格需放名詞。有鑑於選項皆為名詞，需從單字解釋作為判別的依據。其中 variety（多樣化、變化）能以 a variety of 表「各式各樣的」，所以 (A) 是正確答案。

字彙 catalog 目錄 lace 蕾絲
come in 有（商品以某種形式出現）
a variety of 各種的；各式各樣的
priority 優先 dimension 方面；維度

5.

翻譯 為了回應這款藥物安全性的疑問，藥廠召開緊急記者會。

解說 空格位在介系詞後，由此可知空格須放名詞。有鑑於選項皆為名詞，需從單字解釋作為判別的依據。其中 response（回答、回應）能以 in response to 表「回應」，所以 (C) 是正確答案。

字彙 in response to 因應；回應
drug 藥物　safety 安全
pharmaceutical 藥的；配藥的
hold 舉行　urgent 緊急的
press conference 記者會
departure 離開；出境
exception 除外　conclusion 結論

Mini Test **Chapter 02** p. 032
代名詞

1. A　2. C　3. C　4. B　5. B

1.
翻譯 節儉了好幾年之後，萊利女士終於有能力在熱門郊區買下自己的房子。

解說 空格在 home 之前，用以修飾名詞。選項的人稱代名詞中，唯一能修飾名詞的是所有格代名詞 her，再搭配具強調功能的形容詞 own 形成 her own（她自己的），故 (A) 為正確答案。

字彙 saving 節約　be able to . . . 有能力做
purchase 購買　suburb 郊區

2.
翻譯 客服人員為了福斯女士帳單費用的爭議打電話給她。

解說 空格後是動詞 had disputed，該子句修飾空格前的名詞 charge，由此可知空格前省略了關係代名詞 that。故空格是主詞，(C) 是正確答案。

字彙 regarding 關於　charge 收費
dispute 爭議　bill 帳單

3.
翻譯 葛蘭姆女士手術後，員工買了一張卡片給她打氣。

解說 因為空格位在不定詞 to cheer 之後，所以受格人稱代名詞 her 是正確答案。

字彙 cheer up 鼓舞　surgery 開刀；手術

4.
翻譯 所有職員必須在值班前十分鐘到，確保都穿著正確制服。

解說 因為空格位在名詞 shift（輪班）前修飾它，所以所有格人稱代名詞 their 是正確答案。

字彙 employee 雇員；員工　shift 輪班
make sure 確保

5.
翻譯 經過十多年的努力，葛羅里·史卡特的經理終於提拔他為人力資源部主管。

解說 空格位在動詞 promote 之後，是其受詞，所以受格人稱代名詞 him 是正確答案。倘若選擇 (C) 反身代名詞 himself 的話，就表示經理（manager）晉升了他自己，不符合句意。

字彙 decade 十年　promote 提升；晉升

Mini Test **Chapter 03** p. 039
動詞

1. D　2. C　3. B　4. D　5. B

1.
翻譯 委員會成員必須在 3 月 15 日前敲定季預算。

解說 空格在助動詞 must 之後，所以空格要放原形動詞，又因空格後接可以當作受詞使用的名詞片語 the quarterly budget，故應選主動語態的 finalize 比較適合。

字彙 committee 委員會　quarterly 每季的
budget 預算　finalize 完成；定案

2.
翻譯 布蘭特製造公司宣布回收的產品，適用於今年一月到八月購買的洗碗機。

解說 空格是修飾名詞 dishwashers 的過去分詞。由於選項皆為過去分詞，要透過字義加以判斷。選項意思分別為 (A) 被

議價的 (B) 被執行的 (C) 被購買的 (D) 被承認的。根據句意，答案為 (C)。

字彙 recall 召回 issue 發出
apply to 適用於 dishwasher 洗碗機
bargain 交易；划算 conduct 辦理
purchase 購買 acknowledge 承認

3.

翻譯 工作坊成員被分成小組，並針對被分配的主題討論激盪。

解說 空格位在不定詞的 to 之後，應選原形動詞。有鑑於選項皆為原形動詞，所以要找符合句意的。選項意思分別為 (A) 描述 (B) 刺激 (C) 拒絕 (D) 計算。根據句意，答案為 (B)。

字彙 workshop 工作坊 participant 參加者
divide A into B 將 A 分成 B
assign 指定；分派 discussion 討論
describe 描述 stimulate 刺激
deny 否認 calculate 計算

4.

翻譯 導覽結束時，我們會有一位工匠示範如何將玻璃塑形成珠子、容器和雕塑品。

解說 空格位在助動詞 will 之後，應選原形動詞。有鑑於選項皆為原形動詞，所以要找符合句意的。選項意思分別為 (A) 允許 (B) 說 (C) 提供 (D) 示範。根據句意，答案為 (D)。

字彙 artisan 工匠 bead 珠子
container 容器 sculpture 雕刻；雕像
allow 允許 provide 提供

5.

翻譯 行銷主管試圖說服董事出資升級網站。

解說 空格位在不定詞的 to 之後，應選原形動詞。有鑑於選項皆為原形動詞，所以要找符合句意的。選項意思分別為 (A) 結論 (B) 說服 (C) 等待 (D) 贊同。根據句意，答案為 (B)。

字彙 board 董事會 provide 提供
funding 資金 conclude 下結論
persuade 說服 await 等待
endorse 贊同；背書

1. B 2. B 3. D 4. B 5. D

1.

翻譯 上個月弗瑞德・嘉蘭德一舉當選市議會議員，遞補下台的議員。

解說 句子裡沒有動詞，所以可以知道空格內要填的正是動詞。Last month 是過去的時間，主詞 Fred Garland 被選為市議員，故要用被動語態 was elected，(B) 是正確答案。

字彙 city council 市議會 replace 取代
step down 下台

2.

翻譯 如果你無法親自出席董事會，請指派一位人員代表出席。

解說 空格位在 please 之後，該子句是以 please 起始的命令句，應使用原形動詞，所以 (B) 是正確答案。

字彙 attend 出席；參加 board 董事會
represent 代表 appoint 指定；指派

3.

翻譯 包裝正面使用的照片會吸引各種顧客。

解說 空格位在助動詞 will 之後，應選原形動詞，所以 (D) 是正確答案。

字彙 front 前面；正面 package 包裝
a range of 一系列 appeal 吸引

4.

翻譯 會計職務的應徵者必須證明他們通過了專業考試。

解說 根據句意，考生必須證明他們「已經通過」專業考試，故應選擇現在完成式 have passed，(B) 是正確答案。

字彙 apply for 申請；應徵
accountant 會計師 prove 證明
professional 專業的

5.

翻譯 規定企業提供醫療保險的政策，僅適用於雇用 25 人以上的公司。

解說 空格接受指示代名詞 those 的修飾，後接可當作受詞的名詞片語，所以空格要放動名詞，(D) 是正確答案。

字彙 business 企業；公司
medical insurance 醫療保險
apply to 適用　employ 雇用

Mini Test Chapter 05　p. 059
動狀詞

1. A　2. C　3. D　4. C　5. C

1.

翻譯 倉庫工人被要求在貨物抵達時要通知經理。

解說 空格位在被動型態的 were asked 之後，空格又後接名詞片語 (the manager)。be asked ＋不定詞是固定用法，表「被要求去做」，所以 (A) 是正確答案。

字彙 warehouse 倉庫
shipment 運送的貨物　notify 通知

2.

翻譯 領班杰克・海恩斯將寄送程序化繁為簡進而提升效率，因而受到讚許。

解說 空格位在介系詞 for 之後，所以空格要填名詞／動名詞。又因空格後接名詞片語 (several shipping processes)，故應選動名詞，(C) 是正確答案。

字彙 foreman 工頭；領班　praise 讚美
shipping 運送　process 步驟；程序
improve 改善　efficiency 效率
consolidate 合併；鞏固

3.

翻譯 作家葛羅莉亞・哈金斯的才華受到讚美，她能創造出這種文類最特殊的角色。

解說 空格位在介系詞 in 之後，所以空格要填名詞／動名詞。又因空格後接名詞片語 (the most unique characters)，故應選動名詞，(D) 是正確答案。

字彙 unique 獨特的　character 角色
genre 文類

4.

翻譯 放鬆療法雖然大幅降低了崔佛女士的焦慮，卻無法完全解決問題。

解說 空格在 eliminate the problem 之後作為修飾之用，所以空格應是副詞。選項意思分別為 (A) 外部的 (B) 不像 (C) 完全 (D) 整個的。根據句意，答案為 (C)。

字彙 relaxation therapy 放鬆療法
reduce 減少；降低　anxiety 焦慮
eliminate 消除；消滅

5.

翻譯 克爾女士找專業人士來搬家，含稅共付了 949 元。

解說 空格用以引導名詞片語 (applicable taxes)，故應選現在分詞，(C) 是正確答案。

字彙 belongings 個人物品
professionally 專業地
applicable 適用的　include 包含

Mini Test Chapter 06　p. 079
介系詞

1. A　2. D　3. C　4. A　5. D

1.

翻譯 貴賓受邀坐在演講的前排。

解說 空格位在 sit 之後，空格後接 the front row，表「貴賓受邀坐在前排」，在前排是 in the front row，所以最合適的介系詞是 in。

字彙 guest 客人；賓客　invite 邀請
front 前面　row 排　during 在……期間

2.

翻譯 執行長雖然在入住時對訂房有點困惑，但下榻在哈里森飯店的經驗還是愉悅的。

解說 空格是引導從屬子句的連接詞，從句意推斷，表「儘管、不顧」的 (D) notwithstanding 是正確答案。其他選項分別為 (A) 至於 (B) 反之 (C) 再者。

字彙 confusion 困惑　reservation 預約
stay 暫住；停留　pleasant 愉快的
as for 關於　on the contrary 反之
in addition to 除了
notwithstanding 雖然

3.

翻譯 旅客如果沒有航空公司發的登機證，就無法登機。

解說 空格是引導名詞片語（a boarding pass from the airline）的介系詞，表「沒有登機證，就無法登機」這句意。(C) 是正確答案。

字彙 passenger 乘客　allow 允許
board 上（船、飛機）　aircraft 飛機
boarding pass 登機證
airline 航空公司　against 反對
owing to 由於；因為　without 沒有

4.

翻譯 水從破水管濺到地面上，造成小損害。

解說 空格位在動詞 spilled 之後，後又接名詞片語（the floor），根據句意，正確答案是 (A) onto，表「……上面」。

字彙 broken 破損的　spill 濺出；溢出
minor 次要的；小的　damage 損害
until 直到　aside 到旁邊；在旁邊

5.

翻譯 報到櫃台會提供名牌給科技會議的與會人員。

解說 動詞 provide 可以寫成 provide ＋ A ＋ for ＋ B 或 provide ＋ B ＋ with ＋ A，表「提供 A 給 B」。本句是「提供名牌給與會人員」，所以 (D) for 是正確答案。

字彙 provide 提供　name tag 名牌
participant 參加者　conference 會議

Mini Test　Chapter 07　p. 096
形容詞

1. A　2. D　3. B　4. D　5. A

1.

翻譯 拉古納國家公園的眾多營地，使它成為戶外活動愛好者的熱門景點。

解說 空格修飾複數名詞 campsites，故能修飾複數名詞的 (A) many 是正確答案。

字彙 national park 國家公園　campsite 營地
popular 受歡迎的　destination 目的地
outdoor 戶外的　enthusiast 熱衷者

2.

翻譯 西側入口在施工期間無法通行，顧客必須使用主要出入口。

解說 空格是 be 動詞後的主詞補語，要放名詞或形容詞。從句意推斷，表「無法通行」的 (D) inaccessible 為正確答案。其他選項分別為 (A) 不負責任的 (B) 不合邏輯的 (C) 出乎意料的。

字彙 duration 持續期間　construction 施工
entrance 入口　customer 顧客
irresponsible 不負責任的
illogical 不合邏輯的
unexpected 出乎意料的
inaccessible 得不到的

3.

翻譯 太陽能電廠將供應乾淨的可再生能源給附近上千戶家庭。

解說 空格是修飾名詞（energy）的形容詞，故選項中唯一的形容詞 (B) renewable（可再生的）是正確答案。

字彙 solar power 太陽能　plant 工廠
provide 提供
surrounding 鄰近的；周圍的

4.

翻譯 泰勒百貨公司的商品選擇依分店有所不同。

解說 空格是 be 動詞後的主詞補語，要放名詞或形容詞。選項意思分別為 (A) 全部的 (B) 偶爾的 (C) 連續的 (D) 多變的。根據句意，(D) 是正確答案。

字彙 selection 選擇　merchandise 商品
depend on 依……而定　branch 分店
entire 全部的　occasional 偶爾的
successive 連續的　variable 可變的

5.

翻譯 保險公司不會承保這個區域的房子，因為這些房子易受水患侵擾。

解說 空格是 be 動詞後的主詞補語，要放名詞或形容詞。選項意思分別為 (A) 脆弱的 (B) 可得的 (C) 結構的 (D) 密集的。根據句意，(A) 是正確答案。

字彙 insurance 保險　insure 保險
flood 水災；淹水　damage 損害
vulnerable 易受傷害的；脆弱的
obtainable 可得的
structural 結構的　intensive 密集的

Mini Test　Chapter 08　p. 106
副詞

1. C　2. B　3. B　4. C　5. B

1.

翻譯 為了吸引年輕人，高蛋白飲品的包裝設計大膽。

解說 空格位在 be 動詞 was 和過去分詞 designed 之間，應放修飾動詞的副詞，所以 (C) boldly（大膽地）是正確答案。

字彙 packaging 包裝
protein shake 高蛋白飲品　bold 大膽
in order to 為了　appeal 吸引

2.

翻譯 萬雷柯 360 吸塵器的輕量設計，使它能在各種表面上輕易地滑行。

解說 空格是修飾動詞 glides 的副詞。選項意思分別為 (A) 潛在地 (B) 不費力地 (C) 專心地 (D) 慷慨地。根據句意，(B) 是正確答案。

字彙 due to 由於；因為　lightweight 輕量的
design 設計　vacuum cleaner 吸塵器
glide 滑行　surface 表面
potentially 有潛力地
effortlessly 不費力地
attentively 專心地　generously 慷慨地

3.

翻譯 這些菜餚全部以當地種植的有機材料製作，不含任何加工製品。

解說 空格是修飾動詞 made 的副詞。選項意思分別為 (A) 不情願地 (B) 專門地 (C) 負面地 (D) 輪流地。根據句意，(B) 是正確答案。

字彙 dish 一道菜　locally 當地地
organic 有機的　ingredient 成分
contain 包含
reluctantly 勉強地；不情願地
exclusively 專門地　negatively 負面地
alternatively 輪流地

4.

翻譯 梅納先生貼心地寄謝卡給為專案貢獻心力的志工。

解說 空格位在主詞 Mr. Menard 和動詞 sent 之間，應放副詞。故 (C) 是正確答案。

字彙 thank-you card 感謝卡
volunteer 志工
thoughtfully 貼心地

5.

翻譯 技術人員建議不要只靠基礎防毒軟體來保護電腦網路。

解說 空格是修飾動名詞 relying 的副詞。選項意思分別為 (A) 殘酷地 (B) 僅僅 (C) 基因地 (D) 而且。根據句意，(B) 是正確答案。

字彙 technician 技師；技術人員
advise against 建議不要　rely 依賴
anti-virus 防毒的　harshly 嚴厲地
solely 僅僅；單一　genetically 基因地
besides 此外

Mini Test Chapter 09 p. 113
比較級與最高級

1. B　2. A　3. B　4. B　5. B

1.

翻譯 這些電纜是用全世界最強韌的材質做成。

解說 空格修飾名詞 materials，再加上副詞片語 in the world，推知空格應放最高級。故 (B) strongest 是正確答案。

字彙 cable 電纜；繩索　material 物質；材質

2.

翻譯 網時為線上企業和其他網站提供最創新的設計。

解說 空格位在冠詞 the 之後，又位在名詞 designs 之前，是修飾名詞的形容詞最高級。故 (A) 是正確答案。

字彙 innovative 創新的

3.

翻譯 這項研究的驚人發現顯示，握手會散布細菌，其潛在危險不亞於抽菸。

解說 as . . . as A 是比較級片語，表「像 A 一樣……」，所以要放形容詞。故 (B) dangerous 是正確答案。

字彙 finding 發現　due to 由於
potential 潛在的　spread 擴散；散布
germ 細菌

4.

翻譯 這家公司遭遇的最嚴重問題，是最新手機的電池安全性又出包。

解說 空格位在冠詞 the 之後，又位在名詞 issue 之前，是修飾名詞的形容詞最高級。故 (B) 是正確答案。

字彙 latest 最新的；最晚的　face 面對

5.

翻譯 手機網的新智慧手機系列非常成功，因為其產品比競爭對手的更輕薄。

解說 空格位在表比較級的 than 之前，所以 (B) slimmer 是正確答案。

字彙 range of 系列　competitor 競爭對手

Mini Test Chapter 10 p. 120
假設語氣與被動語態

1. B　2. C　3. A　4. A　5. A

1.

翻譯 汽車業務如果能提出保證，買家就會自在地入手。

解說 空格位在 if the car salesperson should give 這個子句中，該子句省略 if，並將主詞和動詞 (should) 倒裝。空格是 give 的受詞，故名詞 assurance 是正確答案。

字彙 salesperson 售貨員
comfortable 舒適
purchase 購買　assurance 保證

2.

翻譯 哈林頓營造最出名的是，他們能快速提供各種服務的合理估價。

解說 空格位在 be 動詞 is 之後，表「以……聞名」，動詞 know 要用過去分詞，故 (C) 是正確答案。

字彙 fair 合理的　estimate 估價
a range of 一系列

3.

翻譯 消費者調查結果顯示，消費者非常滿意新的產品系列。

解說 空格是 be 動詞 were 的補語，表「感到滿意」，動詞 satisfy（使滿足）要用過去分詞，故 (A) 是正確答案。

字彙 highly 非常

4.

翻譯 為了避免我們的生產設備受損，嚴格的安全方針已經到位。

解說 空格位在 be 動詞的過去分詞 been 之後，為被動語態，故 (A) 是正確答案。

字彙 in order to 為了　avoid 避免
manufacturing 製造
equipment 設備　strict 嚴格的

5.

翻譯 線上行銷團隊成功地讓我們的產品，
接觸到原本不曾聽過我們的消費者。

解說 在假設語氣中，條件子句可以省略先行
詞或連接詞。otherwise（否則）可當作
假設語氣的連接詞來用，表提出一個和
主要子句相反的條件。本句用來表「不
然不會聽過我們的產品」。

字彙 expose 使接觸到
otherwise 不然；否則

Mini Test　Chapter 11　p. 126
連接詞

1. D　2. A　3. D　4. D　5. B

1.

翻譯 吳先生待過好幾個海外分公司，而布
朗寧女士則一直只在總部工作。

解說 空格是連接兩個完整子句的連接詞，揭
示「對照」的兩者，故 (D) 是正確答案。

字彙 overseas 海外　branch 分公司
station 駐紮　exclusively 只限於
headquarters 總公司
regardless of 儘管　aside from 除了
whereas 然而；反之

2.

翻譯 維加斯貨運的送貨員送來一個包裹，
接待員就簽收了。

解說 空格位是連接兩個完整子句的連接
詞。根據文意，(A) 是正確答案。

字彙 courier 送貨員；快遞員
drop off 把……放下　package 包裹
receptionist 接待人員　sign 簽名
whether 不管

3.

翻譯 當雙方在文件上簽名，併購案就將被
視為完成了。

解說 空格是連接兩個完整子句的連接詞，表
「簽名的當下」，所以 (D) 是最合適的。
(B) during 是「在……期間」，與句意
不符。

字彙 merger 合併；併購　consider 視為
document 文件　sign 簽名
party （合約）當事人一方

4.

翻譯 除非經理同意其他付款方案，不然所
有客製的費用都必須預先支付。

解說 空格是連接兩個完整子句的連接詞，表
可能性或條件。根據句意，(D) 是正確
答案。

字彙 charge 費用　customize 客製
in advance 事先；預先　approve 同意
throughout 遍及；從頭到尾
rather 而不是　unless 除非

5.

翻譯 租車時，駕駛要出示有效駕照。

解說 空格是連接兩個完整子句的連接詞，表
「租車的當下」，所以 (B) 是最合適的。

字彙 be required to 被要求　present 出示
valid 有效的　license 執照　rent 租

Mini Test　Chapter 12　p. 130
關係詞

1. D　2. D　3. B　4. D　5. B

1.

翻譯 欲瞭解更多新創公司在稅務機關登
記前的應做事項，請撥打熱線電話。

解說 根據句意，空格應該放 what（什麼）。表
場所的 where 和表特定事物的 which
均不能和 do 搭配使用。how 除了表某
種程度外，還可表方法或方式，所以可
能會誤選到它。但如果將 how 用在這
裡，是主詞「應該要如何做、如何自處」
之意。即使文法沒錯，但在句意上卻完
全說不通。故 (D) 是正確答案。

字彙 hotline 熱線電話　register 登記

2.

翻譯 阿魯加航空公司全體人員將盡力確保飛行的安全與舒適。

解說 包含空格在內為一名詞字句，是以空格的作用在於引導該名詞子句。故最合適的是表「無論什麼事、任何事」的複合關係代名詞 whatever 了。

字彙 ensure 確保；保證

3.

翻譯 全女士留了語音訊息給我，說她開走一部公司車，但沒說是哪一部。

解說 句中的 one 是關鍵，一旦了解立刻就能解題，而 one 是指全女士開走的公司車，所以空格後的 one 可以換寫成 car was taken by her。因為不是在談兩輛汽車中的一輛，所以 (C) 可以不用考慮。(A) 是用來代替人的複合關係代名詞，因此也不對。(B) 是用來修飾 one 的關係形容詞，which one 表「哪一輛」，故 (B) 是正確答案。

字彙 voice mail 語音訊息

4.

翻譯 不分晝夜、不論何時，監看閉路電視的保全都會迅速對可疑活動做出反應。

解說 選項意思分別為 (A) 即使如此 (B) 好像 (C) 彷彿 (D) 無論。根據句意，(D) 是正確答案。

字彙 respond to 做出反應
security staff 保全　suspicious 可疑的

5.

翻譯 有興趣加入公司壘球隊者，請在週五前發電子郵件給朱利安。

解說 從空格到壘球隊 (softball team) 都是主詞，所以空格應放能當作名詞使用的字。根據句意，最適合放進空格的是複合關係代名詞 (B)。若放 (D) 的 someone 或 (C) 的 anyone，會變成一完整句；softball team 就不能當作主詞使用，所以都不能選。

字彙 be interested in 對……有興趣

278

1. A	2. B	3. D	4. D	5. A
6. B	7. B	8. B	9. A	10. D
11. C	12. D	13. C	14. B	15. B
16. B	17. A	18. C	19. B	20. A
21. D	22. C	23. B	24. D	25. D
26. B	27. C	28. A	29. D	30. D

1.

翻譯 國際機場的保全主管行駛他的權限，拒絕讓一位可疑乘客登機。

解說 空格在所有格人稱代名詞 his 之後，所以要放名詞，故選項中唯一的名詞 (A) authority（權限）是正確答案。

字彙 security officer 安全人員
international airport 國際機場
deny 拒絕給予　suspicious 可疑的
passenger 乘客　right 權利
board 上（船、飛機）　authority 權限
authoritative 有權威的

2.

翻譯 人事經理在找能主動開發新客戶的業務拓展老手。

解說 空格是動詞 take 的受詞，所以要放名詞。選項的字彙中，initiative 可以成為片語 take the initiative in，表「主動；帶頭」，故 (B) 是正確答案。

字彙 hiring 徵才的　look for 尋找
experienced 有經驗的
developer 發展者；擴展者
take the initiative in 採取主動
client 客戶　supplement 補充
circumstance 情況；情勢　advice 建議

3.

翻譯 除了能減少居家異味外，這款清潔劑還有許多實用用途。

解說 空格接受形容詞 practical 的修飾，所以要放名詞，且這名詞要能接受 other 修飾，應為複數名詞。(D) 是正確答案。

字彙 aside from 除……以外　reduce 減少
household 家庭的；家用的
odor 臭味　practical 實際的

4.

翻譯 貝里斯燒烤餐廳供應多種牛排、海鮮和麵食。

解說 空格位在冠詞 a 之後，所以要放名詞。選項的單字中，selection 可以成為片語 a selection of，表「各式各樣」。故 (D) 是正確答案。

字彙 provide 提供　a selection of 各式各樣　beneficiary 受益人　preference 偏好　maintenance 維持；保養

5.

翻譯 艾克索通訊將與孟買的電話公司合夥，強化它在印度的能見度。

解說 空格接受所有格人稱代名詞 its 修飾，所以要放名詞。選項意思分別為 (A) 存在 (B) 重複 (C) 禮貌 (D) 描述，根據句意，(A) 是正確答案。

字彙 form 形成；構成　Mumbai 孟買　solidify 鞏固　presence 能見度　repetition 重複　courtesy 禮貌　description 描述

6.

翻譯 可汗飲料公司的全職員工人數，最近因新廠房的開設而增加一倍。

解說 空格是動詞。選項意思分別為 (A) 聚集 (B) 翻倍 (C) 收費 (D) 釋放，根據句意，(B) 是正確答案。

字彙 full-time staff 全職員工　recently 最近　plant 工廠　convene 聚集；集會　double 兩倍　charge 收費　release 釋放；發行

7.

翻譯 尼可遊戲公司的員工始終致力於創造能吸引大眾、獨特而有娛樂性的軟體。

解說 空格是動詞。選項意思分別為 (A) 指派 (B) 努力 (C) 遲疑 (D) 假定，根據句意，(B) 是正確答案。

字彙 employee 雇員　create 創造　unique 獨特的　entertaining 娛樂的　appeal 吸引　public 大眾　designate 指定；指派　strive to 努力　hesitate 猶豫；遲疑　assume 假定

8.

翻譯 為評估年輕人對線上教學的興趣，執行了一項消費者調查。

解說 空格位在不定詞的 to 之後，所以要放原形動詞。選項意思分別為 (A) 說服 (B) 估計 (C) 結合 (D) 執行，根據句意，(B) 是正確答案。

字彙 consumer 消費者　survey 調查　carry out 執行　interest 興趣　persuade 說服　gauge 測量；估計　combine 結合　administer 管理；執行

9.

翻譯 建森顧問公司有些員工住在離辦公室幾里遠的地方。

解說 空格是動詞。選項意思分別為 (A) 居住 (B) 拿 (C) 使用 (D) 擁有，根據句意，(A) 是正確答案。

字彙 within 在……之內

10.

翻譯 這篇報紙報導確認這些指控將在下週接受指定委員會的調查。

解說 空格位在 that 子句中，且是子句的動詞，且空格後沒有可當作受詞的名詞片語，而是直接接介系詞 by，由此可推論為被動語態。透過副詞片語 next week，可以知道為未來式，所以 (D) 是正確答案。

字彙 article 文章　confirm 確認　allegation 指控　appointed 指定的　committee 委員會　investigate 調查

11.

翻譯 安德魯‧格雷是受人景仰的作曲家，寫了許多獲獎的音樂劇作品。

解說 空格位在冠詞 an 和名詞 composer 之間，可以知道是形容詞。選項中只有動詞 admire（尊敬）的過去分詞可當作形容詞使用，表「值得尊敬的」。故 (C) 是正確答案。

字彙 composer 作曲家　a number of 一些　award-winning 獲獎的

12.

翻譯 候選人面試時，必須清楚說明自己的長處與短處。

解說 空格位在連接詞 when 之後，when 引導省略主詞（candidates）的分詞片語。省略主詞後將動詞變成現在分詞。故 (D) 是正確答案。

字彙 candidate 候選人　clearly 清楚地　express 表達　strength 長處；優點　weakness 短處；缺點　attend 參加

13.

翻譯 有兩位需要接受新人培訓才能上工的新員工。

解說 go through 是「經過（一系列的方法、順序等）」，後要接名詞。故 (C) 是正確答案。

字彙 employee 雇員　orient 朝向　orientation （對新進人員的）培訓

14.

翻譯 該國最大的汽車銷售商剛宣布他們將進軍亞洲。

解說 空格是以形容詞最高級修飾的名詞，所以 (B) 和 (D) 可以考慮。因為句後出現了複數人稱代名詞 they，故同為複數的 (B) 經銷商是正確答案。

字彙 distribute 分配；分發

15.

翻譯 如果公司今年夏天要舉辦領袖訓練營，我們都應該要確定地點。

解說 表有計畫的未來時，要用 be going to。故 (B) 是正確答案。

字彙 retreat 靜修

16.

翻譯 我們到目前用過的所有策略都對我方有利。

解說 該句的動詞出現 have employed，為現在完成式；so far 表「到目前為止」，指從過去的某時間點持續至今，所以要用現在完成式。(B) 是正確答案。

17.

翻譯 對於改進我們的廣告，你有沒有任何建議？

解說 介系詞後接名詞，所以 (A) 的動名詞 improving 是最合適的答案。

18.

翻譯 如果公司打算以合理價格購置必要原料，就必須採取更積極的作為。

解說 介系詞後接名詞，所以 (C) 的動名詞 acquiring 是最合適的答案。

字彙 aggressive 積極的　raw material 原料

19.

翻譯 我們的首要之務是服務社區內最需要幫助的人。

解說 不定詞放在補語的位置，當作名詞來使用。所以 (B) 的原形動詞 serve 是正確答案。

字彙 priority 優先

20.

翻譯 市中心的新噴泉是為了吸引城外的人進來商業區。

解說 不定詞放在補語的位置，當作名詞來使用。所以 (A) 的不定詞 to attract 是正確答案。

字彙 fountain 噴泉　downtown 市中心

21.

翻譯 當處理多家公司的理賠申請時，與相關各方的充分溝通是很重要的。

解說 空格用以修飾各方（parties）。根據句意，各方的參與是被動的，用過去分詞來修飾，故 (D) 是正確答案。(A) 和 (C) 皆不能作修飾之用，所以都不能選。

22.

翻譯 收視率的上升讓我們下了這個結論：我們已打動了目標觀眾。

解說 空格修飾名詞收視率（ratings），選項中唯一能修飾名詞的是過去分詞，故 (C) 是正確答案。

23.

翻譯 升級後的網路讓員工能更順利地編輯和傳送文件。

解說 透過 more 可以知道空格要放修飾動詞 edit and transfer 的副詞，選項中唯一的副詞是 easily，故 (B) 是正確答案。

字彙 ease 放鬆　transfer 傳送　edit 編輯

24.

翻譯 如果教授決定做研究，她可能會結束和校方延長的休假。

解說 空格修飾名詞 leave（休假），所以要放具形容詞功能的字彙。因為 leave 不是行為的主體，所以 extend 要用過去分詞的型態。故 (D) 是正確答案。

字彙 wind up 結束　leave 休假

25.

翻譯 傳輸敏感資訊時，應在加密伺服器上進行。

解說 空格位在連接詞 when 之後，when 引導省略主詞（you）的分詞片語。省略主詞後將動詞變成現在分詞。故 (D) 是正確答案。

字彙 encrypt 加密

26.

翻譯 據引述，執行長說 KG 公司不應和 Hub 公司合併，因為大不相同的企業文化整合起來有困難。

解說 空格是 that 子句的動詞，空格後沒有名詞片語，而是直接接介系詞 with，merge with 為固定用法，表「合併」。所以正確答案是 (B)。

字彙 quote 引述　difficulty 困難 integrate 整合　vastly 巨大地 corporate culture 企業文化

27.

翻譯 你在描述新的銷售計畫時，真的說服了我相信它會很有效。

解說 空格是動詞。從屬子句的動詞時態是過去式（were described），所以主要子句的時態也要是過去式。故 (C) 是正確答案。

字彙 describe 描述　sales 銷售 convince A of B 使 A 相信 B effectiveness 有效性

28.

翻譯 政府正在推動一個促進觀光的新計畫。

解說 空格位在 be 動詞 is 之後，且空格後有可當作受詞的名詞片語 a new program。能放在 be 動詞後且可接受詞的，只有現在分詞。故 (A) 是正確答案。

字彙 government 政府　promote 促進 increase 提升；增加　tourism 觀光

29.

翻譯 自從我們在市區開了新分店之後，市占率每年都在成長。

解說 since 表「自從」，從過去某一個時間點開始直到現在，所以要用現在完成式。本句的完成式之後又接現在分詞，形成現在完成進行式。故 (D) 是正確答案。

字彙 market share 市場占有率　since 自從 branch 分店

30.

翻譯 在投遞履歷給潛在雇主前，務必要仔細校對。

解說 before 引導的是省略了主詞（you）的分詞片語，空格不能填動詞，要填現在分詞。故 (D) 是正確答案。

字彙 be sure to 肯定；必定 proofread 校對　résumé 履歷 carefully 小心地　potential 潛在的 employer 雇主

Actual Test p. 172

1. C　2. B　3. A　4. C　5. B　6. C
7. B　8. A　9. A　10. B　11. A　12. B
13. C　14. D　15. A　16. C

參考以下電子郵件回答問題 1–4。

收件人：鮑勃 ・ 強森
　　　　　<bjohnson@happy.net>
寄件人：卡斯柏 ・ 瑞克斯達
　　　　　<kr@human source.net>
日期：11 月 29 日
主旨：退款？

強森先生您好：

我上週在市區克萊蒙大道上的快樂百貨買了幾條褲子。褲子的標籤説腰圍 **38** 吋，褲襠以下的褲管長 **32** 吋。但我哥試穿時，顯然是尺寸是不對的。我的收據還在，可以帶過去換貨或退款嗎？如果您願意寄給我正確尺碼，我可以去店裡歸還它們。請回覆並讓我知道可不可以。我不住在瓦靈福德，必須特別跑一趟，我不想浪費時間白跑。

卡斯柏 ・ 瑞克斯達 敬上

字彙 pant 褲子　receipt 收據
gain weight 增胖；變胖

3.
(A) 如果你願意寄給我正確尺碼，我可以去店裡退還它們。
(B) 我討厭開車，但如果必要我願意再跑一趟。
(C) 我哥哥已經不需要這種褲子。
(D) 我想我哥一定變胖很多。

解説

1. 因為主詞是 they，所以單數的 (A) 和 (B) 可以不考慮。從句意來看，標籤上的尺寸是過去已經標示好的，所以用過去被動式。(C) 是正確答案。

2. 空格是加強語氣的副詞。(A) 和 (D) 皆為形容詞，與文法不符。(C) 是現在分詞，表「褲子正在弄清楚錯誤的尺寸」，完全不通。(B) 是正確答案。

3. 空格和前一句的退換貨有關，由後面的文意可知作法尚未確定，所以 (C) 不對。標籤尺寸的錯誤跟哥哥的體重沒有關係，故 (D) 也不對。(B) 與後續的文意不符。使用假設語氣的 (A) 是正確答案。

4. 要跑一趟的人，就是寫這封信的人，所以正確答案是 (C)。

參考以下通知回答問題 5–8。

湖木社區中心

湖木社區中心正在調查如何改善設施和服務，以嘉惠湖木住戶。社區中心正在規劃完整的重整計畫，計畫大約會耗時兩年。從調查蒐集到的資訊將有助於本計畫。

調查表將在大廳櫃台親取，或上網 www.lakewoodcommunity.com/survey 填寫。

歡迎大眾參與。您的參與可能會直接影響社區要做哪些改變。湖木社區中心每日開放時間是上午 9 點到下午 7 點。欲知詳情，請參閱網站或撥打 555-1234 與我們聯繫。

字彙 conduct 實施　survey 調查
improvement 改善　facility 設施
resident 住戶；居民　restructure 重建
gather 收集　in person 親自
in face 面對面　finalize 完成；敲定

8.

(A) 您的參與可能會直接影響社區要做哪些改變。

(B) 沒有您的支持，中心就不會存在。

(C) 我們需要更多義工。

(D) 計畫確定後，我們會立刻公布

解說

5. 掌握要讓（make）「什麼對象」進步（improvement），立刻就能解題了。對象是 facilities 和 services，因此要用被動語態。而且，改善、進步的作業不是正在進行中，而是計畫要進行，所以要用未來被動式。正確答案是 (B)。

6. take 和時間搭配，是「花費……時間」的意思，所以本句應是重建計畫（restructuring program）將花兩年的時間。因此 will take about two years 是重建計畫的形容詞子句，空格不能放表時間的關係副詞，要放表事物的關係代名詞。(A) 和 (D) 不能選，最合適的答案是 (C)。

7. 取得問卷（survey）的方法有兩種，兩種方法以 or 劃分。第一種是「以……的情況（in ＋空格）」在大廳的櫃檯（information desk）找到，第二種是上網。從文意來看，最合適的答案是 in person（本人親自）。這裡的介系詞 in 不是「在……裡面」的意思。如果要選 (A) 為正確答案，則要去掉 in。

8. 因為空格前的句子是鼓勵去取得問卷，說明填寫問卷的優點並予以肯定的 (A) 是正確答案。(B) 則把 survey 想成是

support，沒有支持中心將不會存在，就文意來看有點牽強，所以不能選。(C) 與上下文皆無關，也不能選。根據文意，鼓勵填寫問卷以後，應該會告知要做些什麼改變（change），但 (D) 的計畫（plan）並沒有在公告中被提到，故文義不順，也不能選。

參考以下報導回答問題 9–12。

（哈葛羅夫市，10 月 23 日）搬運家公司剛剛宣布，他們的運送服務下個月要擴張到鄰近的牛頓市。這是搬運家公司東山再起的跡象。當搬運家在哈葛羅夫市建立設備先進的工廠後的一個月，將會開始進行展店事宜。

超過 25 年，搬運家一直都是哈葛羅夫市的大公司。去年的這個時候，搬運家還擔心自己會結束營業。幸運的是，哈葛羅夫市通過了一個法案，將資助搬運家，並允許他們升級所有設備。有了市議會的介入，搬運家得以更新許可並繼續營運。

字彙 expansion 擴張；膨脹
grant 給予；同意　funding 贊助；資金
city council 市議會
turnaround 大轉變；轉好（或壞）
divest 賣掉；售出

9.

(A) 這是搬運家公司轉好的跡象。

(B) 牛頓市是一個跟哈葛羅夫市互相競爭的城市。

(C) 這對競爭者來說不是好事。

(D) 這會讓送貨時間更久。

解說

9. 選項 (B) 提到了牛頓市和哈葛羅夫市的關係，和文意不符，首先刪除不予考慮。剩下的選項只要掌握 this 是指什麼，立刻就能解題了。this 指的是搬運家公司的業務擴張至牛頓市這件事，而 (C) 和 (D) 的內容並沒有在本文中出現，所以均不能選。只剩下 (A)，在文意上和第二段搬運家公司在去年遭受了危機，意思上有連貫，故為正確答案。

10. 空格是形容詞，修飾搬運家公司是怎麼樣的雇主（employer），可選的形容詞為 (B) 和 (D)，但是 (D) 缺少形容詞前應有的冠詞。故正確答案是 (B)。

11. 根據文意，「去年的這個時候，搬運家還擔心（fear）……」，所以應該是擔憂發生不好的情況。選項意思分別為 (A) 關門 (B) 擴展 (C) 改組 (D) 撤資。(A) 和 (D) 皆為負面的狀況，但 (D) 為及物動詞，後面需要加受詞。故 (A) 是正確答案。

12. 有了資金之後會做什麼，掌握了這點立刻就能解題了。正確答案是 (B)，收到了金援後會更新許可證，並繼續「經營下去」。要特別注意文法結構，選項 (A) 用了過去式，表示已經經營結束了，不符合句意。care on 是「擔心什麼」，和搬運家公司的情況也不符。

參考以下通知回答問題 13–16。

我們歡迎全國業餘運動員來報名在紐約大球場舉辦的友誼錦標賽。歡迎各年齡的棒球選手代表你們的家鄉出賽。這個活動由艾迪馬斯和酷佳裝備贊助。參加者將可獲得贊助商提供的免費帽子和外套。此外，你還有機會遇到前來參加的職業棒球球星，報名的團隊將有機會贏得各種獎項和獎品。

詳情請參閱我們的網站 www.gstournament.com/baseball。團隊必須在截止日期前報名才符合資格，而職業運動員不符合本賽事資格。大球場的見面會訂於 4 月 20 日舉辦。期盼你來報名，一同共襄盛舉這場刺激的活動！

字彙 athlete 運動員　sign up 登記；報名　represent 代表　attendance 出席　deadline 期限；到期時間　qualify 符合資格　competition 競爭　gear 配備　athlete wear 運動服裝　distinct 明確的；鮮明的　diversified 多元的；多樣的　eligible for 有資格；符合資格

14.
(A) 請考慮選購他們的產品。
(B) 他們已經大方同意支援我們的活動。
(C) 這兩個廠商的棒球配備和運動服都很有名。
(D) 參加者將可獲得贊助商提供的免費帽子和外套。

解說

13. 根據文意，該賽事尚未舉辦，且「正在」招募業餘的運動選手，應選現在進行式，故正確答案是 (C)。

14. 空格前一句揭示了贊助商，(A) 和 (C) 皆不符合文意，另 (B) 等於是把同樣的話再說一遍，也不對。所以空格放贊助公司提供的服務是最合適的，故正確答案是 (D)。

15. 要找一個最適合修飾獎項（awards）的形容詞，正確答案可以考慮表「各式各樣的」的 (A)，或是表「多樣化的」的 (D)。然而 (D) 特指「單純地在型態上衍生出了很多種型態」，並不適合用來說明獎項，所以不能選。故正確答案是 (A)。其他選項意思分別為 (B) 明確的 (C) 分開的。

16. eligible for 是「合法的、有資格的」。因為公告一開始提到招募業餘（amateur）運動員，所以專業運動員（professional athlete）不能參加。suitable 是「符合……用途的」或「適合……狀況」，句意上並不足夠精確，故正確答案為 (C)。其他選項意思分別為 (A) 可接受的 (D) 偏好的。

實戰應用 **Chapter 01** p. 182

1. 表格、圖表、折價券

參考以下問卷調查表回答問題 **1–4**。

1. A　2. B　3. C　4. C

多佛良品

多佛良品恭喜您購買了新商品。本公司歷史悠久,由葛林家族經營,至今已超過三代。如果您——我們尊貴的客戶——願意填寫以下調查表,我們將無比感激。調查結果將有助於我們改善服務和顧客經驗。當我們收到您完成的表格後,Q1 您會收到我們回饋的小謝禮。謝謝您。

姓名:傑米・布里吉

電子郵件:jbridges@frescosh.com

地址:55929 明尼蘇達州多佛鷹高大道98 號

產品編碼:F4556Y56

Q2 產品說明:滾筒洗衣機

Q3 問題:您是如何得知本公司呢?

答:同事推薦。

問題:您對我們的服務感覺如何?

答:客服人員態度很好。

問題:您對本公司有沒有其他建議?

Q4 答:如果能有一個容易使用的線上論壇可以發問,會很有幫助。

字彙 time-honored 悠久的
thank-you gift 謝禮　agent 專員
giveaway 贈品　home appliance 家電
orderly 整齊的　warranty 保固

1. 布里吉先生寫完問卷會得到什麼?

(A) 免費禮物

(B) 一些抵用金

(C) 折價券

(D) 終生會員資格

解說 在問卷引言的最後,once 起始的副詞片語揭示了「一旦收到完成的表格,就會收到回饋的謝禮」。

2. 布里吉先生買了什麼?

(A) 一個娛樂設備

(B) 家電用品

(C) 流行飾品

(D) 備用零件

解說 問卷調查表中揭示了產品編碼和產品說明,從這裡可以確認布里吉先生購買的是滾筒洗衣機(front-loading washing machine)。(A) 是在戶外從事休閒活動時使用的裝備,(D) 是零件,所以這些都不能選。(B) 是正確答案。

3. 布里吉先生如何知道這家店?

(A) 看到電視廣告。

(B) 他在附近一家店工作。

(C) 同事跟他提起。

(D) 他逛到商店的網站。

解說 正確答案在問卷的第一個問題中。問卷中布里吉先生回答「一位同事推薦」,(C) 將「推薦」這個動詞換成了「提到」,所以正確答案是 (C)。

4. 布里吉先生認為多佛良品可以如何
   改善？
   (A) 維持商店整齊
   (B) 僱用更多店內人員
   (C) 增加顧客服務的項目
   (D) 延長保固期

   解說 正確答案在問卷的第三道問題中。布里
   吉先生寫說「希望能有一個容易使用的
   線上論壇可以發問」，找到最符合此
   意思的選項即可。問卷調查的說明及填
   寫均未提到選項 (A) 的使商店更加整
   齊，所以不能選。(B) 和 (D) 同樣也無法
   從本文中確認，所以也不對。正確答案
   是 (C)，布里吉先生的要求是「可以在線
   上問問題與溝通」，這包含在 (C)「增加
   顧客服務的項目」中。

實戰應用 Chapter 01   p. 186

2. 簡訊

參考以下訊息串回答問題 **1–2**。

1. B   2. C

陳・華特利（下午 1:23）

嗨！蓋兒，我需要你明天早點進來工作，
可以嗎？

蓋兒・賽耶斯（下午 1:34）

早一點，是多早呢？ᴼ¹ 我早上六點就會
到了，大部分的客人至少要到七點才會進
來喝咖啡。

陳・華特利（下午 1:45）

沒錯，我知道，但我們要大盤點，盤點完
要確定全部整理乾淨了，才可以開店門。

蓋兒・賽耶斯（下午 2:00）

了解。所以……ᴼ² 要幾點到？

陳・華特利（下午 2:10）

那就五點好了。

蓋兒・賽耶斯（下午 2:15）

好，明天見。算你欠我喔！

---

1. 陳・華特利最有可能從事什麼工作？
   (A) 車行
   (B) 咖啡店
   (C) 午餐餐廳
   (D) 畫廊

   解說 在下午 1:34 蓋兒・賽耶斯的訊息，提
   到了早上上班的時間，還有客人來喝咖
   啡的時間，由此可知這兩個人工作的地
   點是客人來喝咖啡的地方，也就是咖啡
   店，所以正確答案是 (B)。

2. 下午兩點十分，陳・華特利的訊息
   「Let's make it five（就約五點吧）」是
   什麼意思？
   (A) 應該有五個人到。
   (B) 他們應該花五分鐘想一下。
   (C) 早上五點碰面。
   (D) 他認為蓋兒需要五杯咖啡。

   解說 在下午 1:34 的訊息中，蓋兒問說「早一
   點，是多早」。在下午兩點的訊息中，蓋
   兒同意會早點到店裡，並詢問何時要
   到。在下午 2:10，陳說 Let's make it
   five，由此可推知他們敲定了時間，也
   就是早上五點碰面，所以正確答案是
   (C)。

實戰應用 Chapter 01   p. 189

3. 公告與通知

參考以下廣告傳單回答問題 **1–4**。

1. C   2. A   3. D   4. D

亞斯本信用合作社
卡爾頓街 55 號
亞斯本，科羅拉多州 25234
www.aspencreditunion.com

ᴼ¹ 從亞斯本信用合作社成立以來，已經十
年過去了，感謝您的長期支持。我們想通
知您，從新的一年起，亞斯本信用合作社
要引進幾項新的金融服務。

字彙 inventory 盤點；存貨　owe 欠

新的服務有：

• Q2D 行動金融 APP，讓您更方便地查詢餘額、轉帳、繳款。

• Q2C 開放週六營業，以提供客戶更好的服務。

• Q2B 我們將提供更多的貸款方案和諮詢服務，以滿足個人借貸需求，並針對小企業推出融資方案。

亞斯本信用合作社目前有一個促銷活動，Q4 任何在一月申請新開銀髮儲蓄帳戶的銀髮客戶，只要登錄就可獲得 100 元存款金！

欲知更多本設新的金融服務相關細節，請翻至傳單背面。

字彙 loyal 忠實的　establish 建立；創辦
inform 通知　balance 餘額
bill 帳單；法案　loan 貸款；借出
promotional 促銷的
registration 登記；註冊
relocate 轉換地點；重新安置
interest rates 利率　convenient 方便的
withdraw 提領　rotate 轉動；循環
operate 經營；操作
apply 適用；實施　survey 調查

1. 本文指出亞斯本信用合作社的什麼事？

(A) 最近搬到新址。

(B) 正在招募新血。

(C) 已經營業十年了。

(D) 將會在一月開新分行。

解說 傳單的第一句話提到，從亞斯本信用合作社成立以來，已經十年（decade）過去了，感謝您的長期支持，由此可知 (C) 是正確答案。(A) 和 (B) 無法從本文中確認，所以不能選。雖然傳單中提及了一月，但那是關於最近的促銷活動，而非 (D) 所說的開設新分行。

2. 下列何者不是亞斯本信用合作社明年會提供的服務？

(A) 較低的利率

(B) 更多的貸款方案

(C) 延長營業時間

(D) 更便利的行動服務

解說 根據傳單的內容，亞斯本信用合作社明年啟用的新服務有三者。唯有 (A) 的較低利率沒有被提及，故不能選。

3. 第三段第一行的 running（進行）一字意思最接近下列何者？

(A) 提領

(B) 轉動

(C) 移動

(D) 運作

解說 running 在此處所指並不是跑步，而是「進行、運作」，後接受詞一個促銷活動（a promotional event），故可從文意中推斷正確答案為 (D)。

4. 根據傳單內容，銀髮客戶如何能獲得 100 元存款金？

(A) 申辦信用卡

(B) 填寫問卷

(C) 下載行動 APP

(D) 在一月開一個特殊帳戶

解說 傳單的第三段提到，只要申請新開設的銀髮儲蓄帳戶，即可得到存款金。選擇意思最接近之選項，故 (D) 是正確答案。

實戰應用 **Chapter 01** p. 192

4. 電子郵件

參考以下電子郵件回答問題 1–4。

1. A　2. B　3. C　4. C

寄件人：約翰・斯蒂爾
　　　　<jsteele@starburst.com>

收件人：瑪莉・漢普頓
　　　　<mhampton@starburst.com>

日期：9 月 22 日

主旨：媒體關係經理一職

漢普頓女士您好：

我是行銷部門的約翰・斯蒂爾。Q1 這封電子郵件是關於近期貴部門的媒體關係經理職缺。我想推薦潔西卡・哈蒂。我認為她非常適合這個角色。Q2 身為行銷部門主管，我過去三年來都督導她的工作，她是

一位出色的團隊成員。在我們行銷部門，她曾主導過許多行銷活動，增加了我們產品的獲利。

我認為哈蒂女士在貴部門也能有所發揮。她是一位身經百戰的行銷專家，常與這領域的許多記者和播報員往來。Q3 她有強大的溝通技巧，能在媒體關係的經理職位上有出色表現。

Q4 由於我們的公司規模持續擴張，我認為我們必須提拔資深員工到較高的位置。如果您想多多了解哈蒂女士，請不要猶豫與我聯繫。我的分機號碼是 2315。除了週一和週三上午之外，我通常都會在辦公室。

期盼得到您的回覆。

約翰・斯蒂爾
行銷部主任
光芒四射公司

字彙 job opening 職缺
media relations 媒體關係
suitable 適當的
oversee 監督；管理；俯視
exceptional 優秀的；特殊的
marketing campaign 行銷活動
profitability 收益　field 領域
superb 一流的；頂尖的
therefore 因此；所以
managerial 管理的；經理的
promote 提升；推動
extension number 分機號碼
long-term 長期的　downsize 縮減

1. 這封電子郵件的目的是什麼？
   (A) 舉薦員工擔任某一職務
   (B) 提供顧客購買建議
   (C) 提出議程
   (D) 推動投資機會
   解說 第一段的第二句闡明了想推薦潔西卡・哈蒂來擔任公司出缺的媒體關係經理人。正確答案是 (A)。

2. 這封信提到哈蒂女士什麼事？
   (A) 她與漢普頓女士在同一部門。
   (B) 她目前在行銷部門工作。
   (C) 她過去曾是報社記者。
   (D) 她週一上午沒空。
   解說 本電子郵件的寄件人是行銷部門主任，想要舉薦哈蒂女士去漢普頓女士部門下所開的職缺，並在過去三年來都督導哈蒂女士的工作。由此可知 (A) 不對，而正確答案為 (B)。(C) 是過去哈蒂女士在工作上時常接觸的人。週一上午沒空的是行銷部主任約翰・斯蒂爾，而非哈蒂女士，故 (D) 也不能選。

3. 根據這封電子郵件，媒體關係經理需要什麼條件？
   (A) 創新的行銷策略
   (B) 長期規劃
   (C) 高明的人際手腕
   (D) 電腦程式能力
   解說 電子郵件的第二段，揭示了哈蒂女士的優點為強大的溝通技巧(superb communication skills)，能在媒體關係經理職位中有出色表現，也就是說這正是該職位所具備的特質。故 (C) 為正確答案。(A) 是哈蒂女士所具備的能力，並非該職位所需要的條件，所以不能選。

4. 從這封電子郵件可得知光芒四射公司什麼事？
   (A) 正在考慮縮減人員編制。
   (B) 最近得到一張合約。
   (C) 公司營運正在擴張。
   (D) 成立於三年前。
   解說 在最後一段提到，因為公司持續擴張(as our company continues to grow in size)，所以必須提拔資深員工到較高的位置。由此可知正確答案是表達相同意思的 (C)。除此之外，其他選項均無法在文章中找到。

實戰應用 Chapter 01　p. 197

5. 廣告

參考以下廣告回答問題 1–2。

> 1. B　　2. C

申請貝克斯頓創業者組織會員

現在就加入本區最具影響力的商業領導者和創業者社群。

Q1A 申請者必須是企業主，Q1D 其年收入須達至少一百萬元。此外，Q1C 公司必須有五名或五名以上的員工。

加入這個社群將有助您擴展事業，增加競爭力。誠如您所知，與其他企業主互動是商場上重要的一環。Q2 我們的資料庫會讓你與各行各業的企業主建立人脈，這些人樂於分享經驗和知識。不要低估會員夥伴的眼光和專業。我們對於您的事業有成也很有興趣。

如果您在九月申請加入，第一個月將免會費。詳情請見我們的網站 www.bextoneo.com 或撥打 555-8974 與我們聯繫。

字彙　influential 有影響力的
entrepreneur 創業者；企業家
earn 賺得；贏得　competitive 競爭的
interaction 互動　factor 因素
underestimate 低估
insight 眼光；洞察 expertise 專業
waive 撤回（不強制）；放棄（權力）
fee 費用　requirement 規定；條件
ownership 擁有權
academic degree 學位
conveniently 便利地

1. 以下何者不是申請入會的必要資格？
   (A) 擁有事業
   (B) 擁有學位
   (C) 員工要達到特定人數
   (D) 年收入最低限制

解說　廣告的第二段提到了申請成為會員的資格，揭示申請人必須是企業所有人，每年收入最少達一百萬元，且至少有五名員工，惟沒有提到 (B) 的學歷。所以正確答案是 (B)。

2. 根據本文，參加貝克斯頓創業者組織會員有什麼好處？
   (A) 每月電子報
   (B) 交通便利的辦公空間
   (C) 人脈機會
   (D) 較低廉的年租金

解說　廣告的第三段中介紹了加入會員的優點，強調與其他企業主的互動（interaction with other business leaders），並揭示會員能透過資料庫（database）和其他企業主交流，建立溝通網絡。所以 (C) 是正確答案，其他選項則皆未在廣告中被提及。

實戰應用 Chapter 01　p. 201

6. 新聞報導和社論

參考以下文章回答問題 1–4。

> 1. C　　2. C　　3. D　　4. A

解決住屋短缺問題

梅頓市，6 月 23 日——梅頓市正召開一連串市政會議，Q1 針對愈來愈多市民無法在預算內購置房屋，提出解決之道。根據市府官員的說法，必須採取措施，透過立即性的政策倡議方案和其他改革計畫，在短期內增加住屋供給。

Q2D 為了要讓房價變得更合理，市府官員建議執行一項通盤調查，了解最新住屋需求。接著，Q2A 對於低收入市民，市府將以稅收提供住房補貼。此外，Q2B 據說市府正考慮通過一項法律，要求地產開發商的新公寓建案，必須提供低價位住宅給低收入市民。

市府官員和本地居民希望這些措施有助於緩解住屋短缺問題，此問題已對梅頓市市民造成影響。Q4 住屋問題將會是下次市長、市議員、學校董事會成員選舉的重點議題。

字彙 city council 市議會　housing 住宿　budget 預算　measure 措施；方法　initiative 倡議；新措施　reform 改革　reasonable 合理的　comprehensive 全面的；綜合的　income 收入　subsidized 補貼的　tax revenue 稅收　unit 單位　alleviate 緩解　housing crunch 房屋短缺　school board 學校董事會　shortage 短缺　influx 湧入　legislation 立法　conduct 帶領；實施　solicit 索求；請求　attest 證明　facilitate 促進；幫助　relieve 緩和；使放心　municipal 市立的　attract 吸引　postpone 拖延；延後

1. 梅頓市目前遇到什麼問題？

   (A) 勞工短缺

   (B) 難民湧入

   (C) 人們買不起房

   (D) 人口減少

   解說 本文第一段便開宗明義揭示主旨，指出愈來愈多市民無法在預算內購屋（growing number of citizens who cannot find housing that fits within their budget）。故正確答案是 (C)。

2. 以下何者不包括在建議事項裡？

   (A) 補貼房價

   (B) 通過新法律

   (C) 建新學校

   (D) 執行調查

   解說 本文第二段即是為了解決房價問題所提出的方案。選項 (D) 將文章中的進行一項調查（carry out a comprehensive survey）的動詞 carry out 換成了 conduct。在該段也可以找到補貼房價與考慮立法，與 (A) 和 (B) 相符。所以正確答案是本文隻字未提的 (C)。

3. 第三段第一行的 alleviate（減輕）意思最接近下列何者？

   (A) 請求

   (B) 證明

   (C) 促進

   (D) 緩和

   解說 根據本文，alleviate 後接受詞「以對梅頓市市民造成影響的房屋短缺問題（the housing crunch that has been affecting Mayton residents）」，所以正確答案是表「減輕；緩解」的 relieve。

4. 從本文可得知梅頓市什麼事？

   (A) 很快就會有個全市選舉。

   (B) 市政府不負責任。

   (C) 試圖要吸引更多觀光客。

   (D) 延緩一項工程。

   解說 本文第三段預測了梅頓市未來會發生的狀況，並提及住宅居住問題會是之後選舉（election）的重要議題，所以 (A) 是正確答案。(C) 和 (D) 均無法從本文中確認。(B) 則和市政府所提出的各種各種方案意思相反，所以也不能選。

實戰應用 Chapter 01 p. 205

7. 線上聊天與討論區

參考以下網路聊天室回答問題 **1~4**。

1. D　2. B　3. A　4. C

佩佩・華瑞茲（上午 10:12）

嗨，今天員工會議是幾點？我下午一點要去看牙醫。

柯林・寇沃德（上午 11:00）

佩佩，你在哪裡？會議再 30 分鐘就要開始了。快來。

佩佩・華瑞茲（上午 11:01）

我稍早傳過訊息給大家，但沒人回應。會要開多久？

尤阿契姆・費茲傑羅（上午 11:02）

一直開到所有的草案都定案為止。

柯林‧寇沃德（上午 11:04）

佩佩，你有重要工作，Q1 要安排活動的保全。不要搞砸了。

理查‧伯頓（上午 11:06）

大家都會 11 點半到吧？如果準時開始，我們應該可以在一點前結束。我會點名。

柯林‧寇沃德（上午 11:08）

Q3 是，老闆！我已經在這邊準備會議室。尤阿契姆，記得帶投影機過來。

佩佩‧華瑞茲（上午 11:12）

好，我會取消我的門診。你們可以相信我，我會到的。放心。

尤阿契姆‧費茲傑羅（上午 11:15）

投影機已經在那邊，只是先藏起來了。我不希望被別人拿走。Q4 開始之前我會拿出來。大家待會兒見。

字彙 response 回應；反應
blow something 搞砸 on time 準時
take roll 點名 investment 投資
caterer 外燴業者 retrieve 取回

1. 這個會議的主題是什麼？
   (A) 投資銀行
   (B) 安全篩檢
   (C) 休閒運動規劃
   (D) 籌備一個活動

解說 透過上午 11 點 02 分費茲傑羅的訊息可以知道，他們召開員工會議是為了要寫某會議的議程。另外，從上午 11 點 04 分的訊息，可以看出佩佩負責籌備該活動（會議）的保全工作。由此可知這是會議工作人員的討論群組，討論即將舉行的活動。所以 (C) 和 (D) 的動詞 planning（計畫）和 organizing（籌辦）可以考慮，不過從本文中，無法確認活動是否和運動或娛樂有關，所以正確答案是 (D)。

2. 11 點 12 分，佩佩‧華瑞茲寫的 Just chill（冷靜；沒關係）是什麼意思？
   (A) 他想喝一杯冷飲。
   (B) 希望其他人不要擔心。
   (C) 他想去看病。
   (D) 他希望其他人等他。

解說 chill 當作動詞使用時是「冷掉、冷卻」的意思。佩佩在一開始的訊息中說他約了要去看牙醫，暗示也許不能參加員工會議。但柯林強調了好幾次他必須參加，最後佩佩說他會取消看牙，並說 just chill，故依照文意是要柯林冷靜，不用擔心。所以 (B) 是正確答案。

3. 理查‧伯頓的工作最可能是什麼？
   (A) 總籌畫人
   (B) 外燴業者
   (C) 布置組經理
   (D) 秘書

解說 理查‧伯頓的訊息只出現過一次，他的簡訊結束後，緊接著柯林用敬語回答他，由此可知理查的職位比其他人都高，故只有 (A) 和 (C) 可以考慮。透過上下文可知這些人正在籌備活動，所以 (A) 較 (C) 更為合適。

4. 尤阿契姆‧費茲傑羅接下來最可能會做什麼事？
   (A) 上教堂
   (B) 打給佩佩問最新狀況
   (C) 取出投影機
   (D) 聯絡理查‧伯頓

解說 柯林叫費茲傑羅要帶投影機（projector），費茲傑羅回覆他會在會議開始前去拿，所以正確答案是用取回（retrieve）來表此意思的 (C)。

實戰應用 **Chapter 01** p. 209
8. 網頁

參考以下網頁回答問題 1–3。

```
1. B   2. B   3. A
```

歡迎來到驚奇動物網，Q3 這是「唯一」能依您的寵物，來客製填充玩偶的網站！

我們提供服務給各種寵物的飼主。貓和狗當然是最受歡迎的，但我們也做過魚、蜥蜴、蛇，甚至豬娃娃！

只要填好表格，上面有付款和寄送説明，再上傳三到五個您的寶貝寵物的照片檔，要 JPEG 格式。24 小時內我們會寄出數位圖檔和報價。如果您確定要訂製，我們會即刻處理您的付款並開始動工。

驚奇動物網為您製作很棒的禮物，Q2 這些寵物娃娃對剛剛痛失心愛寵物的飼主來説更是有幫助。

請參閱以下價目表，評估您的客製寵物娃娃！

- 小型寵物（重量三公斤以下，體積低於一立方公尺），價格 24.95 元。
- 中型寵物（重量十公斤以下，體積小於二立方公尺），價格 59.95 元。
- 大型寵物（重量十公斤以上，體積超過二立方公尺），價格 89.95 元＊。

＊Q1 本網站不接受體積超過四立方公尺的訂單。

今天就馬上下單吧！

字彙 quote 報價　custom-made 客製的
stuffed animals 填充動物玩具
cubic meter 立方公尺
get an estimate on 估價
supervise 監督；指導
state-of-the-art 最先進的

1. 驚奇動物網不會製作以下何種動物？
   (A) 蛇
   (B) 大象
   (C) 鳥
   (D) 貓

   解説 網頁中並沒有具體提到，有哪些動物可以提供製作填充玩偶。不過參考定價説明，即可找出解題的線索。在星號的注意事項中，特別提及體積超過四立方公尺無法訂做，符合該條件的是 (B)，為正確答案。

2. 從這個網頁可以得知什麼事？
   (A) 這個產品針對兒童。
   (B) 這個產品能幫助痛失愛寵的飼主。
   (C) 這個產品必須受到監督。
   (D) 訂購流程很複雜。

解説 網站的第三段揭示了產品用途有兩種，第一，可當作很棒的禮物（make great gifts）。第二，提供剛失去愛寵不久的飼主心靈慰藉（can really help people who have recently lost a beloved pet）。所以 (B) 是正確答案。(A) 和 (C) 在本文中並未被提及，(D) 則是和文章中所説的簡單訂貨説明事實相反。

3. 文中提及驚奇動物網什麼事？
   (A) 他們是唯一一家在線上提供客製動物玩偶的公司。
   (B) 保證滿意。
   (C) 他們使用最先進的設備。
   (D) 他們正擴大服務，製作有異國感的寵物娃娃。

解説 網站的第一句話便揭示了驚奇動物網的服務，是「唯一」能依委託人的寵物，來客製填充玩偶的網站。根據這句話，可以很清楚地知道正確答案是 (A)。其餘選項均無法從本文中得到確認。

實戰應用 # Chapter 01　p. 214
9. 信件

參考以下信件回答問題 1–4。

1. B　2. D　3. C　4. C

溫莎戶外活動服飾專門店

9 月 27 日

珍妮・泰勒

福樂街 12 號

克羅斯比，密西根州 49618

泰勒女士您好：

為了慶祝秋季的到來，Q1 溫莎戶外活動服飾所有秋季時裝正在打折！希望您把握這個大好機會，來店參觀選購！

Q3A 活動將在十月一日星期一在蘭興門市開跑。底特律門市也會在十月二日開始提供優惠。活動將在兩家店進行，大約持續一週，Q2 在十月七日同時結束。

Q3D 我們會銷售各式秋季流行服飾，包括外套、裙子到帽子、圍巾等。同時也會販售專業戶外活動，針對露營、單車活動、慢跑等設計的服飾。很多商品都是全新品項，預計很快就會售罄。我們也會加派人手到各店，以服務湧入的顧客。

Q3B 蘭興門市位於柳樹街 45 號，就在福頓百貨公司再過去一點點。底特律門市位於松樹街 137 號，也就是麥斯威爾戲院和星（日式料理餐廳）的中間。

Q4 更多優惠資訊，請參閱隨信附上的宣傳冊。下禮拜別忘了來店看看！

約翰‧華特斯 敬上

行銷經理

溫莎戶外活動服飾專門店

字彙 apparel 服裝　discounted 打折的
take advantage of 利用
a wide variety of 各式各樣的
run 進行　specialized 專門的
accommodate 容納；使符合
enclose 附上　brochure 小冊子
hesitate 猶豫；遲疑　stop by 路過停留

1. 這封信的目的為何？
(A) 宣傳新的線上商店
(B) 宣傳季節優惠
(C) 介紹新雇員
(D) 蒐集客戶意見

解說 信的第一段說，該店正在做秋季服飾的促銷活動，所以要找符合此意思的選項。(B) 說這是一個季節折扣（seasonal sale），所以是正確答案。從信中可知所有商品都是在實體賣場進行買賣，不能網購，所以 (A) 不能選。(C) 和 (D) 則無法從本文中確認。

2. 溫莎戶外活動服飾專門店的活動何時截止？
(A) 九月二十七日
(B) 十月一日
(C) 十月二日
(D) 十月七日

解說 第二段提到了兩個門市的活動開始和結束時間，而結束時間都是在十月七日，所以正確答案是 (D)。

3. 關於溫莎戶外活動服飾專門店的優惠活動，文中沒有提到下列何者？
(A) 日期
(B) 地點
(C) 價格
(D) 商品品項

解說 在第二段已經提到活動開始和結束時間。在倒數第二段也提到了兩個門市的位置，所以 (A) 和 (B) 都不能選。第三段提及某些商品依定價而有折扣，卻沒有提及商品的價格，所以正確答案是 (C)。

4. 如果泰勒女士想知道更多細節，最可能會做什麼？
(A) 聯絡華特斯先生
(B) 上溫莎戶外活動服飾專門店的網站
(C) 參考信內所附的文件
(D) 跑一趟店面

解說 在最後一段揭示了，想要欲知更多資訊可參閱附在信封裡的宣傳冊，所以正確答案是 (C)。本題所問不是看了廣告以後會做的事，而是要獲得更多訊息（more information）會做什麼，所以要仔細閱讀題目來解題。

Actual Test　p. 244

1. D　2. C　3. C　4. C　5. C　6. A
7. C　8. C　9. A　10. B　11. A　12. B
13. B　14. D　15. B　16. C　17. D　18. C
19. B　20. C　21. A　22. B　23. C　24. D
25. C　26. B　27. D　28. D　29. A　30. B
31. C　32. A　33. C　34. A　35. B　36. A
37. C　38. D　39. B　40. C　41. C　42. A
43. C　44. A　45. C　46. C　47. A　48. A
49. C　50. B　51. C　52. A　53. C　54. B
55. B　56. C　57. C　58. B　59. C　60. D
61. A　62. C　63. C　64. B

参考以下通知回答問題 1–2。

凱勒社區中心歡迎朵那・匹茲女士

我們很興奮地宣布，Q1 朵那・匹茲女士即將在凱勒社區中心開辦狗狗訓練工作坊，時間訂在 7 月 22 日、23 日這兩個週末日。匹茲女士是受歡迎的動物訓練師，最近出現在許多談話節目上，如《早安，陽光》和《今晚報報》。Q2 打算參加工作坊者，務必要攜帶狗繩，並要隨時管好愛犬。

在匹茲女士的長期專業訓練師生涯中，曾和許多名人合作，如歌手吉娜・溫士頓和演員傑森・昆恩。匹茲女士教導他們動物行為和服從訓練。您可以上她的網站 www.donapitts.com 觀賞教學影片，並了解更多匹茲女士的訓練方法。

活動預計很快就會額滿，有興趣的人要趁早打給社區中心，為愛犬把握機會報名。

字彙 dog leash 狗繩　restrained 受限制的
obedience 順從；服從
instructional 教學的；教育的

1. 本通知宣傳哪種類型的活動？

(A) 愛犬節目頒獎典禮

(B) 寵物店開幕

(C) 電視節目首播

(D) 動物訓練課

解說 本通知第一句即提到，凱勒社區中心將開辦一個狗狗訓練工作坊。正確答案是 (D)。

2. 參加者必須做什麼事？

(A) 在正式開始時間前到場

(B) 提供個人資料

(C) 管好自己的寵物

(D) 聯絡社區中心

解說 在第一段的最後一句提到，要參加的人必須攜帶狗繩，並在訓練期間管好自己的狗，所以正確答案是 (C)。選項 (A)、(B) 和 (D) 很容易被誤以為是正確答案，但這並不是「參加者」必須做的事，而是想參加的人須具備的條件，所以不能選。

参考以下訊息串回答問題 3–4。

保羅・紐曼（上午 8:00）

史蒂芙，有沒有機會在這個禮拜後面幾天碰面，Q3 看一下新的輪胎規格？

史蒂芙・簡森（上午 8:13）

好啊，你什麼時候方便？

保羅・紐曼（上午 8:23）

星期三可以嗎？

史蒂芙・簡森（上午 8:33）

收到。

保羅・紐曼（上午 9:10）

太好了。那就倉庫見，要記得把存貨清單帶過來。

史蒂芙・簡森（上午 9:11）

好，我會從辦公室帶一張過去。

字彙 go over 查看；檢查　spec 規格
inventory sheet 存貨清單
automotive 汽車的

3. 史蒂芙・簡森最可能在哪一種公司上班？

(A) 金融公司

(B) 建設公司

(C) 汽車公司

(D) 程式設計公司

解說 傳遞簡訊的兩個人見面，是為了檢查新進的輪胎。之後又說要在倉庫見面，並要帶存貨清單（inventory sheet）。將這些連接起來便可知，正確答案是會做輪胎庫存的汽車公司，故選 (C)。

4. 在早上 8 點 33 分，史蒂芙・簡森說的 Roger that（收到）是什麼意思？

(A) 她認為羅傑應該要來做。

(B) 她了解他的訊息。

(C) 她星期三會到。

(D) 羅傑已經完成了。

解說 前一個訊息詢問說星期三見面可以嗎，必須回答同意不同意。roger 起初用在無線電通訊中，不僅表達接收到這則資訊，也有同意的正向含意。另也可以從

後文保羅説的太好了（Great）得知史蒂芙同意星期三見面。所以 (C) 是正確答案。由於必須給予對方肯定答覆，不能回答了解（understanding），所以 (B) 不能選。

參考以下電子郵件回答問題 5–7。

收件人：產品研發部門全體人員

寄件人：大衛・史汪森

日期：8 月 28 日

主旨：顧客意見

你們大概知道，我們最新的玩具正在接受 JD 顧問集團的測試。Q7A/Q7B 維斯塔的熱銷玩具持續穩定銷售，但我們已經有六年多的時間，都沒看到銷售量成長。所有我們推出的新玩具，銷售結果都讓人失望。為了瞭解消費者到底要什麼，我們連繫了 JD 顧問集團，請他們協助我們找出消費者會喜歡什麼玩具，以及他們對我們的新產品有什麼不喜歡的地方。

Q5/Q7C 我很開心地告訴大家，我們針對五歲以下兒童推出的最新玩具原型，看起來大有可為。這類多重學習和教育類型的玩具似乎很受消費者喜愛，如果這個潮流不變，我想讓這個原型繼續發展，並開始生產，趁假期購物旺季之際上市。這款玩具可望成為假期間最熱門的必買商品。

感謝諸位辛勤的工作，期待你們能繼續將創新商品帶進我們的陣容。

大衛・史汪森 敬上

資深主任

字彙 assess 評估
promising 可行的；有機會成功的
survey 調查 arrange 安排
essential 必要的

5. 這封電子郵件的目的是什麼？

(A) 徵求調查參與者

(B) 安排會議

(C) 提供一個新的開發商品資訊

(D) 鼓勵員工更努力工作

解說 第二段第一句話使用了動詞 note（通知），揭示全文主旨，是以務必留意這句話。寄信人大衛・史旺森説「針對五歲以下兒童推出的最新玩具模型看起來大有可為」，所以正確答案是 (C)。儘管本文最後一段表達了對員工的感謝之意，但不能視為本文主旨，故 (D) 不能選。

6. 從文中第二段第六行的 must-haves（必買）意思最接近以下何者？

(A) 必要商品

(B) 引領潮流者

(C) 應該買的

(D) 有創意的

解說 must-have 在日常對話中通常被當作名詞使用，表「必須具備的東西、一定要買的東西」。最符合此意的是 (A)。(B) 是「引領潮流的東西」，也就是決定之後流行趨勢的「流行先導者」，與 must-have 的意思不同。

7. 從文中可得知維斯塔玩具公司什麼事？

(A) 過去幾年來，銷售量穩定成長。

(B) 過去幾年來，銷售量持續下跌。

(C) 研發中的新玩具看起來前景可期。

(D) 專攻於電子玩具。

解說 從本文第一段可知，維斯塔玩具公司數年來銷售穩定卻沒有成長，所以不能選 (A)，而本文也沒有提到下跌，故 (B) 也不對。而第二段（也就是本電子郵件主旨）提到新開發的產品原型看起來大有可為（look to be promising），所以 (C) 是正確答案。

參考以下網路聊天室回答問題 8–10。

萊絲莉・艾普頓（下午 8:09）

好，各位，我們這次交易的條件是什麼？

喬西・金（下午 8:17）

批發公司的人説，倉庫裡所有東西都打八折，Q8 包括所有高爾夫用品。

羅伯特·傑克森（下午 8:21）

八折？真是有誠意的開價。我們有能耐處理所有存貨嗎？

喬西·金（下午 8:22）

一定可以，我們的倉庫沒那麼大，^{Q8} 但我想他們的庫存大多可在 13 日的「春季健身大作戰」活動中銷出。

羅伯特·傑克森（下午 8:25）

太好了，^{Q11} 我會聯絡搬運公司，安排幾臺卡車在他們倉庫那邊跟我們碰頭。

喬西·金（下午 8:35）

太棒了，我會開始把他們的商品放到我們的促銷廣告中。

萊絲莉·艾普頓（下午 8:45）

聽起來真是不錯，各位。^{Q9/Q10} 我知道我才當頭第一個禮拜，但每件事情都如夢般順利。

字彙 term 條件 wholesale 批發
inventory 存貨 stock 庫存；存貨
at the helm 掌舵；領導
pickup 開車載送或領取

8. 這些人最可能在以下何地工作？

(A) 銀行

(B) 電玩公司

(C) 運動用品公司

(D) 外燴服務

解說 根據下午 8 點 17 分的簡訊，提到倉庫裡的貨品包含了高爾夫設備。之後 8 點 22 分簡訊又提到，大部分的庫存都預計可以在春季健身大作戰活動（Spring Fitness Blastoff）中銷出。所以正確答案是 (C)。

9. 在晚上 8 點 45 分時，萊絲莉·艾普頓說 everything is running like a dream（如夢一般進行順利）的意思是什麼？

(A) 她認為所有事情都進展順利。

(B) 她不相信這一切是真的。

(C) 她希望事情能更順利。

(D) 她有起床障礙。

解說 該句的動詞 run 並非是「跑步」的意思，而是「經營、進展」。從上下文可以知道，所有事情都上了軌道，因此此處是感嘆事情如夢一般運作良好。所以正確答案是 (A)。

10. 萊絲莉·艾普頓最有可能做什麼工作？

(A) 貨運秘書

(B) 經理

(C) 倉儲人員

(D) 貨車司機

解說 最後一句話中的 at the helm，原來是「在船長的位置」。一般生活中則是表「在最高的職位、負責人」。並由整個網路對話串由她開頭詢問進度可知，萊絲莉是主管階級，故選項中最符合此意思的是 (B)。

11. 羅伯特·傑克森接下來最可能採取什麼行動？

(A) 安排載貨

(B) 弄一杯咖啡

(C) 製作宣傳品

(D) 聯繫萊絲莉尋求指示

解說 在晚上 8 點 25 分羅伯特說會連絡搬運公司，安排一些卡車在倉庫碰頭。由此可推知答案。選項 (A) 將安排搬運貨物，說成是 pickup（開車載送或領取），所以 (A) 是正確答案。選項 (C) 的製作宣傳品是喬西·金的工作，至於 (B) 和 (D) 則沒辦法從本文中得到確認。

參考以下報導回答問題 12–14。

羅森咖啡是一家人氣咖啡店，七年前創立於丹佛，^{Q12} 正計畫明年在鄰近的奧羅拉鎮新設分店。這個消息是昨天湖木新店的開幕活動上宣布的。羅森咖啡行銷公關經理詹姆士·海勒表示：「我們覺得很興奮，要在科羅拉多州的主要城市布點，並與社區建立長期關係。」

羅森咖啡由琳達·羅森所創立，她當時還是大學生，滿懷特殊使命：在舒適放鬆的環境，提供平價的優質咖啡。羅森女士的咖啡店因社區內口耳相傳而逐漸成名，是當地居民和上班族的熱門聚會地點。特別是從它去年獲得國家咖啡董事會頒發最佳咖啡店獎之後，人氣和名聲迅速飆漲。

羅森咖啡正在奧羅拉鎮尋找適當的地點來展店。Q13 羅森女士強調，新的地點必須要有足夠空間放置舒適的桌椅，並且要面南，以引進明亮日光，也必須有寬敞的停車場。

Q14 歡迎有餐飲服務或料理經驗的人應徵奧羅拉鎮新店的職缺。可直接與客服經理伊娃·萊特女士聯絡，電話是 720-555-2349。詳情可參閱羅森咖啡官網：www.lawsoncoffee.com。

字彙 specific 特定的　affordable 買得起的
gradually 逐漸地　emphasize 強調

12. 這篇文章的目的為何？

　(A) 宣布獎項得獎人

　(B) 報導某企業擴展版圖

　(C) 宣傳新產品

　(D) 說明一項政策調整

解說 本文第一句開宗明義，由「羅森咖啡正計畫新設分店」開始。由此可知正確答案是 (B)。

13. 以下何者不是奧羅拉鎮新店要求的必備條件？

　(A) 足夠的座位空間

　(B) 冷暖空調系統

　(C) 大量停車空間

　(D) 充足的自然光

解說 本文第三段提到了新店應有的條件，惟冷暖空調系統未被提及，所以應選 (B)。

14. 根據本文，歡迎哪一類型的人與萊特女士聯絡？

　(A) 餐飲設備供應商

　(B) 有興趣的投資客

　(C) 食物報導者

　(D) 潛在員工

解說 本文最後一段提到，有餐飲服務或料理經驗的人，可來應徵相關職位，並致電客服經理伊娃·萊特。所以 (D) 是正確答案。

參考以下新聞報導回答問題 15–17。

普雷斯科特每日新聞

（11 月 2 日）經過七個月的施工，Q15 普雷斯科特會展中心將於明天對外開放。此會展中心將服務大普雷斯科特地區，除了提供最先進的設施外，會展中心將有能力承辦萬人規模的活動。[1]

瑪新公司耗資一千多萬美元設計和規劃這個會展中心。[2] 儘管這是一筆可觀金額，普雷斯科特市還是必須補足經費才能使其完工。普雷斯科特會展中心可望透過明年已排定的一連串會展活動，回收其建設成本。[3]

開幕典禮將於中午舉行，Q16/Q17 普雷斯科特市長會出席剪綵。[4] 歡迎所有社區居民共襄盛舉，現場備有免費餐點，由已進駐會展中心的永久店家所提供。

字彙 construction 施工；建設
public 大眾　provide 提供
in addition to 除……之外　offer 提供
facility 設施　be able to 能夠
host 主辦　north of （數量）超過
substantial 大量的　match 補足
recoup 取回（成本）
opening ceremony 開幕典禮
complimentary 贈送的；恭維的

15. 本篇文章的主旨是關於什麼？

　(A) 一個新的工程即將展開

　(B) 一個新的商業設施將開幕

　(C) 在普雷斯科特區完成的工作

　(D) 瑪新公司的投資

解說 本文的第一句話就揭示，會展中心將在明天對外開放，也就是 (B) 中提到的新的事業機構(a new business facility)，所以正確答案是 (B)。由於該工程已經完工，並非 (A) 所說即將展開新的工程，所以 (A) 不能選。另 (C) 所說

已經完成的工作，對照本文不夠精確，因此也不能選。雖然普雷斯科特會展中心是瑪新公司的投資，但本文並非以該公司的投資為主，故 (D) 不能選。

16. 普雷斯科特市長將會做什麼事？

(A) 介紹瑪新公司董事長

(B) 提供免費食物

(C) 正式宣布會展中心開幕

(D) 舉辦會議

解說 文章的最後一段說市長會出席普雷斯科會展中心的開幕剪綵，宣告會展中心正式啟用。所以正確答案是 (C)。

17. 文中的 [1]、[2]、[3]、[4] 四個位置中，何者最適合插入 This will mark the fourth time a new facility has been opened by her this year.（這將會是她今年第四個開幕的新設施）？

(A) [1]

(B) [2]

(C) [3]

(D) [4]

解說 該句使用了代名詞 her，所以要找有可代稱的先行詞對象。[1] 沒有 her 所指稱的對象，所以不能選。[2] 和 [3] 既沒有 her 所指稱的對象，也沒提到新設施開幕的內容，故也不合適。[4] 有指稱的對象，也就是前面出現的普雷斯科特市長（the Mayor of Prescott），且主詞 this 也可以指前面出現的「出席開幕典禮」這件事。正確答案為 (D)

參考以下信件回答問題 18-19。

荷頓大學

1 月 20 日

琳達・格特

羅斯福路 2789 號

明尼亞波利斯，明尼蘇達州 52985

格特女士您好：

很高興您願意在今年堪薩斯州商業會議中擔任講者，Q18A 本會議將在堪薩斯州的威奇托舉行。我相信，Q18D 這是讓投資銀行家、稅務分析師、財務審計師和其他專業人員齊聚一堂、彼此切磋的好機會。

會議將於 2 月 13 日週一舉行。請在上午 10 點前抵達會場，Q18B 並到會議服務櫃檯報到，我們會在那邊分發名牌、議程和旅館房間鑰匙。您會在會議第一天上臺分享，因此可能會想要提早抵達做準備。同時也請記得，所有賓客必須在 2 月 17 日週五下午 3 點前退房。

威奇托會展中心距機場只有 10 分鐘車程。如果你從機場搭計程車過來，應該沒有問題。

Q19 我很喜歡您在科羅拉多州最近一個會議上的演講，期待能在威奇托再一次聽到您的演說。如果您在演說之後有時間，我們可以一起享用午餐，享受彼此的陪伴。再讓我知道您的計畫。

麥可・崔頓 敬上

堪薩斯州商業會議總策畫

字彙 conference 會議　specialist 專家

18. 本文沒有提到以下何者？

(A) 活動地點

(B) 報到手續

(C) 旅費

(D) 人際交流的機會

解說 本文第一段第一句即提到活動地點，將在堪薩斯州的威奇托舉行。並在第一段最後提及了，這是一個讓大家齊聚一堂彼此切磋的好機會。所以 (A) 和 (D) 都不能選。本文第二段則提及詳細的報到手續，故 (B) 也不對。正確答案是 (C)，在本文中完全沒有出現。

19. 崔頓先生如何知道格特女士？

(A) 透過一位共同朋友的介紹。

(B) 他在之前的活動見過她。

(C) 他讀了她最近的書。

(D) 他跟格特女士就讀同一所大學。

解說 最後一段崔頓先生便提到，先前在科羅拉多州聽過格特女士的演講，並非常喜歡。所以正確答案是 (B)。其餘選項在本文中完全沒有提及。

參考以下傳單回答問題 20-22。

Q20 **國際學生新生訓練**

翠登大學熱烈歡迎新學年的
新進國際學生。

翠登大學學生會

9 月 3 日 上午 9 點到下午 1 點

新生訓練時程表	
上午 9 點	選課：如何決定上什麼課程（108 室）
上午 10 點	學業成功：學業及校園生活經驗談（202 室）
上午 11 點	移民：了解簽證規定（114 室）
	在美國生活：如何適應新文化（111 室）
中午 12 點	宿舍生活：宿舍生活相關規定（120 室）

請注意，Q21 所有國際學生都要參加新生訓練。新生訓練的第一階段會發學生證和課程表。不克參加者，請事先撥打 432-555-8924，與朱·奈爾森聯絡。

有任何問題都歡迎詢問我們的同仁。新生訓練就是讓國際學生有機會感受校園的舒適和歡迎。

Q22 新生訓練結束後，歡迎國際學生與我們行政人員一起在學生餐廳享用免費午餐。參與者將會領到餐券，僅限當天於學生餐廳進行兌換。

再一次謝謝您選擇就讀翠登大學。

字彙 student identification card 學生證
distribute 分配；分發　hesitate 猶豫
voucher 禮券；兌換券

20. 這張傳單針對的對象可能是以下何者？
(A) 客座教授
(B) 歐洲移民
(C) 來自國外的學生
(D) 崔登大學的教職員

解說 從本傳單的標題可以知道，這是國際學生的新生訓練。所以正確答案是 (C)。(B) 把國際學生限定為歐洲移民，這是不對的，所以不能選。

21. 從本文可得知這個活動的什麼事？
(A) 一定要出席。
(B) 已安排好座位。
(C) 事前要購票。
(D) 入場需要身分證件。

解說 表格下方的第一句提到，所有國際學生都必須參加，所以正確答案是 (A)。(B) 和 (C) 在本文中沒有提到，所以不能選。表格下的第一段提到，新生會在第一階段的訓練中拿到學生證，故 (D) 也不對。

22. 根據這張傳單，活動結束後，參與者可以馬上做什麼？
(A) 選課
(B) 問職員問題
(C) 與一些教授碰面
(D) 享用免費午餐

解說 根據本文倒數第二段，新生訓練結束後國際學生可與行政人員，前往餐廳享用免費午餐，所以正確答案是 (D)。會不會問職員問題以及會不會見教授，兩者皆無法確定，所以 (B) 和 (C) 都不能選。

參考以下報導回答問題 23-25。

喬治城博物館理事會很開心地宣布，Q23 本市新科學博物館的破土典禮將會在 3 月 21 日週六上午 11 點舉行。博物館位於喬治城西側，緊鄰喬治·楊紀念公園。新的博物館有五層樓高，Q24A 這將會是喬治城第三高的建築物。此外，博物館會有一整層樓作為教育用途。博物館理事會長期致力於激發小朋友對科學的興趣。

Q24D 多虧許多贊助者的資助，喬治城科學博物館才得以建造。其中最大筆的兩百萬元捐款，來自於本地知名慈善家布蘭敦·波特。波特先生是著名科學家，在韓森大

學教授遺傳學長達 20 多年，並創立跨國農產企業「波特食品公司」。他在許多訪問中表示：「我一直在想，要怎麼做才能回饋我的故鄉」，為了表示對他慷慨捐獻的敬意，Q24C 科學博物館的自然歷史區將命名為「布蘭敦．波特自然歷史展示廳」。

動土典禮將對外開放。喬治城市長桂格．萊特及 23 位包括波特先生在內的捐款人都會出席這場典禮。Q25 更多詳細內容、博物館與活動的照片，將會在下週一於官方網站 www.georgetownsciencemuseum.org 上公布。

字彙 groundbreaking ceremony 破土典禮
philanthropist 慈善家
generous 大方的；慷慨的

23. 本文主要跟什麼有關？
   (A) 科學研究的結果
   (B) 新的政府單位開幕
   (C) 工程開工
   (D) 科學活動的時程表

解說 本文的第一句話，宣布將舉行新科學博物館的動土典禮。所以正確答案是 (C)。

24. 從本文可得知喬治城科學博物館什麼事？
   (A) 是當地最高的建築物。
   (B) 下週將完工。
   (C) 博物館為波特先生所有。
   (D) 由私人捐款提供資金。

解說 本文第二段第一句提到，科學博物館獲得許多個人捐款的支持而得以興建。所以 (D) 是正確答案。其餘選項皆與本文事實不符。科學博物館是本市第三高的建築物；正要舉行動土典禮，與完工相去甚遠；為感謝波特先生的捐款而將其中一展示廳由其名命名，並非波特先生擁有了博物館。故 (A)、(B) 和 (C) 都不能選。

25. 根據本文，如何能更了解科學博物館建案？
   (A) 到工地
   (B) 看當地報紙
   (C) 造訪網站
   (D) 與萊特先生聯絡

解說 本文最後一句提到，更多詳細資訊及博物館照片，都將放到博物館官方網站上。所以正確答案是 (C)。

參考以下電子郵件回答問題 26–29。

寄件人：黛博拉．斯蒂爾斯
　　　　<dstills@comclast.com>
收件人：亨利．沃德
　　　　<hward@kansasbuilders.com>
日期：12 月 18 日
主旨：滿意
附件：廚房 .jpg

沃德先生您好：

我是黛博拉．斯蒂爾斯，我住在亨德森維爾。這封電子郵件是想對貴公司「堪薩斯建造專家」為我家提供的服務，表達我的謝意和滿意。Q26 我們請貴公司重新設計客房浴室，讓其面目一新，成果讓我們非常滿意，不只完全符合我先生和我想要的樣子，還讓我們在預算內完成。

Q27 我們會有親戚來家裡過節，他們將住在客房。感謝你們能在他們造訪之前就迅速完工。你們團隊的專業讓我打從心底佩服。

一如之前所說，我們剛搬進去的新家還需要一些整修。由於我們對於貴公司的服務非常滿意，Q29 我們計畫未來的修繕也委請你們幫忙。請先寄給我重新裝潢廚房的估價單。附上一張廚房照片給您參考。

再次感謝並祝佳節愉快

黛博拉．斯蒂爾斯 敬上

字彙 gratitude 感謝　thoroughly 徹底地
estimate 估計　budget 預算

26.「堪薩斯建造專家」是什麼公司？

(A) 會計師事務所

(B) 裝潢修繕公司

(C) 健身中心

(D) 不動產仲介

解說 黛博拉・斯蒂爾斯在第一段提到，她委託了該公司來重新設計並裝潢客房浴室，由此可知正確答案是 (B)。

27. 為何斯蒂爾斯女士希望工程盡速完成？

(A) 她要搬出去。

(B) 她要辦一個派對。

(C) 她正要出租客房。

(D) 她的親戚要來造訪。

解說 本文第二段提到，有些親戚會來家裡過節，且他們將會住在客房。所以正確答案是 (D)。

28. 第二段第二行的 thoroughly（完全地）意思最接近下列何者？

(A) 小心翼翼地

(B) 逐漸地

(C) 一般地；通常

(D) 完全

解說 thoroughly 在是「徹底地、完全地、十分地」的意思。從本文的上下文來看，其餘選項均無法確切表達文意，故 (D) 是正確答案。

29. 斯蒂爾斯女士在電子郵件中隱含什麼事？

(A) 她會再找堪薩斯建造專家來幫忙。

(B) 她正拍版定案一個預算。

(C) 她希望沃德先生能在假期時過來住。

(D) 她這幾天會付款。

解說 在本文的最後一段提到，未來也計畫將請堪薩斯建造專家來幫忙，並提供廚房照片，請他們寄給她廚房裝修的估價單。所以正確答案是 (A)。

參考以下廣告和表格回答問題 30–34。

鞋櫃公司

Q30 鞋櫃公司年度清倉特賣將於 2 月 6 日到 8 日舉行。以下這些鞋款都是零售價下殺 2.5 折，售完為止。欲購從速，以免向隅。

喬治亞女用踝靴採真皮製作——有黑色硬皮、黑色麂皮、棕色皮、灰色皮、紅色專利皮等款式可供選擇。鞋跟九公分高。不管是上班或外出旅遊穿都舒適時尚。貨號：GB387。售價 85 元。

肯辛頓女用及膝長靴——有黑色硬皮、黑色麂皮、海軍藍麂皮可供選擇。側邊有拉鍊設計，鞋跟 10 公分高。這款俐落的靴子是必備款，搭配整套服裝，讓您整體有型又大膽。貨號：KB472。售價 129 元。

貝德福男用樂福鞋——有黑色或棕色皮款可供選擇。羊毛內襯讓您在冬天倍增溫暖。百搭任何休閒衣著，不論是辦公或出遊皆可足蹬本鞋款。這個經典鞋款將會是櫃內未來幾年的基本配備。貨號：Q33 BL327。Q34 售價 99 元。

貝德利男用工作靴——採耐用牛皮製作，只有棕褐色。其特色是防水橡膠鞋底和溝槽，適合在冰天雪地的冬季使用。羊毛內襯，舒適暖和。這雙鞋是冬日完美鞋。貨號：WB382。售價 125 元。

Q34 以上價格均不含稅。稅款會在結帳時計入。

寄送資訊：Q34 購物百元以下，運費一律七元。購物超過百元免運。僅適用國內送運。貨品將於三到五個工作天送達。

鞋櫃公司

收件人：強納森・布朗

地址：歐瑞恩大道 3827 號

市：西雅圖

州：華盛頓州

電話：101-555-1234

電子信箱：jbrown@email.com

貨號：BL327　　　尺寸：11

顏色：黑　　　　數量：1

如果您想購買的品項已輸入完畢，Q34 請按「提交」以計算總金額，含稅和運費。

字彙 clearance sale 清倉拍賣　retail 零售
patent leather 專利皮
sleek 線條流暢的　must-have 必備品
staple 必需品　sole 鞋底
groove 溝槽
lined with . . . 以……為內襯
flat 均一的　domestic 國內的
business day 工作日

30. 從本文可得知鞋櫃公司什麼事？

(A) 針對上班族而廣告。

(B) 每年都有清倉拍賣。

(C) 專賣女用鞋款。

(D) 專門販售靴子。

解說 四個選項分別顯示對鞋櫃公司所賣商品的描述，所以要詳細閱讀第一篇文章的商品介紹。廣告中四雙鞋並非都純為商務場合而廣告，所以 (A) 不能選。銷售的產品除了靴子以外，還有樂福鞋，女性和男性的鞋子也皆有銷售，所以 (C) 和 (D) 也都不對。本文第一句提到，這是年度清倉（annual clearance sale），由此可知 (B) 是正確答案。

31. 廣告中沒有提到下列哪個資訊？

(A) 品項顏色

(B) 產品材質

(C) 尺寸

(D) 商品名稱

解說 廣告中提到的許多產品，揭示了它們的顏色、材質、品名、編號、價錢等，但並沒有提到尺寸大小，所以 (C) 是正確答案。

32. 清倉拍賣主推的是何種鞋款？

(A) 冬季鞋款

(B) 女鞋

(C) 男鞋

(D) 工作鞋

解說 廣告中提到的產品，女鞋和男鞋各有兩款。男鞋是工作鞋和便鞋，女鞋是短靴和長靴，由此看不出鞋子的種類集中在某種鞋子上，所以選項 (B)、(C) 和 (D) 都不對。不過在描述男鞋時都提到羊毛內襯，且打折期間是冬天的二月，所有

產品都是皮製品。雖然沒有直接說明，但可以肯定全是冬季鞋款。所以正確答案是 (A)。

33. 布朗先生在鞋櫃公司買了什麼？

(A) 踝靴

(B) 及膝長靴

(C) 樂福鞋

(D) 工作鞋

解說 從布朗先生填寫表格中的產品編號（Item Number），再對照廣告文中的產品編號，就可以知道答案了。所以正確答案是 (C)。

34. 布朗先生應該要付多少運費？

(A) 0 元

(B) 7 元

(C) 99 元

(D) 125 元

解說 廣告的最後一段提到了購買金額在 100 美元以下，必須付運費 7 美元，100 美元以上免運費（shipped for free）。布朗先生購買的貝德福男用樂福鞋是 99 美元，運費應為 7 美元。不過表中的最後一句話提到，結帳時會再計算稅金，通常 99 美元的稅金一定會超過 1 美元（美國大部分地區都是課 7 至 9% 的稅金），所以適用超過 100 美元的免運費，正確答案是 (A)。

參考以下網頁和表格回答問題 35–39。

歡迎來到《新聞線週刊》網站

Q35/Q36《新聞線週刊》提供本地企業廣告空間及專為社區公告設置的網頁。

價目包括在紙本雜誌和線上訂閱曝光的週、月、年三種廣告方案。其他選項如完整雙開頁廣告、整頁廣告、50 字數限制小篇幅廣告。詳見以下價目表。

雙開頁廣告：週方案 600 元；月方案 650 元，年方案 800 元。

全版廣告：週方案 400 元；Q37 月方案 450 元；年方案 600 元。

小篇廣告：週方案 100 元；月方案 150 元；年方案 300 元。

請在下表提供您的資訊，並附上圖片。

訂購者：夢想旅行社

廣告版面：全版廣告，月方案

提交日期：7 月 1 日

發布日期：7 月 8 日

文字內容：

Q38 夏威夷完整套裝行程只要 500 元，五天四夜，住宿四星旅館，享免費飯店早餐、貝爾航空來回機票、參觀威基基博物館、浮潛、文化展覽、魔術表演。Q39 這檔促銷只在八月。今天就下訂你的行程！

照片：夏威夷圖

其他：全彩照片

字彙 dedicated to 為……而設；奉獻於
publication 出版；發行
complimentary 贈送的；恭維的
round-trip 來回行程
promotion 促銷；晉升
subscription 訂閱

35. 廣告內容是什麼？
(A) 免費夏威夷旅遊
(B) 廣告業面
(C) 電子郵件通知
(D) 訂閱雜誌

解說 本題問的是廣告的內容，所以跟第二篇的夏威夷旅遊廣告申請表無關。所以 (A) 是錯的。第一篇文章揭示了在雜誌上刊登廣告的種類及價格，所以廣告的是雜誌的「廣告頁」。正確答案是 (B)。

36. 由此可知《新聞線週刊》的什麼事？
(A) 這是一本區域性雜誌。
(B) 每個月出版。
(C) 新訂戶有折扣優惠。
(D) 這是一本商業雜誌。

解說 《新聞線週刊》說明和特色在第一篇文章第一段中已經揭示。即在地企業和社區團體可以在上面刊登廣告。所以可知正確答案是 (A)。雜誌種類和訂戶優惠均沒有提到，因此 (C) 和 (D) 都不能選。雜誌名稱的週刊（weekly）可以知道它每週出版，所以 (B) 也不能選。

37. 《新聞線週刊》大概會跟夢想旅行社收多少錢？
(A) 650 元
(B) 400 元
(C) 450 元
(D) 150 元

解說 從廣告價目表中揭示了廣告刊登的期限和價格，而在表格中也清楚顯示廣告版面為全版廣告，採用月方案。對照回價目表，(C) 是正確答案。

38. 夢想旅行社想要廣告什麼？
(A) 便宜機票
(B) 旅館促銷
(C) 四星餐廳
(D) 旅遊套裝行程

解說 表格中廣告詞的第一句話，寫到去夏威夷的套裝行程（full package deal to Hawaii）。所以正確答案是 (D)。

39. 從夢想旅行社的廣告可得知什麼事？
(A) 夏威夷是蜜月的好地點。
(B) 促銷只有持續一個月。
(C) 飛行包括商務艙座位。
(D) 行程包括所有餐點。

解說 套裝行程的文字說明只提到來回機票，但並沒有提及艙等，所以 (C) 不能選。另外，套裝行程中免費提供的只有早餐，不能說所有餐點（all meals）都包含在內，(D) 也錯了。而廣告詞的最後，有說到該優惠僅限於八月有效，所以正確答案是 (B)。

參考以下網頁和表格回答問題 **40–44**。

山谷國際機場

山谷國際機場失物招領處位於 A 航廈二樓。A 航廈服務檯旁的電梯可直達失物招領處。所有在機場、等候區、停車場、接送載客區和機場內商店餐廳拾獲而未認領的物品，會在招領處保管 90 天。失物如果 90 天後依舊無人認領，就會在年底拍賣。機艙內拾獲的物品則由個別航空公司保管，請旅客直接連絡航空公司。

如需協尋失物，請點選頁面上的「失物招領」按鍵。填寫申請表格，愈詳盡愈好。請務必提供了連絡資訊和失物的詳實描述。當您的失物被拾獲時，會有專員跟您連絡。Q44B 貴重物品必須親自領取，且必須簽名才能領回。Q40 其他物品會寄送到您的住所，並酌收運費，Q44A 當然，也還是要簽收。

山谷國際機場
失物通報

今天日期：6 月 20 日

遺失日期：6 月 19 日

姓名：克勞蒂亞·李

地址：伊利諾州山谷市米爾頓街 482 號

住家電話：101-555-2837

Q43 工作電話：

電子信箱：lee837@email.com

方便的聯絡方式：住家電話

方便的聯絡時間：隨時

描述失物和遺失地點：

多倫多機場免稅商店的購物袋，裡面有個全新普契亞手提包。它是黑色的皮革肩背包，上面有金色配飾。Q41 我當時在 8D 門等我先生，後來跑去幫他拿行李和包包，不小心把購物袋放在 8D 門附近長椅上。Q42 那是我先生出差回來買給我的禮物。

字彙 lost and found 失物招領處
unclaimed 未認領的
curbside area 接送載客區
auction 拍賣　airline 航空公司
residence 住所
business trip 商務旅行；出差

---

40. 根據網頁說明，什麼狀況會收費？

(A) 打給航空公司

(B) 請求協尋失物

(C) 保管失物

(D) 寄送失物

解說 第一篇文章第二段的最後，提到酌收運費（for a small shipping fee），這裡揭示了答案，也是在文中唯一出現費用的部分，所以正確答案是 (D)。

41. 關於克勞蒂亞·李的描述何者正確？

(A) 她出完差要返家。

(B) 她買了一個包包給自己。

(C) 她去機場接她先生。

(D) 她在機場工作。

解說 根據克勞蒂亞的描述，手提包遺失於等待出差回國的先生途中。並根據上下文，該手提包是克勞蒂亞的先生出差時回來買給她的。所以 (A) 和 (B) 都錯了。(D) 則沒辦法從文中辨別。僅表接機（pick up from the airport）的 (C) 是正確答案。

42. 文中提到失物什麼事？

(A) 是一份禮物。

(B) 是舊貨。

(C) 是一件行李。

(D) 遺失在飛機上。

解說 從克勞蒂亞的描述，可以得知關於這個手提包的細節。包括其外觀和遺失的時間、地點與情況。它是一個全新的手提包，所以 (B) 不能選。而最後一句話提到，該手提包是先生出差時送給她的禮物。所以正確答案是 (A)。因為是遺忘在登機門附近的長凳上，所以 (D) 和這事實不符。

43. 根據網頁資訊，李女士的表格少提供什麼資訊？

(A) 地址

(B) 班機號碼

(C) 工作電話

(D) 日期

解說 表格中空白的地方只有工作電話這一欄，所以正確答案是 (C)。選項 (B) 則不是表格上詢問的事項，故不能選。

44. 為何李女士需要簽名？

(A) 確認收到物品。

(B) 確認是本人。

(C) 確認班機。

(D) 提供資訊給機場。

解說 有關簽名的內容在第一篇文章的最後提到了兩次，即歸還失物必須要本人簽收。選項 (B) 看似符合此意，不過李女士遺失的物品是手提包，不能算是貴重物品，所以應該適用第二個要求簽名的情況。由此推想，一定是失物送到府後，失主確認收到了失物再簽名，所以 (A) 是正確答案。

參考以下報導和電子郵件回答問題 45–49。

年輕藝術家夢想成真

Q46 天才畫家馬汀‧桑德斯年僅 18 歲，其作品售價已達一萬元以上。他曾被《藝術生活雜誌》報導，甚至也曾出現在歐普拉‧溫德斯的節目上。

長期擔任桑德斯美術老師的華倫泰‧桑默斯說：「他有非常特別的才能，是唯有少數人能夠企及的。他從十歲起就創作了鉅作，我十分為他驕傲。」

桑德斯的父母也深知他的天賦，但就像桑默斯先生所言：「我怎麼樣也想不到受到大家喜愛的歐普拉，會花錢買他的畫作。甚至還有企業執行長來電詢問他的作品。」

馬汀‧桑德斯的畫作詢問度很高，Q47 他現在只在藝廊廣場新的工作室販售畫作。他的作品也成了波蒙特美術館內的觀光熱點，展期只有這個月。訪客將有機會目睹他作品中那活潑的色彩和如夢般的特質。有興趣購買者，必須聯絡馬汀‧桑德斯，預約參觀工作室的時間。非誠勿擾。

寄件人：比爾‧葛蘭特

收件人：馬汀‧桑德斯

日期：9 月 3 日

主旨：請問

桑德斯先生您好：

我是比爾‧葛蘭特，是園景市市區史蒂文生飯店的負責人和總經理。我想購買一幅您的作品，放在旅館辦公室。Q49 最初我在同事住處牆上看到您一幅畫，當下便印象深刻。我上週也去了波蒙特美術館，對您的作品更加喜愛。我對您的風景畫情有獨鍾。Q48 不知是否有機會參觀您的工作室，並挑一幅待售的畫作呢？我在旅館的工作時間很彈性，除非臨時有會議，因此我可以配合您的時間來安排碰面。希望您考慮我的請求。靜候佳音。

比爾‧葛蘭特 敬上

字彙 prodigy 天才
make an appearance on 出現
talent 天分；才華　masterpiece 傑作
workshop 工作坊　dreamlike 如夢的
general manager 總經理
flexible 有彈性的

45. 本篇文章是關於什麼？

(A) 一個美術館

(B) 一位年輕生意人

(C) 一幅美麗的畫作

(D) 一位美術老師

解說 這是一篇和馬汀‧桑德斯有關的報導，所以描述他的選項就是正確答案。由文章可知馬汀會販售自己的作品，因此 (B) 說他是一位年輕事業家，也說得通，所以 (B) 是正確答案。文章的焦點是販賣作品的人，而不是他被販賣的作品，所以 (C) 不能選。

46. 文章中第一段第三行的 made an appearance（露臉）的意義最接近下列何者？

(A) 選擇

(B) 贏得名聲

(C) 作畫

(D) 出現

參考以下報導、網頁和獎狀回答問題 50-54。

解說 made an appearance 是「露臉」的意思,所以 (D) 表「出現、登場」的片語 show up 意思最接近。

47. 根據本文,關於藝廊廣場的描述何者是正確的?

　　(A) 藝廊廣場是馬汀工作室所在地。

　　(B) 此處展出馬汀作品一個月。

　　(C) 這是著名的博物館。

　　(D) 這是馬汀上繪畫課的地方。

解說 藝廊廣場出現在文章中的第四段,是馬汀・桑德斯工作室(workshop)的所在地,也是唯一一個販賣他作品的地方。所以符合此意的是 (A)。展出馬丁作品的地方是貝爾蒙特美術館,因此 (B) 是錯的。

48. 比爾・葛蘭特寄這封電子郵件的目的是什麼?

　　(A) 為了提出請求

　　(B) 提供建議

　　(C) 表達祝賀

　　(D) 確認會議

解說 電子郵件的內容由自我介紹開始,之後提出了想拜訪工作室的要求,以及拜訪工作室的目的,就是想購買馬汀・桑德斯的畫作。所以 (A) 是正確答案。因為無法確認這兩個人見面會不會開會,所以 (D) 不能選。

49. 葛蘭特先生最早是在哪裡看到馬汀的作品?

　　(A) 博物館內

　　(B) 歐普拉・溫德斯的節目上

　　(C) 同事住處

　　(D) 雜誌上

解說 電子郵件中有說,比爾・葛蘭特是在同事家的牆上看到馬汀的畫(saw a painting of yours on the wall of a colleague of mine),由此可知 (C) 是正確答案。

---

10 月 8 日——有機食物超市公司網路商店已經上線,消費者在家裡就能輕鬆採買,不需在鄰近社區找實體店面。Q50C 有機食物超市以販售公平交易產品、有機食物、全素和素食食物,Q50B 並捐贈 2% 利潤給慈善機構而著名。Q51D 有機食物超市是少數將社會責任視為優先的企業,Q51A 這使他們愈來愈受歡迎,尤其是千禧世代和 X 世代族群。新的線上商店將提供有機物超市販售的所有商品,但新鮮農產品、肉類、乳製品只會運送到配送中心附近區域。Q51B 公司希望先看看線上商店的市場反應如何,再決定是否擴大營運。目前為止的反應都很正面,愈來愈多消費者接觸到有機食物超市。Q50A 目前有機食物超市在全國只有 128 家店。詳情請上網站 www.organofoods.com。

Q53D 有機食物超市一開始是個八個農人的小團體,他們在華盛頓州賓斯黎小鎮舉辦農人市集,Q53B/Q53C 只販售當地生產的農產品、手工藝品和商品。Q53A 農人市集很快就成了常態性的全年市場。這些農人於是決定開合作商店,將產品銷售到更大的市場,就有了有機食物超市。至今,賓斯黎的農人市集還是吸引了大群顧客。農人都同意,企業利益和貪婪將不會出現在合作商店內。有機食物超市引以為傲的是,其所販售的產品百分百有機、環保且公平。

公司誠信組織很榮幸
頒出認證書給有機食物超市

這個獎項不只肯定有機食物超市的不凡成就,也讚賞其在企業充斥的環境下依舊信奉的誠信原則。我們樂見貴公司回饋社會,並鼓勵對農人和工人的道德對待。最重要的是,這個獎項表彰貴公司宣揚社會責任的重要性。

凱文・拉孟
Q54 主席

字彙 comfort 舒適　neighborhood 街坊
organic 有機的　vegan 全素的
vegetarian 素食的　donate 捐贈
priority 優先權　produce 農產品
dairy 乳製品　year-round 一整年的
integrity 廉政；誠信

50. 從本文可得知有機食物超市的什麼事？

(A) 到國外開設新的經銷店。

(B) 會捐出一部分營收給慈善機構。

(C) 只銷售全素和素食食物。

(D) 是一家老公司。

解說 有關有機食物超市的內容在三篇文章中都有，所以要將選項一一對照來確認。關於超市規模在第一篇文章的最後，揭示了全國有 128 個賣場，由於無法知道國外有沒有展店，選項 (A) 不能選。關於超市販售的產品有在第一篇文章被提及，選項 (C) 的全素和素食食物只是其中之一，所以 (C) 是錯的。關於超市過去的歷史可在第二篇的網頁文章中找到，但並沒有提到創立的時間，所以 (D) 無法確認。正確答案是 (B)，在第一篇文章講述超市之所以成名，提到它將百分之二的利潤捐給慈善機構。

51. 關於有機食物超市的敘述何者錯誤？

(A) 受到年輕族群歡迎。

(B) 是一個成長中的公司。

(C) 商品很便宜。

(D) 重視社會責任。

解說 第一篇文章中超市深受千禧世代和 X 世代人的喜愛，選項 (A) 的年輕族群可以概括這群人。由此可知道 (A) 是事實。並從公司決定推線上商店，且有可能擴大營運的訊息，這符合 (B) 所說它是個成長中的公司。而在第三篇獲獎文和第一篇文章中，提到好幾次該超市社會責任視為己任的精神，所以 (D) 也不能選。因此正確答案是無法從文章中確知的 (C)。

52. 網頁中的 draw（吸引）字義最接近以下何者？

(A) 吸引

(B) 油漆

(C) 想像

(D) 檢驗

解說 draw 用 在 continues to draw large crowds 中，是「持續吸引大批群眾」的意思，所以要在選項中選出最符合此意的做正確答案。所以選 (A)。

53. 關於賓斯黎農夫市集的描述，以下敘述何者正確？

(A) 已不復存在。

(B) 販售各種進口商品。

(C) 只販售農產品。

(D) 成為有機食物超市。

解說 網頁的文章中提及有機食物超市的歷史，揭示由八位農人所組成的農人市集，販售當地生產的農產品、手工藝品和商品，並發展成持續開常態性的全年市場，最後他們決定擴大規模，於是有機食物超市誕生。選項中和本文內容一致的 (D) 是正確答案。

54. 凱文·拉孟是什麼人？

(A) 有機食物超市總裁

(B) 公司誠信組織的主席

(C) 是農人協會會員

(D) 是一個顧客

解說 該人物在第三篇的獎狀中出現，最下方署名後面的頭銜是主席，由此可知他是某機構的總經理。在獎狀的第一行，標題處點出授予該獎項的機構名稱是公司誠信組織。將該機構名縮寫成 OIC 的 (B) 是正確答案。

參考以下報導、廣告和電子郵件回答問題 55–59。

紐約（2月9日）——韓系美妝這幾個月橫掃美容界，隨之而來的是美國對韓國商品需求愈來愈高。Q55C 這就是為何韓國化妝領導品牌美麗佳人已宣布，Q56 他們會在紐約市開第一家門市和供應中心。Q55B 目前已有百貨公司專櫃銷售該公司的商品，但是專門店要到夏天才會開張。這些銷售的商品在諾曼·馬可斯、哈林斯、賽克大道百貨公司都登上熱銷排行榜。諾曼·馬可斯總經理說：「韓國彩妝和保養品的已供不應求。我們很開心知道供應商將會在紐約設點，這肯定會讓顧客開心。」

美麗佳人紐約分店徵才

美麗佳人急徵 100 多個職缺，包括倉庫、行政、管理、客服、銷售和美妝顧問等。Q57 除了管理職要求必須有管理經驗之外，所有職缺有經驗佳，但無經驗可。應徵管理職者，在其他公司類似領域至少要有兩年經驗，且要提供兩份不同來源的推薦信。欲從事客服工作者，必須要有流利的英文和其他語言能力，特別是法語、西班牙語、中文或韓語。有興趣的求職者應將完整的求職申請和履歷表請寄到 www.arumdaunbeauty.com。團體面試將會在 3 月 15 日於荷頓飯店會議 B 廳和 C 廳舉行。通過初試的求職者將參加複試，時間地點會另行公布。

寄件人：茱蒂·漢米爾頓
收件人：琳達·馬克斯
日期：4月3日
主旨：特別感謝

琳達妳好：

Q59 非常謝謝妳幫我寫去美麗佳人求職的推薦信。我通過了兩次面試，也錄取了應徵的職位。如果沒有妳的協助，我不可能成功。我在美麗風尚學到很多，不敢相信我已經在這裡工作五年了。時光飛逝。雖然我很興奮地要開啟人生的新頁，但也會非常想念這裡的大家。

我下禮拜會開始新工作，這比我預期的快。我知道我兩週後才會離職，我會繼續在這個崗位上，直到正式離開。但我下週一需要參加新進人員訓練。我請莎曼珊幫我代班。我希望這不會造成困擾。

再次感謝您的諒解。

茱蒂 敬上

字彙 sweep 橫掃；大勝　demand 需求
dedicated to 為……而設；奉獻於
overwhelm 擊敗；壓倒
administrative 行政的
consulting 顧問　field 領域
reference letter 推薦信
fluency 流利　leave 告別　shift 輪班
manufacture 製造　export 出口

55. 本文提及關於美麗佳人什麼事？
　(A) 是紐約的一家公司。
　(B) 有些產品已可在美國購得。
　(C) 是韓國第一家美妝產品公司。
　(D) 是美國的美妝大廠。

解說 第一篇報導在開頭即說明美麗佳人是一家韓國品牌，所以 (A) 和 (D) 都可以不用考慮。美麗佳人只是韓國化妝界的領導品牌，不是韓國第一間化妝品公司，所以 (C) 也錯了。另該篇文章也提到，已經有些產品在美國的百貨公司銷售。所以正確答案是 (B)。

56. 根據本文，美麗佳人計畫做什麼？
　(A) 在紐約開一家官方店面
　(B) 在美國生產產品
　(C) 從韓國進口更多產品
　(D) 拓展到其他國家

解說 從第一篇的報導可以找到正確答案。其中明示了美麗佳人宣布將在紐約開設第一間門市。所以選項 (A) 是正確答案。化妝產品的出口、製造、銷售到其他國家，則都沒有在文中提及，所以 (B)、(C) 和 (D) 都是錯的。

57. 以下職位何者非低階職位且需要經驗？

(A) 行政

(B) 客服

(C) 管理

(D) 美妝顧問

解說 在第二篇徵才廣告中提到有關經驗的部分，是說除了管理職位外，其他職位對於經驗的要求皆非必要；接著直接提到，要應徵管理職需要兩年以上經驗，並需要兩封推薦信。由此可知正確答案是 (C)。

58. 電子郵件第一段第五行的 how time flies（時光飛逝）意思最接近下列何者？

(A) 有鳥飛過。

(B) 時間過得很慢。

(C) 茱蒂覺得年紀大了。

(D) 時間過得非常快。

解說 本句和一般的感嘆句型「How ＋形容詞／副詞＋（主詞＋動詞）」順序不同，省略了其中的形容詞／副詞（fast），所以很容易讓人混淆，不過它的確是感嘆句，是「時間飛（fly）得多（how）快啊」。也可以用 Time flies.（光陰似箭）此平述句來表感嘆。所以正確答案是 (D)。

59. 漢米爾頓女士最可能錄取什麼工作？

(A) 行政職

(B) 客服

(C) 管理

(D) 售貨

解說 從第三篇的電子郵件可以知道，茱蒂・漢米爾頓對琳達・馬克斯表示感謝，謝謝她寫了推薦信。由此可知，茱蒂應徵的工作需要推薦信。在第二篇廣告中，有關應徵職位的說明，唯一提到需要兩封推薦信以及兩年以上經驗的職位是管理職，所以正確答案是 (C)。

參考以下網頁、電子郵件和通知回答問題 60–64。

磚屋餐廳

歡迎來店享用本週午間與晚間套餐。您可以從以下菜單選擇，用優惠價格就可以大啖各式特製餐點。

午間 A 套餐

享用大番茄義大利麵、烤雞、花園拌沙拉和香草冰淇淋。一人 12.99 元。

午間 B 套餐

內含本店獨特奶油蘑菇湯、香烤明蝦、義大利麵沙拉、拌沙拉和新鮮水果塔。一人 19.99 元。

晚間 C 套餐

享用本餐廳受歡迎的蛤蠣巧達湯、香蒜麵包棒、磚屋特製六層起司千層麵、花園拌沙拉和招牌巧克力蛋糕。一人 29.99 元。

晚間 D 套餐

享用本餐廳熱銷的凱薩沙拉、自製番茄湯、磚屋火烤起司漢堡佐大馬鈴薯塊、烤蔬菜和檸檬塔。一人 36.99 元。

＊請注意，套餐菜單僅適用於團體顧客或兩位以上的顧客。

寄件人：磚屋餐廳

收件人：羅德尼・史密斯

日期：9 月 28 日

主旨：Re: Q63 商業晚餐餐敘

史密斯先生您好：

感謝您來信詢問。我們確實有私人包廂供商業會議使用。包廂可容納 12 人，Q62 相信以您的八人團體來說，空間相當足夠。我們有團體菜單，比單點划算。Q61 您提到您對海鮮過敏。Q60 我希望第二組晚間套餐符合您的需求，因為每道菜都不含海鮮。

至於您其他的問題，可惜我們目前沒有午餐時間以前的套餐菜單，但我已附上本店特餐和最熱門的菜色與價格，供您參考與未來在此舉辦餐會時用。

謝謝您，並期待您的回覆。

欣蒂・婓蘭 敬上

字彙 discounted 折扣的
tossed salad 拌沙拉
prawn 明蝦；大蝦　signature 招牌
potato wedge 馬鈴薯塊
seafood 海鮮
for further references 未來參考

60. 史密斯先生最可能會點什麼餐？

(A) 午間 A 套餐

(B) 午間 B 套餐

(C) 晚間 C 套餐

(D) 晚間 D 套餐

解說 第二篇的電子郵件揭示史密斯先生為了舉行商務會議，而向餐廳預訂包廂和訂餐，但文中並沒有提到史密斯先生的喜好或選擇，只在電郵中出現了唯一一個暗示，這點要好好掌握。文中提到史密斯先生對海鮮過敏，且信件主旨是「商業晚餐」，所以四組推薦套餐中，唯一符合的是晚間 D 套餐，正確答案是 (D)。

61. 從本文可得知史密斯先生什麼事？

(A) 他有食物過敏的問題。

(B) 他是嚴格的素食者。

(C) 他是公司執行長。

(D) 他去過磚屋餐廳。

解說 如同上一題的解說，已經知道史密斯對於海鮮過敏，因此 (A) 是正確答案。(B) 和 (C) 均無法從本文中獲得確認。從史密斯詢問餐廳的包廂和菜單，可以看出他沒來過，所以 (D) 也和本文不一致。

62. 有多少人會出席餐敘？

(A) 2 人

(B) 4 人

(C) 8 人

(D) 12 人

解說 在第二篇的電子郵件的第一段，回答了史密斯先生先前詢問的兩個問題。第一個問題：有沒有可以開商務會議的包廂；有的話，可以容納多少人；第二個問題：他詢問了中午以前的套餐菜單。第一個問題給予了肯定的答覆，並說可以容納 12 人，容納史密斯開會的八人是綽綽有餘。由此可知正確答案是 (C)。

63. 關於這場餐會，以下敘述何者最可能是真的？

(A) 時間在早上。

(B) 時間在中午。

(C) 時間在晚上。

(D) 會取消。

解說 從電子郵件的主旨便可以得知，商業餐會的時間是在晚上舉辦。並從磚屋餐廳推薦史密斯先生第二套晚餐組合可確認，正確答案是 (C)。

64. 附件傳單的 sneak peek（搶先看）意思最接近下列何者？

(A) 秘密菜單

(B) 局部觀看

(C) 照片

(D) 試吃

解說 按照字面來解釋，sneak peak 是「偷偷地看一眼」的意思。在文章中它當作名詞來用，所以不能按照字面翻譯。將附件和第一篇的網頁對照，可以發現，網頁的菜單完整列出套餐內容，而附件扼要地以簡短的幾個字條列餐點品項。所以 (B) 是正確答案。由於該表所列出的品項，並沒有提到秘密菜單、照片、試吃等等，所以 (A)、(C) 和 (D) 都不對。

新制多益閱讀考題完全戰略 Basic

作　　者	Ki Taek Lee
譯　　者	彭尊聖／陳依辰
審　　訂	Richard Luhrs
編　　輯	王婷葦
主　　編	丁宥暄
校　　對	申文怡
內文排版	謝青秀／林書玉
封面設計	林書玉
製程管理	洪巧玲
出 版 者	寂天文化事業股份有限公司
電　　話	+886-(0)2-2365-9739
傳　　真	+886-(0)2-2365-9835
網　　址	www.icosmos.com.tw
讀者服務	onlineservice@icosmos.com.tw
出版日期	2021 年 1 月 初版再刷 (160103)

Mozilge New Toeic Basic RC

Copyright © 2016 by Ki Taek Lee, The Mozilge Language Research Institute

Originally published by Book21 Publishing Group.

Traditionally Chinese translation copyright © 2018 by Cosmos Culture Ltd.

This edition is arranged with Book21 Publishing Group through PK Agency, Seoul, Korea.

郵撥帳號 1998620-0 寂天文化事業股份有限公司

劃撥金額 600 元（含）以上者，郵資免費。

訂購金額 600 元以下者，請外加郵資 65 元。

〔若有破損，請寄回更換，謝謝。〕

國家圖書館出版品預行編目 (CIP) 資料

新制多益閱讀考題完全戰略 Basic /
Ki Taek Lee 著；彭尊聖，陳依辰譯 .
-- 初版 . -- ［臺北市］：寂天文化，2018.03

　　面；　　公分

ISBN 978-986-318-654-0(平裝)

1. 多益測驗

805.1895　　　　　　　　　　107000444